Praise for *Strong Light of Day*

"Jon Land is a writer's writer. . . . He packs every story with menace and peril, providing a feast for any thriller aficionado."　　　—Steve Berry, *New York Times* bestselling author of the Cotton Malone series

"*Strong Light of Day* lives up to its name, an adrenaline-packed, tension-soaked thrill ride that's a top-notch addition to an already terrific series."

—Lisa Gardner,
#1 *New York Times* bestselling author of
Crash & Burn

"The suspense rises page by page until all the pieces crash together in an epic, high-tech finale. . . . *Strong Light of Day* is an intelligent thriller that combines the insight and subtlety of the great literary masters with the vivid imagery and heart-pounding action of a big-screen blockbuster. This is one for the shelves of English professors and thriller lovers alike."

—*New York Journal of Books*

"Caitlin Strong is a kick-ass Texas Ranger and one of the toughest female protagonists in crime fiction. . . . This is a complex, multifaceted tale, but it moves at lightning speed. Fans of the series and readers who like their women fearless and smart will love this story."

—*Booklist*

"Exciting . . . Land pulls out all the stops in the latter chapters. More than a few bombshell revelations and jaw-dropping plot twists will satisfy longtime series fans."

—*Publishers Weekly*

"Demonstrates why [Land] is one of the best action thriller writers in the business. The mix of history, character development, and baffling story lines will enthrall readers."　　　—*RT Book Reviews* (Top Pick!)

"For years I've been a fan of Jon Land's books, but with *Strong Light of Day* he's outdone himself. Great plotting, incredible character development, and all the key ingredients for a great mystery novel."

—*The Strand Magazine*

"A globe-spanning criminal plot with several dark twists, historical parallels with deep ties to the protagonists, a dash of sci-fi, a sprinkling of the fantastic, and plenty of gunplay for the die-hard Texas Ranger enthusiasts in the readership." —*San Francisco Book Review*

"Electrifying . . . filled to the brim with mesmeric plot twists and an unforgettable cast of characters, both good and bad. Suspense is expertly sustained in a masterfully developed plot as Jon Land affords fans of this superb series another dynamic novel with a truly unique protagonist." —*Fresh Fiction*

"Jon Land, the master of nuance, has outdone himself with his latest Caitlin Strong thriller. . . . Caitlin Strong proves that justice is not about being politically correct; it's about caring for the underdog and doing what's right, no matter the cost." —*Suspense Magazine*

"A nonstop, heart-pounding, no-holds-barred book that doesn't let up even the slightest until the very last loose end is tied up tight. This is the best thriller of the year and one of the best you will ever read, a tour de force of reading entertainment at its very best."

—*Bestsellersworld*

"A rollicking roller-coaster ride of nonstop adventure."
—*The Jewish Voice*

"A suspenseful, fast-paced tale apparently constructed by a writer so obsessed with James Bond movies, Stephen King novels, Clint Eastwood Westerns, Marvel Comics, and *The Matrix* that he tried to combine all of them into a single book. Logic suggests there's no way this should work, but somehow it does, making *Strong Light of Day* at once preposterous and wildly entertaining."

—Associated Press

"Land masterfully keeps many balls in the air at once in a novel full of breathtaking suspense and extremely relevant current topics. . . . Readers will marvel at how all of these events, as well as a handful of other subplots, are deftly weaved together to produce another terrific Caitlin Strong mystery. I can't wait for the next one!"

—*Bookreporter*

"Explosive action, heart-pounding drama, and a mystery steeped in history that will keep readers guessing until the final pages . . . The dialogue between characters maintains a true grit and Southern-born honesty that only adds layers to an already atmospheric thriller. Caitlin Strong is back in all her glory, proving her worth as an honest and bare-knuckled fighter for justice against the greatest of foes."   —*Literary Inklings*

"Land has done it again in this riveting, suspense-riddled yarn. . . . [He] keeps you on the edge of your seat with his cliff-hanging chapters and sudden revelations. Multiple climaxes occur that will chill the blood and stop the heart. The novel is simply terrific."

—*The Providence Journal*

"One of the few female leads in the thriller category, Caitlin has boots that few others can fill. . . . Land is an experienced and skilled author who keeps finding new highs to reach, and Caitlin Strong is at her best in *Strong Light of Day*. Five stars!"

—*Manhattan Book Review*

STRONG
LIGHT OF DAY

OTHER BOOKS BY JON LAND

The Alpha Deception

Betrayal (nonfiction)*

Black Scorpion: The Tyrant Reborn*

Blood Diamonds*

The Blue Widows*

The Council of Ten

Day of the Delphi*

Dead Simple*

Dolphin Key*

The Doomsday Spiral

The Eighth Trumpet

The Fires of Midnight*

The Gamma Option

Hope Mountain*

Keepers of the Gate*

Kingdom of the Seven*

Labyrinth

The Last Prophecy*

The Lucifer Directive

The Ninth Dominion

The Omega Command

The Omicron Legion

Pandora's Temple

The Pillars of Solomon*

The Rising*

The Seven Sins: The Tyrant Ascending*

Strong at the Break*

Strong Cold Dead*

Strong Darkness*

Strong Enough to Die*

Strong Justice*

Strong Rain Falling*

Strong Vengeance*

Takedown (nonfiction)*

The Tenth Circle

The Valhalla Testament

The Vengeance of the Tau

Vortex

A Walk in the Darkness*

The Walls of Jericho*

*Published by Tom Doherty Associates

STRONG
LIGHT OF DAY

·

A CAITLIN STRONG NOVEL

Jon Land

A TOM DOHERTY ASSOCIATES BOOK • NEW YORK

This is a work of fiction. All of the characters, organizations, and events portrayed in this novel are either products of the author's imagination or are used fictitiously.

STRONG LIGHT OF DAY

Copyright © 2015 by Jon Land

A Forge Book
Published by Tom Doherty Associates, LLC
175 Fifth Avenue
New York, NY 10010

www.tor-forge.com

Forge® is a registered trademark of Tom Doherty Associates, LLC.

ISBN 978-0-7653-7028-0

Our books may be purchased in bulk for promotional, educational, or business use. Please contact your local bookseller or the Macmillan Corporate and Premium Sales Department at 1-800-221-7945, extension 5442, or by e-mail at MacmillanSpecialMarkets@macmillan.com.

First Edition: October 2015
First Mass Market Edition: August 2016

Printed in the United States of America

0 9 8 7 6 5 4 3 2 1

For my father

Acknowledgments

Before we start, it's time to give some much deserved shout-outs to those who make it possible for me to do what I do, as well as do it better.

Stop me if you've heard this before, but let's start at the top with my publisher, Tom Doherty, and Forge's associate publisher, Linda Quinton, dear friends who publish books "the way they should be published," to quote my late agent, the legendary Toni Mendez. The great Bob Gleason, Karen Lovell, Elayne Becker, and especially Natalia Aponte are there for me at every turn. Natalia's a brilliant editor and friend who never ceases to amaze me with her sensitivity and genius. Editing may be a lost art, but not here thanks to both Natalia and Bob Gleason, and I think you'll enjoy all of my books, including this one, much more as a result.

My friend Mike Blakely, a terrific writer and musician, taught me Texas firsthand and helped me think like a native of that great state. And Larry Thompson, a terrific writer in his own right, has joined the team as well to make sure I do justice to his home state along now with his son-in-law, a state trooper who was part of Governor Perry's protective detail and would make a great Texas Ranger himself. I want to thank all the organizers of the Books in the Basin book festival for giving me my first taste of West Texas and, especially, Brenda Kissko of the Midland Convention and Visitor's Bureau and Randy Ham from the Odessa Council for the Arts and Humanities for introducing me to that wonderful city I hope I've done justice to in these pages. You'll also find more info on how *Strong Light of Day* came to be in my author's note that follows the epilogue here.

Check back at www.jonlandbooks.com for updates or to drop me a line, and please follow me on Twitter @jondland. I'd be remiss if I didn't thank all of you who've already written or e-mailed me about how much you enjoyed the first six tales in the Caitlin Strong series. And if this happens to be your first visit to the world of Caitlin, welcome and get ready for a wild ride. I promise you the greatest one yet this time out, so enough already and let's get started.

P.S. For those interested in more information about the history of the Texas Rangers, I recommend *The Texas Rangers* and *Time of the Rangers,* a pair of superb books by Mike Cox, also published by Forge.

We can easily forgive a child who is afraid of the dark; the real tragedy of life is when men are afraid of the light.

—PLATO

STRONG
LIGHT OF DAY

PROLOGUE

Perhaps the earliest confirmed existence of a true Texas Ranger company was in January 1827. [Stephen] Austin had taken his militia out to maintain order during the Fredonian Rebellion in Nacogdoches. To protect his colony from surprise Indian raids in his absence, Austin ordered Captain Abner Kuykendall and eight other men (John Walker, Early Robbins, Thomas Stevens, Barzillai Kuykendall, John Jones, William Kuykendall, James Kiggans, and John Furnash) "to range the country" between the Brazos and the Colorado along the San Antonio Road.

—Stephen L. Moore, *Savage Frontier, Volume I,*
1835–1837: Rangers, Riflemen, and
Indian Wars in Texas

Jim Strong entered the Menger Bar via the street entrance, the Texas Ranger badge pinned to the lapel of his shirt struggling to glisten in the dull light. The patrons, mostly tourists mixed with a smattering of locals, paid him little heed, except for the solitary figure seated at the bar itself, who followed his approach the whole way in the mirror.

"Boone Masters," Jim said, taking the stool next to the man and noticing the melted ice dotting his auburn-shaded bourbon.

"Buy you a drink?" Masters asked, eyes fixed on Jim Strong in the bar's mirror, which was streaked with cleaning solvent.

"I come to talk, not drink."

Masters finally turned toward him. He was a raw-boned man with tawny-colored skin like stitched leather, courtesy of several years spent as a dockworker and railway foreman before another livelihood had claimed his attention. Crime, robbery in specific, had produced far better earnings without giving his complexion the texture of a darned sock.

"So talk, Ranger," he said.

Jim Strong ran his eyes about the polished wood

and elegant glassware for which the Menger Bar, located off the lobby of the Menger Hotel and with a direct entrance off the street as well, was known. "Not the kind of place I'd expect to find you, Boone."

"We on a first-name basis now?"

"You offered me a drink, so I figure we must be."

Masters turned back to the mirror and sipped from his glass. "Except you didn't take me up on it."

"I could do with a Dr Pepper."

"I almost forgot. You gave up booze after your wife got gunned down by those Mexicans in front of your little girl."

Jim stiffened. "That's no concern of yours."

Masters turned on his stool to better face him. "That's right. Now that I recall, it was your wife getting Swiss-cheesed by those bullets that turned you *to* booze, not away from it."

Jim Strong's upper lip started to curl upward and his eyes narrowed with a focused intensity that made them look like the twin bores of a double-barreled shotgun. Boone Masters felt a pressure settle between the two men that seemed ready to topple him backwards off his stool.

"Me turning to booze after my wife's murder is a fact," Jim managed, clinging to his calm, "just like you beating yours senseless when you had too much whiskey inside you. I heard tell the emergency room kept her records in a separate drawer, the file was so thick."

Masters pushed up against the pressure that felt like a stiff wind blowing straight out of Jim Strong. "That what you come in here to discuss?"

Jim Strong waved the bartender over and ordered a Diet Coke, settling more easily onto his stool. "This is the very spot where Teddy Roosevelt recruited his Rough Riders for the Spanish–American War."

"Is that a fact?"

"Sure is. Word is he got them drunk before sticking the enlistment papers before them with pen in hand."

Masters gazed toward a brass spittoon sitting at the far end of the bar. "That's an original, you know, dating back to 1887. The mirrors, too. Guess we're both students of history, Ranger."

"I'm here to talk about your history, Masters," Jim Strong said, as the bartender set his Diet Coke down on a napkin before him, complete with a lime he hadn't ordered bobbing atop the foam.

"What history would that be?"

"Criminal, mostly. Heard you been enlisting your own teenage boy in heisting major appliances in those warehouse jobs."

"You working for Social Services on the side now, Ranger?"

"Nope, just talking recent history. My daughter's a few years younger than your boy. I'm trying to square how any father worth his salt could risk getting his son sent to Huntsville, where he'd be poked more than those whores your daddy pimped back in the oil boom days."

Masters had already gone back to sipping his drink, not even bothering to regard Jim Strong in the mirror anymore. "Your daughter—that be Caitlin, right?" he asked, with just enough of a gleam in his eye. "Hope she can take care of herself, what with you gone so often and only old Grandpa Earl Strong to watch her. She know not to answer the door for strangers?"

Jim Strong unpinned the badge from his shirt lapel and laid it on the bar. "She knows an asshole when she sees one, just like her dad."

With that, he reared back and punched Boone Masters in the jaw so hard that Masters flew off his stool and upended three more that had been occupied just seconds before. He stayed down until the Ranger hoisted him back up by the hair, riding the move close enough to head butt Jim Strong square in the nose. Blood exploded from both the Ranger's nostrils, his eyes gone shiny with tears.

Masters seized the advantage by trying to slam Jim Strong's face into a wooden pillar left over from the bar's original construction. But Strong slipped from his grasp and smashed the back of Masters's skull into the pillar instead. Then he punched him hard in the jaw. Masters started to slump, only to hammer a knee into the Ranger's groin, dropping him in a heap to the shiny floor, which was the same cherrywood as the walls.

Masters grabbed a chair from a nearby table, now vacated, slashing it downward on an angle meant to smash its legs over Jim Strong's spine. But the Ranger shifted at the last moment. Chunks, splinters, and shards coughed up into the air on impact with the floor, as Jim scissors-kicked Masters's legs out from under him.

Masters went down fast, still managing to grasp the remnants of a stool leg, which he promptly splintered against Jim Strong's skull, slowing the Ranger not in the least. Before Masters realized the stool leg had been stripped from his hand, he was being jerked backwards, up and over the bar, with Jim Strong landing on top of him amid a shower of glasses toppled from the shelves.

Several bottles had smashed on the floor as well. Boone Masters grabbed the neck of one and thrust its fat, jagged end up toward the Ranger's face. Jim deftly deflected it and jammed his thumbs hard into the outlaw's throat. Masters's neck muscles were so taut and hard it felt like squeezing gristle. The man grinned at him and spit, even as his face darkened and wispy, guttural rasps pushed out his mouth.

Jim realized too late that Masters was going for the heirloom .45-caliber automatic holstered on his hip. Should've left it in his truck, of course, locked in the glove box. Because now he felt it coming free of its holster, already cocked, and Jim just managed to get a thumb wedged before the hammer to forestall any thoughts Masters might have had of firing. But he had his breath back now. The Ranger, left with only a single hand, stretched up to grab hold of a bar gun.

Jim Strong jerked the bar's soda gun dispenser downward and jammed it into Masters's open mouth, which was still gasping for air. He hit a plunger, with no idea which of the available choices was now flooding down the outlaw's throat. Jim felt Masters give up his hold on the .45, thrashing wildly to work himself free, and finally managing to latch a hand onto the hose dangling downward from the bar works. Masters yanked and the hose came free, a fountain of soft drinks erupting from beneath the bar in a geyser and spraying into the smoky air.

He started punching at Jim, even as huge gulps of fluid mixed with spittle coughed from his mouth, further soaking his clothes. The Ranger punched right back, the two of them poised on the floor behind the bar, hammering each other silly, until Boone Masters's final strike died in midair and his arm flopped back to the floor. His gaze grew glassy, somewhere else entirely now, as Jim Strong cocked a fist for a final blow meant to avenge his busted nose.

Then the world before him froze up solid and Jim Strong collapsed atop Boone Masters, who'd preceded him into unconsciousness.

"You never did tell me what you came into the bar to talk about," Boone Masters said from his gurney, alongside the one on which Jim Strong rested in the back of the ambulance summoned to take them both to the Southwest General Hospital. Normally, each would have gotten his own transport, but a pileup on the 410 had left emergency services short of vehicles.

"You busted my nose," Jim said, feeling about the thick wad of bandages the paramedics had wrapped in place to stanch the bleeding.

"I did you a favor, on account of it already being bent to one side. Now you can get it fixed for free."

"I'd like to fix you, same way they fix a pup before it knows any better."

Masters continued to regard him, gaze lingering on the bandages crisscrossing the Ranger's face, stretched over his nose. "You come into that bar already fixing to clean my clock?"

"Nope. I come because I need your help," Jim Strong told him, his voice nasally from his broken nose.

"My *help?* I know I got my bell rung pretty bad, but now I'm hearing things."

"You heard right."

"Help you, the *Texas Rangers?*"

"It's in your best interests."

"How you figure that?"

"We may not have any of the same friends, Masters, but we got a few of the same enemies."

"Who that be exactly?"

"The gang you use to move all that stolen merchandise through."

"What stolen merchandise?"

Jim tried to sit up, but the IV the paramedic now seated on the ambulance's rear bench had hooked into him didn't have enough slack to allow the effort. "Let me put it this way: a few months back I heard a warehouse full of major appliances got boosted— funny thing, being those appliances had been boosted before that. Ironic, don't you think?"

"What's that mean?"

"What's what mean?"

"*Ironic.*"

"Couldn't tell you. Just that I know what it is when I hear it." Jim let Masters see him staring at him through still-watery eyes. "Just like I know what I'm looking at now."

"What's that?"

"A man I could put away for a stretch if I had a

mind to, which I'll do if you don't have a mind to help me out with something."

"You mean you'll try, Ranger, just like plenty others who weren't up to the task neither."

"Then let's do this another way: How you think your boy Cort Wesley would do behind bars until his midtwenties, if he's lucky?"

Boone Masters stiffened. "Don't go there, Ranger."

"You already did, when you made him an accomplice on your heists. Very considerate, to just have him stand lookout, but make sure you have him wear a mask next time. Turns out we can identify the boy clear as day, thanks to one of them newfangled video surveillance systems."

Masters tried not to show how concerned that left him. "Hard being a single parent, ain't it?"

"We got that much in common, anyway—'long with something else."

"And what would that be exactly?"

"The Russian mob. I intend to take them down, and you're going to help me. Otherwise, your boy's going away for a time."

Now it was Boone Masters who tried to sit up, working to tear the IV from his arm until the paramedic, who'd played three years of college football, stopped him. "You're a real son of a bitch, Ranger, just like Teddy Roosevelt. You came into that bar to recruit me, the difference being you didn't buy me a drink."

"Comes with the territory, Mr. Masters. And right now that territory is running Russian red. They're up to something a lot bigger than fencing major appliances. I believe they're fixing to kill a whole lot of

Americans, and we just might be the only ones who can stop them."

EASTERN AFGHANISTAN; 2002

"Empty," Navy SEAL Lieutenant Mark Grasso said, standing just outside the cave entrance in the darkness that had fallen like a blanket over the area. One moment there was light draining from the sky and the next there wasn't. Grasso continued, not bothering to disguise the disgust in his voice. "Just like the whole nest of them."

"It happens, Lieutenant," said the big man who'd remained at the holding point until the all-clear sign was given. He looked more like a shadow silhouetted against the night, like some sort of holographic figure projected onto the scene instead of standing within it. "Get used to it."

"What, you spooks fucking up? Sending us after ghosts over and over again with lousy intelligence?"

"You expect to turn over a rock and have Osama pop up with hands in the air? You sign up for this shit, you need to stop figuring the rules are yours to make up. We're playing by the rules of others, Lieutenant, but we're getting close. Whoever was here left in a real hurry. We probably missed them, *him* even, by a couple hours at most. Maybe next time."

"I don't give a shit about next time."

The night smelled of a combination of soot and ash, a perpetual burned odor that hung in the air as if residue of bomb blasts that had torn these mountains apart had become a permanent fixture on the scene. Every shift of the breeze seemed to intensify the scent that reminded Grasso of driving through a burned-out forest, lingering long after the fire itself was done.

"That's the business I'm in, son," the big man told the SEAL Team 3 leader, his tone abrasive and condescending. "Giving a shit about the next time, since I can't do anything about the last."

"You need to see this, Lieutenant," a voice called from inside the cave.

The SEALs had stormed the mountain just before dawn on intelligence that high-asset targets and large stores of munitions had been located in a cluster of caves hollowed out like entrances to a hive. But the SEALs had found no guns, no explosives, and no targets, high asset or otherwise.

Grasso entered the cave, followed by the big man, who moved, acted, and spoke like someone who hadn't always used his desk as a staging ground, to the far wall, where a collection of documents had been found inside a hole covered by a nest of rocks. Pages and pages of them; hundreds by the look of things.

"Like I said," the big man noted. "They must've left in a hurry. Arabic," he continued, scanning some of the pages.

Grasso handed him a fresh batch. "Not all of them."

The next set of documents looked like some kind of field or technical manuals. The pages felt brittle and warped, smelling of musk and mold. At the bottom of that pile lay something else. Drawings, the big man noted; skilled and detailed. No, not drawings at all.

Schematics, plans. Whoever had been in this cave was apparently planning something in the very minutes before the raid descended on his lair. Bin Laden himself, maybe, or at least somebody high up the al-Qaeda organization food chain.

Damn! the big man thought. *How close they'd been. . . .*

He peeled back the drawings to find fresh documents, written not in Arabic at all but in English. Fresh with a familiar stamp and logo. And beneath them rested another set, in a third language.

Russian.

"You need to get on your sat phone, Lieutenant," the big man said, studying these documents much more closely than he had the others. "You need to get me Washington on the line five minutes ago."

Grasso freed the satellite phone from his vest. "Pentagon, sir?"

"No, Lieutenant, the White House. Let me give you the number."

Part One

Charged with the mission of operating beyond the boundaries of civilization, with minimal support and no communication from higher authority, they lived and often died by the motto "Order first, then law will follow."

—Thomas W. Knowles, *They Rode for the Lone Star: The Saga of the Texas Rangers, Volume 1*

I

ZAVALA COUNTY, TEXAS

Caitlin Strong stopped her SUV at the checkpoint on Route 83 heading toward Crystal City. The sheriff's deputy approaching her vehicle seemed to recognize her as soon as she slid down her window, well before he could see her Texas Ranger badge. He was an older man, long and lean, with legs crimped inward from too much side-to-side stress on his knees while riding horses.

"You got no call to be here, Ranger," the deputy said, having clearly been warned to expect her, his light complexion a rosy pink shade from the sun and heat.

"You mean driving on a public highway, Deputy?"

"I mean heading into the shit storm that's unfolding a few miles down it." He had brownish-purple blotches on the exposed flesh of his right forearm, the kind of marks that cry out for a dermatologist's attention. Then she noticed the bandages swathed in patches on his other arm and realized they were probably already getting it. "We got enough problems without you sticking your nose in," the deputy continued. "Wherever you go, bullets seem to follow, and the last thing we need is a shooting war."

"You think that's what I came here for?"

The deputy folded his arms in front of his chest so the untreated one stuck out, the dark blotches seeming to widen as his forearm muscles tightened. "I think you've got no idea how Christoph Russell Ilg will react when a Texas Ranger shows up. You don't know these parts, Caitlin Strong, and no stranger known for her gun is gonna solve this problem the sheriff's department has already got under control."

"Under control," Caitlin repeated. "Is that what you call an armed standoff between sheriff's deputies, the highway patrol, and that militia backing Ilg? I heard they've been pouring in from as far away as Idaho. Might as well post a sign off the highway that reads, 'Whack jobs, next exit.'"

"If the highway patrol had just left this to the sheriff's department," the deputy groused, face wrinkling as if he'd swallowed something sour, "those militia men never would've had call to show up. We had the situation contained."

"Was that before or after a rancher started defying the entire federal government?" Caitlin asked him, unable to help herself.

"The goddamn federal government can kiss my ass. This here's Texas, and this here's a local problem. A Zavala County problem that's got no need for the Texas Rangers."

The deputy tilted his stare toward the ground, as if ready to spit some tobacco he wasn't currently chewing. Then he hitched up his gaze along with his shoulders and planted his hands on his hips, just standing there as if this was an extension of the standoff down the road.

"You should wear long sleeves," Caitlin told him.

"Not in this heat."

She let him see her focus trained on the dark blotches dotting his arm. The breeze picked up and blew her wavy black hair over her face. Caitlin brushed it aside, feeling the light sheen of the sunscreen she'd slathered on before setting out from San Antonio. She'd taken to using more of it lately, even though the dark tones that came courtesy of a Mexican grandmother she'd never met made her tan instead of burn.

"Better hot than dead, Deputy," she told the man at her window. "You need me to tell you the rate of skin cancer in these parts?"

He let his arms dangle stiff by his sides. "You really do have a nasty habit of messing in other's people business."

"You mean trying to keep them alive, sometimes from falling victim to their own stubbornness."

"Who we talking about here, Ranger?"

"Christoph Russell Ilg. Who else would we be talking about?"

2

Caitlin reflected on what she'd learned about Christoph Russell Ilg, for the next two miles down the road. His second wife had just given him his ninth child, his sixth son, even though he was somewhere close to either side of seventy. His parents were German immigrants who came to Texas as migrant farmworkers. He'd been born on one of numerous farms they worked in the years immediately after World War II, when birth certificates were optional. Ilg himself swore he didn't even know his own birthday and, as a result, he celebrated his and all his children's on the same day in June, exactly six months after Christmas.

For more than a century, ranchers and feedlot operators had been grazing their cattle on South Texas grasslands. Then the Environmental Protection Agency, working in concert with the Army Corps of Engineers, interpreted the Clean Water Act as giving them the right to redefine cattle ponds, and even ponds formed over flooded land, into what they called "waterways of the United States." The Bureau of Land Management then crafted a law requiring ranchers to get permits for land on which they once free grazed. Short of that, they could be fined for polluting or contaminating those newly proclaimed federal properties.

The fact that the EPA's efforts were as well inten-

tioned as the ranchers' protests were strident probably hadn't registered with Ilg, who'd paid none of the
two dozen citations he'd been issued, amounting to
nearly fifty thousand dollars in fines. In fact, he'd been
purposely setting his cattle to graze near those waterways on a regular basis, including the day the sheriff's
department came to serve him with an arrest warrant
for the unpaid levies. The first of the militiamen who'd
come in expectation of exactly that moment sprang
from positions of cover, training their guns on the
four deputies, who had the sense not to draw theirs in
response.

By the time the reinforcements they summoned arrived, more militiamen had spilled in, and more continued to show up, seemingly by the hour. They formed
a perimeter around the area Ilg had staked out and
returned with his cattle every day to graze, further in-
citing the potential for violence the militiamen seemed
to thirst for while pawing the triggers of their AR-15s
and hunting rifles. One had been arrested during a
routine traffic stop after a highway patrolman had
spotted a Gatling gun in the back of his pickup.

The stand-off had been going on for three days
now, with neither side showing any signs of giving in
or up. For his part, Ilg had no reason to acquiesce
either to the demands of the EPA to stop grazing his
cattle amid federally protected waters or to the attempts of the Bureau of Land Management rangers
to collect the bulk of the fines levied against him. For
their part, the militiamen who'd gathered at Ilg's
ranch not far from Uvalde likely saw his faux crusade
as another last stand to preserve the so-called real and

free America. They wore the fatigues and gear of real soldiers, imagining themselves to be as brave and skilled as true servicemen fighting real wars instead of imaginary ones. Anointing themselves as the only just moral arbiters, when all they really wanted was an opportunity to parade around with their weapons in the hope of someday getting an actual chance to use them.

Caitlin saw the second roadblock at the head of a side road off the highway leading straight to Christoph Russell Ilg's ranch. From this distance, the scene had the look of a child's play scene with toy soldiers staged to confront each other on a papier-mâché battlefield. Drawing closer, Caitlin was able to see the true scope of the danger. Heavily armed highway patrolmen were poised in flak jackets behind their vehicles, while even more heavily armed militiamen peeked out from behind various boulders, trees, and thick fence posts. A television truck bearing the markings of a national cable news channel, meanwhile, was parked between the rival fronts. A technician unloaded equipment while a reporter Caitlin thought she recognized looked on casually.

She pulled her SUV over and was met by a highway patrol captain she'd worked with before, as soon as she climbed out.

"Morning, Frank," she said to Captain Francis Denbow.

"You got no call to be here, Caitlin," he said, mopping the sweat from his brow with a sleeve.

"That's what they told me at the checkpoint back up eighty-three."

"Well, you should have listened to them."

"Thanks, anyway."

"For what?"

"Not telling me you have the situation under control."

"Because we damn well don't. A car backfiring could set off a whole shooting war here over waters not fit to drink. Last thing we need is you stirring the pot. Hope you don't mind I called Austin to get them to call you off."

"Too bad my cell phone's not working," Caitlin told him, reaching back inside the SUV to grab a set of trifolded pages from the visor.

3

ZAVALA COUNTY, TEXAS

Caitlin continued into the open space of road and land between the two armed camps, ignoring the threats shouted her way by the militiamen. She walked on without slowing, heading straight into more guns than she could count, while making sure her SIG Sauer P-226 remained in plain view in its holster. She held the pages before her as well, feeling them rustle in the breeze lifting off the prairie. It picked up briefly, hard enough to whisk the hat off a militiaman lying prone over the rim of an arroyo, holding a rifle with telescopic sight fixed on her. She caught the heavy *whomp-whomp-whomp* of a helicopter circling overhead—this network or that sure to be getting shots of the stand-off.

That's when she spotted the man with the light-colored suit and graying, ginger-shaded hair, striding her way from the side of the road where most of the media had gathered, hands tucked into his pants pockets.

"Well, well, well," grinned Congressman Asa Fraley, who represented Texas's seventeenth district, voice droning as if he were still giving an interview. "Look who it is. Just what we need right now, some gasoline sprayed on the fire."

"I'm just here doing my job, Congressman," Caitlin said, standing stiff before him.

Fraley stopped close enough to Caitlin for her to be able to smell the spearmint lacing his breath. "The problem, Ranger, is I'm here doing my job, too. In this case that means putting out a fire, not fanning the flames."

Caitlin nodded. "I couldn't help but notice which side you're standing with, sir."

"I'm just trying to defuse the situation. That man's a patriot, Ranger," Fraley said, looking back toward Christoph Ilg, who was holding court with any media type who'd listen. "I would've thought you of all people would see that."

"Really? Why?"

"Because the Texas Rangers were birthed to lend justice to a frontier not all that much different than this one."

"Oh, it was plenty different, Congressman," Caitlin said, blowing out her own breath to chase the spearmint back. He'd stopped close enough to leave them contending for the same space, Fraley treating her more like another reporter with whom he needed to establish an instant familiarity. "Back then, my ancestors had their hands full with Mexican bandits and marauding Indian tribes. They never had to deal with the likes of antigovernment militias and politicians looking for any soapbox to shoot off their mouths." She spotted a man glaring at her, having drawn closer to Ilg's right flank, and packing a cannon-size pistol. "Do you have a brother, sir?"

"That's none of your business."

"Because I just noticed a man who looks an awful lot like you. That twin of yours, maybe, the one who can't keep himself out of trouble? As I recall, even in Texas a felon carrying a gun is a violation. Maybe I should run him in."

Fraley took a step back, aware suddenly that the space wasn't his to command as he was normally accustomed. His gaze grew flat and harsh, his eyes narrowing to mere slits barely revealing his grayish pupils. Caitlin had never seen a man with gray eyes before, nor one with a dye job gone so wrong; Fraley's strands of coarse hair were evenly mixed between shades of orange and corn yellow.

"How many men have you killed, exactly, Ranger?"

"One less than maybe I should have, Congressman."

"Is that a threat?"

"No more than that subpoena you keep promising to slap me with to drag me before that committee of yours in Washington."

"It's called the Committee on Oversight and Government Reform, and you're going to find that we take our work very seriously."

"So do I, sir," Caitlin said, peering past him. "Speaking of which, please step aside so I can do my job."

4

ZAVALA COUNTY, TEXAS

Fraley fell into step behind her as Caitlin headed straight for Christoph Ilg, who'd just started his interview with the cable television reporter. He held his big, thick hands on his hips, bracketing a stomach that stretched the bounds of his plaid shirt well over his belt. Ilg was bald and had pinkish, babylike skin that made his utterly round head look like an unfinished basketball with a cowboy hat riding its top. The wind was stiff enough to make him use a hand to keep it pinned in place.

"Christoph Russell Ilg," Caitlin said, in range of both Ilg and the reporter, interrupting their interview, "I'm here to serve you with a warrant for your arrest."

Ilg grinned, clearly unbothered by the warrant she'd extended toward him. His gaze locked on her badge.

"They got girl Texas Rangers now?"

The cable news camera swung her way, making Caitlin realize that the sounds of a chopper overhead had grown louder as it hovered closer to the ground, likely so the cameraman inside could get a better shot of whatever was transpiring. She noticed that the man she took for Asa Fraley's twin brother had slipped away.

"Apparently, sir."

Ilg took off his cowboy hat and fanned the air with it. "Well, I'll be a pig in a poke. Now I've seen everything. Little lady like you with such a big gun. And I ain't taking your warrant."

Caitlin was conscious of the camera still on her, ignoring it. "That's okay, sir, because I'm gonna arrest you anyway."

Time froze, seized up solid. And in the moment before it jump-started again, the color seemed to wash out of the scene. Everything was reduced to grayish halftones as hushed whispers were exchanged on the backs of gun barrels being steadied on both sides. It was like watching a storm racing across the sky while waiting for the first clap of thunder.

"Those highway patrol and sheriff's deputy boys out there already tried that and didn't fare so well. What makes you think you can do any better?" Ilg smirked with the bluster of a man who had a hundred guns backing him up.

"Oh, my presence has nothing to do with those federal trespass charges. I'm here on a state matter. This warrant here details the charge, if you'd like to read it."

"And what charge is that, Ranger?"

"Cattle rustling," Caitlin told him.

Ilg stared at Caitlin for what seemed like a very long time, the camera now shifting back and forth between them. The microphone the reporter had stuck out toward her was now hanging in a kind of limbo. Around her, Caitlin was aware of the almost preternatural quiet that had descended on the scene. No sounds whatsoever, other than what the breeze could rustle up, Caitlin imagining she could hear the gravel and light stone being blown across the two-lane.

That silence scared her more than anything as she continued to eye Ilg, gauging his intentions.

"That blue truck over there yours, sir?" she asked him, noting the old Chevy with a pair of Ilg's teenage sons, both armed with hunting rifles, poised behind it for cover. "I'm going to assume that it is," Caitlin continued, when the rancher remained silent. "This warrant entitles me to search it. But I don't have to do that to know I'll likely find a running iron somewhere inside. You know what that is, sir?"

Ilg swallowed hard, his expression confirming that he did, but Caitlin resumed anyway.

"You seem like an old-school sort to me, Mr. Ilg, so running irons would be just your style. Allow you to brand freehand under cover of night." She cocked her gaze toward the teenage boys with rifles laid over the bed of Ilg's truck, having to raise her voice over the still-descending chopper now. "Something you could teach your boys to do, making them accessories subject to the same ten years in jail as you. I'm betting your iron's got a hooked tip, since the anonymous tip we got says you been changing esses to eights and bars to fours. My warrant also entitles the Rangers or other designated authority to impound your cattle for evidence."

Ilg cupped a hand over his brow and pretended to stare back down the two-lane, trying so hard to look casual and nonchalant that the gesture had the look of a badly rehearsed stage move. "Well, I don't see no trucks. You fixing on squeezing my herd into that German half-track of yours?"

"It's a Ford Explorer, sir, and the trucks will be here any minute to haul your cattle away, accompanied by federal marshals who won't take to you as kindly as the local sheriff's deputies." Caitlin let him see her run her eyes about the gunmen protectively enclosing Ilg in a wide semicircle. "And those marshals have orders to arrest any of your friends here who attempt to impede their efforts, on accessory charges—meaning they'd face the same ten years as you, too. How do you think that'll sit with them? Guess you're going to find out just how good friends they are."

"This won't wash, Ranger," Ilg said slowly, and so softly the reporter had to stick the microphone closer to his mouth.

"Maybe this will," Caitlin told him, extracting a set of pictures from her pocket. "The resolution of these isn't great, but you'll notice that they're all close-ups of the brands on the cattle you claim to be yours. The tampering is evident in all that discoloration."

Caitlin extended the pictures forward but Ilg didn't take them, tried not to even look. Then he swept a hand out and brushed them from her grasp. They fluttered through the air and landed, all face up, strangely, on the bleached concrete.

"Pictures is pictures," was all he said. "And if it interests you any, I got plenty pictures of my own, showing what the government did to half my herd. Picked 'em clean to the bone to make it look like aliens or something, to scare me off. Well, I ain't scared of them and I ain't scared of you, neither."

Caitlin stooped to retrieve the pictures, never taking her eyes off Ilg. "I've also got an affidavit from a local vet who inspected your cattle and found a number of the brands to have fresh scarring. How do you think that could be, exactly?"

Ilg's pale skin had turned a shade of sunburned red, and he was breathing noisily now through his mouth. He seemed to suddenly remember the microphone stabbing the air before him and he cleared his throat, trying to get back the bravado that had won him his sudden celebrity.

"This is free land, Ranger," Ilg spoke her way, going back to his canned lines and raising his voice to be heard over the increasing volume of the helicopter that was just a few hundred feet over them now. "My cattle can graze on it as I see fit. You hear?"

"They're not your cattle, sir," Caitlin said, reaching for the handcuffs clipped to her belt. "And you're under arrest."

Caitlin kept her eyes on Ilg the whole time Frank Denbow and his deputies approached to take him into custody. The tension between the armed camps felt like a hot summer wind blowing through her. But something had changed, uncertainty settling over Ilg's supporters, as if they were suddenly questioning the reason they'd gone to guns.

"I ain't going nowhere," Ilg said through puckered lips, hands tucked behind his back to avoid the handcuffs Caitlin was holding. "Let the lead fly."

So Caitlin circled behind him while Ilg primped for the cameras that had converged like a third army onto the scene. As she snapped the handcuffs on, he swept his gaze about the blocked portion of the two-lane, expression crinkled in dim confusion over his militia protectors, none of whose names he actually knew, holding their ground but not his stare.

"He's all yours, Captain," she said to Frank Denbow, as if it were only the three of them now.

While the cable news camera continued to roll, Congressman Asa Fraley had made himself conveniently scarce, and Caitlin found herself scanning the lines of the militiamen in search of the man she took to be his brother.

Before she could spot him again, the helicopter she'd figured had been dispatched by another television network set down on flat stretch of ground on the empty side of the road, its rotor wash kicking up a storm of dust and gravel, which left forces on both sides shielding their eyes. Caitlin watched as the thin, knobby figure of Texas Ranger Captain D. W. Tepper climbed out of the chopper and ducked low to avoid the blades still spinning in a blur as he made his way toward her, getting only so far as the pavement of the two-lane.

"We got trouble, Ranger!" Tepper yelled over the sounds of the still-churning helicopter. "Come on, the meter's running!"

"Where we headed, Captain?"

"An empty school bus was found just outside of Houston."

"Since when do the Rangers get called in to investigate empty school buses?"

"Since all the students who'd been riding it are missing. Since those students come from a fancy Houston prep school." He paused, his dour expression making the furrows lining his face seem deeper than ever. "Since one of the missing students is the youngest son of that boyfriend of yours, Cort Wesley Masters."

5

DALLAS, TEXAS

"Hey, baby, you like what you see?"

Cort Wesley Masters smiled back at the dancer who'd just tossed her top into his face, stopping short of feeding her the ten- or twenty-dollar bill she'd been expecting for the effort. When that failed, she ran her hands through his thick hair, now tinted gray at the temples, and let her fingers trace the lines of the deepest sun wrinkles dug into his face. Then she backed off, flashing an even more forced smile that slipped from her face so fast it seemed the gesture must've hurt her.

Cort Wesley sat at a table squeezed against the stage, which was scuffed by heels and discolored in patches by spilled drinks. The girl whose top he dropped onto an empty chair was one of three performing now at the Pleasure Dome, the reddest of all the establishments in Dallas's red-light district off Harry Hines Boulevard, just steps away from a family-oriented area of stores, shops, and restaurants. Several blocks were jam-packed with massage parlors, adult book and video stores, rooming houses that rented by the hour, and establishments that ranged from truly seedy to those attracting a reasonably respectable crowd of businessmen and college students, like the Pleasure Dome.

The marquee outside advertised a free luncheon buffet and a daily morning attraction called Legs and Eggs, for those either getting off work, on their way to it, or simply suffering from insomnia. He'd heard that much of this section of Harry Hines Boulevard was owned and operated by the Russian mob, after the Branca family out of New Orleans, in whose employ Cort Wesley had once served, had pulled up stakes due to either eradication or imprisonment of its leaders. He'd never given that much thought, until he'd gotten the call that brought him here this afternoon.

Hey, it's a living.

Cort Wesley didn't know who coined that phrase originally, but truer words had never been spoken.

A second dancer was tempting him by leaning over and spreading her butt cheeks as far as they would go. Cort Wesley flirted with the notion of wedging at least a dollar bill into the space revealed, then decided on a cocktail napkin instead, in keeping with the true purpose behind his presence here.

The dancer shot him the finger before moving on down the line.

Cort Wesley figured the cocktail napkin would do the trick for sure, and he sipped at his ginger ale, which was now watery with melted ice. The Pleasure Dome didn't charge a cover during the day, relying solely on food and alcohol sales to justify the show. Proper tipping was an unwritten rule here, as much as the fifteen percent added to a restaurant tab was, the difference being that the amounts swayed wildly depending on the level of a customer's drunkenness, desperation, and depravity.

Cort Wesley saw one of the dancers look toward him but not quite his way. He realized that this was the first time in the hour he'd been at the stage-front table, for which he'd paid twenty bucks, that none of the girls were anywhere near him. Then a trio of broad shadows fell over his table.

"We need you to leave the premises," the biggest of the shadows said, with knuckles laid on the table in simian fashion.

"I do something?"

"No," the big man said. "That's why we need you to leave."

"I paid twenty bucks to get this table."

"It's also customary to tip the ladies."

"Ladies?" Cort Wesley smirked. "Really?"

"How hard do you want to make this?"

How hard do I need to? Cort Wesley wanted to say, but that would have broken the illusion he needed to cast.

"I want my twenty bucks back first," Cort Wesley

said, not budging from his chair. "You can buy me a drink on the way out."

The biggest shadow leaned across the table and spilled Cort Wesley's ginger ale in his lap. "There's your drink, and this is me tossing your ass out of here."

Cort Wesley let himself be jerked out of the chair by the other two hulks squeezed into dark suits that looked ready to burst at the seams. "I wanna see the manager."

"This is close as you're gonna get," said the biggest one doing all the talking.

"The owner, then. I want my twenty bucks back or I go straight to my lawyer. He won me a bunch of cash in a personal injury case. It's all I've got to live on—that's why I'm not tipping. Tell your boss to show some compassion or my lawyer will serve him before the next shift goes on tonight. So what'll be, bub?"

"Bub?"

"Hey, I didn't mean anything by it. Does your boss have any idea how you treat customers?"

And, just as expected, the commotion had drawn that boss, a burly older Russian named Alexi Gribanov, from his back office down a short hall just off the bar.

"Hey!" Cort Wesley called to him as the three thugs dragged him off. "Hey, you! You think I don't know who you are, what you're really doing here? Smarten up, bub. I can turn your lights out forever."

Gribanov must've passed some signal to his thugs to stop them in their tracks, because that's what they did. Then they started dragging Cort Wesley toward the bar instead of toward the exit, slicing past tables where seated patrons barely looked away from the stage antics they'd come here to see.

"Hey!" Cort Wesley made himself protest, forcing himself to go limp in the thugs' grasp. "Who the fuck you guys think you are?"

They tossed him into Gribanov's office and planted him in a chair, didn't close the door until their boss was inside.

"So," he said to Cort Wesley, "tell me why I shouldn't have you killed?"

6

DALLAS, TEXAS

"Hey, bub," Cort Wesley started fearfully, hands held out almost as if he was praying to the Russian, "I made a mistake, okay?"

"No, this is not okay in my establishment. And 'bub,' what is this 'bub'?"

"I don't know. It's like calling somebody 'sir' or 'friend.'"

Gribanov slapped Cort Wesley across the face with a hand that stank like sardines. "Am I your friend now?"

Gribanov crouched down, face-to-face with him now, smelling lightly of cologne instead. He was a dapper man with well-coiffed white hair and a perfectly groomed mustache. In his late sixties probably, short and heavyset to the point where Cort Wesley guessed he must've had his suits custom made, unlike his thugs, who probably bought their matching black ones off the rack in the big-and-tall-man section of the nearest department store.

"You know the Russian word for 'bitch'?" Gribanov sneered at him.

Cort Wesley noticed his eyes looked set too far back in his face, as if they'd been somehow pushed out of place. And one of them seemed to lag behind the other when they blinked.

"No."

"It's *cyka.*" He slapped Cort Wesley again, harder. "And you're my *cyka* now; you're my bitch because you ask to be treated like one. You disrespected my establishment, my home, and that means you disrespected me."

"Hey," Cort Wesley pleaded, pulling back. "I got problems, okay? I told your men here I was in this car accident, and ever since—"

Gribanov slapped him a third time, the hardest blow yet, and easily hard enough for Cort Wesley to sell being thrown from the chair to the floor, where he lay cowering on his back, waiting for the stars to clear from before his eyes.

"Can we just forget this, please?"

Gribanov stared down at him.

"I get my next installment check on my settlement the third of the month. I'll come make good with the girls then, I promise. Hand to God, man, hand to God."

And Cort Wesley stuck a trembling hand up to enunciate his point.

Gribanov glared at him. "They're not girls; they're ladies. You understand me?"

"Yes. Yes, I do."

"They deserve your respect. And the way you show respect is with money, and when you don't, you pay a different way."

Cort Wesley saw the biggest thug's foot coming and prepared for it as best he could. But it still rammed his torso with the force of a jackhammer splitting concrete, compressing his ribs enough to rip his breath away and leave him gasping for real. The thug kicked him again, Cort Wesley taking the blow square on his hip, sparing his ribs and soft tissue this time. Then Gribanov was in his face, Cort Wesley sucking in a lungful of his cologne, mixed with the sardine stench when he let out his breath.

"We leave things here, eh, *bub?*" He pronounced it *boob*. "But you come back here it gets much worse. Your lawyer shows up and it gets even worse than that—for him, too. Nod if you understand."

Cort Wesley nodded.

"Now, get out of my sight . . . *bub.*"

Which drew a chuckle from all three thugs, none of whom lowered a hand to help him up. So Cort Wesley stretched a hand up to the sill of Gribanov's desk, spilling the contents of a pen holder to the floor, making a desperate show to replace everything inside and put it back in place when he finally got to his feet.

He said nothing further, just raised his hands in that same conciliatory fashion he couldn't remember ever doing before in his life and backed out the door. Still seething, his ribs still fiery with pain, Cort Wesley pushed through a side exit into the parking lot and headed toward an innocuous SUV parked in a darkened corner, climbing in and slamming the door hard enough to startle the big shape behind the wheel.

"Whoa, easy does it there, *bub*," smirked the man Cort Wesley knew only as Jones.

7

DALLAS, TEXAS

Cort Wesley had met Jones through Caitlin Strong and, like a bad penny, he just kept coming back. "Well," he said, closing the door behind him, "at least I know the bug's working."

"Where'd you plant it?"

"Under Gribanov's pen holder."

"You're kidding."

Cort Wesley shook his head. "It hurts too much to laugh."

Jones took out his cell phone and jogged it to an application already on the screen. He hit a single key on the keyboard, transferring Cort Wesley's considerable fee for letting the Russian assholes kick his ass, and stuck the phone back in his pocket.

"There you go. Not bad for a day's work."

In his mind, Cort Wesley was already parceling out the money between his son Dylan's college bills and son Luke's tuition for the prep school he attended in

Houston. "Easy for you to say, Jones; they're not your ribs."

"Just don't go running to the Ranger and tell her I mistreated you."

"Afraid she might shoot you?"

Jones smirked, the gesture seeming to lengthen the rectangular face dominated by crystal-colored eyes. Cort Wesley thought his hair looked more like individual strands of straw sewn onto his scalp.

"If she was going to shoot me, cowboy, she would've done it a long time ago."

"What's all this about, Jones?"

Jones started to turn the key. "You've been paid for your efforts. Let's just leave it there."

"Why does Homeland Security care about a two-bit Russian gangster like Alexi Gribanov? What's their interest? And why bother planting what they called a tin ear in my old man's time when you've got the goddamn NSA on speed dial?"

Jones started the engine and gunned it. "Because maybe the fiasco that went down here in your lovely state last year changed the equation some. Maybe Homeland, in general, and yours truly, in particular, lost a little juice and gumption. Maybe I'm persona non grata and the NSA isn't taking my calls anymore."

"Cry me a river, agent man."

"You were special ops in the first Gulf War?"

Cort Wesley nodded. "Long before it came into fashion."

"So, does the fact we're cut from the same cloth irk you at all?"

"Different tailors, though," Cort Wesley said, and

noticed two of Gribanov's thugs, including the biggest one, whose shoe imprints he was currently wearing on his ribs, emerge from the same exit and light up cigarettes as they clung to the slight shade provided by an overhang.

"You mind giving me a minute here?" Cort Wesley said, easing the door open. "I think I left something inside."

Cort Wesley looped the long way around the parking lot, clinging to the edges and approaching the two thugs from outside their line of sight. Add that to the distraction of them making small talk, probably joking about the loser whose ass they'd just kicked, along with the fact that each had a hand occupied working a cigarette, and this was going to be over very quickly.

They didn't see Cort Wesley, even at the last, didn't see him at all until he'd angled himself to sweep in off their rear. The one closest to him—not the one who'd done the kicking—must've caught a hint of motion out of his peripheral vision. He swung, both hands coming round with him to leave his cigarette dangling free in his mouth. Cort Wesley hit him so fast with a blow to his face that his mouth gaped and he swallowed his cigarette, gagging and retching when he slammed back against the side of the building.

By then, Cort Wesley had taken the other thug's leg out, the leg attached to the very same foot that had pummeled his ribs. Turned out the cliché about the bigger they are, the harder they fall couldn't have been more accurate. The bigger thug went down with a force that seemed to rattle the very parking lot, coughing up a thin cloud of gravel and dust on impact.

"How's it feel, bub?" Cort Wesley asked from over him, before bringing his boot down against the side of the same knee, feeling something in the joint snap.

The bigger thug was screaming, rolling back and forth across a swatch of the parking lot that was now cleared of debris, sticking to his suit instead. His flailing hands seemed to have trouble grasping his wounded knee.

The smaller thug's guttural roar alerted Cort Wesley he was coming, a millisecond before he would've realized it anyway. The man lashed out with one wild strike, and then another, the second missing so badly his momentum actually cracked him against the same wall he'd already struck once. Ready to hit him again, Cort Wesley simply watched as he slumped to the asphalt, one side of his face riding the brick the whole way.

Cort Wesley made sure to free the still-writhing thug's gun from its holster and toss it into a nearby Dumpster, which stank to holy hell. Then he cut a straight line across the parking lot, back to Jones's SUV, not noticing or caring if anyone saw him.

"You are one piece of work, cowboy," Jones said, shaking his head when Cort Wesley closed the door behind him.

Cort Wesley opened the glove compartment and felt around for the cell phone he'd left in there. He had six missed calls and two voice mails, all from Luke's school, which had come in while he'd been getting his ribs worked on inside the Pleasure Dome and then had paid the kicker back in spades.

"Okay if we leave now?" Jones asked him, starting the engine again.

"You mind shutting up for a minute?" Cort Wesley said. "I got a call I need to return."

8

ARMAND BAYOU, TEXAS

The empty school bus sat in a cordoned-off area of the parking lot, surrounded by more law enforcement officials than students who'd been inside the bus when it departed the Village School thirty minutes away yesterday. Luke Torres, just short of his sixteenth birthday and a sophomore now, had chosen the Houston-based prep school himself, after his older brother, Dylan, had been accepted to Brown University. Luke wasn't half the athlete his older brother was, but he was twice the student, and he knew he'd need all of that to follow Dylan to an Ivy League university, maybe Brown too.

And now he was missing, along with thirty-five of his classmates.

"Could you give me that again, Captain?" Caitlin had asked, once the helicopter was airborne over Christoph Russell Ilg's farm.

"Luke Torres, thirty-five other students, two teachers, and three chaperones are missing from an overnight field trip in the Armand Bayou Nature Center," Tepper told her, moving his mouth as if he were chewing gum for want of a Marlboro. "Parents reported receiving phone calls and texts right up until around midnight, when the adults likely got fed up with all the chatter. After that—nothing. They were camping out on the preserve farm at the time. According to reports, their stuff and supplies are gone, too, like they just flat-out vanished into thin air and took everything with them."

"What else, Captain?"

Tepper took off his hat and scratched at the bald patches of his scalp that looked red and scaly. He sucked in some breath and let it out as a sigh that dissolved into more of a growl. "That's all we really got right now. The Ranger chopper was available, so as soon as I got the word Luke Torres was one of the missing, I commandeered it and headed to pick you up. Just do me one favor when we get to the scene, Ranger," Tepper said, glancing down at the scene below, where the big trucks had arrived to tote Christoph Ilg's stolen cattle away. "Stay away from anything that even looks like a camera."

The chopper's landing pod settled with a *thunk,* Caitlin needing no coaxing to throw open the door and step down, starting toward the lot where the bus was parked without waiting for Captain Tepper.

"There's been no ransom demands," he said, breathing hard from the mere effort of keeping up with her.

"Not yet," Caitlin told him, the school bus square in her sights. "How about we go have a talk with the driver?"

9

ARMAND BAYOU, TEXAS

The Armand Bayou Nature Center boasted an ideal and beautifully bucolic setting in which to fulfill its mission statement, which was to open the door to numerous elements of the natural world, cutting across various disciplines. It was situated in its own little world, right on the Texas Gulf Coast, which didn't feel like Texas at all. Essentially, the 2,500 acres the center now claimed was an outdoor classroom rich with virtually every ecosystem imaginable, available for study. Amazing how so much of the food chain that made up the world and helped define civilization was contained in various parts of the grounds, from the coastline and further in. All a mere thirty-minute drive from the city of Houston.

A bit more for a school bus.

Nestled in the Clear Lake area, Armand Bayou strove to make visitors appreciate the various wetlands, prairie, forest, and marsh habitats enough to join the fight to preserve them in their pristine form.

A trio of sophomore science classes from the Village School had taken a field trip to learn about plant and animal inhabitants, bird-watch, hike on the trails lifted from another time, or view live animal displays of snakes, alligators, turtles, hawks, and bison.

From the itinerary D. W. Tepper had explained to her, the day had finished with a visit to the center's Martyn Farm, which elegantly recreated the lifestyle just as it had been in late-1800s Texas. They were to set up camp in an open field and sleep under the stars. The next morning they'd take a ride on the *Bayou Ranger,* a pontoon boat moored at the nearby docks, prior to heading back to school, with a stop for lunch planned on the way. The students, faculty, and chaperones were to rendezvous at the bus promptly at eleven o'clock and, toward that end, the driver made sure she was back in the lot by ten thirty.

"Bad weather would've brought me back here earlier," the woman explained to Captain Tepper and Caitlin from the school bus's shadow.

Her name was Sara Ann Hoder and she had mousy blond hair that looked fashioned from thin string, reaching just past her ears. She had a big, round face and blue eyes that looked too small for it. She was dressed in ill-fitting jeans and a baggy top that couldn't quite hide the muffin shape of her midriff. Caitlin noticed she was wearing worn sneakers that looked like a man's and smelled of a combination of musty clothes and cigarettes that might've been Marlboros, just like Captain Tepper smoked.

Caitlin checked the bus's markings again. "So you don't work for the school."

"No, the bus company. First Student. We've got a contract with the school for sporting events, field trips, and the like."

Caitlin glanced at Tepper, making a mental note of that. "So who would know you were coming out here?"

"My gosh, all kinds of people. Places like the Village School reserve buses long in advance. Of course, they may provide the itineraries later, closer to the ride in question. But to answer your question, let's see, the dispatcher for sure, the booking office—heck, pretty much anyone at the company who's got a computer."

"Let's turn our attention back to the events of today, when you came to pick the kids up, and yesterday, when you dropped them off. Did you notice anything that sticks out in your mind?"

Sara Ann Hoder tucked her hands into the pockets of her smock Caitlin had taken for a shirt, waiting for her to continue. "No, Ranger, I didn't."

"On either occasion, especially yesterday, did you notice anyone lingering about, maybe in a way that made them stand out in your mind?"

The woman puckered her lips, features squeezed taut as if she were searching for just that, and looked disappointed when she didn't find it. "No, ma'am. I'm sorry."

"Don't be sorry, Sara Ann. You're doing great here. This isn't your doing in any way whatsoever. But that doesn't mean there wasn't something that sticks out, something maybe just a little off, that could help us get to the bottom of things."

The bus driver swallowed hard. "You figure something bad happened to those kids?"

"It's too early for speculation of any kind, but they're missing, and that's bad in itself. What about vehicles?"

"Vehicles?"

"In the parking lot, when you pulled in yesterday."

"I didn't pull in then. I let the kids out at a drop-off point, like a staging center."

"Okay," Caitlin said, keeping her tone reserved and gentle. "There then."

"Other vehicles, you mean?"

"Yes, ma'am."

"Hmm, let me think some more on that. It's all I've been doing since the kids didn't show up when they were supposed. Running things through my head, knowing somebody'd be asking me these very questions."

"Take your time, Sara Ann."

The woman buried her face in her hands, starting to break down. "It's so darn hard. My brain's all seized up like a bad bearing."

"Then let's leave it for now. Try again later. How's that sound?"

The woman nodded, sort of. Caitlin tried to look reassuring before she slid away with Tepper in tow.

"Any security cameras, Captain?"

"Not a single one back out on the road, and just four to cover all these grounds, one of which is inside the souvenir shop that just opened." Tepper ran his tongue around the inside of his mouth, pushing it about as if feeling for something. "Guess shoplifting around here is considered a bigger crime than thirty-six missing students and their chaperones."

"Let's go have a look at the campsite where they were last seen."

10

ARMAND BAYOU, TEXAS

The Martyn farmhouse offered a perfect re-creation of the past, specifically life on an 1890s farm. One of the few trips her father had taken Caitlin on was highlighted by a stop in the Amish country of Pennsylvania, featuring an actual working farm and exhibit residence that, like this, was period perfect. No electricity or running water, which was also how the Amish continued to live today.

The Martyn farmhouse reminded Caitlin of that. Only a bit too staid, perfect, and clean—more like an exhibit lifted out of a museum. The actual farm displays, including various gardens, were scattered through other areas of the grounds that, in Caitlin's mind, made for the possible routes the perpetrators had used to make forty-one hostages vanish into nowhere. The lone exception was a single interactive field a stone's throw from the farmhouse, laid out to allow visitors to work the crops as if they were real farmers. Only there were no crops, just a dead field with only dried, untended soil where whatever had once grown here had been. The field was rimmed on three sides by trees known as desert willows, which looked weak and sallow, as if starved of nutrients by the parched ground.

"There's rooms upstairs you can arrange to sleep in," Tepper told her when they entered the stuffy confines of the replica farmhouse, the windows closed against the day's building heat. "School administrator I talked to told me that was the plan for the kids."

"Probably too hot, too steamy. And it was a beautiful night to sleep out."

"They all had sleeping bags with them, part of the stuff everyone was supposed to bring."

"You got that list, D.W.?"

"Why?"

"Because it may be helpful to our cause. Won't know exactly how until I see it."

"I'll order it up."

"Let's check out where the kids did end up sleeping, first."

The field between the Martyn house and the sample farmland reminded Caitlin of the one where the chopper had landed, except the grass was browning here as well. The entire perimeter where the kids had bedded down had been sectioned off by yellow crime scene tape looped between sawhorses arranged in a de facto circle. Police, both uniformed and plainclothes, swarmed the area, along with crime scene technicians covering every square inch of area. Several of these held high-intensity lights that could detect blood or other secretions. Others dabbed at the ground with brushes that made them look like some kind of artists. Still more were taking samples of grass and soil at regularly spaced junctures, clacking off photograph after photograph, or measuring some impression they'd found in the grass.

A Houston patrolman in uniform held up the crime scene tape at their approach, Caitlin watching it stiffen and then flutter in the wind above her.

"What do you notice, D.W.?" she said to Captain Tepper.

"Nothing, absolutely nothing."

"Right. No sleeping bags, backpacks, personal items. Whoever took them wanted to make it seem like they were never here. You ever know, seen, or heard of a kidnapping scene like this?"

Caitlin ran her eyes about, hoping to see something that had escaped her so far. The grass flattened or broke away under her boots, and the sound of the wind rustling through the trees that enclosed the field on three sides would've sounded even louder after dark last night. A few of the law enforcement types nodded toward Tepper and Caitlin as they passed, the crime scene techs paying them no heed at all.

"Not exactly," Tepper said finally. He took off his hat and fanned himself with it. "Closest was a case I worked with your dad once. Couple kids got snatched from a playground. Whoever did it doused the scene in bleach. I could smell it as soon as I stepped out of my truck. I don't smell anything like that here."

"What happened to those kids?"

"Found dead in the perp's trunk a week later. He'd pulled his car into the garage in midsummer. A neighbor called the locals when the stench got to be too much." Tepper turned his face to the sun, then swung it away just as fast, as if that brief moment was all it took to burn his skin. "Guy takes bleach to a crime scene and then leaves the bodies to rot in the trunk of an old Chevy. Can you explain that to me?"

Caitlin couldn't, something else on her mind. "What kind of security they have at night here?"

"Couple rent-a-cops crisscrossing the roads, doing routine rounds. Only one of them was on duty last night. The other called in sick and is already in custody. Locals are sweating him, but so far they've got nothing except a trash can full of vomit. I guess he really was sick." Tepper paused and felt about his pockets for his Marlboros, until he remembered he'd left them somewhere else. "Maybe we're thinking about this the wrong way."

"How's that, Captain?"

"Maybe we should be focusing on how they got them out and away from here. Would have taken another bus or a truck, and the two-lane offers only two choices once they were off the grounds: right and left."

Caitlin continued to survey the scene, picturing forty-one students and adults bedding down for the night, climbing into their sleeping bags, with some sweeping their flashlight beams across the night sky. "This all goes down and not one of the now missing managed to get any word out?"

"So?"

"Assume they were all asleep. Assume they all got

snatched so fast nobody had a chance to make a call or send a text."

"What we got is what you see," Captain Tepper told her. "No footprints, tire tracks, socks, underwear. No evidence whatsoever anybody was ever here. Jesus H., Ranger, maybe those kids got sucked up into the sky by space aliens."

"Or a team of professionals who'd done this kind of thing before, not necessarily in these parts."

"Foreign terrorists?"

Caitlin shrugged. "Something we need to consider."

"Then where's the ransom call, Ranger, or call to the press to claim credit?"

"Give it time. How long did it take when that nut job grabbed a school bus and buried it in the ground, kids and all?"

Before Tepper could respond, walkie-talkies started squawking across the field. The uniformed officers canted their heads toward their shoulder-mounted radios and the detectives jerked the handheld variety from their belts, one of them turning toward Tepper and Caitlin as he jogged past.

"Two of the missing kids just wandered out of the woods," he said.

II

Guillermo Paz leaned across the plank-wood table, his huge legs squeezed uncomfortably beneath it, with knees left to rub up against the underside. "Don't take this the wrong way, but I need to know you're not a fake."

Madam Caterina narrowed her gaze at him. "Test me, child."

"It's been a long time since anyone called me 'child,' " Paz reflected, still wondering what exactly had attracted him to this storefront off East Houston Street in east San Antonio, which featured a sign outside that read, "Psychic Readings by Madam Caterina. Satisfaction Guaranteed."

"We're all God's children, and God knows no age," Madam Caterina told him.

She was a shapeless woman, her bulk concealed beneath a baggy black dress that looked more like a housecoat. Her face was patchwork of tone and texture, darker skin intermixed with lighter, as if her genes couldn't make up their mind which race actually claimed her for its own. Her eyes were light, almost silvery, a strange complement to her raven hair. But her eyes seemed to change color depending on how the light from the single lamp dangling directly over the table struck them, sometimes seeming as dark as her hair. The lighter patches of her complexion looked shiny, almost translucent, as if she was the result of an unfinished portrait. Her hair was tied tightly up in a bun, with a woven silk scarf concealing it tight against her scalp.

The plank table before them, Paz noted, was empty. No crystal ball, tarot cards—not even a Ouija board. Just a box of tissues.

"The last person to call me 'child' was a priest back home in Venezuela," he picked up.

Madam Caterina seemed to look at him differently, as if suddenly seeing someone else seated across from her. She reached across the table and grasped Paz's hands in hers, kneading them. "He's dead, isn't he?"

He resisted the temptation to pull his hands away. "Yes."

"And you witnessed it, you watched him die, this priest," Madam Caterina said, eyes straying off Paz as if surprised by her own words.

"Right again."

"He was murdered. He was carrying something at the time. Two bags. He was walking back to the church with them. Something to eat."

"Bread," Paz said, louder than he'd meant to.

Madam Caterina looked into his eyes and something changed in hers. "Oh."

"What?"

"You should leave," the psychic said, letting go of his hands and pulling away.

"We haven't finished."

"We haven't even started, and we're not going to,"

Madam Caterina said, rising to her feet in an unspoken signal for the giant across from her to do the same.

But Paz stayed in his chair, his knee knocking up against the underside of the plank table. "You answered my question."

"You didn't ask me one."

"I meant about you being a fake. You're not. You're the real thing. That must've been what brought me here. Back in the La Vega slum where I grew up, the people thought my mother was a *bruja,* a witch. She had visions, saw things that weren't there. For a long time I thought she was crazy."

Madam Caterina sat back down. "What changed, child?"

"A few years later, I found her crying when I got home. She knew what I'd done."

"You killed the man who shot the priest."

"He had it coming."

"You did it with a knife, *his* knife, a knife you still carry."

"How do you know all this? Who told you?"

"Would you like to speak to your mother?"

"I speak to her all the time."

"You talk, but you don't hear what she's got to say. She's here now. Do you have something to ask her?"

"No," Paz said, his voice taking on the sheepishness it always had in his mother's company as a boy, because he knew he could never lie to her. She could always tell and would scold him with her eyes that could pierce his soul.

"Then what did bring you here . . . *Mo?*"

"That's what my mother called me. Short for Guillermo."

"I know. She just told me."

Paz suddenly felt very cold and realized he was trembling, an entirely foreign sensation for him. "I'm not the same person I became after killing the man who murdered my priest. I killed a whole lot of people after that—in service to my country, I told myself, but mostly because I enjoyed it."

"Your mother says as much," Madam Caterina told him. "But she also agrees you're not that man anymore."

"You don't even know me."

"Your mother does, and those were her words, not mine. You sure you don't want to talk to her? Maybe about these other paths you've taken in search of the truth?"

Paz found himself leaning forward, his chair creaking from the strain. "I audited college classes for a while, but that didn't work out too well. Then I tried teaching English to Mexican immigrants, but that worked even worse. I always end up back with my new priest at the San Fernando Cathedral near Main Plaza. Thought I was done seeking my answers elsewhere, until I showed up here."

Madam Caterina seemed to study Paz briefly, then looked down at the plank table. "You came to this country to kill," she said, eyes remaining poised that way. "And you've done plenty more killing since, but not toward your original purpose in coming."

Paz nodded, even though she wasn't looking at him.

"Toward a different purpose entirely." Madam Caterina looked up but squeezed her eyes closed. "I see a woman wearing a badge."

"My Texas Ranger."

"She's the one you came here to kill. I see you both with guns, aiming at each other."

Paz couldn't believe what he was hearing. "That was a long time ago. I look in the mirror now, I see an entirely different man looking back. Still a work in progress, though."

"How's that?"

"I want to see in my eyes what I see in my Texas Ranger's."

"And what's that?" Madam Caterina asked, her tone different, the otherworldly forces that had grabbed her ear likely quieting themselves to listen as well.

"I don't know. I'm still working on that, too."

"Now you find purpose in being her protector, in searching for the light you see in her eyes, Colonel."

Paz found himself taken aback again. "How'd you know that?"

"Know what?"

"That I was once a colonel. My Texas Ranger calls me that."

"You didn't tell me?"

"No."

"Someone else did, then. Your mother maybe. Wait," Madam Caterina signaled. "Something's wrong. . . ." Her eyes sharpened. "Does this Texas Ranger have children, a son?"

"Yes and no. Two boys."

"One's in trouble. Danger," Madam Caterina corrected quickly. "She's going to need you."

"My Texas Ranger?"

Madam Caterina nodded. "And this boy."

Paz started to rise, when Madam Caterina clamped a hand on his forearm from the other side of the table. He'd been captured by antigovernment rebels back home in Venezuela once, manacled to a tree while they tried to figure out what to do with him. That's what the woman's grasp felt like—a steel manacle fastened over his flesh, squeezing tight enough to shut off the blood flow until his fingers went numb.

"Wait," she said again, "there's a light, a strong light, a blinding light. Everywhere at once, swallowing everything."

"A nuclear blast maybe," Paz reasoned.

"In my experience, it's more likely metaphorical, the strong light a sign of something that's coming."

"In my experience," Paz told her, as she finally released her grasp so he could rise as tall as the single light fixture dangling from the ceiling, "they're the same thing."

PART TWO

One Ranger who has come to epitomize the Ranger service of the early 1900s was Bill McDonald, captain of Ranger Company B. One reason McDonald is still so well known today is that he had a knack for hard-boiled talk. . . . Perhaps less known is McDonald's statement to a large mob that confronted him as he left a jail with two prisoners in custody. "Damn your sorry souls!" growled McDonald as the men surged forward, intent on hanging the prisoners in his custody. "March out of here and get away from this jail, every one of you, or I'll fill this yard with dead men." The mob quickly dispersed.

—Jesse Sublett, "Lone on the Range: Texas Lawmen,"
Texas Monthly, December 31, 1969

12

The bright light shining on the stage kept Calum Dane from seeing the protester storm down the aisle and yank off his own leg. The move had the look of a performance to it, slapstick comedy maybe, until Dane saw that it was a prosthetic leg he was now trumpeting over his head like a flag, while the audience hooted and hollered.

"You did this to me, Mr. Dane!" the young man yelled up toward the stage, holding the leg still to keep himself from falling. "You just said you're in the business of giving back. How about it then, sir? Give me back my leg!"

Dane cupped a hand over his brow to shield his eyes from the lighting. He'd taken the stage just a few minutes earlier, the wires of the lavalier microphone threaded up under his shirt to emerge at his lapel like a clipped-on insect. He'd straightened it one last time in the mirror before he'd taken the stage. His own expression stared back at him, Dane amazed by how little different he looked from year to year. His coarse black hair showed barely a touch of gray, and his skin tone held just enough color and leathery stitching to capture his rough-hewn spirit and experience as a mere boy working farm fields and offshore oil rigs before he owned a damn thing.

Now he owned lots of things, though not this ballroom, where he'd taken the stage to give the keynote address to his company's shareholders and was greeted with hoots, hollers, and boos. Dane had just managed to get the audience to simmer down, just a few catcalls about the lawsuits and controversies in which Dane Corp was embroiled stubbornly shouted his way, when the kid holding his leg hopped up the center aisle, much to the angry crowd's delight.

"I'm glad to see we've got a packed house today, ladies and gentlemen," he said to the cluster of faces and frames squeezed into the hotel ballroom's tightly packed chairs, the shareholders he'd made rich who'd booed his entry. "And I appreciate the opportunity to address you, although I wish I could do it one stockholder at a time to better explain how Dane Corp is affecting, sometimes dramatically, your everyday lives."

He paused long enough to meet as many stares as he could, doing his best to ignore the smattering of fresh boos that resounded, and to ignore the one-legged young man at the same time.

"You sleep on mattresses treated with a Dane Chemical solvent to repel bedbugs," Dane continued, his long legs aching from standing for practically two days straight doing damage control. "You drive cars made safer by the new air bags Dane Technology invented. You talk on phones and communicate on the

Internet more clearly and safely because of Dane Advanced Electronics. The food you eat costs less because of the advances in farming made possible by Dane Petrochemicals and Dane Pharmaceuticals. We are in the business of giving back—primarily to you, our shareholders."

"Then give me back my leg!" the kid yelled up at him, and the crowd roared with delight, cheering and applauding as he waved his prosthetic lower leg in the air at the foot of the stage.

He was probably in his midtwenties but his long, shaggy hair and soft, buttery features made him look young enough to pass for high school. Almost immediately, dark-suited members of Calum Dane's private security force stormed down both aisles. But Dane held them back with a simple gesture of his hand while he moved to the front of the stage to address the protester personally, seeing the headlines that would surely result if he let his security team have its way.

"What's your name, son?"

"Brandon McCabe."

"How'd you lose your leg, Brandon?"

"You took it from me. And I'm not your son."

Dane crouched in front of the protester so they were face-to-face. "By me taking your leg, I assume you're referring to the unfounded claims that one of our pesticides caused cancer."

"It's not unfounded. This is living proof of that," the young man added, addressing the crowd more than Calum Dane as he pumped the air with his leg. "My epithelioid sarcoma is living proof of that."

"Not according to a joint investigation conducted by the EPA and FDA."

"Bullshit. And that's what the investigation amounted to: bullshit."

"I'd ask you to watch you language, young man."

"You didn't ask me if I wanted to get cancer. There was no warning label on whatever it was that gave it to me, just all those reports I read later about people getting the same or similar disease, all linked to a pesticide your company produced."

"And that has now been removed from the market on a purely precautionary basis. We take our role and our responsibility at Dane Corp seriously, son."

"I'm not your son."

"No, you're not; my boy died serving in Afghanistan. If he'd lived he'd be about your age now. A land mine took his leg, too, along with pretty much everything else."

"Shit happens, man. I should know."

"It happens to everyone," Dane said, stopping short of mentioning his other son, who a court order prevented him from seeing. "And Dane Corp is in the business of making sure it happens less. You may not believe this but, thanks to us, your food is safer than it's ever been. When you travel, you're safer than you've ever been. And if, by chance, you work around hazardous or toxic materials, you're safer because of the improvements we've made in the protective gear you wear. We are in the business of making your life better."

"Not all the time," said Brandon McCabe.

13

Dane stood back upright and moved to address the rest of the crowd, turning his back on the kid who was becoming a royal pain in the ass.

"You can't ignore me!"

"Yeah, yeah!" parts of the audience barked, supporting Brandon McCabe, as more boos and catcalls echoed.

"I'm not, and I'm not going to ignore *you,* either," Dane told the audience. "You know the two most valuable commodities on the planet? Food and water. Maybe not now, or in the immediate future, but soon, and for the rest of our lives."

The crowd quieted a bit.

"If we can't find better, more efficient ways to grow food, as much as half the world's population will be starving before the end of this century. Think about that. And think about this: on average, a quarter of crops worldwide are currently lost to pests, mostly insects. Eliminating the loss of that twenty-five percent would be enough on its own to reduce hunger and starvation by half."

Dead quiet now; not a single sound of protest resounding.

Dane seized the moment to swing back toward the protester, his big hips swiveling so suddenly, and the motion so abrupt, that the young man lurched back from the stage and almost fell over.

"This young man, Brandon here, believes that our efforts in that regard made him sick, even though there's nothing to scientifically back up his claims. But it's still enough to make lesser companies think twice about the risks they're taking and rethink their priorities. Not so at Dane Corp. At Dane Corp we know the ability to succeed comes from not being afraid to fail. We take risks so you can enjoy the fruits of our labors in your wallets and the world can enjoy them in their next meal, next fill-up, next doctor's checkup, or next drink of water. Our goal is to leave everything behind better than it was when we found it. That includes the environment."

Calum Dane stopped there. He could see the attention of the audience was still rooted on the young man now standing on one leg with his prosthetic leg tucked under his arm. Dane never had a chance today. All the great news he had to report on increased profits and the bottom line of Dane Corp fell on the deaf ears of investors, some of whom had seen triple-digit returns on their original investments.

Maybe he should show them the scar on his back from when a well cap blew out into it. How about the nose that was still bent, and the capped teeth, from when a horse he was trying to break to earn money as a teenager kicked him in the face? Or the cigarette burn marks left on his arm during one of his drunken dad's rages about the unfairness of the world. His old man had beaten him good, and Dane was convinced that, in the end, it had toughened him up and helped define all the success he'd achieved. Who could blame him, then, for taking a belt to his own boy, the younger, ne'er-do-well one, who needed it more than mother's milk?

Apparently, lots of folks, including his wife, who'd now won full custody—awarded it by a pissant judge who would've fit in just fine among the collection of commoners squeezed into the chairs before him, who thought Calum Dane was somehow beholden to them.

Didn't they know he'd started with nothing? Grew up dirt poor, the son of migrant sharecroppers who moved from shack to shack wherever and whenever they could find land to work? Calum Dane had never spent a full year in the same place until high school, had gotten used to lugging his records home under his arm when the time came to hand them over at whatever school came next.

What would these people think if they knew how other kids had made fun of how he smelled, or that day's clothes, dirtied by yesterday's work in the field after he got back from school? He'd pick or plant, hoe or rake, dig or flatten, all the time imagining himself as the person giving the orders instead of taking them. He'd saved every penny he'd ever earned, starting back then, to buy a whole bunch of Texas land everyone else thought had been bled of oil. Dane had bought the land for pennies on the dollar, the owners walking away figuring they'd just conned a big, dumb hick. Then, not long after, both slant and horizontal drilling came into vogue, and those thousands of worthless acres laid the foundation for all his success and the basis of his fortune.

What had Brandon McCabe done, besides lose a leg to cancer? And what was Dane supposed to do about it? He'd already withdrawn the pesticide in question from the market, replacing it with one that came with a significantly smaller profit margin to the point where he was actually losing money by doing everything he could to keep families like the one-legged kid's fed. Calum Dane wished he'd lost his tongue instead, pictured himself yanking it out of Brandon McCabe's mouth with a pair of pliers.

"Who of you out there can feel their bellies rumbling with hunger?" Dane heard himself asking the audience, unsure himself where this was going when no hands went up, as expected. "Nearly half the world would be raising their hands now. At Dane Corp we are committed to eradicating hunger."

A smattering of applause followed his thinly veiled stab at self-justification.

"We are committed to making food more safe, wholesome, and plentiful than it's ever been before."

A slightly louder ripple of applause.

"And at Dane Corp, as you can find in that prospectus I can see lots of you holding on your lap, we are committed to doing all that while still making our investors money in the process."

Much louder applause, even a few cheers.

"So, folks, this may seem like no more than a shareholders meeting, sure. But it's actually plenty, plenty more than that. Because you *are* Dane Corp. And when *we* do good by the world, *you* do good by the world. Think about that the next time you open a dividend check, and remember that money came from doing good, from putting more and better food on the table, cheap and better oil in your tank, and energy to run this big world that's plentiful and cheap, too."

His final words were drowned out by applause that grew louder as plenty of the shareholders in attendance at the annual meeting leaped to their feet. In that moment, Calum Dane forgot all about Brandon McCabe and the prosthetic leg he was holding like some trumpet of truth. The kid was gone, and the ballroom was his to own again.

Until the kid wasn't gone anymore. Dane glimpsed him reaching into his hollow limb and coming out with handfuls of tiny pieces of plastic that looked like the remains of a child's toy.

For good reason. Because the pieces were the sliced-off legs of toy soldiers. Dane could see the little foot poking out from painted-on army pants on one that landed on the stage and skittered close to him.

"Now everybody can have a severed leg of their own," Brandon McCabe called out, hurling a final handful of the things out into the audience which gobbled them up, hooting and hollering all over again. "Difference being you didn't have to have yours amputated."

And then the kid went hopping up the center aisle of the ballroom, propelling himself along from chair back to chair back. He stopped at the very back of the hall, close to a set of open double doors, and shot Calum Dane the finger.

"Good thing you didn't take my hands, too!" he

shouted to the delight of the crowd, and then hopped out the door.

But Dane wasn't watching anymore. His attention was claimed by a big, rough-hewn man not unlike the man he'd been maybe twenty-five years before, when he'd had no debt, responsibility, or cripples stalking him. The man stood rigid, stiff and board straight just offstage, entirely out of view of the audience. He'd stopped just short of the light radiating down onto the stage floor, as if its brightness might burn him and he preferred the shadows instead.

Dane joined him in those shadows, suddenly glad to be out of the light and all it revealed.

"Talk to me, S.," he said to the man, using the man's first initial, as had long been his custom, trying to beat back the hammering in his chest.

"The situation in Texas has been contained, sir," reported Sev Pulsipher. "The operation was a success."

"Thank God," Dane said, feeling his breathing steady itself. Then he noticed the big man's taut expression. "What else you got to tell me?"

"There's been a complication."

"I don't understand, if you got all the kids."

"Turns out we didn't, sir. *That's* the complication."

14

ARMAND BAYOU, TEXAS

Houston PD was holding two boys from the Village School at the visitors' center located just off the entrance to the grounds. That's all Caitlin knew as she approached: two boys, no further information provided.

Law enforcement officials had already begun to cluster around the one-story building, a majestic A-frame structure built out of trees cut from these very grounds. Those officials found themselves battling for space with all manner of television and print reporters, who'd turned the parking lot into a staging ground for camera trucks and prep areas for the on-air personalities to grab whoever they could for an interview.

"Man oh man," Tepper groused. "I miss the days when we had three channels and UHF was the new big thing."

"Long gone and forgotten by nearly everybody else, Captain," said Caitlin.

"That's the problem with this world. People take progress for improvement, when I'm of the opinion we're going backwards in more ways than forwards."

They eased their way through the growing swarm, avoiding the microphones, cell phones, and recording devices thrust in their faces when reporters spotted their Texas Ranger badges. For his part, Tepper bummed a pair of filterless cigarettes off a newsman Caitlin recognized as an on-air reporter since she'd been a little girl. She thought she remembered him interviewing her grandfather at a Fourth of July celebration, when his hair had been black instead of silver.

Her and Tepper's badges were enough to get them into the visitors' center without having to flash their IDs. They were directed toward a back office, where she glimpsed a pair of youthful figures beyond a half-wall of glass, her angle precluding view of their faces.

Caitlin felt her heart hammering against her ribs, her mind working fast, calculating the odds that one of the found boys was Luke.

Please let it be, just please. . . .

She couldn't remember praying a single time in her life, a little girl who slept with her grandfather's empty Colt Peacemaker instead of a doll. All of a sudden, though, she found herself hoping against hope that some higher power would hear her words and grant her that much. A long time ago she'd witnessed her mother gunned down by Mexican druggers, and not all that long ago had watched her father die a slow death from heart failure. But this, she thought to herself, was the worst moment of life, all of it filled with a dread fear that if one of these boys wasn't Luke Torres, son of Cort Wesley Masters, she might never see him again. That he'd been swept away into the ether that defined the violence of the world, which had so long defined both her and his father.

The figure of a Houston detective she recognized moved in front of the window, blocking her view. He bent over, to tie his shoe maybe, and she got her look at both boys, their faces turned away and still indistinguishable.

Her stomach was fluttering and her knees had gone weak when one of the boys turned and peered through the glass, meeting her gaze with a face coated with grime, streaked with tears.

Luke Torres.

15

ARMAND BAYOU, TEXAS

Caitlin burst through the door, no thought given to protocol or to disturbing any evidence the boy's clothes may have shed. Luke had already bounded off the office couch by then, practically leaping into her arms, his hair smelling of tree bark, wood smoke, and the outdoors when she hugged him. She felt his tears soaking into her shirt before his sobs even became audible.

In her mind she said lots of things, comforting words meant to ease his plight, his confusion, make all this right. But in reality she said nothing at all, just hugged the boy tighter and didn't let go until he did first, sniffling as he backed off slightly.

"Is it true?" he just managed to utter, swallowing hard. "What they're saying about the other kids?"

Caitlin looked toward the Houston detective she recognized. "I suspect it is."

She turned her gaze toward the couch and the second boy, who was shivering beneath a blanket wrapped over his shoulders. He had ice-blue eyes, big and full, his hair hanging in wavy ringlets past his shoulders. Looked like some kind of model or something, except she also seemed to recall him starting on the school soccer team, for which Luke casually described himself as a "scrub."

"You okay, son?" Caitlin asked the boy on the couch, knowing it sounded lame, because of course he wasn't.

The boy's eyes quickly turned from fearful and longing to furtive, turning away from hers as if she'd spotted something in them he didn't want her to see. She let it go, cursing herself for feeling the Texas Ranger in her creeping back in to wonder exactly how this boy and Luke had gotten separated from the rest.

What were you doing in those woods, son?

She posed that question only in her mind, knowing there'd be plenty of time for answers later.

"My dad know?" Luke asked, swabbing a long-sleeve shirt over his eyes and nose.

"Got a message from him saying he's on his way."

The office's overly bright fluorescent lighting made his face look shiny through the stitches of grime streaking it. Compared to his older brother, Dylan, just short of his twentieth birthday now, Luke had always been a little kid to her. Except he wasn't anymore. He looked older and more mature than Dylan had at this age and was just as good looking, even more so. Both boys had inherited their mother's beauty—a curse as much as a blessing, in her mind.

Something made Caitlin glance back at the boy still

seated on the couch, trying to remember his name, until Luke repeated his question.

"He should be here shortly," Caitlin resumed.

"Ranger," the Houston detective whose name continued to slip her mind started, "we need to talk to these boys now, if you don't mind."

"Well, I do mind, sir, after all they've been through. And they're both minors to boot."

"I said 'talk,' " the detective said gently, "not question or interrogate."

"Is there a difference?"

She could see the detective start to stiffen, everyone else crammed in the office seeming to freeze solid.

"Tell you what," she said to the detective, before whatever she felt building inside her spilled out, "why don't we 'talk' to them together?"

16

ARMAND BAYOU, TEXAS

"Frank Pepper," the detective said, extending his hand as everyone else filed out of the office, leaving her and Pepper alone with the boys.

"That's right," Caitlin remembered, finally. "They call you 'Doctor.' "

Pepper shrugged. "Ever since junior high."

"I apologize for forgetting, and for my tone earlier."

"That's all right. And, for what it's worth, I'm a big admirer of yours."

"It's worth a lot, Doctor."

"Frank, please."

Caitlin nodded, that one word having sucked up whatever tension remained between them. Pepper dragged one chair over in front of the couch, where Luke was again seated next to the other boy, and positioned another next to it. Neither boy was looking at the other. Luke's arms were folded tight against his chest, as if he'd tucked something beneath them.

Pepper waited behind his chair for Caitlin to take hers. She remained silent, deferring to him out of protocol, since this was technically Houston's case until the FBI or Rangers assumed jurisdiction, which would surely be the case.

"I want you to know," he started, leaning forward to bring himself closer to the boys, "that we're doing everything we can to find your friends. But we need your help, anything you can tell us." He paused, resuming when the other boy finally looked up. "Luke, Zach . . ."

Zach, Caitlin thought, remembering.

"I'm not gonna lie to you, boys. Right now, we don't have a lot to go on, so anything you've got to say, anything at all, is sure to help us."

The boys shrugged in unison, their expressions slipping into twin frowns.

"Well then," Pepper picked up, sitting more upright in his chair, "is it okay if I ask you boys a few questions, see if that might spur something?"

Both of them nodded.

"Let's start with how the two of you got separated from the group. I'm guessing somebody would've done a count, once you were all settled in that field, am I right?"

Luke nodded slightly. Zach just shrugged again, his big eyes looking darker, as if somebody had taken a color stick to them.

"Okay, so you were all together at that point. Do you remember what time that would've been?"

"Eleven thirty," Zach said first.

"When they told us to turn off our phones and flashlights," Luke added, "and did—what'd you call it?—a count."

"One of them, the adults, was supposed to stay up all night."

"Like in shifts," Luke added, again. "I had to go to the bathroom. Zach said he'd come with me, so I wouldn't get lost."

"Then we both got lost," Zach filled in.

But Caitlin was focusing on Luke. His eyes were locked on Pepper, as if trying to paint her out of the scene.

"Luke?"

He looked toward her. Reluctantly.

"I thought you had permission to use the bathrooms in the farmhouse," Caitlin resumed.

"They're not bathrooms; they're outhouses out in the back. I wasn't going in there, not the way they smelled. I just had to, you know, piss. It seemed easier to just use the woods."

"And what time would this have been?" Pepper asked both of them.

Luke turned to look at Zach for the first time since he'd reclaimed his place on the couch. "Midnight?"

"I think so," Zach said.

"You ask permission, at least tell whatever adult was awake you needed to use the bathroom?"

Zach shrugged.

"They were all asleep," Luke said, "even the one who was supposed to stay awake."

"That your recollection too, Zach?"

Zach took a deep breath. "I forget now. I've got ADD. I forget lots of things."

"Well, son, you won't be tested on any of this." Pepper smiled, trying to sound comforting. "Let's go back a bit further, to earlier last night. Do either of you recall seeing or noticing anything that didn't appear right, that stood out for any reason, like something or someone that didn't seem like they belonged?"

Caitlin watched Zach shake his head and then look down again, sighing.

Luke nodded. "There was one thing," he said, looking at Caitlin.

"Go ahead, Luke," she coaxed.

"I saw lights."

"Lights?" Pepper asked.

"More like flickers. Out in the woods to the right of the field where we were sleeping—to the west, I think. They were there and then they were gone. Then they came back again."

"You mean like flashlights?" Caitlin asked him.

The boy shrugged, then shook his head. "I don't know what they were, but they weren't flashlights. I don't know. I remember thinking maybe it was fireflies."

Caitlin took her penlight from her pocket and ran its thin beam about a bare wall. "Like this?"

"Yeah," Luke said, leaning forward, "something like that."

"So it was after midnight when you had to take a leak," Pepper started, taking the discussion back a bit, "and Zach came with you."

"After midnight, for sure."

"And when did you see those lights, those flickers?"

"A while before that."

"You were awake the whole time?"

"Well . . ."

Caitlin could see Zach stiffen as Luke groped for words, working his boots back and forth on the floor.

"I don't like sleeping outside," he said, leaving it there.

Another detective, carrying what looked like Luke's backpack, entered and whispered something to Pepper as he pressed a small ziplock bag into Pepper's hand. Caitlin watched something change in the detective's expression, gleaming like a predator's with prey suddenly in his sights.

"You boys want to tell me whose backpack this is?" he asked, ignoring her.

"Mine," said Luke.

"And this?" Pepper continued, opening his hand to reveal a joint inside the ziplock bag.

Luke swallowed hard. Zach looked away.

Pepper rose from his chair and stepped closer to the couch. "Did you hear what I just asked you, son?"

"I did," Caitlin interrupted, rising too. "And I'm

going to assume you had a warrant to search that backpack."

"Do I need one?"

"According to the law you do, Detective."

"What happened to Doctor?" Pepper asked, behind a frown.

"I'm still waiting for an answer."

"I thought I told you I don't need one, since the search involved imminent danger in the commission of a crime."

Caitlin almost said, "Bullshit," but kept her tone professional, as her blood began to boil. "Even if that were true, Detective, you have no evidence of any such crime."

"Hey, maybe thirty-four missing kids doesn't qualify as a crime to the Texas Rangers, but it does in these parts."

"Not if these parts are located in the state of Texas and United States of America, it doesn't, and you know it. Please give the boy back his backpack, sir. You can keep the joint. What we have here is two kids doing their best to help us out in a very trying situation. Why don't we keep things there and avoid the distractions?"

"You call possession of drugs on a school field trip a distraction, Ranger?" Pepper challenged, flashing the ziplock bag before her.

Caitlin pretended not to see it. "What drugs? All I see is something obtained illegally that you might as well throw out before the court does. We on the same page here yet?"

Pepper closed his fist around the ziplock bag and

returned his attention to the boys. "You say you went into the woods after midnight, which makes it more than twelve hours before you walked out again."

"I told you," Luke said, "we got lost."

Pepper turned his gaze on Zach, who glanced at him with hooded eyes. "Is that true, kid. You got lost?"

Zach shrugged again, stopping just short of a nod this time.

"Long time to be lost in these kind of woods. You finish up something else you hid in your backpacks? Bottle of mouthwash, or Gatorade mixed with vodka maybe, something like that?"

Caitlin stood up and stepped out right in front of Pepper, planting herself between him and the boys. "I believe we've gone as far as we can right now, Detective."

Pepper rose and looked slightly down at Caitlin, the two of them so close they could feel each other's breath. "And I believe that's my call. Stand aside, please."

"I can't do that, sir." Caitlin felt the distinctly familiar flush of heat building inside her, an early warning signal that she needed to reel her emotions in. "If these boys knew anything that could help us, we'd know it now, too. If you can't see that, what you need is a pair of glasses to go with a class in etiquette and compassion."

Pepper's face was turning red, his eyes gone jittery, as if he were trapped between intentions. "I believe I should continue the interview alone. You have a problem with that?"

"I have a problem with bullies. That's why you won't be continuing the interview at all."

Pepper's expression came up just short of a smirk. "You gonna draw on me, Ranger, get into your comfort zone?"

"You're not worth the price of the bullet, Detective, and I believe you have another nickname, don't you? Mr. Peepers, on account of your proclivity to make female suspects strip naked to make sure they're not hiding a weapon somewhere in their privates. Now that I think of it, I saw the complaint one filed when you made her do that after arresting her on a traffic warrant. She came to the Rangers when nobody at Houston PD would give her the time of day."

Before Pepper could respond, a commotion erupted out beyond the room. Caitlin noted the rapid shifting of bodies through the window as something like a dark streak of energy cut straight through them. An instant later the door to the office burst open, and Cort Wesley Masters surged inside.

17

ARMAND BAYOU, TEXAS

"Get over here, son," Cort Wesley said to Luke.

Captain Tepper followed in his wake, must've been running interference when Cort Wesley made his presence known at the visitors' center entrance without a badge or any law enforcement ID. Luke bounded up off the couch and practically leaped into Cort Wesley's arms.

"We're gonna sort this out. We're gonna make some people pay for whatever they did here," Cort Wesley said, hugging him.

"What did he just say?" Pepper snapped, his face an even deeper red.

"Rangers are running lead on this now, Detective, until the FBI sets up shop," Tepper informed him, sizing up the situation. "You got a problem with that, take it up with the Department of Public Safety. But this is Ranger business, so thank you for your service and please stand aside."

Pepper's eyes fell on Cort Wesley, who was holding Luke against him with a single arm now, the other one held low by his hip with fingers bent, clawlike, halfway to a fist. Then he turned to D. W. Tepper, who'd just recovered his breath.

"Nice zoo you're running, Captain. How's teaching the animals the limits of their cages going?"

"Why don't you step inside mine and find out?" Caitlin asked him.

"Well," Tepper said, planting his hands on his hips when Pepper closed the door behind him, "some things don't change. Hurricane Caitlin blows again."

"That man's lucky he's not swallowing his teeth."

"Maybe so. He's an asshole, for sure, but you're not the conscience of Texas, Hurricane, and it's not your place to dispense judgment, even on a depraved asshole like Pepper. That's my job," he added as an afterthought, stealing a glance first at Luke and then at Zach, who'd remained in the same position on the couch, looking forlorn and lonely there by himself. "Your parents coming, son?"

"They're divorced."

"Has either of them been called?"

"Nobody asked me for their number, and that detective took my phone."

"Well, I'm asking now, and I'll get your phone back straightaway." He widened his gaze to include both Caitlin and Cort Wesley. "We're gonna need to bag the clothes both boys are wearing, so forensics can give them the once-over. There's a bathroom where they can change."

Tepper opened the door and summoned a pair of Houston patrolmen standing just outside it to escort the boys. Caitlin watched Zach finally relinquish his claim on the couch, his shoulders staying slumped as he followed Luke out the door.

"And Detective Peepers is not to come anywhere near them," Tepper instructed the uniforms. "Is that clear?"

"Who, sir?"

"Sorry, I meant Detective *Pepper*." He turned back around, shaking his head as his gaze locked on Caitlin again. "Either of the boys say anything could prove helpful?"

"Something about penlights in the woods," she told him. "I'm still putting it all together."

Tepper stuck one of the unfiltered cigarettes he'd bummed outside in his mouth, only to realize he'd left his lighter back in his truck at the Department of Public Safety's San Antonio heliport.

"Somebody made off with those kids, Captain," Cort Wesley said, his breath trailing the words like a growl. "My son got lucky, unlike his friends. That means I won't rest until they're found."

Tepper fished a pack of matches from a desk drawer in the office and lit his cigarette. "You and Hurricane teaming up to hunt down bad guys?" He shook his head. "Well, wouldn't be the first time for a Masters and a Strong. . . ."

Caitlin took a single step forward. "Come again, Captain?"

"I never did tell you how Boone Masters and Jim Strong joined forces once, did I? Well, I suppose this is as good a time as any. . . ."

18

SAN ANTONIO, TEXAS; 1983

"Looks like we take ours the same way," Jim Strong said, as Boone Masters twirled a spoon through his mug. "Except I prefer a bit more coffee with my sugar."

Boone dumped one more spoonful, his fifth, in. "What is it they say, 'I ain't happy until the spoon stands straight up'? Least of all the things that makes us different, I suppose, considering we stand on opposite sides of the law."

"Not this time, Boone. Not this time."

They'd been stitched up, bandaged, and released

from Southwest General within minutes of each other. Jim Strong was waiting outside when Boone Masters emerged.

"You want to get a coffee, Boone?"

"I'd prefer a beer, Ranger, something to chase down those painkillers they gave me."

"I never take them."

"Never?"

Jim shook his head. "Nope. I go by one simple rule: if it affects the way I shoot, I don't do it."

"How about sleep? You do that?"

"Never had to shoot anybody in my sleep."

Boone winked at him. "I'll keep that in mind."

A San Antonio police cruiser was parked across the street and Jim asked the rookie patrolman inside to give them a ride back to their trucks. The kid gushed the whole time about how thrilled he was to meet his first Texas Ranger, spouting off legend after legend that taught even Jim Strong a thing or two. Finally, regarding Boone almost as an afterthought, he asked, "You a Ranger, too?"

"I'm undercover," Boone said softly. "Keep it under your hat."

There was an all-night diner not far from where their trucks were parked, and Boone relented, deciding to join Jim for that coffee, only after checking the time.

"Didn't realize it was this late," Boone said, finally setting his spoon down on the saucer. "Shit, I missed last call and all to come afterwards, thanks to you."

The diner was housed in a stripped-down, hollowed-out old train car that had served as a parlor car on the famed Sunset Limited, which had once made its leisurely way west, straight through these parts. The counter was formed by the ledge that ran the car's length, padded polished wood with the authentic brass fittings still in place. The windows, too, were authentic, and it wasn't hard, in quieter times, for Jim Strong to sit by one and imagine the world passing by before him as it had for the passengers aboard the Sunset Limited.

"Remember what I said in the back of the ambulance?" he said to Boone Masters, who sat across from him before one of those very windows. The night beyond was just empty and dark, the world not moving at all.

"Something about Russian gangsters."

"The ones you been fencing your merchandise through; same ones who you're still gunning for after they ripped off one of your warehouses."

"Hold on there, Ranger. That would make me a criminal, when, last time I checked, I was a free man with no charges pending."

Jim Strong sipped his coffee, considered ordering something to eat to go with it, except his mouth felt too sore to chew. "Let me put it this way, just between the two of us, a couple Texas boys born and bred shooting the shit. And there was a time when Rangers were more like you than me. Those Russians did you wrong, and Boone Masters is hardly the kind of man to just let that go."

"Well, Boone Masters also ain't the kind of man who joins up with the law."

"Might want to give that notion some more thought, on account of you having the bad sense to involve your son in your dealings. Something I didn't tell you before, Mr. Masters, but San Antonio PD's got a witness ready to testify they saw your boy playing lookout when you boosted that storage depot in Lubbock."

Masters tried not to appear rattled. "Do they now?"

"Rent-a-cop was watching the whole thing, too scared to move an inch. That's in addition to the security tape that pictures Cort Wesley clear as a bell. Makes him an accessory to grand larceny." Jim raised the coffee cup to his lips and continued speaking through the steam rising from it. "That's serious time if they try him as an adult."

"You're a piece of shit, Ranger."

"Only doing my job, Masters, just like you."

"So what's the deal?"

"Like I said, SAPD's got the case now, in tandem with the highway patrol. That can change with one phone call when I inform the parties that be that the Masterses, both father and son, are working with the Rangers in exchange for making that investigation go away."

Boone gave up trying to look nonchalant about the whole thing. "You can do that?"

"I'm a Texas Ranger. I can do anything I want." Then, after a pause, "So long as you do something for me."

"This Russian thing."

"Yup."

"Bastards ripped me off."

"I know."

"And I'm not the only one, neither."

"I know that, too."

Boone leaned forward, his big chest canted over the table. "They think they can ride into Texas and pull the same shit they been pulling in New York. Don't give a shit about anybody but themselves."

"New York's where they got their American business started. Heard about this Potato Bag Gang, where a bunch of them disguised themselves as merchants selling antique gold rubles on the cheap that ended up being bags of potatoes. Made themselves a fortune. That was the midseventies. And it only got worse from there, when the Soviet government freed a whole bunch of dead-enders from their prisons who found their way to the West."

"You ask me, Ranger, the Statue of Liberty ought to read, 'Give me your assholes, your shitheads, and your huddled misfits.'"

"The bottom line, Mr. Masters, is that it should be an easy choice between your boy going to prison and you helping me to put those very same assholes, shitheads, and misfits there instead."

Masters leaned all the way back, resting his coffee cup against his chest. "And what's the real reason?"

"Real reason for what?"

"The Rangers' interest in these mobbed-up Russians. What you're saying doesn't square with a man of your history. How am I supposed to take you at your word when you're not telling me everything I need to know?"

"I am," Jim Strong told him. "For now."

Before Masters could respond, something out the

window claimed Jim's attention: a coyote prancing off with the shredded corpse of a skunk in its mouth. The sight made him think the animal had assured itself a fine meal at the expense of an odor that would stick to it for days. A trade-off. A metaphor for life itself that Jim found to be oddly appropriate. You pay a price for what you want the most, and sometimes you pay an even steeper price to keep it.

"Let me make it simple for you, Ranger," Boone Masters was saying. "You wanna go up against these Russians, be ready to go to guns. And I mean lots of them."

Jim Strong peeked out the window again. "In my experience, one's more than enough to do the trick." He leaned forward. "Now, how long before you can get this set up?"

"How long before you can tell me what's really going on here?"

19

ARMAND BAYOU, TEXAS

Tepper stopped when Luke Torres and the kid named Zach reappeared, wearing the change of clothes they'd brought for the morning that had never really come for them, which pretty much looked like what they'd been wearing before.

"So, what was it?" Caitlin asked him.

"What was what?"

"What was Jim Strong really up to with these Russians, what he really needed Boone Masters for?"

"Story for another day, Ranger," Tepper said evasively, taking a quick look at Cort Wesley, who'd listened to the tale as entranced as Caitlin. Then his eyes darted between the two of them, far away and still there in the same moment. "Can you imagine, your two daddies like that, working together?"

He stopped when Luke moved into his line of vision, the boy stopping between Caitlin and Cort Wesley. "I wanna go home now," the boy said, holding both of them in his stare. "Can we go home?"

Cort Wesley didn't look for some signal from anyone in purported authority, just nodded. "You bet. Anything they want from you, they can get later."

"And we need to take Zach with us. There's nobody at his house."

"Where your parents at, son?" Cort Wesley asked him.

"My mom and stepdad are traveling," was all the boy said, leaving it there. "I don't talk to my real dad."

"Then grab your stuff," Cort Wesley said. "You're coming home with us."

Caitlin looked toward Captain Tepper. "I'll expect you to finish that story another time. I'm gonna walk Cort Wesley out, in case some fool like Detective Pepper gets in his way. Then we can take another look at the grounds, see whatever it was we missed."

"How you know we missed something, Hurricane?"

"Because I just thought of something. About those lights Luke thought he saw."

*   *   *

Caitlin trailed Cort Wesley and the boys from the visitors' center, immediately noticing Guillermo Paz leaning casually against his massive, extended cab pickup truck, impervious to the stares being cast his way by everyone who passed. Paz stood silent and still as a pillar, not even moving his eyes or seeming to breathe.

"What's he doing here?" Cort Wesley said, unsure of how to react to Paz's presence.

"You get these kids home, Cort Wesley, and let me find out. I'll be there as soon as I can."

"Whatever you say." He followed, hardly enamored by the prospects, and then slid stiffly away.

Luke trailed after him, then stopped and turned back toward Caitlin, suspended in that moment between her and his father. His eyes looked tentative and longing at the same time, filled with uncertainty, words forming in his head that never quite reached his mouth.

"We'll talk when I get back," Caitlin said simply.

The boy blew the hair from his face out of the side of his mouth, just like his older brother, and nodded. Then he jogged off to catch up with Zach, the two of them following Cort Wesley to wherever he'd parked, leaving Caitlin to steer toward Guillermo Paz.

20

"How'd you know, Colonel?"

Paz pulled a business card from the lapel pocket of his olive-shaded shirt and handed it to Caitlin.

"What's this?"

"Psychic I saw earlier today. I told her I'd give you her card. She said there's a long line of people on the other side waiting to talk to you."

"Most of whom I probably put there ahead of their time."

"According to Madam Caterina, the line stretches too far into the past for her to know for sure."

"Madam Caterina?"

"The psychic's name. It's on the card, Ranger."

Caitlin pocketed the card without checking. "You're visiting psychics now?"

"When you're lost on the road, you stop in as many places as it takes to find your way."

She let Paz see her gaze past him into the truck; its tires were so high she really couldn't see anything. "Even though you've got navigation installed on your dashboard, Colonel? Means you don't have to stop and ask anyone for directions. You can get where you're going all on your own."

"Too bad we don't have something like that wired into our brains."

"We do," Caitlin told him. "It's called instinct, and you should know that better than anyone."

Paz ran his eyes around him, seeming to take in a scene hidden by the trees, far out of range of the human gaze. "Madam Caterina told me one of the Torres boys was in trouble. She asked if they were your sons."

"Close enough, I suppose. Don't tell me she told you exactly where to come."

Paz stepped away from the truck, turning so the host of police and media types starting to grasp his presence could only view him from behind. From this angle, the width of his shoulders seemed to match that of the driver's side door, and the truck riding on tires almost as high as Caitlin's waist seemed normal in size when measured in relation to him.

"No, I was going to make a few calls after I left," he told her. "When I started the car, the radio came on with a bulletin of those missing kids up here. It was a Spanish station. Details were sketchy but so is everything really. I knew right away that's what Madam Caterina was talking about."

"You going back to see her again?"

"Would you like to join me?" Paz took a quick glance behind him at some media types passing by. "That's how people looked at me back in Venezuela."

"You're a lucky man, Colonel. About as lucky as they come. You got a second chance when you came here, and a third one when Homeland Security hired you to lead their personal assassination squad. And now you can stand out here in the open, your whole past wiped off the board. The ultimate mulligan."

"All because of you, according to Madam Caterina."

"What else did she have to say on the subject?"

"She told me she saw a strong, blinding light that swallowed the world."

"Uh-oh."

"That was my thought too, Ranger."

Before Caitlin could respond, D. W. Tepper reached them in a slow jog, so out of breath he dropped his hands to his knees in a crouch.

"We got to get a move on, Ranger," he wheezed. "Chopper's already warming up. There's somewhere else we need to be, and fast."

21

New York City

Brandon McCabe returned to his room upstairs, a bit wobbly after a stretch spent in the hotel bar to celebrate his victory. Because that's what embarrassing the shit out of the asshole who'd cost him his leg felt like. Of course, thanks to that leg, a few of Dane Corp's stockholders staying at this hotel insisted on paying for his drinks—out of guilt. He could see it in their eyes; the money they'd put into the company was partially responsible for the pesticide that had disabled him, no matter what the courts had to say on the subject. He'd taken Calum Dane down like an opponent on the wrestling mat back in high school, before he understood the depths of phantom pain, something that wasn't there throbbing incessantly.

What sense did that make? No more than him becoming a crusader on behalf of those with their own ax to grind against Dane Corp.

His thoughts slurring the way his words must have downstairs, McCabe stepped into his hotel room, thinking how his missing leg never throbbed when he was wearing his prosthetic, as if the space-age plastic somehow fooled his nervous system. He was pretty sure he must've left some of the toy soldier legs inside it, because he could hear something clacking about when he walked, like the sound of pennies dropped into an old-fashioned piggy bank.

McCabe closed the door behind him and flicked on the light.

"Evening, son," greeted Calum Dane, as he wedged a toothpick between his teeth.

Dane sat in the room's easy chair, draped in the thin spray of light that left him mostly lost to the shadows.

"Oh, that's right," Dane continued, the chair's leatherlike material creaking as he pushed himself out of it, "you're not my son. I wish you were, since then I'd have a chance to say good-bye. Didn't get that with the boy I lost in Afghanistan."

Dane started the kid's way, Pulsipher falling into step behind him as if held on a leash.

"Sit down," Dane ordered Brandon McCabe, his words a bit garbled by the toothpick wedged in his mouth. "I said, sit down."

McCabe eased himself to the edge of the bed, gingerly, to avoid putting too much weight on his prosthetic.

"Nice performance today. Tell me who put you up to it and I won't break your other limbs."

"You're guilty and you know it, you son of a bitch," McCabe said, trying to sound brave.

"Not so easy sounding tough when you're not in public anymore playing to the crowd, is it, son?"

"Huh?"

"I'm going to say it again. Give me the name of whoever put you up to this."

McCabe laid his palms down on the bedcovers, seeming to hold himself up. "I have no idea what you're talking about."

"I'm talking about a setup, son," Calum Dane said, easing his arms from the sleeves of his jacket and handing it to Pulsipher as if he were a coatrack. "I'm talking about someone sending you to disrupt Dane Corp's shareholders meeting. Since I don't know who, I also don't know why. Could be it's somebody with a plan to short my stock, hoping to depress its value. Could be a competitor looking to fuck us in the marketplace or with the FDA." He stopped and shook his head, seeming displeased with himself. "Please excuse my language, me setting a bad example for a fine, upstanding young man like yourself who's already suffered enough."

"What's that mean?"

"That you're a solid citizen, son."

"I was talking about what you meant by 'suffered enough.'"

Calum Dane took another step toward McCabe, his broad shoulders blocking the bulk of the room's light shed by the single desk lamp, before it could reach him. "I meant that you don't need to suffer anymore."

McCabe tried to look like he wasn't scared, and failed. "I don't know what you want from me."

Another step. "Yes, you do, 'cause I already told you. I want to know who put you up to this, who's paying the freight. Right now you're the guy trapped in the middle. In over his head, let's say, through no fault of his own. I'm going to assume somebody sold you a bill of goods, took advantage of your disability by using you to get me. I imagine they may have auditioned others for the role, but you're the one who got the call and a decent paycheck to go with it."

Dane started tapping the hotel room's stuffy air with a fresh toothpick, in rhythm with his thinking, some revelation apparently striking him.

"Tell you what, son, I'll make you a deal. Whatever those folks paid you to pull this charade, I'll double if you give up their names. What do you say?"

"You owe me a leg," the kid said. "How about you give me back what the doctors sawed off and we'll call it even?"

"We back there again?"

McCabe made himself look as strong and sure as he could. "I never left. You took my leg with that poison you spread, and unless you can give it back to me we've got nothing to talk about."

Dane shook his head, looking honestly disappointed. He looked down at Brandon McCabe sitting on the edge of the bed and thought of his own boy getting blown to pieces in Afghanistan for no good reason at all. McCabe looking at him smugly, secure in the degree of insulation and protection being disabled afforded him. Who picks on a cripple, right? Dane had no idea what exactly was in the coffin the army sent back. It had been a closed casket at the funeral that had drawn thousands, and plenty of his boy's friends looked a lot like Brandon McCabe.

Calum Dane looked down and found himself looming directly over the kid, with no memory of taking the steps that had gotten him there. His breath felt hot as it pushed out of his mouth, noisy since it was suddenly the only sound in the room.

"Who put you up to this?"

"Nobody."

"That's a load of shit, son. Pissant like you couldn't have come up with that show you put on by yourself. Hell, maybe they paid you to cut off your leg, too."

McCabe tried to make himself look defiant. "Get out of my room."

"Be glad to. Once you tell me who's behind this."

"Nobody. Maybe your boy stepped on the land mine on purpose to avoid ever having to set eyes on you again. And I heard you got another boy they took away from you because you beat the shit out of him." McCabe tried for a smirk that didn't quite materialize. "But I heard that wasn't the only thing you did to him."

Calum Dane had never had an out-of-body experience, didn't believe such things existed. Which is why it felt so strange to him when he seemed to *see* himself lurch downward and punch Brandon McCabe square in the jaw.

Time froze.

Then it started up again.

Dane's knuckles erupted in fiery pain an instant after feeling the crunch of bone beneath the skin that split into a neat gash between the kid's cheek and jaw. The kid plopped backwards atop the bedcovers, eyes going glassy as they fixed on the ceiling. Then Dane watched himself reach down to McCabe's jeans and thread his hands up to find where his prosthetic was fitted into place. He twisted, pulled, yanked, twisted again, and pulled harder until he felt it come free.

And watched the kid's face fill with fear and shock, eyes bulging as if they were seeing what was to come next.

Calum Dane saw it a moment later, saw himself raising Brandon McCabe's prosthetic leg into the room's stale air and bringing it down hard.

Thwack!

He wasn't sure what cracked on impact, the kid's face or the plastic leg. Decided it must've been the leg when the next three impacts yielded the same sound and the upper portion of the prosthetic seemed to be breaking away from the lower.

Dane didn't care, just kept hammering the kid with it, left to right and back again, feeling his own breath deserting him from the exertion and only then realizing he had no idea how many times he'd actually struck McCabe. He thought he remembered the kid first crying out in pain, begging for him to stop. That was followed by a gasping, a wheezing, and then nothing. All of it a blur amid a reality caked over by a thickening haze, like mist from hot water steaming up a glass shower so you can't see what's outside it.

The mist finally cleared from Calum Dane's vision.

And he saw the kid's face reduced to what barely passed for pulp, flesh-colored splinters and shards protruding from it. Dane realized he was still holding the fractured remnants of the prosthetic leg by half a foot, all that remained of it, coated in blood and skin and sinew, some dripping down to the bedcovers in thick globs.

Dane tossed it aside and realized he was gasping for breath, awakening as if from some kind of trance that left him looking at Brandon McCabe's face pulped into mashed potatoes. He remembered hammering a frog to death with a rock as a young boy, how much he loved hearing the plopping sound and feeling skin and bone smashed under his control. He'd never felt so powerful and strong as in that moment and had sought to recover that same sensation his entire life. He'd come close numerous times, but this was the first time he'd ever replicated the feeling in its entirety, actually exceeding the original one.

But I heard that wasn't the only thing you did to him.

The kid's hands and feet were still twitching, and Dane watched until they spasmed, seized, and stopped. The scent of blood was like heavy copper hanging in the air, sweet and sour at the same time. He remembered there'd been no scent with the frog, other than something acidic and bitter rising from beneath the rock. Standing there over the remains of Brandon McCabe, Calum Dane remembered for the first time how that had disappointed him.

That's why this time was better.

Dane felt Pulsipher's hands on his shoulders for the first time, trying to draw him backwards. He swabbed a sleeve across his own brow, feeling it pick up a thin bit of bone, and realized he was still holding what was left of the kid's leg.

"Here you go," Dane said tossing it atop the kid's corpse. "So you can't accuse me of taking this one from you too."

22

AUSTIN COUNTY, TEXAS

"Here we are," D. W. Tepper said, gazing out the helicopter at the sea of revolving lights churning through the late afternoon's fading sun. "This is a day for the ages, Ranger. If I had it to do all over again, I would've stayed in bed."

Caitlin followed his gaze as the chopper settled into a brief hover over a ranch belonging to one Karl Dakota. They had taken off from one crazed scene only to land in another—and worse, potentially, given that Dakota was currently walled up in his house threatening to kill his wife and four children. Local sheriff's deputies had been summoned by a cattle buyer who'd showed up for an appointment, only to have his tires and windows shot out when he was heading for the house. He'd called 9-1-1 from behind the cover of an old-fashioned well, right down to the rope and pail.

"Are you in immediate danger, sir?" the operator had asked him.

"If that's what you call getting shot at, you bet your ass."

The deputies arrived to a similar greeting, screeching their shot-up cruisers in reverse to what seemed to be a safe zone before calling for backup, and lots of it. The hostage negotiator had gotten absolutely nowhere with Dakota, who claimed he needed to shoot his wife and kids in order to save them from a far more horrible death.

"Pick 'em to the bone they will, just like they did my cattle!" he ranted.

Neither the negotiator nor any of the deputies had any notion what the rancher was talking about. According to reports, he owned a stockpile of weapons and ammunition, accumulated when his survivalist leanings led him to build a shelter off the back of his house—until the backhoe busted a shovel, striking shale, and he postponed the effort. That was five years ago now and Dakota had chosen today, apparently, to put those weapons to use. In addition to traditional ordnance, he was rumored to have purchased hand grenades, a pair of fully automatic M16s, and a vintage .50-caliber machine gun from illegal dealers, who were as common in Texas as ice-cream trucks.

"How'd he come by that name, exactly?" Caitlin asked Tepper, as their chopper set down in a barren field across a thin dirt road from his farmhouse and surrounding land. "Karl Dakota."

Tepper waited for a belch, spawned by his acid reflux, to surface before responding. "Legend has it that the man's great-grandmother was kidnapped by a Cheyenne Indian chief she ended up marrying, while insisting that their children maintain at least a semblance of their native German heritage. That's how his name came to combine German with the one the chief had taken, after the US Army finally conquered the plains and shipped the disenfranchised Indians out to settlements that became the reservation system, seen by them as a scourge and source of misery to this day."

"Can't argue with them there, D.W."

"I can't stomach any more kids getting hurt today," Tepper said, his expression pained and uneasy, as if another belch was building. "Austin asked for you specifically after that police negotiator's family almost got early death benefits for his efforts."

Caitlin also suspected her presence here was due to the proximity of Karl Dakota's farm to Lonesome Pines, a world-famous ranch resort and top tourist attraction, similarly located in the rolling hills of Austin County. It was among the most beautiful country Texas had to offer, lush and full and green. Viewing it from the air in the chopper almost made her think there was no way anything bad could happen down there.

And now it had, or was very close to.

Captain Tepper and Caitlin hurried up to the perimeter, erected clumsily by sheriff's deputies most concerned with not getting shot.

"We didn't call for any Rangers," the local sheriff

told Tepper, spitting a wad of tobacco juice close enough to Tepper's boot to make him pull it back.

"Then it's a good thing Austin did, Sheriff. We know our way around these sorts of things and we'll be running lead now."

The sheriff took a long, sliding gaze about the rim his deputies formed, poised protectively behind their cars. "Maybe I'll just pull up stakes, then."

"Feel free to take the rest of the day off, Sheriff. But your deputies are now under our command and ain't going nowhere."

The sheriff fingered the big wad of tobacco from his mouth and tossed it behind him as far as he could. "Can't you see we know what we're doing here?"

"From what I can see," Caitlin told him, "your men don't know what they're doing at all. If they did, they'd be well aware that the kind of load Karl Dakota is packing will cut straight through those car doors like they're Swiss cheese. But you take our advice and do what we say and they're liable to make it out of the day alive."

"You think I don't know who you are, Ranger?"

"I hadn't given it much consideration, sir."

The sheriff stepped forward, close enough for Caitlin to smell the stale tobacco odor lacing his breath. "Well, let me share some truth with you, little lady. Any mess you make here, I'm gonna have to clean up. But you won't find me nearly as hospitable as all those other towns you left with blood drying on your boots."

"I'll keep that in mind, Sheriff. Now tell me where we're at here."

The sheriff's expression crinkled, reducing his eyes

to mere slits. "Where are we at? A crazy man's got his family held hostage and all he talked about when our negotiator got him on the phone is aliens eating his cattle to the bone."

"Aliens?"

"Yes, ma'am, as in from outer space, not illegals."

"I'm familiar with the term."

The sheriff pulled a pack of tobacco from his pocket and worked the flap open, packing a fresh wad in his mouth. "Dakota said he had to kill his wife and kids to keep them from the same fate of getting eaten to the bone."

"That's what he said, in those words?"

"Close enough, for Pete's sake. Jeez, it's hard to hear clearly when you know there's a rifle barrel bearing down on you."

"That depends on who's doing the listening, Sheriff."

Caitlin couldn't tell if the sheriff's snarl spread in reaction to her comment or to the wad of tobacco that was too big to fit in either cheek.

"You want an excuse to gun somebody down?" he said. "Just walk straight ahead toward that house and wait for Karl to start shooting."

"You know," Caitlin said, glancing toward Tepper, "that's not a bad idea."

23

Caitlin moved in front of the haphazardly arranged police cruisers, into a clearing set between them and the farmhouse where Dakota and his family lived. She approached, keeping herself between two centrally placed windows on the first floor, expecting Dakota and one of his rifles likely to be poised behind one of them.

Drawing close to what she judged to be comfortable shooting range for any reasonable gunman, Caitlin eased her SIG Sauer from its holster and placed it on the ground between a flatbed and a pickup truck. She kept her hands in the air as she addressed whoever was listening inside.

"I'm a Texas Ranger, Mr. Dakota, and I just want to talk. Listen up, sir. I understand until this point nobody's been hurt, most of all your own family. Why don't you let me help keep it that way?"

"How do I know you're real?" a muffled voice called through a window opened barely a slit.

"A real Texas Ranger?"

"A real *person*, as in not one of the space aliens that picked my cows down to the bone like they was chicken. I figure they must look like us to have been getting away with this with nobody knowing."

"I'd like to come inside, sir, so you can tell me more

about what happened to your cows, while we're looking at each other. That okay?"

Silence followed; the only sound was the wind
whistling through the open space between the bevy of
police cars and the farmhouse.

"What do you say, Mr. Dakota? How about you let
me help you out here?"

More silence, and Caitlin had started to figure the
rancher was done talking, when his voice returned.

"You got handcuffs?"

Caitlin yanked them from her belt. "Right here, sir."

"Snap them on. In front of you, so I can see."

Caitlin did as she was told, imagining D. W. Tepper
cursing her out for it, back behind the perimeter.

"Now come forward," Dakota's voice cracked.
"But keep your hands where I can see them."

She started walking.

Caitlin sized up the scene as soon as Dakota kicked
the door closed behind her, shoulders pressed against
a slab of wall between the door and the window
opened just a crack. He came around in front of her,
lugging a .30-06 hunting rifle with sight, careful to
avoid the drawn drapes. A dog, some pit bull mix,
rode his right side like an extra appendage, baring its
teeth at Caitlin and growling in a low rumble that
seemed to come from deep inside it.

"Easy, boy," Dakota said, in a tone more fit for a
lover than a dog.

The dog closed its mouth, but Caitlin continued to
hear the low rattle of its growl, which sounded a bit

like a car caught in first gear. By that time, she'd accounted for the man's wife and all his kids. It wasn't hard, given that they were huddled together on the plank floor, hands and feet both bound, the youngest kids sobbing. Her problem was she now had a dog and a rifle to contend with while she was handcuffed and weaponless. Not a good scenario if Caitlin couldn't talk Karl Dakota back off the ledge.

"It's for their own good, me tying them up, so they stay put," he explained to her. "What those aliens did to my cows, they could just as easily do to my kids if they catch 'em."

"I'd like to see those cows, Mr. Dakota."

He looked beyond her toward the covered windows, seeming to measure up the light beyond them. "Gonna be dark soon. That's when they come, after dark."

"Then we better hurry."

"Even the Texas Rangers can't win this one."

"I don't know about that, sir. There's lots of Indians and Mexicans in the old days who fully believed that and went to their graves for it."

"What ate my cattle ain't Mexicans or Indians."

Caitlin kept her eyes off Karl Dakota's terrified wife and kids, nothing that might draw his attention to them as well. Instead, she eased her hands out straight before her.

"Mr. Dakota, the key to these cuffs is in my back pocket. Now why don't you take these off me so we can see about doing ourselves some good?"

"They'll shoot me."

"Not if I tell them not to."

"I grew up with that damn Sheriff Lee. He was born an asshole and his crack's only got wider with age. And we can't even be sure that really is Sheriff Lee."

"Sir?"

"I think maybe these aliens walk among us. I believe they're able to replace human beings and pretend to be just like us. Sheriff Lee wants me dead because I've figured that out." His eyes narrowed suspiciously. "You could be one of them too. That's why I had you cuff your wrists." He cocked a gaze back toward his wife and kids sitting on the kitchen floor, terrified. "I believe it may be too late for them, too. I need to do what I gotta do."

"Take off these cuffs and let me help you, sir," Caitlin said, and took a step closer to him, only to be chased back by the dog baring its teeth again.

"No way, no how," Dakota told her, holding the rifle between her and his family now. "Can't take that chance. If you seen what's left of my cattle, you'd know why."

"Then show me."

"Nope. Could be a trap."

Caitlin shook her head. "They've got you where they want you, sir. Not trusting anyone else to help, not even your own family."

But Dakota didn't seem to hear her. His eyes fixed on nothing and his head canted oddly to the side as if he were hearing other voices.

"I need to do this," he said, to no one in particular.

"Do what, sir?"

"What I gotta do. It's for their own good, so they

can be at peace. Save their souls from the aliens, even if I can't save their bodies."

He twisted toward his family, the dog backing up alongside him to keep Caitlin in its sights. Caitlin watched Dakota take a big step that placed him within a yard or so of his wife, as he steadied his rifle. He angled the barrel down toward her, seeming to have forgotten Caitlin was even there.

"I gotta do this," he said to his wife, starting to sob. "For your own good. To save you all that pain later and save your soul while I still can. You and the kids. I got no choice. You may not feel it, but one of them's inside you, taking you over."

Caitlin watched his finger paw the trigger. "Mr. Dakota? Karl? Look at me, Karl."

He didn't seem to hear her.

"Close your eyes," Dakota told his wife.

His oldest son and daughter began to beg and plead, wailing loud enough to batter Caitlin's eardrums. All the commotion had the dog swinging around that way as if to seek out the source, neglecting Caitlin in that moment, just as his master was.

So she sprang.

Caitlin lurched into a dash, with no idea exactly what she was going to do. But Dakota's trembling finger was curling inward on the trigger and his whimpering wife had ducked her head to stare at the floor.

The dog turned at the last moment before Caitlin slammed into its master. She looped the center of the chain cuffing her wrists together around the man's throat, twisting him before her as protective cover from the dog.

The hunting rifle roared, further bubbling her eardrums in the tight confines, the bullet blowing out a back window and taking some of the old wood frame with it. Caitlin jerked Karl Dakota backwards, the pit bull mix whipped into a frenzy, trying to reach her, with its master still pinned between them. She kept using Dakota as a shield and realized she was choking off his air at the same time. Her shoulders smacked the wall and she pulled tighter, certain the gunfire would have the deputies storming the farmhouse at any moment.

Might as well have taken forever under the circumstances.

Caitlin felt Dakota stiffen and start to slump in her grasp from having his oxygen shut off. The rifle finally slipped from his grasp and clattered to the tile floor below, his kids screeching loud enough to make Caitlin flinch, while his wife remained still and silent, frozen in shock.

The dog was snapping and barking up a storm as it tried to reach Caitlin. Drool flew from its muzzle in thick, frothy clumps, its sights set on Caitlin and nothing more.

Including an old kitchen hutch, dragged awkwardly against a big bay window so no one could see through it from the outside.

Caitlin jerked Dakota that way, sliding back into the open, which meant jerking the man from side to side to shield herself, and dancing from the path of the dog's snapping jaws when it ventured too close. Dakota's legs gave out under him just as she drew even with the hutch. Caitlin felt herself dragged downward by his weight, the dog readying another charge before her. She imagined the inviting target she must make, glimpsed the dog launch itself airborne, straight for her.

In the same moment, she snapped her cuffed hands from Karl Dakota, sideward, tucking both behind the already teetering hutch and pushing. It toppled much faster than she'd expected, directly into the path of the dog, when it was close enough for Caitlin to see its browning teeth and feel its hot breath upon her.

Then the dog was gone, vanished beneath the tumbled hutch with a single yelp.

24

AUSTIN COUNTY, TEXAS

"I don't know what pisses me off more," said D. W. Tepper, as he used his own key on the cuffs still fastened to Caitlin's wrists, "you using your gun or dropping it." He shook his head and handed them back to her. "Doesn't seem to matter which way those hurricane force winds blow for my acid reflux to kick up a meal or two."

The sheriff's deputies had crashed through the front door while dust and splintered flecks of wood from the toppled hutch were still staining the air. Paramedics summoned to the scene as a precaution were still tending to Karl Dakota, who'd just regained consciousness, while more of the deputies worked first to untie and then to comfort Dakota's wife and children. A few others, meanwhile, started to lift the hutch off whatever was left of the dog.

"You may want to hold off on that, boys," Caitlin signaled, gesturing toward the Dakota children.

The deputies got her point and eased it back down.

"Well, I am amazed at one thing," Tepper said to her.

"What's that?"

"You getting through a whole week's duties without shooting anybody."

"Don't jinx me, Captain. We're not done here yet."

"How's that, Ranger?"

"We need to take a look at Karl Dakota's cattle."

They borrowed flashlights from the sheriff's deputies, to cut through the first of the night, walking off alone toward the grazing fields that rimmed the rear of the Dakota property.

"What time was it when I picked you up outside Christoph Ilg's ranch?"

"I don't remember for sure," Caitlin told Tepper. "Around eleven maybe?"

"What a day. . . ." Tepper took off his hat and mopped his brow with a shirtsleeve. "You hear that buzzing sound?"

"Yes, I do. Can't tell you what it is, though, sir."

"Well, can you tell me why you figure the Torres boy went missing for so long, Ranger?"

"No, I can't—at least not right now."

"But you don't believe he and his friend were lost, do you? Woods on that nature preserve aren't very thick and don't extend very far. They might well have been in somebody's backyard."

"You hear anything, Captain?" Caitlin asked him, instead of trying to explain what she'd gleaned from Luke's gaze.

"Just that buzzing. Why?"

"Because where exactly are Karl Dakota's cattle?"

The next sweep of their flashlights illuminated a series of clumps that looked like swollen mounds of dirt or field grass at first glance, but at second were something else entirely.

"Is that . . ."

"Holy shit," Captain Tepper finished for her.

25

AUSTIN COUNTY, TEXAS

The buzzing, it turned out, was flies, swarms and swarms of them, looking like patches of ink in the air of the night's thickening darkness. Caitlin and Tepper froze in their tracks, aware immediately this was some kind of crime scene into which they didn't dare wade for fear of disturbing any evidence.

"Get Doc Whatley on the line," Tepper instructed. "My hands are shaking too much to press out the keys."

Caitlin followed the now-shuddery ribbon of light cast by his flashlight into the grazing fields, trying to make sense of what she saw beneath the multitude of swarms as her eyes adjusted to the darkness.

"Are those . . ."

"Yup," Tepper affirmed, after her voice tailed off without completing the question. "Karl Dakota's cattle—what's left of them anyway. Maybe he's not as crazy as we thought."

As luck would have it, Bexar County Medical Examiner Frank Dean Whatley was in Houston for a forensics conference for the week, none too happy to be roused from a dinner by Caitlin's call.

"Why can't you just call the locals? Houston had a police department of their own last time I checked."

"Because this is a Ranger case now."

"It wasn't before?"

"How fast can you get out here?"

It turned out to be just over an hour before Whatley arrived on the scene. By that time, Sheriff Lee's deputies had secured the area and ordered up outdoor construction lighting powered by generators from a local contractor well versed in providing them. They had just been switched on when Doc Whatley was escorted onto the scene beyond the fence line from where he'd parked his car.

He carried an ancient forensics case in hand, the leather worn and discolored in stray patches. Caitlin could only imagine what the original contents of that case must've looked at when Whatley began carrying it. Frank Dean Whatley had been Bexar County's medical examiner since the time Caitlin was in diapers. He'd grown a belly in recent years that hung out over his thin belt, seeming to force his spine to angle inward at the torso. Whatley's teenage son had been killed by Latino gangbangers when Caitlin was a mere kid herself. Ever since then, he'd harbored a virulent hatred for that particular race, from the bag boys at the local H-E-B to the politicians who professed to be peacemakers. With his wife first lost in life and then death to alcoholism, he'd probably stayed in the job too long. But he had nothing to go home to, no real life outside the office, and remained exceptionally good at performing the rigors of his job.

Whatley had seemed to resent Caitlin in her first years on the job, warming up to her only after they'd worked closely on a few cases together. Caitlin always let him know how much she appreciated his persistence and professionalism, inevitably treating the victims of violence with a dignity that belied the coldness of his office. He'd purchased floral bed linens with his own money to better dress the steel slabs on which he performed his autopsies, because he believed those with the misfortune of ending up there deserved at least that much comfort and respect.

"Your description didn't do this justice, Ranger," he told her, swallowing hard. "The scene's even worse than what you indicated."

He pulled three pairs of pull-on plastic booties from his case and passed sets to both Caitlin and D. W. Tepper, the three of them leaning up against the wobbly fence to put them on. Caitlin held Whatley's stare through much of that process. The man's eyes looked much too big for his face from this angle, and she could read what was in them as well.

Because something had ravaged Karl Dakota's

entire herd, eaten each and every animal down to the bone.

Caitlin and Captain Tepper didn't say a word while Doc Whatley slipped into his medical examiner's role, first extracting fluids, sprays, and tools neither of them could identify. They looked on as he disappeared into the task of studying what remained of the animals scattered through the field, in positions identifiable by the swarms of flies dotting the air above them.

Even what her visual inspection told her seemed impossible: Each head of cattle had been picked clean to the bone with not the slightest bit of flesh remaining. Made it look like the animals had been dropped into a tank of piranha fish that left only their skeletons behind. Whatley took dozens of samples, allocated into individual plastic bags or tubes for further scrutiny later. Kept shaking his head through the process, obviously having a difficult time remaining detached from findings he'd yet to verbalize.

"Okay, Doc," Tepper started finally, "what do you make of all this?"

"I don't. I don't make anything out of it. At least not yet." He started to dip down again, then looked up and found Caitlin in his gaze instead. "How long is stuff like this gonna follow you around?"

"I wasn't aware it had been."

"Check the record, Ranger. Chances are the bulk of your cases are filed under either the impossible or the apocalypse."

"That what you think we're facing here, Doc?"

Tepper asked him. "The apocalypse? Because if we are, I wanna get in a whole lot of smoking 'fore the end times arrive. And you just try stopping me, Hurricane."

"Give us something, Doc," Caitlin urged.

"In this case, Ranger," he said, continuing the process of running a portable UV light in a crisscrossing grid around one of the stripped carcasses, "nothing *is* something."

"You've lost me."

"Figure of speech," he said, with grass, dirt, and dead flies staining the knees of his trousers. "Accurate in this case, nonetheless."

"Accurate how?" Tepper asked him.

"Tell me what you see, Ranger," Whatley said to Caitlin, shining the brightest flashlight she'd ever seen down on one of the carcasses.

"Bones."

"How about what you don't see?"

"Skin, blood, hair, grizzle, sinew—how long you want me to go on?"

"That was long enough," Whatley told her, moving the sweep of his beam off what was left of the animal. "Your turn, Captain. Tell me what you see now."

"Gravel and grass."

"Anything else?"

"Not a damn thing."

Whatley held both of them in his gaze. "That's what I meant by the impossible."

"You said the apocalypse, too," Tepper reminded.

"True enough, and still as good an explanation as any I can give you right now. I'm guessing your first thought when you saw the flies and bones were animals got these things. Wolves, cougars, bears—something like that."

"Actually," said Caitlin, "I was thinking *T. rexes* or velociraptors."

"Well, even they would've left *something* behind—plenty in fact. Look, I can't tell you what happened in this field, but I can tell you what didn't. You see how the remains are spaced?" Whatley raised and swept his flashlight about to highlight the dark mounds with fly swarms buzzing over them. "Normally, animals—even cattle—cluster defensively when attacked. Not these. They look to have been standing there eating up grass, blissfully unaware that they were about to get eaten down to the bone."

Caitlin considered that in the context of what was already on her mind. "And if they'd been attacked from the outside in, normal practice, the animals away from the perimeter would've had some time to back off and cluster."

"What's that suggest to you?"

"The impossible, just like you said."

"Besides that, Ranger."

Caitlin let her eyes roam the field as she responded. "They were all attacked at once, by something they never heard, saw, or smelled."

"First part of my preliminary report precisely," Whatley told her.

"What about the second part?" Tepper asked him, as if he really didn't want to know.

"I haven't decided how to word it exactly, without sounding like I've flown straight off the handle."

Tepper felt for the second cigarette he'd bummed off a patrolman back at the nature center, only to find it had slipped out of his pocket somehow. "Talk to Hurricane here," he said, gesturing toward Caitlin. "She's an expert on flying off the handle."

"Here's how it plays," Doc Whatley continued, not absorbing the humor. "I come across a scene even resembling something like this, a mass animal slaughter, I'm thinking about how they died and who did it. Here, there's no evidence on the corpses to give me any notion as to what happened. . . ." He stopped here, as if still struggling to form his next thoughts into words. "And also no evidence to suggest anyone or anything did it."

Tepper and Caitlin exchanged a befuddled glance.

"You want to give us that again, Doc?" she asked, before Tepper had a chance to.

"I can't find a single track of any kind, not a one," Whatley said, like he was trying to believe it himself. "If a predator got to these animals, you'd see evidence of that in the form of blood and remains scattered all over this field. But there's nothing, absolutely nothing. Almost like whatever did this just swooped in from the sky and then swooped back up when they were done."

"How many head of cattle we talking about?" Caitlin wondered.

"Somewhere around sixty'd be my nearest guess, Ranger, but it's hard to say."

"How's that compare to the wild animal kills you've come across in the past?"

"It doesn't, not in any way, shape, or form. I believe

the worst cattle kill I ever saw was by a starving wolf pack that had wandered onto the Texas prairie all the way from Oklahoma. Six head torn to shreds," Whatley told Caitlin and Tepper. "But there was still flesh and fur left over, and enough tracks to make me estimate three times the actual number of wolves had been involved. No tracks anywhere on this scene, though. And as for flesh and fur, well . . ."

Whatley let his comment tail off, the rest obvious.

"Can I give you a word of advice, Captain?" he resumed, after a pause he used to steady his breathing.

"You're going to anyway, Doc." Tepper frowned. "Everybody else does."

Whatley let his eyes roam the fields again, awash in the glow of the construction lights, which made Karl Dakota's grazing field look like an airport tarmac finished in grass instead of macadam. A dull heat radiated off him that had nothing to do with the temperature of the night.

"You may want to call the FBI in on this one," Whatley finished.

"Yeah, Doc? And what good are the G-men supposed to do me? Believe what happened here is more in Homeland Security's or the CDC's realm—hell, maybe NASA, based on the fact that whatever did this seems to have vanished into thin air."

PART THREE

Born in Lockhart, Texas, William Lee "Will" Wright (1868–1942) was small in stature but relentless in nature. The bespectacled Ranger, called El Capitán Diablo (the Devil Captain), and the members of his company guarded the border in World War I, went after liquor smugglers, tamed oil boomtowns, and took part in shootouts. In his career as a law officer, Wright witnessed the transition of the Rangers from their horseback days to the modern era after 1935. His belief that there should be less political interference and patronage in Ranger affairs became one of the axioms of the new order.

—Bruce A. Glasrud and Harold J. Weiss, Jr., eds.,
Tracking the Texas Rangers: The Twentieth Century

26

"You should look at me as a friend," Vyacheslav Beriya said, another finger plopping into the children's plastic pail set before the groveling shape seated on the couch. "After all, they're not your fingers."

The man seated before him, in the chair in the living room of his own sprawling mansion, was sobbing now. He had blond hair that looked ridiculous for a man his age, and Beriya was more convinced than ever that it was a dye job, or maybe even a hairpiece. The man could afford the best money could buy, anywhere in the world, because he had as much money as anyone in the world.

"Surely, you can understand why Moscow is upset with you, turning your allegiance and your investment capital to such poor and wasted use. Consider this an intervention. Consider me your financial counselor, trying to assure your billions are not pointlessly squandered on risky investments promising negative returns."

Beriya rose to his full height of six and a half feet and sighed, straddling the plastic pail that currently held six of Tutalev Krichenko's oldest son's fingers. The fall of the Soviet Union had left Beriya mostly isolated and ostracized, banished to the world of free-lance jobs that paid well but provided little satisfaction or respite from the drudgery of his days. Then Vladimir Putin had come along, the mind-set that accompanied him into office having offered Beriya a lifeline. Officials, journalists, holders of office at all levels who stood in the way of the government's vision of the new Russia faced elimination if they couldn't be coaxed to toe the line. Others handled the coaxing; Beriya's involvement came only when subtler methods had failed.

Eventually those subtler methods were abandoned altogether.

"Would you like to hear about the first time I killed something, comrade?" he asked Krichenko.

The man couldn't manage a nod; he was trembling so much that the figurines on the table next to the couch clattered against the glass.

"I was twelve years old and there was a vicious dog that lived next door to my house. Both yards were tiny and the dog was outside behind the fence all the time, barking and growling. One day it got loose somehow when I was walking by, and attacked me. It sunk its teeth into the arm I'd managed to raise. I don't remember being scared, just furious. I started hitting it again and again with my other hand, but it wouldn't let go. We tumbled to the ground, rolling. I found a rock and smacked it in the head and it padded off, whimpering. I could've just let it go, but I didn't. I caught up with it and kept hitting it with the rock until its face was gone. You know what I remember most?"

Krichenko was sobbing now.

"Feeling the dog's bones crack," Beriya told him. "And I didn't stop hitting it until there were none left to crack. I've never killed a man that way."

The Federal Security Service, or FSB, through which Beriya operated, was much more than just an ordinary security service. Combining the functions of an elite police force with those of a spy agency, and wielding immense power, it had come a long way since the early 1990s, when it was on the brink of imploding. Thanks to Vladimir Putin, it had been restored to the glory and power of the former KGB, in large part to make sure men like Krichenko cooperated, and to take proper action when they didn't.

Beriya lived for the pleasure of his work, but lately he had found himself bored with assignments like the one that had brought him here to Krichenko in his sprawling Mezhyhirya estate, once owned by former Ukrainian president Viktor Yanukovych. The gated grounds had featured six guards and two dogs. Beriya had spared the dogs and effortlessly killed the men who'd been trained to expect a much larger and more overt attack, never considering a single man breaching their perimeter. He'd squeezed the uniform top and trousers of the largest over his own clothes, leaving the blood in place to aid in his disguise as he stumbled and staggered toward the front door before collapsing before it. Three guards burst to his aid from within the mansion, and Beriya left them in the very place he'd pretended to collapse. Inside, he unleashed a pair of Strizh pistols on anyone and anything that moved, sparing only Krichenko's wife and children so he might utilize them later, after binding the oligarch to a chair positioned to ensure he could hear the screams coming from upstairs.

Beriya rustled a hand through the ash-colored hair rising just enough from his skull to form a stiff, bristly stubble. "I must say, I am disappointed in you, comrade," he continued, shaking his head at the cowering man beneath him. "I shouldn't need to be here. Pride and gratitude for all your riches should have made my visit unnecessary. But you ignored all the warnings, shrugged off all the overtures made by the civilized sorts who, even in Russia, would never believe men like me exist. You didn't think so either, did you? Thought your dogs and former soldiers were enough to keep you safe. You should have known, comrade, that a traitor like yourself is never safe," Beriya finished, and dropped another finger into the pail.

"What do you want?"

"I already told you. You need to sign your oil leases over to the state."

"And I told you such things take time."

"You have one week, comrade. If the leases are not signed over, you will force me to return—if not here, then anywhere you feel safe. No one is safe from me, do you understand that? And for each visit you force me to make, another of your children's fingers will end up in the pail," Beriya said, as the final finger belonging to Krichenko's oldest son plopped atop the others. "So, what will it be?"

Sobbing uncontrollably now, the billionaire managed a nod, the awful screams that had echoed through the house still ringing through his ears. "I'll do whatever you ask." Krichenko stopped his sobbing, looking more mystified than anything, in that moment. "You're smiling."

"Because I'm enjoying this. Like you, I take great pride and pleasure in my work."

Krichenko started to look down at the pail, then stopped. "How could you?"

"How could I what?"

"Do that," Krichenko said, his voice quaking as he tried to look down into the pail. "To a child . . . my son."

His business done, Beriya took the knife from its sheath and wiped it clean with the traitor's pocket square, which he then stuffed back into his lapel pocket. "It was easy, comrade. He was already dead."

Beriya strolled casually across the estate grounds upon which the bodies of Krichenko's guards still rested. The pair of dogs he'd spared bounded to his side, as if hoping he'd take them along with him. He petted both shepherds and handed each of them one of the fingers he'd plucked from the plastic pail before leaving. The dogs pranced off happily, already working their teeth.

All too easy. It had been so long since Beriya had been tested by a true challenge—all the way back to his days serving with Russia's Spetsnaz, when he'd tracked down and killed every one of the Chechen rebels behind the Beslan school massacre, in 2004. A lifetime ago.

He felt his phone vibrate in his pocket and jerked it to his ear. "I was just going to call you. Comrade Krichenko has had a change of heart."

"Excellent work, Major," his former commander in the FSB complimented. "You are needed elsewhere now, immediately, something of an emergency. In America."

Beriya felt something stir inside him, anticipation mixed with excitement. "I like working in America."

"Ever been to Texas, comrade?"

27

SHAVANO PARK, TEXAS

Caitlin sat on the porch swing, holding it still and silent while Cort Wesley was talking to his oldest son, Dylan, over his cell phone.

"Dylan's in a cab on his way here from the airport now," he said, voice still heated as he squeezed the phone hard enough for Caitlin to hear a cracking sound from the plastic case she'd bought him.

"You didn't tell me he was coming home."

"Because I told him not to, after calling him about his brother, soon as I got the word."

"Sounds like something I would do."

Cort Wesley shook his head. "Yeah, he's learning all the right lessons from you. He must've charged the flight to his credit card—*my* credit card. You have any idea what that must've cost?"

"Not a clue, these days."

"Well, I don't think he does, either, and he's the one who signed the slip. Kid doesn't listen to a word I goddamn say."

"So what else is new?"

"How about the cost of sending him to Brown University?"

"I thought Brown put together a decent financial aid package for him."

"Decent only pays for about half the costs, which still leaves me responsible for around thirty thousand a year."

"Explains why you decided to farm yourself out to Jones, Cort Wesley. What about that inheritance money?"

"Turns out everyone you could shake a stick at must be Maria Torres's cousin," he said, referring to the sister of his boys' mother, who'd been murdered along with her husband and children, a few years back. "Her estate's gonna be tied up in probate forever maybe." Cort Wesley shook his head, looked as if he'd swallowed something bitter. "When I put their mother's insurance money aside for the boys' education, I figured that was one thing anyway I didn't have to worry about. Let me tell you how wrong I was. I can't believe how much this shit costs."

"Why don't you let me help?"

"Because it's not your job."

"And you need to do his yourself."

Cort Wesley's eyes narrowed. "Did I say that?"

"You didn't have to. You're as good a father as there is on this planet, Cort Wesley."

He approached the swing but stopped short of taking the seat next to her. "Then tell me the truth, Ranger."

"About what?"

"About Luke."

"I have no idea what you're talking about."

"Yes, you do. I saw it in your eyes as soon as you heard me say his name. And something's not right with that long-haired kid. What was his name again?"

"Zach."

"Zach claims he still can't reach his parents. What are they, Luddites or something, traveling without cell phones?"

"I wouldn't know," Caitlin told him.

"Then tell me what you do know."

"That he's a damn good soccer player. You've watched him play."

"I have?"

"Up at Village School." Caitlin nodded.

Recognition flashed in Cort Wesley's eyes. "I met his mother and father, didn't I?"

"Stepfather, but yeah."

Cort Wesley dug the heels of his boots into the porch flooring. "What am I supposed to do about this joint that cop found?"

"Illegally, you mean."

"I'm not a court of law, Ranger."

"You should forget all about it, for now anyway. Deal with it later."

"As in how long?" He shook his head. "I never caught Dylan with weed."

"Doesn't mean he didn't have it, Cort Wesley."

He scolded her with his eyes. "If you know something that I should . . ."

"I don't, and I wouldn't tell you right now if I did. Those boys upstairs are already scared enough."

Cort Wesley stiffened and swept his eyes about the street beyond the house where his two sons had witnessed their mother shot to death, where they would've been killed as well, if Caitlin hadn't saved them. "He's around here somewhere, isn't he?"

"Who?"

He moved to the porch railing and continued looking, able to see more of the street from there. "You know who: Paz."

"I suspect he is."

"You suspect."

"What do you want me to say, Cort Wesley?"

"Oh, I don't know. How about that you told him this is a psychopath-free zone? That you believe I'm capable of taking care of my own son."

"Don't blame Paz for something that's already eating at you."

"What's that supposed to mean?"

Caitlin rose and joined him at the railing. "You being gone a lot lately."

"Being gone as in working?"

"Just make sure you wear plastic gloves before you take a check from our friend Jones, Cort Wesley. Whatever he's got, you don't want to catch."

"Yeah, well, there's not a lot of work out there for

special operators who've done time in prison, unless you're willing to go overseas. That leaves me working with Jones, and I make sure every job I do for him knocks off another tuition payment."

"Any bonus if you avoid collateral damage?"

"I'm not a hit man like your friend Guillermo Paz, Ranger."

Caitlin looked away, down the street into the night, as if expecting something to be there. "Paz showed up at that nature center because he knew something bad was happening."

"How can that be, exactly?"

"He said a psychic told him."

"A psychic?"

"Yup. He gave me her card."

"And you believed him?"

"I believe the psychic told him, yes. I don't normally believe in psychics."

"Well, that's a relief," Cort Wesley snapped, with plenty of bite to his voice.

"The psychic also told him something bad was coming."

"Isn't it always, Ranger?"

"She described it as a bright light swallowing the world."

Cort Wesley shook his head again, slower this time. "And that's what Paz is out there protecting us from, a bright light? If I were you, I'd file that psychic's card under Con Artists."

"This from a man whose best friend is a ghost."

"What's the difference between talking to old Leroy or talking to myself?"

"For one thing, last time I checked, you were still alive." Caitlin took a deep breath and joined him in gazing out into the night. "Right now, there's nothing I wouldn't believe. Hell, that crazy rancher in Austin County flat-out believed space aliens have invaded Texas and, based on what we found in his grazing fields, he just might be right."

"Picked to the bone, you say?" Cort Wesley repeated, once Caitlin had finished explaining what they'd found in Karl Dakota's grazing fields.

"When was the last time you finished a piece of chicken with your hands?"

"Last week sometime, at KFC. Why?"

"Because that's what you call picking something to the bone. Point being that you still leave something, even plenty, behind. Those cattle looked shaved of everything except their skeletons. And Doc Whatley can't find a shred of evidence indicating that any of the animals reacted to what was happening. That suggests they were all attacked and done in at once, by something covering the whole of the half-acre the herd was scattered across."

"Sounds like you're describing some dinosaur."

"I raised that point. The problem is even a *T. rex* leaves *something* behind. What did this left absolutely nothing other than bones."

It seemed to have grown cooler since Caitlin began telling the story, and she wondered if it was more a product of rehashing the tale again, with all its mystery and portent, than the weather.

"So let's hear your theory," Cort Wesley asked her.

"Haven't got one. Sorry."

He narrowed his gaze. "You've always got one."

Caitlin shook her head. "Not this time. Maybe you can ask Leroy Epps," she added half-jokingly, in reference to the ghostly specter Cort Wesley sometimes spoke with—or at least thought he did. "If anybody can tell us what's happening here, it's your friend Leroy."

Cort Wesley's gaze pulled off Caitlin a bit, as if trying to judge the level of sarcasm in her voice, ultimately deciding that her last comment had been uttered in frustration instead. "Leroy seems to prefer looking out instead of in. This kind of stuff isn't up his alley."

"And what alley is that?"

"The future, Ranger. That thing that starts every morning you wake up."

Caitlin pushed herself up off the swing. "Think I'll go inside and check on Luke."

28

SHAVANO PARK, TEXAS

As soon as Caitlin had disappeared inside the house, Cort Wesley caught the sweet smell of talcum powder and turned toward the porch rail where he spotted the silhouette of a gaunt figure, the moonlight seeming to pass straight through it.

"Things ain't never boring for you, are they, Bubba?" said Leroy Epps.

They'd let Cort Wesley attend Leroy's funeral, in a potter's field not far from Huntsville's infamous Walls Unit, for inmates who didn't have any relatives left to claim the body. He'd been the only one standing at the graveside, besides the prison chaplain, when the fork-lift had lowered the plank coffin into the ground. Cort Wesley tried to remember what he'd been thinking that day, but it was hard, since he'd done his best to erase those years not just from his memory but from his very being. One thing he did remember was that the service was the first time he'd smelled the talcum powder Leroy Epps had used to hide the stench from the festering sores spawned by the diabetes that was killing him.

Just like now, his dead cellmate standing right there at the porch railing. Epps held a bottle of root beer in a thin, liver-spotted hand. His lips were pale pink and crinkled with dryness. The moonlight cast his brown skin in a yellowish tint. The diabetes that had ulti-mately planted him in the ground had turned Leroy's eyes bloodshot and numbed his limbs years before the sores and infections set in.

As a boxer, he'd fought for the middleweight crown on three different occasions, knocked out once, and had the belt stolen from him on paid-off judges' score-cards two other times. He'd been busted for killing a white man in self-defense and had died three years into Cort Wesley's four-year incarceration. But ever since, he always seemed to show up when needed the most. Whether Epps was a ghostly specter or a figment of his imagination, Cort Wesley had given up trying to figure out. Just accepted the fact of his presence and was grateful that Leroy kept coming around to help him out of one scrape after another.

"How's the view from where you sit?" the ghost asked him. *"Imagine it's the same as over here."*

"What is it you're looking at, champ?"

"Your youngest for starters. Boy's wound tighter than my granddad's watch. I ever show that to you?"

"Not that I recall. Get back to Luke."

"Ask the Ranger."

"Ask Caitlin *what?*"

"She's upstairs hearing it told now. Not for me to say."

"The boy's been through a lot."

"You're not hearing what I'm saying, Bubba."

"That's because you're making less sense than usual."

Old Leroy drained the rest of his root beer and laid the empty bottle down atop the porch railing. *"I'm making the same as I always do. Maybe it's your hearing that's off."*

"I hate when you talk like this."

"Thought you'd be used it by now."

"Get back to Luke."

"Can't."

"Why?"

Leroy reached for the root beer bottle, as if forgetting it was empty. Cort Wesley thought he could actually see through his spectral hand, as if it, too, were made of glass.

"Not for me to say, Bubba. I never thought one man could have so much mystery in his life. Tell you this, though. Things ain't as different on this side as you think; it's the view that's different. You ever climb one of those skyscrapers and drop a quarter into one of those cheap telescope things?"

"Sure, when I was a kid."

"Where I be is like looking at the world through one of those all the time without needing no change at all. It's not that I always understand what I'm looking at, just that I can see a whole lot more and a whole lot farther."

"What's this have to do with Luke, champ?"

"Got a quarter?"

"Sure."

"Then pretend you're using it to see what the world looks like up close from a distance. Whole new perspective that'll show you what you're missing."

"What am I missing?"

Epps brought the empty root beer bottle back to his mouth and blew into it across the top, creating a whistling sound that jibed with the harmonic twang sprayed by the wind chimes hanging from the porch eave. *"Know what else I can see about the world from where I stand? How damn much all this shit is connected. You have no idea."*

"Why don't you tell me?"

"You know I can't do that, Bubba. I can't tell you what to see, only where to look." Epps cast his gaze upward. *"Your boy's safe and sound, and you're fine*

leaving it at that instead of asking the questions you should be. But you gotta watch something else right now, that being your back."

"So what else is new?"

"Know the biggest assholes I ever knew on the inside? Wasn't MS-13 or them racist pigs of the Aryan Nation. Know who it was? Russians. They're an altogether different breed, like their clocks wind through less hours of the day or something. I swear, they hated life so much they didn't care about dying, and that made them more dangerous than any others I ever come across."

Cort Wesley felt something cold grip his insides. "You talking about the ones I messed with outside Dallas today?"

"I'm talking in general, but those'll do for starters."

"Meaning I haven't seen the last of them?"

"Not sure on that account, Bubba. I might need no change to peer through that rooftop telescope, but that doesn't mean I don't see nothing but dark through it sometimes, and this is one of those times. I just don't like the sound of what I see. I don't like it none at all." Leroy set the root beer bottle back down atop the railing, a sudden gust of wind jiggling it a bit, and gazed upward again. *"Just remember what I said about those connections."*

"You didn't say anything."

"I said all you needed to hear if you was listening, Bubba. And I've outstayed my welcome. You don't mind, I need to be off, find myself another root beer. Leave you to your thoughts."

"Anything else on your mind, champ?" Cort Wesley asked Leroy Epps, his insides still twisted into chain mail.

"*Ask the Ranger,*" was all he said, his tired eyes sad, peering out into the night toward something Cort Wesley had no hope of seeing.

29

SHAVANO PARK, TEXAS

Caitlin stopped at Dylan's room first, poking her head in to find Zach sitting on the edge of the bed, face lost in his hands.

"You okay?" she asked him. "You need anything?"

"No," he said, clearing his throat. "I'm good."

"You try your parents again?"

Zach flashed his phone, his hair swimming past his shoulders. "Voice mail."

"What about your real dad? Think you should call him?"

The boy started to look down, then stopped. "No. That's the last thing I want to do."

Caitlin didn't press him on that. "You're a hell of a soccer player."

"I guess," he shrugged.

"You made all-district as a freshman."

"Second team."

"Only freshman who did, though."

Zach narrowed his gaze on her, looking glad that Caitlin knew that.

"Can I ask you a question?" she asked him.

"Sure."

"You see those same lights Luke did? Off to the left of where you were in the woods?"

"I think so. I don't remember for sure now."

"Well, anything you do remember, make sure you tell me, no matter how small. Don't hesitate, okay?"

Zach nodded. "Ms. Strong?" he said, after she'd turned back for the door.

Caitlin swung round again. "It's Ranger. But you can call me Caitlin."

Zach took a deep breath. "There's something I need to tell you, something you need to know. That joint? It was mine."

"What joint?" Caitlin asked him.

Luke was sitting on his bed, reading by a single lamp's light. "Couldn't sleep," he said, before she could knock on the jam of his open door.

"Still scared?"

"You think Dylan'll be pissed?"

"Why would he?"

"For letting somebody sleep in his bed." Luke looked down and then up again, legs tucked beneath the covers and wearing a T-shirt that read "I Heart Texas." "He's on his way home, right?"

"You spoke to him before me or your dad."

"Maybe we should wake Zach up and move him somewhere else before Dylan gets here."

Caitlin took a few steps into the room and stopped. "You ready to talk about last night?"

"You mean about those lights I told you I saw?"

"I mean about anything."

"I can't tell you anything about those missing kids. I've been racking my brain trying to think of something I haven't thought of before. A sound, maybe, or a glimpse I caught of something without realizing."

"I'm not talking about those missing kids, Luke. I'm talking about you."

"I'm here, aren't I?" the boy snapped, an edge creeping into his voice. "I'm not missing."

"Okay."

"Okay *what?*"

"Whenever you're ready."

"Ready to do *what?*" Defensively now.

Caitlin thought she saw Luke's shirt rippling, in rhythm maybe with his heart suddenly hammering against his rib cage. "Whatever it is you've got to tell me," she said, meeting his eyes, which were having trouble meeting hers, "I'll be ready to listen as soon as you're ready to talk."

Caitlin started to turn for the door, then stopped. She watched Luke look down for a time and then look up again, as if expecting to see Caitlin gone, but relieved when she wasn't.

"If you've got a few minutes," he started, "maybe I'm ready now. . . ."

30

"Well?" Cort Wesley posed when she stepped back out onto the porch.

"Luke was asleep."

"Took you a long time to figure that out."

"I just wanted to make sure." She stopped, choosing her next words carefully. "I heard you talking to someone from inside."

"I'll whisper next time."

"Leroy?"

"What do you think?" Cort Wesley asked, and then he started again before Caitlin could answer. "Sometimes *I* think I've gone fully around the bend." He looked toward the porch railing, expecting the empty root beer bottle to still be there, but it was gone. "Only two people in this world who make any sense to me, and one of them's not in this world at all."

"Speaking of sense . . ."

"What were you and Luke talking about?"

"I told you—"

"I know what you told me. Now tell me what you talked about."

Caitlin came up close to the porch swing but stopped short of taking her seat back. "It's been a long day, Cort Wesley."

He rolled his eyes. "You sound like Leroy."

"Maybe you should listen to him more."

He shook his head. "I swear the two of you have joined forces. Maybe it was him you were talking to upstairs, not Luke."

Caitlin remained standing. "Except he was down here talking to you."

"It's been a long day, Ranger." Cort Wesley cracked a smile that seemed to rise out of nowhere. "Wonder if our dads argued like this that time they worked together."

"We'll have to ask Captain Tepper what happened next, after the night of that famous bar fight."

"No, we don't, Ranger," he told her, "because I know a part of the story too."

31

HOUSTON, TEXAS; 1983

"Russian guy I've been dealing with, the one who ripped me off, goes by the name of Stanko," Boone Masters explained from the passenger seat of Jim Strong's pickup truck. "I call him Stinko."

Jim lowered the binoculars from his eyes. "Bet that pissed him off."

"Well, he pissed me off first, and that was even before he ripped off my warehouse."

"Full of those appliances you ripped off from others."

"You saying that made what he did okay?"

"Stealing from a crook? I don't believe that would

get him any sympathy from a court; you neither, Mr. Masters."

They were baking in the August sun on the rooftop level of a parking garage directly across the street from a gleaming downtown building that served as the international headquarters for a company called MacArthur-Rain that Jim had never heard of. The building stood out from the other skyscrapers around it, not only for its ultramodern, sleek look but also for the courtyardlike grounds that adorned a private land-scaped plaza where any number of employees were currently eating a picnic-style lunch. Not bad work, if you could get it, Jim supposed, as the song "She Works Hard for the Money," by Donna Summer, con-tinued playing over the truck's radio.

Down in the plaza, the man Boone Masters had called Stanko was huddled among three other men who were even bigger and broader than he was. The leaders of the Russian gang Masters claimed had ripped off his warehouse seemed to be competing for which man could hold the most smoke in his lungs. They were chain-smoking their lunch, grinning up a storm, and seeming to eye every pretty woman that passed by, in unison, making just enough of a scene to make those women feel uncomfortable. Casting the kind of leering, lurid glares that were enough to make their visual targets eat lunch at their desks for the rest of the week. Their uniformly dark suits worn over light shirts and black ties made them look more like caricatures lifted from an artist's imagination than the real-life violent thugs they were.

"Why do you do that?" Masters asked suddenly.

"Do what?"

"Call me 'mister.' I'd be obliged if you stopped showing me false respect. You figure that, by addressing me that way, it creates some kind of bond between us. I'm here to tell you that it hasn't and won't."

"You finished?" Jim asked Boone Masters.

"Huh?"

"Waving your dick in the air, trying to claim the upper hand when, so long as I got that unsigned warrant on my desk for your boy's arrest, you might as well use that hand to diddle yourself. Now, what else can you tell me about Stanko's gang?"

"They smell like potatoes and piss vodka. I don't know the names of the other three, never exchanged a word with them. What I can tell you is they have no regard for us at all."

"Us as in Texans?"

"No, as *Americans*. They only want to be doctored by a Russian, have their house painted by a Russian, their broken window fixed by a Russian. You don't speak the language and come from a place I can't pronounce, you're just passing through until they have no use for you anymore."

"You describing yourself in that regard?"

Masters frowned, then let the look dissolve into a sneer. The first bars of "Every Breath You Take" by the Police started playing and he switched off the radio. "Never figured you for a Top Forty man, Ranger. Figured you more for the country music type, or maybe news radio."

"Well, as long as my daughter, Caitlin, likes that kind of music, that's what I listen to. Michael Jackson's her favorite right now. He ever plays a concert in these parts, I'll have to put in to work the security detail so I can take her."

Masters gnashed his teeth, his jaws working like he was chewing a nonexistent piece of gum. "That a reference to our relative merits as parents?"

"I never took my kid on a job with me, Mr. Masters. You can do the math on that as good as me. Now, get back to the Russians."

Before resuming, Boone Masters turned the radio back on and spun the dial to a country station playing "You're Gonna Ruin My Bad Reputation" by Ronnie McDowell, the song seeming oddly appropriate enough to leave him easing back a bit on his throttle.

"I thought I was different," he told Jim Strong. "Guess all the others they ripped off thought the same thing. They come at you real friendly. New guy who showed up recently said he liked my jacket, so I gave it to him. Gesture of goodwill, right? I come outside from the meeting and it turns out his crew had stolen the mag wheels off my truck while he was thanking me. Hey, stop laughing."

Jim sucked in some breath. "Sorry. Couldn't help myself."

"It was thirty-five degrees, and I had no coat and no wheels—yeah, I can see the humor there. Problem being, who does someone like me go to when they've been ripped off? Try putting a crew together to take on these Russians, who sleep in their bulletproof vests." The sneer vanished, replaced by an expression so flat it seemed to swallow the wrinkles that too much time in the sun had dug into Masters's brow and cheeks. "That's why I'm sitting here beside you right now. Since I can't get them, helping you is the next best thing."

"Get back to this new guy."

"What about him? He showed up just before they jacked my warehouse."

"I was going to ask you *why* he showed up, not when."

"I know when. Can't tell you why, except to say Stinko didn't seem too happy about it."

Jim didn't seem to hear him; too busy working with the binoculars again.

"When exactly do you plan on telling me what this is really about, Ranger?"

"You asked me that already."

"I must not have gotten an answer worth remembering."

Jim Strong moved the binoculars slightly, staying on Stanko's gang as they moved into the shade from the sun. "It started with an alert."

"What kind of alert?"

"One that tells law enforcement bodies that the Soviets may have sent KGB agents here in the guise of mobsters. Kind of a last stand, since they realized the Cold War was a lost cause."

"Stanko?"

Jim lowered the binoculars. "How long's he been here?"

"I was fencing merchandise through him for over a year before he ripped off my warehouse."

"That would square with the timing mentioned in the alert," Jim said and raised the binoculars again.

Achoo!

"Gesundheit," Jim said across the cab.

"Wasn't me, Ranger."

Jim laid the binoculars down on the bench seat between him and Masters and threw open the driver's door, shaking his head. "Well, shit . . ."

He stepped out of the truck, the sun heating up his skin on contact. He moved to the pickup's bed and yanked back the tarpaulin that should've been covering a toolbox and bag of old clothes he'd forgotten to drop at the Goodwill.

It was covering his six-year-old daughter, Caitlin, instead.

"Hi, Daddy," she said, biting her lip.

"What you doing back there, little girl?"

"Figured you could use some help. 'Backup,' Grandpa calls it."

Jim nodded. "He know you came along?"

"Nope. I snuck past him when he was taking his morning nap." She lowered her voice and leaned closer to him. "Don't tell him I told you, but Grandpa's old."

Jim Strong hoisted his daughter from the bed and placed her down before him.

"I forgot my Colt," she continued, referring to the old Peacemaker Earl Strong was using to teach her how to shoot. "Hit the target with every shot at the range the other day, a couple in the bird's-eye."

"That's *bull's*-eye."

"Isn't that what I said?"

"You can't be doing this, Caitlin."

"What?"

"Coming to work with me."

Caitlin looked up toward the shape of Boone Masters, who had the binoculars pressed against his eyes now. "Is that man working with you?"

"I suppose."

"He got any kids?"

"One son, I believe."

"Does he shoot?"

"I'm sure he does, little girl."

"Bet he's not as good as me," Caitlin said, her upper lip stiffening.

And that's when the shooting started on the plaza below.

Jim Strong pushed Caitlin against the truck frame for safety. "Stay right there and don't move, not even an inch!"

He had his .45 out it the next instant, sweeping around the length of the truck as the distinctive clack of gunfire continue to pour up from the plaza. Jim first saw the bystanders scattering in all directions, having abandoned their picnic-style lunches and looking ridiculously small from this distance. The gunfire ratcheted into a staccato barrage and Jim got a bead on the gunmen as a pair of them was opening up with automatic weapons, assault rifles, blasting away at Stanko and his gang, who were twisting and turning like some crazed dance step before finally crumpling or falling backwards. The gunmen were all wearing ski masks, darting away in opposite directions before the last member of Stanko's crew had hit the plaza ground.

Jim wished he could leap from the top of the parking garage to the ground like Superman and chase the bastards down. As it was, he'd have to charge down six flights, only to emerge back into the day with the stench of urine from the parking garage stairwell stuck to his nostrils—for no good reason now. The shooters would be long gone by the time he got his breath back, and following that plan meant leaving Caitlin in the company of Boone Masters.

So he climbed back into his truck, leaving the door open as he grabbed the radio mike from its stand and called up Houston police. Not that he needed to; sirens were already wailing in the distance, and Jim tossed the mike down in frustration.

"I warned you about these Russians," Boone Masters smirked.

"Yeah? Well, from my angle, Stanko and his boys just got turned into Swiss cheese. It would seem our association has come to an end."

Masters shook his head. "No, it hasn't."

"Come again?"

"That new Russian I told you about, that I gave my jacket to? One of the gunmen we just watched do the shooting down there looked awful familiar to me, because he was wearing that jacket."

32

Caitlin smiled whimsically. "That was your father in the front seat of my dad's truck that day? I never got a good look at him. My dad made me ride home under the tarp, even though it started to rain to punish me."

"You ever stow away like that again?"

"Oh yeah, a couple times, anyway."

Cort Wesley flashed a smile slighter than hers. "So you met my father long before you met me."

"We weren't exactly introduced. How'd you know?"

"It was one of the last things my dad and I ever talked about. He got a kick out of telling the story. He was doped up on painkillers in the hospital at the time, so I wasn't even sure it was true. Until we actually met, that is. Then I knew it had to be."

Caitlin smiled slightly. "Jim Strong would've liked the boys, Cort Wesley."

"Boone Masters would've, too—would've likely seen them as extra hands on the cheap to take on a job, just like he saw me."

"Seems a different man than the one you've told me about often enough."

"That's because I was never sure any of the story about him and your dad teaming up was real, until Captain Tepper confirmed it."

Caitlin realized only then that the swing was rocking

and likely had been through the whole of the story Cort Wesley had just finished. Her stomach felt a little unsettled—more from the memories, though, than the swaying. Most of the time she liked holding them in her mind, but tonight, for some reason, was different.

"Get back to what you were talking about before," she said across the swing, which was slowing now.

"Before what?"

"Before you changed the subject from our friend Jones, the man whose checks you've been cashing to pay for your kids' educations."

"I told you—"

"Right, Homeland Security's using direct deposit now."

"I'm not sure he's even Homeland Security anymore," Cort Wesley told her.

"Then what is he?"

"I'd say kind of acting in a freelance capacity, off the books."

"In other words," Caitin advanced, "free to use men like you and Paz without making any accounts."

"As long as it pays the bills, that works for me."

"You mentioned something about Russians too."

"Yeah, specifically the owner of a strip club off Harry Hines Boulevard, just north of Dallas. I planted an old-fashioned bug in his office. Looked mobbed up to me."

"Why would Jones be interested in him?"

"I didn't ask."

"Since when does Homeland Security, or its various offshoots, care about a Russian mobster? Or the Russian mob in general?" Caitlin stood up, needing to stretch her legs but also made suddenly uneasy by the whole conversation. "Jones is up to something."

"Jones is *always* up to something, Ranger. That's his business."

"Not if it involves Texas. And if something about this mobster caught his eye, that's something I need to be seeing, too."

Cort Wesley joined her on his feet. "So call him."

"Can't. I programmed my phone to blow up if I ever press out his number again."

"Okay, so tell me what you and Luke talked about upstairs."

"I already told you that he was asleep."

A taxi pulled up to the curb, Dylan lunging out of the backseat before it had even come to a complete halt. He slung his backpack over his shoulder and jogged toward them across the front yard. He bounded up the porch in two bounds and surged straight past Caitlin and Cort Wesley as they moved to greet him.

"I can't believe you people," he said, shouldering his way through the front door.

Cort Wesley and Caitlin were just looking at each other when her cell phone rang, "Captain Tepper" lighting up in her caller ID.

"You get any sleep, Ranger?" he asked for a greeting.

"Not yet. Why?"

"Because you're not going to. Dallas authorities got a suspect in the disappearance of those kids."

PART FOUR

While the gunfight [between Texas Ranger Frank Hamer and two men named McMeans and Phillips] was in progress there was a Nolan County grand jury in session. The jury paused from their deliberation to watch the entire street battle from upstairs windows across the street. In a supreme example of the swiftness of Texas justice, while Frank was being treated by the doctor for his wounds, the grand jury convened in the matter of the death of McMeans. In minutes it returned a no bill, ruling Frank Hamer's killing of McMeans was an act of self-defense.

—Dan Marcou, "Frank Hamer, Texas Ranger: Legendary LEO Was a Hard Man to Kill," Policeone.com

33

"What do you hear from your contacts in New York?" Calum Dane asked Pulsipher, who was walking alongside him through one of several oil fields Dane owned in the Permian Basin.

"The situation has been contained," Pulsipher reported. "We've dealt with the security camera footage showing Brandon McCabe returning to the hotel, and right now it's being treated as a missing persons case."

"And the room?"

"I've used these particular cleaners before, sir," Pulsipher said, leaving it there. "You have no concerns on that front."

"But I do on another front, don't I?"

They'd come straight from Midland International Air and Space Port to the first oil field Dane had ever staked, on the grounds of what had been a potter's field graveyard where he'd buried his own father. On a beautiful, clear morning like this, it was easy to forget the land's original roots before the pumpjacks had moved in with their steady clanking. He surveyed the scene, recalling the endless rows of graves marked only with wooden crosses and trying to recall the location of his father's.

"Know the day I got rich, S.?" he asked suddenly, sun blistering his eyes now as it had back then.

"Sir?"

Dane remained facing away from him, gaze fixed toward nothing in particular. "It was the day I buried my father here. It was skin cancer that got him, from too much time spent working the fields right here in Glasscock County. But me getting rich had nothing to do with cotton and everything to do with oil."

To this day, Dane still remembered being transfixed, as a small boy, by the steady chugging of the pumpjack rigs that lined the barren land, sometimes as far as the eye could see. He remembered them so clearly because they'd terrified him at first, sentencing Dane to a week of nightmares the first time he glimpsed a scattered track of them from the back of a pickup truck. His imagination conjured them uprooting themselves from their moorings and waging war on humans the way Martian machines had in some movie whose title he couldn't remember. And, like another horror movie Dane recalled, about giant ants emerging out of the New Mexican desert, you'd know the metallic monsters were coming thanks to their smell. A corrosive, sulfurlike odor that reminded him of smoldering matchsticks.

"The ground was soft and muddy the day they lowered my dad's coffin into a grave already pooling with water at the bottom," Dane resumed. "I'm standing there at my father's grave site and all of a sudden I catch the faint sulfuric aroma and think to myself,

There's oil here; maybe lots of it. By then, much of the Permian Basin was thought to have gone dry, at least insofar as the limits of current pumping technology went. It had been mostly abandoned by the biggest oil exploration and drilling companies in favor of richer finds easier to plum for their riches. But what I couldn't get out of my head was the irony of a father who'd never done shit for me while alive coming through big-time now that he was dead and in the ground."

Dane started to wonder how he compared as a parent, then pushed the thoughts aside because he hated where they took him. A son dead in Afghanistan, then the divorce . . .

"I guess it was fate, S.," he said, to distract himself as much as anything.

"Sir?"

"Smelling that oil coming from my father's grave."

Dane had worked for a year solid, seven days a week, holidays included, living like a pauper in order to put aside every available penny he could. He finished a year of hardscrabble labor, after lying his way into a job on an offshore oil rig, with just the ten thousand dollars he needed to buy up a few small acres in the area around the potter's field—available in large part because nobody wanted anything to do with land packed to the hilt with graves and small wooden crosses rising out of the ground.

"That smell was H-two-S, or hydrogen sulfide," Dane resumed. "Some oil fields, I learned, have sweet crude that contains very little sulfur, while others, like West Texas in particular, have sour crude that contains high amounts of sulfur. And I was particularly sensitive to the scent after hearing stories about people dying in their sleep occasionally, when an oil company accidentally released a gas compound that turned out to be H-two-S. But, officially anyway, they were covered up, with something else being pegged with the blame, at the behest of oil interests that fueled the entire Texas economy. Can't say I blame them; can you?"

Pulsipher didn't say whether he did or not.

Dane had leased the mineral rights to the land he'd sold—not to the highest bidder but to a decently high one that included a percentage of the profits. And those profits created the basis for his entire fortune today.

The problem, to some degree, was that Dane had never lost his thirst for adventure, for being the boy again smelling oil rising from his father's grave. That had produced Dane Corp's expansion into high technology, petrochemical development, and agriculture. He'd started off buying excess farmland about the Permian Basin. Rolling cotton fields mostly, made especially cheap by the fact that he had his own way of getting the price down.

Dane finally turned and locked Pulsipher in his gaze, his eyes tearing up from the sun. "It turned out that besides being buried in oil-rich ground, my father had done me another favor by teaching me how to battle the pesky varmints that preyed on cotton crops. Boll weevils, mostly; insects that appropriately enough entered the United States in the late nineteenth century by crossing the Rio Grande into Brownsville. My father said that some years up to half the state's cotton-producing land was infested. And, in the worst years, the decline of the crop yield had a direct effect on how much food we could put on the table.

"Now, farmers had employed all kinds of strategies to battle the loathsome bugs, from burning their nesting grounds to laying traps to digging moats filled with a combination of water and gasoline to drown them. But it was my dumb-as-a-stump father with a third-grade education who won the war instead of just a battle.

"My family had been farmworkers and sharecroppers since before the Civil War and had passed down a formula mixing a crude form of turpentine made of simple pine resin with powdered tar. Mixed with dirt, the compound worked because the taste of it was like candy to the bugs that devoured it voraciously, poisoning themselves and left to be crushed underfoot by additional advancing hordes. These boll weevils would then consume the remains, while the ground grew rich with the stench rising from the corpses flattened to a pastelike consistency, which snared further hordes in their tracks. Instead of the cotton, thanks to my father, the bugs ended up eating each other."

Dane had never forgotten that, or the fact his father could've gotten rich off his invention but lacked both the initiative and the smarts to do so. Quite the opposite of his son. And that experience had engrained in Calum Dane an appreciation for the additional revenue that could be coaxed from land kept reasonably free of boll weevils and less-pervasive pests. So, once he expanded his interests into petrochemicals, he invested a fortune in synthesizing the turpentine and powdered tar compound into a chemically enhanced pesticide capable of raising cotton crop yields between twenty-five and fifty percent. That pesticide had enjoyed a spectacular debut, distributed all across the state of Texas, until the cancer shit started, on the eve of its national rollout a few years back.

This had been followed, more recently, by something much, much worse, which was the source of Dane's biggest set of problems right now, stemming from a goddamn high school field trip to some goddamn nature preserve.

"Tell me about your father, S.," he said suddenly, needing to hear something other than his own thoughts.

"He was army. We moved around a lot."

"Growing up on military bases. Toughened you up, I bet."

"I believe it did, sir."

"Just like working those cotton fields did me. Your dad still alive?"

"No, sir. He'd just been posted to the Pentagon. Nine eleven was his first day."

Dane turned away again, gazing out into the fields as if searching for his father amid the endless rows of long-gone cotton. "Know what I learned from my father, S.?"

"What, sir?"

"Indirectly, that true power in the future doesn't lie in oil, gas, gold, or the Fortune five hundred. It belongs to whoever controls the food supply. Imagine being the person responsible for doubling the world's food. Imagine the profits involved. All because my father had stopped boll weevils in their tracks."

Funny thing was, Dane could no longer remember the name of the kid he'd beaten to death with his own prosthetic leg just yesterday. As if he'd excised the memory from his psyche, along with all the lawsuits filed by cancer victims like him. He did recall that, while using that prosthetic leg like a club, the kid on the bed morphed into little Calum Dane as a boy. And he knew that if he looked into the mirror in that moment, his father's snarling, drunken face and bloodshot eyes would look back. He understood, in the moment of beating the kid senseless, how much his father had enjoyed beating him, so much so that he couldn't stop until the shattered leg had spit shards of plastic all over the hotel room and the kid lay beaten to a pulp.

"What are we gonna do about those kids, S.?" he asked Pulsipher.

"You can't hold them forever, sir," Pulsipher said suddenly. "And there's a chance that the two we missed saw something."

"What do our sources have to say?"

"The Texas Rangers are supervising the case. We don't have any sources there. And we've got another problem."

"What's that?"

"One of the kids we missed."

"The other one? Don't tell me," said Dane, "the son of a Texas Ranger."

"Close enough," Pulsipher told him.

34

"Maybe you forgot what I told you last night," D. W. Tepper said, when he saw Caitlin approaching.

"What was that, Captain?"

"To be somewhere else. We're here strictly as observers."

"Sounds good to me."

"Just remember that when you get the urge to shoot somebody."

They were standing down the street from the Fountain View office building on Industrial Boulevard in Euless, just outside Dallas. Caitlin and Cort Wesley had set out on the long drive up here from San Antonio almost as soon as Tepper had delivered the news that a potential suspect, with ties to past kidnapping cases as well as to the Village School in Houston, had been identified. According to Tepper, video surveillance showed him entering his suite of offices here in Fountain View late the previous night, with three other men, but never emerging, even after night had bled into day.

Tepper stuck a Marlboro into his mouth and struck a match against his boot heel. Eyeing Caitlin, he repeated the process when no flame sparked.

"What the . . ."

"Looks like somebody cut the match head, Captain."

Tepper rolled the match before his squinted eyes to confirm precisely that, then tossed the match aside. "More great investigative work on your part, Ranger. I imagine that same somebody cut off *all* the match heads."

"That would be my assumption, too."

They both watched Cort Wesley jogging up from where he'd parked his truck, beyond the blockade formed by police and sheriff's department vehicles. He was breathing heavily by the time he got there, his face red in the cheeks and his brow creased from forgetting his sunglasses.

"Good thing the two of you aren't up for parents of the year," Tepper groused, holding the unlit cigarette in his hand right now.

"Dylan came home," Caitlin explained, reading the intent of his words. "He's watching Luke."

"Alone?"

"What's that mean?"

"You call in anybody else; your own personal Frankenstein maybe?"

Caitlin looked toward Cort Wesley, then back at Tepper. "Something's going on here. You know that as well as I do."

"That doesn't answer my question and, truth be told, I don't care. Guess you gotta be a hurricane to know which way the wind is blowing."

"Anything worth snatching thirty-plus kids over is enough to tear the roof off buildings, D.W. You want to stand there and tell me whoever missed Luke and his friend won't bother trying again, go ahead. I'm just not willing to take that chance."

"Nice to have Monsters Are Us on speed dial, I suppose," Tepper scowled. He was about to say more when a man outfitted in black SWAT garb and body armor waved him over. "Dallas SWAT is handling the takedown. Last I heard, their thermal imaging hadn't picked up any movement inside the office in question at all."

"But security cameras didn't show anybody leaving."

"That's why I love technology," Tepper said, starting away. "Maybe we were better off just kicking in doors and letting the chips fall where they may."

Caitlin watched the Dallas SWAT team gathering outside their RV, all with their chests expanded by more than just the flak jackets, and couldn't help thinking of Waco, when the FBI instead of the Rangers had stepped in to deal with David Koresh.

"So long as it's us doing the kicking, Captain."

"Not today," he told her, scowling again.

35

EULESS, TEXAS

"You still haven't told me what you and Luke talked about last night," Cort Wesley said, while they both watched the SWAT team circling into position before the building.

"I told you, he was asleep."

"Which tells me it's something he didn't want me to hear. Or maybe you didn't. Should I take a guess?"

"Why don't you just talk to him yourself, Cort Wesley."

"Because he doesn't talk to me about stuff like this."

"Stuff like *what?*"

"Anything that bothers him. He saves that for you."

"Jealous?"

"Not so long as you keep me informed, which you're not doing right now."

Caitlin watched Captain Tepper remain at the forward command post while the Dallas SWAT continued their approach. The Fountain View building was located up on a slight hill from their position, beyond an overpass at its back side, in a tree grove out of sight from all the windows facing this direction. By now Dallas PD would've quietly and calmly evacuated the remainder of the building, removing bystanders through exits similarly with no view from the third-floor office suite occupied by a company called St. Petersburg Partners.

Caitlin hadn't recognized any of the names associated with it, and hated being out here playing spectator while the Dallas SWAT team handled the takedown. And there was something else nagging at her, as well, something Captain Tepper had just said.

Last I heard, their thermal imaging hadn't picked up any movement inside the office in question at all.

Security cameras had picked up four men entering the office late the previous night.

But not leaving.

Was there some secret exit? Maybe just a malfunction in the camera system or the thermal imaging scanners?

Something felt wrong here; something *was* wrong here. Caitlin could feel it as clearly as the warming breeze sifting through the trees and whipping ground debris through the air.

"You haven't heard a word I've said," said Cort Wesley, his voice finally registering in her consciousness.

"No, sorry. I was . . ."

"Yeah, you had that look."

"What's that mean?" she asked, looking at him now.

"Couldn't tell you. It's what Dylan always says to me. 'You've got that look, Dad.' Usually as he's rolling his eyes."

"He's a good kid, Cort Wesley," Caitlin said, figuring Dallas SWAT must be in position to breach the building by this point, just moments from battering their way into the office of St. Petersburg Partners. "With a good heart," she added.

"Wonder how he and Paz are getting along."

"Just fine would be my guess."

Caitlin turned away again, half expecting to hear the distant clacking din of gunfire. But none came. Nothing came at all, until she spotted D. W. Tepper signaling from the forward command post, waving for her and Cort Wesley to come up.

36

Caitlin smelled the blood, first, its coppery stench thick in the office building's third-floor hallway as Tepper led her and Cort Wesley through the collection of milling police officers. The overhead lighting was off and the air felt clammy, as if somebody had shut the power immediately preceding the breach and had neglected to switch it back on.

She spotted SWAT officers milling about, their rifles slung across their chests and expressions mixed between disappointment and befuddlement. The kind of look displayed by kids who don't find what they were hoping for inside their presents on Christmas morning.

Inside the office suite belonging to St. Petersburg Partners, Caitlin saw why.

The corpses of four men sat on a combination of chairs and a matching couch in the reception area. They all wore dark suits and might have been mistaken for simply waiting to be summoned, if not for the neat, dark holes dripping with dried blood in the center of each of their foreheads. Three looked to have been shot in the chest as well, and one, who likely had tried to run, in the back, dead center between the shoulder blades.

"Jesus H. Christ," she heard Tepper mutter.

She looked his way and saw him scratching at his scalp through his thin hair with his free hand, Stetson clutched against his hip in the other. Caitlin took hers off too, continuing to process the scene, so many of the questions she'd posed outside to herself now answered.

The thermal scan showed no one moving because the four men security cameras showed entering the building late last night were dead.

"Security cameras didn't show them coming out," Tepper said, having moved alongside her, "and also didn't show anyone else coming in or out. You mind telling me how anybody other than the Invisible Man could have pulled this off, with that in mind?"

Caitlin didn't have an answer for that yet. "Dallas PD do a thorough search of the premises?"

"In the process now. Every nook and cranny, Ranger."

"Shit."

"That was my thinking, too."

"What about IDs on the victims?"

"I can help you there," Cort Wesley said, having advanced ahead of them to get a closer look at the bodies.

"How's that, Mr. Masters?" raised Captain Tepper.

But Cort Wesley aimed his response toward Caitlin. "The older one, sitting on the chair? His name is Alexi Gribanov. He's the Russian I bugged yesterday."

37

Caitlin had trouble for a long moment processing what Cort Wesley had just said, like a desktop computer exceeding its RAM. She heard his words clearly enough but they didn't register, at least not right away.

"You're sure?"

Cort Wesley had fixed his gaze again on Gribanov, after briefly studying two of the other corpses, which he recognized as the men he'd left in broken heaps outside the Pleasure Dome strip club. "You bet."

"That mean anything to you, Captain?" Caitlin asked, turning toward Tepper, who looked as if he was someplace else altogether. "Captain?"

"Yeah," he said, without quite looking at her. "It means plenty."

"You intend on going on?"

"Not here and now I don't. Topic for another time and place, Ranger. Right now I want to hear more about what Mr. Masters has to say on the subject of the victims."

"I put two of the other three down yesterday."

"Say that again, please."

"He was working something with Jones, Captain," Caitlin interjected, before Cort Wesley had the chance.

"There's maybe a quarter-million people with that name scattered across this state," Tepper said, holding an unlit Marlboro between cigarette-stained fingers.

"And I'm hoping this particular Jones is one of them, but I got a feeling it's not."

"And you'd be right."

"Care to elaborate, Mr. Masters?" Tepper said, turning back to Cort Wesley.

"He wanted an old-fashioned tin ear bug planted in Gribanov's office. That's all I know."

"So Jones remains a man of few words, and the ones he gets out are still laced with shit. That's what you're saying."

"I suppose I am, Captain."

"How do you read this, Ranger?" Tepper asked Caitlin, who'd begun moving between the corpses, as if she were measuring off distances, something like that.

"Their guns are still in their holsters, shirts tucked neatly down their slacks, which tells me they never even had time to go for them."

"You figure they were outnumbered? Sat here and executed?"

"No, sir. I believe they were posed, the killer's idea of a sick joke."

"Killer *singular?*"

"The shots are nearly identical and so are the holes. Twenty-two-caliber hollow points is what the Dallas M.E. is going to pull out of them. I'd bet next month's salary that they came from the same gun."

"You don't make enough for it to matter, Ranger, but I hope you're not suggesting this was the work of a single gunman."

Caitlin regarded the wound in Gribanov's forehead more closely. "There's something else: a downward angle to this entry wound. Cort Wesley, how tall you figure Gribanov was, standing?"

"Half-foot shorter than me. Say five-eight."

Tepper started to raise the Marlboro toward his mouth, then stopped. "So what you're telling me somebody bigger than six feet tall shot him."

"Plenty bigger. Six inches at least."

"Sounds like your personal Frankenstein monster."

"Posing his victims isn't Colonel Paz's style, Captain."

"No, he prefers to just leave them littering the streets wherever he goes, like some human video game."

"He enjoys it," Cort Wesley said suddenly, looking at neither of them.

"What was that, Mr. Masters?"

"The killer enjoys his work, revels in it even," he answered, still moving his eyes among the victims. "That's what this scene is all about."

"This before or after he made himself invisible, since we got nothing on the security tapes showing anybody else coming in or out?"

"I think this is some kind of message," Cort Wesley said, as if Tepper had made no response at all. "The man's a pro."

"You mean like a hit man, Mr. Masters?"

"No, I mean a pro."

"You keep using the singular."

"Because one man did this. Killed them all and then took the time to arrange their bodies this way."

"And why's that?" Tepper asked, not sounding convinced.

"Because he wanted us to know he's here, that he can do anything he wants and we won't be able to stop him. That he doesn't give a shit."

Tepper felt about his pockets for a stray match but came up empty. "So, Ranger," he said, looking toward Caitlin again, "King Kong's already settled down here, and now, according to Mr. Masters here, Godzilla has moved into Texas to join him. This whole state is turning into a goddamn horror movie."

"There's more," Cort Wesley said. "Russian special forces are called Spetsnaz. I've fought both with and against them, back around the time of the first Gulf War. Saw this kind of thing on both sides, a message basically saying, 'Fuck with us at your own peril.'"

"Wait a minute; you're saying another *Russian* did this?"

"Looks like their handiwork, that's all I'm saying. Russian version of psychological warfare."

"Last time I checked, we weren't at war against Russia."

"Maybe we should check again, Captain," advanced Caitlin. "Cort Wesley already said our old friend Jones was trying to dime these guys for something. He give you any notion as to what?"

"Not a hint or a clue," Cort Wesley told them both.

Captain Tepper drew closer to the two men Cort Wesley had dropped outside the Pleasure Dome. "And the bruises a couple are wearing on their faces, one of whom's got his leg all wrapped up at the knee—they look that way before you met, Mr. Masters?"

"I didn't bother checking before I kicked the shit out of them."

Tepper just shook his head. "Anybody got a lighter?" he called out, flashing his Marlboro.

"Think I'll have a look around," said Caitlin, sliding past him.

38

EULESS, TEXAS

Caitlin moved about the office suites beyond the reception area. There were five in all, the largest belonging to Alexi Gribanov himself, based on the family pictures framed upon his desk. She swept through all five and then circled back again, convinced that if there was anything to find it would be in Gribanov's office, which featured a small conference table beneath a period map of Texas from the late nineteenth century.

Nothing stood out to her at all, but something kept her from leaving the office. She walked it from one side to the other and back again, inspecting everything that came within her sight while being careful not to touch anything, since this remained an active crime scene.

Still nothing. But she still couldn't leave.

Why? What was she not seeing?

Caitlin recalled her grandfather Earl Strong's tales of his heyday as a Ranger during the oil boom years of the thirties, when big swatches of Texas returned to a virtual frontier mentality. How he'd walked into a bar in search of a suspect, having no idea at all who he was looking for until something they did, something that stood out, gave them away. Sometimes he couldn't even say what had alerted him, and it often took a while before the revelation struck him.

That's what she was hoping for now, listening to some nagging voice at the back of her mind telling her there was something in this office that she was looking at but not really seeing.

What was she missing?

It wasn't on Gribanov's desk, and she didn't expect it would be readily accessible on the computer the crime scene technicians had already removed. Besides, the same kind of instincts that once pointed her grandfather in the direction he needed to look were pointing her first at the bare conference table and then at the wall where the historic map of Texas hung. Looked like something you either scored at a yard sale or paid a decent amount for as an authorized reproduction, although this map looked aged and weathered enough to be a genuine antique, likely worth a fortune. In which case, why—

And then it hit her.

"Captain Tepper," she called, poking her head out the door.

Cort Wesley joined her inside Gribanov's office moments later, followed almost immediately by Captain Tepper.

"Crime scene tech just gave the security camera in the hall a closer look. Turns out the picture's frozen up solid. Been that way for hours, maybe on account of somebody sprayed dry ice, Freon, or something on it."

"Our killer," Caitlin ventured. "And I think I know what brought him here. Look around the room and tell me if anything looks wrong to you."

"This some kind of test?" Cort Wesley asked, as Tepper snatched a cigarette lighter shaped like a bear from Gribanov's desk and fired up his Marlboro.

"Is that a good idea, Captain?"

"Not if I want to live until next month," he said, coughing out the initial stream of smoke.

"I was talking about disturbing evidence."

He blew out some more smoke, without incident this time. "Ranger, I've been to maybe a thousand crime scenes in my career and never once saw a cigarette lighter shaped like a bear end up a piece of evidence. Matter of fact, I'm thinking about stealing it, since it'll be a lot harder for you to snatch out of my office than a box of matches."

"You haven't answered my question."

"Why don't you give us a hint?" Cort Wesley suggested.

"Check the walls."

"You mean that map over there?" raised Tepper.

"Anything strike you as odd about it?"

"You mean, besides the fact it's older than me?"

"It's a glass frame," Cort Wesley said, moving closer. "But there's no glass."

"Seems strange, doesn't it?"

"It sure does," Tepper followed, approaching the

map, too. "Now tell me what I'm supposed to be seeing upon it."

Cort Wesley moved up to the conference table to
view it closer. "There's nothing there."

"You mean, nothing we can see without a little
help," Caitlin said, feeling just as Earl Strong must have
before he took down a gunfighter, con man, or criminal in one of those oil boomtowns. "Which we just
happen to have on hand."

Caitlin borrowed a portable ultraviolet light from one
of the crime scene techs and returned to Gribanov's
office, closing the door so they had it to themselves.
She turned the overhead lighting off and shined the
UV beam toward the frontier-era map of Texas.

"Well, goddamn," Tepper managed, his Marlboro
nearly slipping from his lips.

39

EULESS, TEXAS

The UV light seemed to brighten, illuminating the true
purpose of the wall map. Small blue circles had been
revealed, scattered through much of the state. Nothing specific or even meaningful at first glance, but that
changed quickly.

"Armand Bayou," Cort Wesley pointed. "That

circle up there is right where Armand Bayou is located."

"And that spot there," Tepper picked up, "is in the area of Austin County—Karl Dakota's ranch. Can't say for sure about the others."

Tepper scratched at his scalp, forgetting all about the cigarette he was still holding, and scattering ash all about the carpet.

"Damn," he said, kicking it aside and gazing up toward the map again. "You wanna tell me what I'm looking at here, Ranger? You wanna tell me what a bunch of dead cattle got to do with those kids who vanished into thin air?"

"There's more, Captain," Caitlin told him. "Check out that circle furthest to the west."

Tepper leaned a bit closer, squinting. "You're kidding me, right?"

"Wish I was. That's where Christoph Russell Ilg's ranch is located."

"What was it that son of a bitch said again, while you arrested him?"

"That he only rustled because the government killed his cattle. Poured acid on them, he said. Sound familiar?"

"Oh, man," Tepper groused. "I can feel the winds picking up to gale force now as I stand here. Check your boots, Hurricane, because somehow, some way, you've stepped into some crazy, nasty shit again. Know what I wish?"

"What, Captain?"

"That there were Texas Rangers somewhere else so other states could share the wealth. Maybe I could trade you for a one-legged cooch near to retirement as I am so I could nap at my desk without being disturbed."

"When was the last time you took a nap, D.W.?"

He pretended to be snoring, snapping alert again with a start. "What was that? Must've dozed off. Understandable, given that I slept all of four hours last night." He looked toward Cort Wesley. "But I'm not too tired to wonder how it is a Russian mobster Mr. Masters bugged on Homeland's dime is connected to missing kids and dead cattle."

"There's only one person who can tell us that, Captain," Cort Wesley said, turning toward Caitlin. "And he goes by the name of Jones."

Caitlin had fixed her gaze on the map again, switching the UV light back on, remembering something.

"That circle right around Waco," she said, shining the light straight at that spot in particular.

"What about it, Ranger?" Tepper asked her.

"It doesn't fit in with the rest. All by itself, situated away from all the others. I'm just wondering—"

Caitlin's phone buzzed, interrupting her. She checked the caller ID, moving aside to take the call with UV light switched off again.

"What you got for me, Doc?" she asked Medical Examiner Frank Whatley.

"How soon can you get over here?" his craggy, strained voice asked her.

"I'm outside Dallas, so it's gonna be a while. This

about those cattle we found last night stripped to the bone?"

"You bet, Ranger. It's plum crazy. I've never seen anything like this before, and I don't think anybody else ever has, either."

PART FIVE

I remember, as a little boy in Kingsville, Texas, the day my mother pointed out a big man leading a horse along the railroad tracks. "Look, Sonny, there's a Texas Ranger." I can still hear the awe in her voice.

—"Dac Crossley and the Texas Rangers,"
Oak Tree Press Blog, September 8, 2013

40

"This isn't good," Madam Caterina said to Guillermo Paz, after turning over the final tarot card, representing Outcome. "Suggests something very ominous."

"Like what?" Paz asked, studying the assemblage of cartoonlike figures imprinted on the oversize cards arranged in a neat horizontal line.

Madam Caterina had flipped them over from left to right, starting with what she called the Present Position, followed by Present Desires, the Unexpected, the Immediate Future, and finally, the end result, or Outcome she'd just turned. After Paz sat down, she'd had him light a trio of candles to help set the mood, along with the incense that was already burning. It was pleasant, if a bit sour; sage maybe, Paz thought.

Once the candles were going, Madam Caterina had asked him to shuffle the deck, explaining that the size of the cards and the fact there were seventy-eight of them often made that task difficult. But Paz's huge yet nimble hands handled the task effortlessly, after which he proceeded to cut the cards on cue.

"Lay out five in a row," Madam Caterina instructed. Paz did so, all the cards placed face down.

"Now, pick a card and drag it toward you."

That was five cards ago, the interpretation of others temporarily lost with the flipping of a card picturing five male figures holding matching tree branches, without clear sign of what they intended to do with them.

"The Five of Wands," Madam Caterina told him.

"And that's bad?"

"Not necessarily, but taken in the context of the other four, I'm concerned. Typically, the Five of Wands suggests an outcome based on struggle and conflict, and the fact that victory may come at a deep personal cost or sacrifice."

"That's nothing new."

"Even so," Madam Caterina said, gazing at the other four cards Paz had flipped, "you must take this card in the context these other four have created, starting with the first."

"Representing Present Position," Paz recalled.

"And the card in question is the Devil reversed, or upside down," Madam Caterina nodded, pointing toward the card farthest on the left, which pictured a horned devil with furry legs and clawed feet.

"That can't be good."

"Well, this card can represent temptation, addiction, and unhappy outcomes."

"Like I said."

"But your devil is upside down, advising us to look deeper at the situation and suggesting great change is in the offing."

"This have anything to do with that strong light you told me about?" Paz interrupted.

"Let me finish," Madam Caterina scolded, giving no quarter.

Paz remembered his first visit to his priest here in San Antonio, how frightened and intimidated the poor man had been by him. But not Madam Caterina. She was the first woman, besides his Texas Ranger, he didn't scare the hell out of.

"The Devil reversed," the psychic said, continuing her reading, "in this case suggests control. You're feeling you've lost some measure of control but will be taking action to regain it."

"You said 'in this case.' What's that mean exactly?"

Madam Caterina pointed to the second card in, picturing a regal woman seated on a throne in the open air, right next to the Devil reversed. Paz thought she looked sad.

"This," she told him, "is the Queen of Pentacles. Remember the meaning of the second position?"

"Present Desires," Paz recited, a bit sheepishly.

"And the Queen of Pentacles, like all the court cards, often stands in for an actual person in your life. In that regard, she would represent a woman, likely with dark hair and dark eyes."

Paz felt a bit of a chill. "You're describing my Texas Ranger."

"Am I? Interesting, because taken in context here, the Queen of Pentacles suggests that it's critical that you trust yourself. You may not see things spiritually the way everyone else does, but your belief system works for you, and that's what's most important."

"And how's this relate to that Devil card?"

"Let's move on to the center card," Madam Caterina said, already eyeing it.

"Oh yeah, context . . ."

"That's right."

"Whatever that means. . . ."

"In this case, it means a new beginning."

"Life is full of those," Paz said to the psychic.

"Not like this. The Ace of Swords calls on us to not be afraid to make a leap if it's in our best interests. You have a good idea already of what must be done. The hard part is the doing of it."

"Not for me."

"It might be different this time. The way you flipped the card tells me it may have originally been reversed and, that being the case, you must be leery of being drawn into a battle that is not of your making. The sequencing suggests it lies elsewhere."

"With the Queen of Pentacles maybe?" Paz raised, thinking of Caitlin Strong.

"Taken with the Devil reversed, I'd say someone confronting a great dilemma or, more likely, a great enemy, especially in the context of the fourth card here," Madam Caterina said, pointing at it.

Paz recalled its title easily from memory. "The Chariot. Right side up."

"The Chariot is one of the most complex cards to define. On its most basic level, it's about getting what you want. It implies war, a struggle, and an eventual, hard-won victory over enemies, obstacles, nature, the uncertainties inside you. But there is a great deal more to it. The charioteer wears emblems of the sun, yet the sign behind this card is Cancer, the moon. The chariot is all about motion, and yet it is often shown as stationary."

"So," Paz surmised, "if the sun represents that strong light . . ."

"The moon suggests it will shine somehow at night. That's symbolic of an enemy that can't be seen."

"As in invisible?"

"More like out of sight. Hiding from view. Does that mean anything to you?"

"It will," Paz said, assuredly. "And when placed in the *context* of the Outcome card here?"

"The Wheel of Fortune."

"You said that wasn't good."

"Because it represents something that stands beyond the realm of our understanding and control. Notice that the Wheel of Fortune hovers in the clouds, showing that you can try to reach it but that you can never fully understand it. That indicates some change, a dramatic change from the established order, is not only likely to happen, it is certain to happen, and soon."

Paz nodded. "'Are these the shadows of things that will be, or things that may be?'"

"Excuse me?"

"It's a line from *A Christmas Carol,* a question Scrooge asks the Ghost of Christmas Future. I read the book a whole bunch of times as a boy. First book I ever read in English. My first priest gave it to me."

"Flip the next card," Madam Caterina told him.

Paz did, revealing the Hierophant figure, a holy man holding a cross in a vague position of prayer.

"This priest was your teacher—"

"I watched him murdered in the street for trying to help kids like me. We discussed that last time, remember?"

"Stop interrupting me," Madam Caterina ordered. "I was going to say his death was his final lesson to you, setting you unalterably on the road to the man you are now."

"That question Scrooge posed," Paz said to her. "The ghost from the future never answered it. You haven't answered it either."

"The future isn't set. If it was, people like me wouldn't exist to warn people about it."

"So whatever this thing is that's beyond our understanding and control . . ."

"You can defeat it. That's what the entire context of this reading suggests. A battle against a great foe you can defeat . . . but not alone." Madam Caterina pointed toward the second card again. "The Queen of Pentacles."

"My Texas Ranger."

"Flip another card."

Paz snared one between a pair of thick fingers and turned it over.

"Justice," Madam Caterina noted.

41

Standing on the sidewalk outside Madam Caterina's office, Guillermo Paz realized he felt hot, his skin so superheated that he could barely stand the sun and retreated into the shadows. A trio of Hispanic gang-bangers wearing tight tank tops to show off muscles likely primed behind bars, bandanas tied around their bald skulls, moved into the street to avoid coming anywhere near him, but Paz ignored them anyway.

Paz couldn't get Madam Caterina's tarot reading out of his mind, how spot-on it had seemed to be.

Change, a dramatic change from the established order, is not only likely to happen, it is certain to happen, and soon.

Paz had been feeling that for a while now, but it was the clarity supplied by the psychic's next words that had put him on edge, concerning the Chariot card in particular.

The moon suggests it will shine somehow at night. That's symbolic of an enemy that can't be seen. . . . Hiding from view.

What did that mean exactly? Who was this new enemy he was going to be facing alongside his Texas Ranger?

Paz found himself distinctly unnerved, offered just enough glimpse of the future to fear what was coming. Violence and danger bothered him not at all; they were the things upon which he thrived. But the unknown was something else again. The unknown set him sweating and roasting inside his skin, like it was an extra layer he wished he could strip off.

Thinking of that reminded him he'd forgotten to pay Madam Caterina before taking his leave. That's how much her reading of the tarot cards had unsettled him. So Paz retraced his steps from the shadows, back through the sun. He rang the buzzer, and then knocked on the door when she still didn't answer.

Paz thought about simply paying when he came for his next session, but he felt himself opening the door and entering the tiny reception area rich with the smell of incense. He didn't announce himself for fear of disturbing another client's reading and resolved to retrace his steps if it turned out he was interrupting. And then he heard an accented voice that told him he was indeed doing just that.

"You're late with your fees, senora, two months late. We can't have that, eh? If we're going to keep the neighborhood safe. That takes resources. You understand."

Paz moved through the beaded curtain, leaving the beads clacking against each other as he entered Madam Caterina's reading room. The three gangbangers he'd glimpsed outside were facing her from the other side of the table. The now-flickering candles sat between Madam Caterina and them, as if this was a session instead of a shakedown.

"You boys here to have your fortunes told?" Paz said, just as they noticed him. "Because I can do that for you for free. Gratis. As in no charge."

They'd all pulled back their flannel shirts to show-case nine-millimeter pistols stuck in the waistbands of their sagging pants, but made no move for them as he stood there.

"I'm afraid your futures are bleak," Paz continued. "Lots of pain and broken bones. I see ambulances and rescue wagons and jaws wired shut. But this is your lucky day. Know why?"

None of the gangbangers seemed intent on an-swering.

"You ever read *A Christmas Carol,* maybe saw one of the movie versions? See, old Scrooge learned he could control his own future, alter the path he was on, by changing his ways, rethinking his decisions. That's what you can do today. Alter your path by walking out of here and never coming back. *Comprendes?*"

"Mind your own fucking business, man," the one Paz took to be the leader said, swallowing hard when he finished, as if drained of bravado.

Paz smiled. "So you wanna choose a different path, muchachos? Fine by me."

Two of them went for their guns, but they never even touched steel. Paz lurched forward, a single stun-ningly long step, more like a leap. He had the wrists of the two who went for their guns in hand by then, jerking down and in at the same time and hearing one splintering crack followed by another.

The third gangbanger used that moment to go for his gun and actually managed to strip it from his pants, leaving them to sag even lower. Paz grabbed the gun as it swept toward him, a toy in his hands as he stripped it free and tossed it aside.

"Fuck you!" the banger leader screeched at him. "Fuck you-u-u!"

His lips were still puckered forward when Paz snatched a lit candle from Madam Caterina's table and jammed its flickering end through them, straight into his mouth, shoving the wax down his throat. He saw the banger's neck expand, his eyes bulging desperately as his face purpled.

"You can't breathe," Paz said, holding him up. "That's your present. You're going to die—that's your future."

The other two bangers were trying for their guns again by then, using their off-hands now in place of their ruined ones. Paz took an oversize plastic tarot card in either hand and lashed them outward. He had no idea where they were going exactly before the cards sliced through the air and dug home beneath the bangers' brow level, carving thin, razorlike lines through the eyelids of both men. Blood pooled outward, the pain throwing both men into a squint even before the blood blinded their sight. They began to howl in agony, crumpling to their knees.

"Guess you can't see your own future now," Paz grinned, and proceeded to smash their heads together with a bone-crunching rattle as skull met skull. "You can't see anything."

Madam Caterina had lurched backwards, shoulders pressed against the wall, peering at Paz as if she were seeing him for the first time. A glimpse into his soul, far beyond what cards, intuition, even the counsel of the spirits could provide. She seemed to be looking through Paz as much as at him. But he couldn't stop himself, even though he might be scaring the psychic more than the gangbangers had.

The tarot cards had been sprayed to the floor in his initial assault on the bangers, most of them ending up scattered between the two of them now cowering next to each other with blood running down their faces.

Paz knelt between them, taking a card in hand. "Time to take a good look at your future, amigos. Let's see what we've got here. . . . Hey, it says Judgment. How fitting is that? But do you know what it means?" he asked one of them, flashing the card before his blood-filled eyes. "No? Let's see if this helps."

With that, Paz stuffed the card into his mouth.

"Spit that out, amigo, and I'll break your teeth."

He snatched another card from the floor, focusing on the other banger now. "Hey, the Six of Cups. I don't know what that means, but I'm guessing it's the asshole card, since you're a serious asshole."

Paz crumpled the Six of Cups and stuck it through his teeth. "How's the future taste to you, amigo? I'm betting not so good. But here's the lesson of today. The future's ours to control. That's why people come to Madam Caterina, so they learn what's coming. You didn't give her the chance to tell you boys about that, so it's a good thing I was around to fill in the gaps. Starting now, you can change your future. And if you don't, I'm going to come back and change it for you. *Comprendes?*"

One nodded. The other tried to.

Paz looked up at Madam Caterina. "When does the trash get picked up?"

"Today," she managed, seeming surprised she'd found her voice. "Any time now."

"Good," Paz said, hoisting the two bangers up by the scruffs of their necks, "I'll put these *perdedors* out on the curb. I'll be right back for the other one."

"You didn't have to do this," Madam Caterina said, when he reached the door.

"Yes, I did," Paz told her. "There are some things nobody can change."

42

SAN ANTONIO, TEXAS

"So what am I supposed to be seeing here, Doc?" Caitlin asked Frank Whatley, peering up from the microscope he'd told her to check.

"What's it look like to you?"

Caitlin pressed her eye against the lens again, left it there as she spoke. "Some kind of insect larvae is all that comes to mind."

"Close," Whatley nodded, as she raised her gaze to meet his. "It's insect dung, better known as frass. What you're looking at is consistent with beetle frass, specifically bess beetles. I found it all over the skeletal remains of those cattle, which makes sense, since this kind of beetle uses its dung as a kind of defense mechanism."

"How's that exactly?"

"Well, when feeding on plants, the beetles ingest alkaloids that are toxic to animal predators. The toxins get excreted in their frass. Then, as the beetles poop, they contract muscles to direct the flow of feces onto their backs, rendering them utterly unappetizing to animals that would otherwise snack on them."

"I can see why," Caitlin told him. "Now tell me what it all means."

The Bexar County Medical Examiner's Office and morgue was located just off Loop 410, not far from the Babcock Road exit on Merton Mintor inside the Bexar County Forensic Science Center on the University of Texas Health Science Center campus. Caitlin had been coming here for over twenty years, and what struck her was how it always smelled exactly the same—of cleaning solvent, with a faint scent of menthol clinging to the walls like paint. The lighting was overly dull in the hallways and overly bright in offices like Whatley's.

The lab he supervised never changed, at least not in Caitlin's memory. It was sparkling clean everywhere, not a speck of dust or grime anywhere to be found, the cheap tile floors so shiny she could see the outline of her shadow. It smelled of the powerful antiseptic cleaner Whatley insisted his staff use after every examination and procedure, in a concerted effort to pay homage and respect to those who crossed his slabs. It was almost as if he was trying to make some kind of moral amends, especially to the victims of crime, who had already been treated with the ultimate indifference and cruelty.

"It means I found inordinately large concentrations of beetle frass over the remains of those cattle,"

Whatley explained, "the condition of which stoked my suspicions as soon as I examined them in that grazing field."

"How's that, Doc?"

"The skeletons were entirely intact."

"Okay. . . ."

"You've seen what happens when predators lay siege to livestock."

"Sure, and first of all they tend to leave some meat on the bones, not pick them dry."

"They also wrench at those bones themselves, often shredding or dislodging them. That's why scattered bones are more normally associated with animal remains, not entire, whole skeletons picked to the bone."

Caitlin checked the view through the microscope lens again, as if something might have changed. "Where you going with this, Doc?"

"I wish I knew. That farmer's herd wasn't wiped out by coyotes, wolves, mountain lions, or the boogeyman, Ranger," Whatley told her. "It was wiped out by something we can't identify, and what we *can* identify doesn't make any damn sense at all."

She was about to ask the doc to elaborate on that when his phone buzzed with an incoming text message he excused himself to check.

"Looks like this is for you as much as me, Ranger," he said, looking up from his phone. "It appears we've got a firm location on that unidentified circle near Waco, from the map back at that Dallas crime scene."

"I'm listening, Doc."

43

"Life's about the future, S., not the past," Calum Dane told Pulsipher, trying to sound convincing as they climbed out of the Suburban in the company of three other plainclothes security men. "That's why we're here today. I understand a breakthrough has been made."

The parking lot on South County Road, off Interstate 20 in Midland, sat adjacent to a flat-roofed warehouse slab of a building that had once been used by a now-bankrupt distributor of industrial plumbing parts. Once emptied out and refurbished, its nearly ten thousand feet of open space was perfect for another of Dane Corp's latest pursuits. In addition, its isolated location and fenced perimeter made it easy to secure and kept the locals away—a key component, given the secretive nature of the ongoing research and development going on inside, virtually nonstop.

Dane considered it no small irony that buying the building for a relative song represented a kind of homecoming, since the land was located in what had once been the same county as the farm his family sharecropped. If he squinted, maybe he'd be able to see the pauper's grave where he'd buried his father, a straight shot across the flat stretch of parched land to the south.

The fifth technical team he'd hired to make his latest

technological dream a reality had phoned that morning insisting they had big news to report, insisting that they meant it this time. Dane sincerely hoped so. The profit projections of this particular Dane Corp spin-off were staggering, not to mention the ancillaries and fresh market share this new venture would bring the company.

If it worked, which so far hadn't proven to be the case.

His investors and corporate team told him he was crazy, when Dane told them he was branching off into the video game industry. Of course, people had said the same thing when he bought up millions of acres of mineral rights for supposedly dry oil wells, now lined with pumpjacks for as far as the eye could see. Or when he built the largest petrochemical plant in the country, which had reaped billions of dollars in profit worldwide from the production of agricultural supplies and pesticides.

Dane had learned not to listen to them.

He'd gotten the idea while attending an annual electronics and technology convention in Las Vegas. There he noticed that the biggest crowds by far were attracted to the next generation in video gaming, multiplayer and three-dimensional graphics. There was even a less-elaborate display by Samsung of a room-based gaming system in which players found themselves confronted by life-size figures springing from what the company called "electronic wallpaper" displays. It may have been the next step in virtual reality, but it left Dane impressed more by the graphics than by what was essentially a standard gaming experience played out between walls instead of on a big screen. A letdown, in other words.

But it gave him an idea.

"Impossible," one expert said.

"Come back in twenty years," another told him.

"Twenty years and a billion dollars," surmised a third.

"I've got the billion dollars," Dane said. "But not twenty years."

After four other teams had spent various fortunes building systems with more kinks and breakdowns than functionality, Dane found the Bass brothers, twins generally regarded as outcast rebels in the gaming industry. Utterly identical save for a mole on the cheek of one, with matching wild shocks of curly red hair, the twins, though in their midtwenties, still dressed the same and remained fond of completing each other's thoughts.

"Far out, man," said Frank Bass.

"Deep," added Fred, "truly deep."

"But can you do it?" Dane said, explaining where he'd gotten the idea, after they'd scribbled their names on a confidentiality agreement without reading it.

"Fucking A we can," from Frank.

"We'll nail this bastard," Fred added.

"Start with the wallpaper thing—"

"And build from there. Build you something truly immersive."

"Not like what you saw at the tech shit show," Frank explained.

"That was based on this dome-shaped system, covered with projectors, wall to wall," Fred picked up. "Uses surround sound, augmented reality—"

"And other technologies to fabricate a real world. Emphasis on 'fabricate'—"

"Because there's no real interaction between players and figures."

"That's total immersion."

"What we intend to build for you."

That led to the challenge of moving the characters off the wall by creating artificially intelligent wallpapers that were expanded to include the floors and ceiling. Dozens and dozens more projectors, light-refracting mirrors, and display tubes needed to be added to the mix. All built from scratch at a mind-numbing cost and all controlled by a supercomputer capable of a trillion computations per second, at an even more mind-numbing cost.

Dane never flinched, never blanched. He was building something the world had never seen before. If the proprietary technology worked, the profits would be staggering—as well as unregulated in any respect whatsoever. The video game industry was the Wild West of business, the ancillaries and international arena alone turning the potential from vast to unlimited.

The problem was, every time the Bass twins surmounted one obstacle, another surfaced.

"This artificial intelligence is for shit, man," was Fred's analysis.

"You got a hundred thousand permutations for every movement and action," Frank added. "A hundred code writers working twenty-fours a day would take a century to write that."

"You've got a year," Dane told them. "So long as you tell me it can be done. So long as you tell me you can do it."

"Fuck yeah!" the brothers said in unison.

44

MIDLAND, TEXAS

The solution the Bass brothers came up with was to rely more on the AI software, not less, to the point that the life-size characters game players would actually be interacting with would utilize learned behavior in their responses. The initial test results after nine months of round-the-clock code writing were incredible, sometimes, and incredibly frustrating at other times. The intensity of the initial realism needed to be dialed back a bit, including turning the surround sound down a notch and making the bad guys less "frigging ugly," as one of the Bass brothers put it. Dane wasn't sure which.

"We got three demonstrations for you," Frank said, after greeting him inside the Midland warehouse that had become the brothers' personal electronic playground.

Fred looked up from a laptop that would be controlling the basic game elements in the sprawling open space that had once been jam-packed with distribution fulfillment stations. "*Man of War, Titans of Terra,* and *History Comes Alive.*"

"Talk to your favorite historical figure."

"Tonto inside an authentic tepee, smoking peyote."

"Tonto wasn't real, Fred."

"He wasn't?"

"Anyway," Frank picked up, "call it the ultimate school field trip."

"We can put the game on demo—"

"Or give you a gun so you can play along," Frank explained, unslinging a futuristic, full-size rifle.

"I think I'll pass," Dane told them. "A demo will do."

"Far out, man," said Fred from behind his laptop. "Fasten your seatbelt."

An instant later the open floor space went totally dark, only to be pierced by a million slivers of light an instant later. And then life-size soldiers appeared in full battle gear, off to fight insectlike beings who'd invaded Earth. Even though they were projections, their artificial intelligence allowed them to skirt around the three visitors to their domain, instead of passing right through them.

"They even appear to acknowledge you," Frank noted to Calum Dane.

"What do you mean, 'appear to'?" Dane asked that brother.

"It's almost like they're self-aware," the other brother answered. "A fringe benefit of the AI code we wrote."

"Which brings us to the demo," Frank picked up. "That was just a graphics showcase. Utterly rudimentary."

"And here we go with the main event," Fred followed in rhythm, starting to work the keyboard.

Predictably, the primary lighting went dark, a fluorescent haze that would soon birth the game dynamic.

"Let's start with *Man of War,*" Fred continued.

"Get ready to be immersed," his twin brother said, as Fred hit a final key.

But nothing happened.

"Like I said," Frank groped, "get ready to—"

And then *something* happened. The warehouse confines suddenly turned from stark white to a war-ravaged and utterly decimated city landscape. The realism was so incredible that Dane imagined he could smell the decay in the air and thought that if he reached down and touched the floor it would indeed feel like concrete instead of tile. Then the life-size, incredibly realistic versions of soldiers fighting the alien enemy—hopefully soon to be accompanied by gamers paying a fortune for the experience—appeared from all directions.

The computer-drawn figures were actually beyond lifelike. Dane could see them sweating, bleeding, breathing with the heaviness of battle. The smaller ones even seemed weighed down by the weight of their extended weapons and packs. It couldn't have been more impressive.

Until the alien outdoor landscape of *Titans of Terra* suddenly claimed the warehouse, from its blacked-out windows on down.

"Oh, shit." Fred.

"Oh, fuck." Frank.

The soldiers from *Man of War* stopped, their images

appearing confused and stopping just short of looking at each other. This as dinosaur-size monsters appeared everywhere and began attacking them.

"Bad." Fred.

"Really fucking bad." Frank.

And then it got worse. The *History Comes Alive*
figures appeared on the scene to be besieged by the
monsters of *Titans of Terra*, while the heroic humans
who'd been programmed to battle them began ex-
changing fire with the *Man of War* rampaging characters instead. The sound was deafening, the gunfire
constant and realistic to the point of expended shells
clanging against the ground as futuristic assault rifles
spat them out, one after the other.

Dane watched figures darting and twisting around
him, close enough to reach out and touch, getting
blown apart in a fashion so realistic he expected to
look down to see his clothes splattered with blood.
The problem was that the victims included the historical figures whose programming shouldn't have
even incorporated that. But he was also conscious of
Fred Bass desperately hitting keys to deactivate the
system—to no avail, as if these projections had found
minds of their own. He noticed Frank Bass moving to
a bank of black, obelisklike structures that served as
visible conduits between the game environment and
the off-site supercomputer actually controlling the action. Dane watched Frank stoop down and do the
simplest thing of all.

He pulled the plug. And instantly the warehouse
Calum Dane had bought for three-quarters of a million
dollars returned to its blank canvas—no blood, bodies,

severed limbs, or any other evidence of battle whatsoever left behind. As if nothing had ever happened.

"Whoops," Fred managed.

"That didn't go well," Frank added.

And then Dane felt Pulsipher come up to his side.
He was tempted to borrow the man's gun to shoot
both twins in the head.

"There's a call from the main office, sir," Pulsipher
reported. "A Texas Ranger has requested a meeting
with you about an ongoing investigation."

"He say what this investigation was about?" Dane
asked, feeling his neck hairs prickle and a slight quiver
in his stomach.

He noticed the concern in Pulsipher's gaze, recalling what he'd told Dane the day before about one of
the kids from the Armand Bayou field trip who'd been
found in the woods.

"It's a she, sir."

45

MARBLE FALLS, TEXAS

Jones was already seated at the counter of the Blue
Bonnet Café, fork digging into a piece of cherry pie,
when Cort Wesley entered. The Blue Bonnet offered
the best pie in the state, made even better by a happy
hour between three and five P.M. on weekdays. Cort
Wesley couldn't tell if this was Jones's first slice or his
second.

"Sit down, cowboy," he greeted. "What can I get you?"

Cort Wesley took the stool next to him. "Man, you really are out of the loop, aren't you?"

"What's that mean?"

"Those Russians you had me bug yesterday? Somebody wasted them."

Jones stopped his next forkful halfway to his mouth. "Did I just hear you right?"

"You did. I was the one who identified the bodies."

Jones tried not to reveal how concerned he clearly was. "Since you kicked the shit out of two of them, I'm wondering if you're a suspect."

"What the hell's going on, Jones?"

Jones turned back to his pie but left his fork on the plate. "Don't ask me. I'm the one whose operation just got fucked."

"And what operation is that?"

"Need-to-know basis, cowboy, and you most certainly do not need to know."

Cort Wesley rotated his stool so he was facing Jones straight on. "Maybe we need to start this conversation again."

Jones dabbed at his lips with a napkin. "You mind if we take a rain check on that pie? I've got some calls to make."

He started to slide off his stool, then stopped when Cort Wesley locked a hand over his knee, pinching just enough.

"Ouch," said Jones flatly.

"I didn't know you could feel pain . . . or anything else."

"You must have me confused with the man I used to be."

"You sound like Paz."

"With good reason, since a certain Texas Ranger has messed up my life big-time, too."

"This would be the same Texas Ranger who saved your life last year?"

"Not exactly my recollection, but you can believe whatever you like. Destroyed my career would be a more accurate way of putting it." Jones turned back toward the counter on his stool and picked up his fork again. "It's happy hour. Why don't you order a slice?"

"Already did: a slice of humble pie. How's it taste, by the way?"

"You think this is funny?"

"You see me laughing?"

Jones shoved his plate aside and twisted his stool to face Cort Wesley. "Alexi Gribanov was a lot more than just a strip club owner."

"Of course he was. Why would you give a shit about him otherwise?"

"You're a regular Sherlock Holmes, aren't you, cowboy? Remind me of a certain Texas Ranger we both know."

"Get back to Gribanov, specifically the reason behind your interest in him."

"Take a guess."

"Based on the circles you move in, Jones, only one thing comes to mind: he's a Russian spook, the strip club thing just a cover."

"Yes and no."

"Can't be both."

"It is in this case."

"That still doesn't explain why you needed to bug his office."

Jones hesitated, as if weighing whether he should tell Cort Wesley any more. The scowl that followed indicated he realized he didn't have a choice.

"Chatter. Something's been going on here in your great state as of late that's attracted Russian attention in all the wrong places."

"As in KGB."

"Technically they don't exist anymore . . ."

"Technically."

"And they go by different initials, FSB, now. But the answer's yes. They might as well still call themselves KGB, based on how they operate."

"So why'd you need me to do your dirty work, a man who's got the NSA on speed dial?"

"I already told you. The number I used to have for them doesn't exist anymore; none of the numbers I used to have exist. Thanks to what went down last year, when I took a stand against them and took three bullets for it."

"Get back to Gribanov."

"I had a hunch."

"Bullshit," Cort Wesley said, watching a tray go by with pieces of banana cream and chocolate cream pie. The sight and smell made his mouth water. "You don't play hunches, Jones, only sure things."

"No such thing in this market, cowboy."

"Then, since you're an agent without portfolio, maybe I should be having this conversation with somebody else."

Jones tried to flash the trademark smirk but came up short. His face was flat and freshly shaved, with a dollop of shaving cream clinging stubbornly behind his right ear. Even in the light, Cort Wesley couldn't quite make out Jones's eye color, as if Jones had been trained to never look at anyone long enough for anything to register. He was wearing a sports jacket over a button-down shirt and pressed trousers that looked like a costume on him. His hair, normally tightly cropped and military style—"high and tight" was the nomenclature—had grown out just enough to make his anvil-shaped head look smaller.

Caitlin had met Jones for the first time overseas, when he was still "Smith." She'd told Cort Wesley back then that she had him made for CIA, but he'd moved on to some shadowy subdivision of Homeland Security and, for a time anyway, had pretty much carte blanche to protect the homeland any way he saw fit. That included utilizing the services of Guillermo Paz and the band of killers the colonel had assembled for any purpose Jones deemed worthy. Their paths had crossed his on several occasions since he became "Jones," and none had ended particularly well.

"Stay awhile," Jones said suddenly. "Order yourself a piece of pie while I tell you a story."

"What story?"

"About what put Alexi Gribanov on my radar to begin with. Believe you'll recognize the other characters too. . . ."

46

A day after watching the shootout in downtown Houston, Boone Masters was waiting outside the headquarters of Texas Ranger Company F, when Jim Strong emerged.

"What brings you to the right side of the law, Mr. Masters?"

"Maybe I've come to confess my crimes."

"I don't have that much time."

"Got enough to tell me what that gunfight in Houston yesterday was all about?"

"An internecine battle between rival gangs. Simple enough in my mind."

"I'm talking about the Russians who ripped me off being targeted by a Russian wearing the jacket I gave him."

"So was I," Jim Strong told him. "And your job's done here, sir. It died with those men. The Texas Rangers, me in particular, and the State of Texas would like to thank you for your service."

"And what if that don't sit too well with me?"

"Sounds like you've seen the light."

"Nope. The enemy of my enemy is an even greater enemy."

"I don't think it goes like that."

"It does to me, Ranger. And maybe I can help you out yet."

"How's that?"

"I can't be sure, until you tell me what it was exactly that happened yesterday."

"You were there, same as me. Russians killing Russians."

Boone Masters nodded. "Like an organized crime war or turf battle, something like that?"

"I don't think, no."

"Then what do you think, Ranger?"

"I think the Cold War suddenly got red hot to the touch. I think the Soviet Union is up to something no good at all, right here in Texas."

Masters looked at Jim Strong for what seemed like a long time after he said that. "Doesn't explain why Russians are killing Russians."

"It does if Stanko's crew was in the way of the new boys in town, who needed him out of the way."

Boone Masters tried to make sense of what he was hearing. "Stinko and his boys ran the Russian rackets in the state. You want to move stolen merchandise, you go to them or you don't go to anybody."

"Something you learned the hard way."

"Just like you did, yesterday, Ranger. I saw the look in your eyes when that gunfight broke out. Or maybe it was 'cause you forgot that yesterday was also Bring Your Kid to Work Day."

"Well, I suppose that gives us something in common, given that describes every day in the Masters household," Jim retorted. "What was your boy's name again?"

"Cort Wesley. And, however this shakes out, I've

done my part, so I'm going to assume he's now absolved of that association with any criminal activities."

"You'd assume correct. Your job's done," Jim Strong said, leaving it there.

"I like to see things through to the finish, Ranger, and we're not even close to that yet, here."

Jim Strong didn't look impressed. "Your contact got gunned down in that park, Mr. Masters. There's nothing more I can see you contributing."

"Then you're not looking hard enough, Ranger."

It was four days later that Boone Masters approached a first-floor storefront in an office park, which had been rented so recently that the FOR LEASE sign still hung in the window.

A Russian looked up from a box he was unpacking. "We're closed."

"Yeah," Boone said, ignoring the two other men, who'd suspended their unpacking chores to eye him tightly, hands moving to the familiar bulges beneath their jackets. "And thanks to you the man I used to do business with is closed permanently."

"Leave your name and I'll get back to you," the man who'd spoken first, who Masters now took to be the leader, instructed.

"Nice jacket," Masters complimented. "Maybe you don't remember me giving it to you."

The Russian looked confused, then straightened up all the way and hitched his shoulders. "Fits perfect."

"I can see that."

"Thank you for the gift."

"You're welcome. Son of a bitch Stanko stole from me," Masters told him. "You returned the favor by wasting the prick."

The Russian tried so hard to look calm that it produced the opposite effect. "Maybe I'm out of practice with my English, but I have no idea what you're talking about."

Masters took a step closer, drawing a flinch from the men he'd identified as no more than muscle. "I heard all about how you Russian gangsters do business, and I don't really give a shit, except for how that affects mine. You knocked Stinko off to take his territory. I'm part of that territory."

"Stinko."

"What I call the man you put a dozen holes in, up in Houston last week."

He was wearing a wire that finished with a tight looping around his balls, making them itch horribly. It was all Boone Masters could do not to start scratching his crotch as if he had crabs.

"Something wrong?" the Russian asked suddenly.

"Sure, plenty. I got merchandise warehoused and I've got no one to move it, on account of you shooting the guy who used to handle that end of things for me. Like I said, he was ripping me off, so I've got no problem with him getting dead in a hurry. My problem is with you standing there playing hard to get, bub."

"*Bub?*"

"Figure of speech, like 'man' or 'dude.'"

"Oh," the Russian said, even though it was clear he didn't understand. "But, *bub,* I know nothing of this Stanko, and I'm a legitimate businessman."

"So how come you just used his real name instead of the one I gave him?"

The Russian stiffened. Boone thought he spotted him exchange taut glances with his two thugs.

"What is it we can do for you, my friend?" he asked, leaving it there.

"Handle any major appliances?"

"I've been known to."

"I was paying Stanko a twenty percent service charge."

The Russian smirked, suddenly looking comfortable. "Closer to forty would be my guess."

"Then we seem to have settled upon thirty percent," Boone Masters said, extending his hand. "The name's Boone Masters."

The Russian took it. "Anton Kasputin."

"So when can you handle the first load, Anton?"

Masters left his son Cort Wesley home the night Kasputin's trucks came to empty a warehouse full of major appliances "borrowed" by the Texas Rangers from Sears on the promise they'd be returned in perfect working condition.

"You gonna move in and bust them when they make the pickup?" he asked Jim Strong from the other side of a diner booth, where they'd met for breakfast. "Maybe find the guns they used on Stinko and his boys right on their persons?"

"Nope, not my intention at all."

"Then what is?"

"I can't tell you any more than I already have."

"You haven't told me shit."

"You wanted to keep playing the game, Mr. Masters, but it's gotta be by my rules."

Boone took his mug of coffee in hand but left it short of his lips. "Know what I think?"

"I'm sure you're gonna tell me."

"I heard your grandfather, William Ray Strong, rode with the Frontier Battalion, and your famous dad, Earl, tamed oil towns that would've put the Old West to shame. I think you're doing the same thing here, going frontier with some kind of one-man show. I think you got a tip from somebody about something and you're running it as far up the flagpole as it'll go, instead of passing it up the ladder. I'm guessing you had a bad experience with such government types before and learned the lesson to keep things where they lie. So tell me, am I right?"

Jim laid his cup down and rested his elbows on either side of a fruit plate he was struggling to get through because his daughter, Caitlin, had made him promise to eat better. "As rain, Mr. Masters."

"How many times I gotta tell you to call me Boone?"

"Not my way, sorry."

"So what's on the docket next?"

"Just let me know once you got the pickup scheduled with your new Russian friends."

"They're not my friends, Ranger."

"And neither am I, Mr. Masters"

But Boone Masters never did tell Jim Strong, once he'd set up the meet with Anton Kasputin to take possession of the major appliances the Rangers had borrowed from Sears. Instead, he took it on himself to follow the four semis, packed with his own boosted merchandise, from the east San Antonio warehouse, north for a good couple hundred miles, until they came to a fenced-in complex of buildings with a rusted FOR SALE sign clanging in the wind against the main gate. He parked down the grade and stowed his truck out of sight and had just started toward the fence line when something rustled in the bed of his truck.

Masters drew the .357 Magnum holstered back on his hip, under the denim jacket he'd had since high school, and yanked back the canvas balled up in the bed of his pickup.

"What's up, Dad?" asked his son, Cort Wesley.

Masters reholstered his pistol. "What the . . ."

Rage swallowed the rest of Boone's words as he jerked his fifteen-year-old son up and out of the bed, the boy's boots scratching against the cargo liner, and slammed him hard against the cab.

"What the fuck, boy?" he finally finished.

"I don't like getting left behind."

"Say that again."

"I don't like—"

A heavy slap across the face froze his words and stung him with pain.

"This isn't a normal run, son."

"Then what is it?" Cort Wesley asked, his eyes tearing up as his hand rubbed his cheek, which felt numb.

"That don't concern you."

"If it concerns you," the boy started, "it—"

He stopped when Boone Masters raised his hand again.

"That's better, boy. What I always tell you?"

"To keep my dick in my pants and tongue in my mouth."

Boone looked down in melodramatic fashion. "Well, one out of two ain't bad, I guess. Now get yourself up in the truck bed, back under the canvas where nobody can see you, and pretend you're not there," he said, realizing Jim Strong had said almost the same thing to his daughter last week in Houston. "It's like you're on the same wavelength as that girl."

"What girl?"

"Caitlin Strong."

"Who?"

"Never the fuck you mind."

"Dad—"

"I can't hear you because you're not there."

Boone waited until Cort Wesley was safely hidden back in place and then approached the perimeter of the warehouse complex along a natural culvert dug out of the ground. He hopped the fence—fortunately not electrified or topped with barbed wire—and moved close to the big doors Kasputin's thugs were hoisting open to off-load the washers, dryers, and refrigerators he'd boosted over the course of the last month. And he got close enough to see what was inside.

"Holy shit," he muttered to himself, already wondering what Jim Strong was going to make of this.

* * *

"Say that again," Jim requested, after Boone Masters had explained what he'd spotted in Anton Kasputin's warehouse.

"I didn't want to waste your time. Come on, Ranger, I did you a favor here."

"That what you call deviating from my instructions?"

"Since when do I take orders from you?"

"Since you got your son jammed up. Do we really need to go over that again?"

"I suppose not."

"Then just tell me what you saw in that warehouse. And it better be good or your boy will be in custody before the day's out."

"Shelves and shelves of tanks, laid out as far as the eye could see," Boone told him. "Looked something like scuba tanks, except they were marked 'Propane.'"

"Propane," Jim Strong repeated thoughtfully.

"Mean something to you?"

The Ranger nodded. "That natural gas shortage the country's been experiencing has led to a panicked surge of propane sales. Definitely a good idea to stockpile it, if you can."

"Bullshit," Boone said, stopping just short of rolling his eyes. "You don't believe it's really propane in those tanks, any more than you believe in Santa Claus or the Easter Bunny."

"I've got my issues with the bunny, but Santa's real as rain. But you're right, Masters. I don't believe for one second it's propane those Russians got tucked in those tanks."

47

"Okay, so what really was in those tanks?" Cort Wesley said, when Jones finished his tale.

"Maybe I'm not ready to tell you yet."

"Maybe that's because you don't know, and that's what you planting a bug in Gribanov's office was all about."

"Except, according to you, Gribanov's dead now."

Cort Wesley finally called the waitress over and ordered the chocolate cream pie. It was a few minutes after five o'clock, but she told him she'd honor the happy hour special anyway.

"Okay," he said, once she'd left with his order in hand, "let me see if I've got this right. The Cold War heats up at the same time Gribanov and his Russian thugs show up in Texas under the auspices of the KGB. First order of business was to wipe out Stanko and his boys. That was to give him the cover he needed, right? One set of gangsters replacing another."

"Warm, cowboy."

"A rivalry maybe? Two warring Soviet factions facing off, with only one left standing?"

"Cold."

"Maybe Stanko or somebody on his crew couldn't be trusted."

"Warm," Jones said, drawing the word out by slurring the *m*.

"Maybe word was one of them was talking to the cops."

"Warmer."

"Or Texas Rangers?"

"Hot as blazes," Jones told him. "Jim Strong was called in when one of Stanko's lieutenants got pinched for statutory rape. I think the girl was fifteen. Anyway, the guy's looking at twenty years in Huntsville and starts singing up a storm. So our favorite gunfighter's dad enlists your dad to do some infiltration for him. The way such things were done in the old days. You really don't remember any of this?"

"I remember stowing away in his truck that night, but that's about it. It was right after he quit drinking, not long before he took sick," Cort Wesley related. "Best memories I've got of the son of a bitch."

"Never knew he was a genuine hero, did you?"

"You still got some blanks to fill in that regard, Jones, starting with how you knew I was there that night."

"I got my sources."

"You expect me to buy that?"

"Let's table that for another day," Jones said evasively.

"The answer have anything to do with how this all ended back in eighty-three?"

"That's classified."

Cort Wesley couldn't believe what he was hearing. "My father involved in something that was classified?"

"It appears he never shared that part of the story with you, either."

"Only thing he shared was his right hand when we got home, to thank me for riding along in the truck bed. And it wasn't too long after that he went into the hospital and never came out."

Jones's expression fluttered, his eyes uncertain for a moment, until he slipped back into the guise he wore like a second skin.

"He didn't take sick, did he?" Cort Wesley challenged. "Something else put him in the hospital."

Jones played with his fork, remained silent.

"Oh, and by the way," Cort Wesley continued, "he made me ride home under the same canvas in his truck bed that night. I damn near froze to death."

Jones wiped his mouth with a napkin. "Get back to the Gribanov murder."

"More like an execution," Cort Wesley told him. "He and the thugs I remember from yesterday killed in identical fashion, pretty much, their bodies arranged like they were getting ready for a birthday party."

"What's that mean?"

The waitress set two pieces of chocolate cream pie in front of Cort Wesley and he went to work on the first with his fork. Jones gave him a longer look, suddenly more interested in Cort Wesley than the second piece of happy hour pie the waitress had just set down before him.

"It means that somebody killed four guys, weighing in at a half-ton, combined, as easily as most men comb their hair."

"Wait a minute, you think it was *one* shooter?"

"He's a hell of a lot more than just a shooter, but yes, that's what I think."

Jones nodded to himself, gritting his teeth and weighing the prospects of what Cort Wesley had just said. "Bad to worse."

"There's more," Cort Wesley resumed. He told Jones about the map with circled areas visible only under ultraviolet light. "That means something to you," he said, studying Jones's reaction when he was done.

"It does, cowboy. It means plenty," Jones said, sighing in resignation, as if prepared to say something he hadn't been before. "Anton Kasputin survived his final run-in with your father and the Rangers, and he never did leave the country."

"That a fact?" Cort Wesley said, swallowing his first mouthful.

"He just became somebody else: Alexi Gribanov."

48

MANHATTAN, KANSAS

Beriya stood in the shadows cast by the streetlights dotting the campus of Kansas State University. He leaned against a tree, fighting the temptation to light a cigarette, which might reveal him to a passing student or a security officer making his rounds. It didn't matter so much now as later, after the explosion, at which point the last thing he wanted was anyone to randomly recall his presence.

Before him, through the trees, he could see lights flickering in the windows of Pat Roberts Hall. The people behind those windows would be dead in mere moments, too, along with Beriya's primary targets, since death doesn't discriminate among its victims, especially in the kind of blast he'd wired in a basement sublevel.

Campus security procedures being what they were, everybody used swipe cards to access every building. The right one could pretty much get you inside any place you wanted to go, and finding one had been as simple as pretending to have dinner in the nearby Sale Barn Café. There, Beriya had spotted a woman wearing the uniform of a Kansas State security officer, seated at the counter, and he had followed her out of the café once she'd finished her meal. But he didn't approach until she was behind the wheel of her truck. He was smiling and friendly, knees crimped and shoulders sagged to disguise his true height and size.

"Say, do you know where I can find . . ."

Beriya didn't remember the rest of what he said; he honestly didn't. Could be, in a sleepy town like Manhattan, Kansas, they hadn't even found her body slumped across the front seat yet, much less noticed that the swipe card was missing from her wallet.

Cards belonging to such officers normally accessed all buildings on campus, and Kansas State was no exception. A single swipe, with his face steered away from the security camera aimed down at him, was all it took to get him inside Pat Roberts Hall and then the basement. Accessing his actual target inside would have proven far more problematic, so Beriya opted for a strategy that took that into account.

The entire process had taken a mere hour, and then

he emerged into the night and made his way to the cover of these trees to trigger the blast. A safe distance from both the shock wave and the debris field, which likely would be quite large, given the power of the shaped charges he'd set. He held the detonator in his hand, reliving the moments that had made him the man he was, freezing them in a mind that considered all the kills that defined his very reason for being to be the same. The victims lacked any discernible features, since Beriya had no recollection of what the killers of his father looked like anymore.

In those final moments before he triggered the blast, Beriya was a young man again, serving with the OMON forces, short for Otryad Mobilny Osobogo Naznacheniya, commited to salvaging as much as they could of the crumbling Soviet Union. His father, a decorated colonel, had pulled strings to get Beriya assigned to his unit during the Latvian revolution of early 1991. He was just twenty years old and Riga was his first real posting, his first exposure to genuine violence, as the crumbling Soviet Union made a last-ditch effort to hold on to whatever it could. Beriya hardly saw the point of futilely trying to hold things together. But men like his father stubbornly, arrogantly, refused to let go, especially with a general's posting in his immediate future.

When the Riga revolutionaries known as the Popular Front erected barricades in the streets to further rally the people, Beriya's father saw his opportunity to cement his status by crushing them and launched an attack on the Latvian Ministry of the Interior on January 20. The revolutionaries proved far better armed and more skilled than anticipated and a fierce battle erupted. Though severely outnumbered, the elder Beriya refused to let his troops withdraw. Beriya himself was wounded in one of the exchanges and watched helplessly from behind a pillar as the mob descended on his father like crazed dogs and literally tore him apart.

Beriya never turned away, not even once, feeling his sadness and desperation recede behind a curtain of obsession and desire for cold vengeance. He watched the horror, making sure to commit the faces of his father's killers to memory.

Beriya pictured the angry mob descending on his father, as he squeezed the detonator tighter in his grasp, moving his thumb over the activator at the top. He felt the warmth of the moment beginning to consume him, as time and space lost all meaning. In that moment he was twenty years old again and slumped behind a pillar with his own wound sucking the life out of him. Helpless to come to his father's aid, lacking the strength even to spray the crazed crowd with machine gun fire when his father's awful screams had finally stopped.

But Beriya did something else instead: he memorized the faces of his father's killers. And in the days, weeks, and months that followed, as the Soviet Union dissolved and OMON was disbanded, he learned their identities and tracked them down. Eleven men, Latvians who considered themselves heroes to their people.

Beriya couldn't just kill them; killing them, alone, wasn't enough. First they had to suffer, just as he had suffered, watching helplessly as his father was executed by an angry mob. So Beriya made all eleven men watch as he murdered their families—wives, sons, and daughters, mostly; parents in a few cases. Killing his final targets actually left him feeling empty in comparison to watching them suffer the deaths of their loved ones.

Ever since then, the work he did was all about trying to recapture the feeling of that day. Beriya understood he never would or could achieve that, but there were reasonable facsimiles. And the impunity with which he operated gave him license to dispense suffering on the same level he'd suffered, whenever possible. Like making an oligarch watch his son's freshly severed fingers pile up in a child's play pail.

It was the only thing that made Beriya feel alive.

And that's when he depressed his thumb, holding his breath instinctively as the first rumble sounded, like a lingering roll of thunder. Pat Roberts Hall on the campus of Kansas State University suffered no flame burst, initially, just a huge wash of ash and debris contained in a gray-black cloud as the explosion's reach stretched upward until it had captured the whole of the building in its grasp. There were no screams yet, nothing but a deafening roar preceding the blast's shock wave, and the flame spout that burst up from the cloud, as blinding as a flashbulb, seemed to suck the air out of the night.

The flames receded quickly and Beriya waited, his heart hammering with anticipation at the product of his labors, which would become clear any moment now. Before it had, he eased a cell phone from his pocket and dialed an American dummy exchange that would automatically route his call to Moscow. It rang once, followed by silence as the connection was made, affording Beriya more time to wait for the view of the destruction he'd wrought. His heart thudded with anticipation, the murderers of his father slain yet again. He could hear screaming now, along with, already, the distant screech of sirens.

Finally, the pole lamps revealed a pile of rubble intermixed with a few walls jaggedly clinging to life. The effects had exceeded his expectations; char, ash, and smoke continued to cloud the air in thick pockets. Then a voice in Moscow answered his call.

"*Da.*"

"It is done," Beriya reported.

"Good, because you have fresh target, a new priority."

"What?"

"Not what, who: a Texas Ranger."

PART SIX

Wheaties presents Joel McCrea in *Tales of the Texas Rangers*. Starring Joel McCrea as Ranger Pearson. Texas, more than 260,000 square miles and fifty men who make up the most famous and oldest law enforcement body in North America. Now from the files of the Texas Rangers come these stories based on facts. Only names, dates, places are fictitious, for obvious reasons. The events themselves are a matter of record.

—Introduction to *Tales of the Texas Rangers*, aired on NBC Radio from August 27, 1955, to December 26, 1958

49

Dylan was sitting on the porch swing, holding his father's twelve-gauge shotgun across his lap, when Caitlin climbed out of her SUV and headed up the walk.

"Where's your dad?" she asked, climbing the stairs.

"Still meeting with 'You Know Who,'" he said. I don't, but I'm guessing you do."

"I've got a few ideas," she said, wondering what was keeping Cort Wesley with Jones so long. She checked her phone to make sure she hadn't missed a text or e-mail from him.

"And I don't need a babysitter."

She sat down on the swing next to him, rocking it slightly, glad the shotgun barrel was facing away from her. "I'm not following."

"Your friend the colonel."

"I thought the two of you would get along just fine."

"We did."

"So what's the problem?"

Dylan pursed his lips, blew out some breath, which rattled the hair from his face, and shook his head. "Do I really need to tell you?" he asked, tilting his gaze up toward Luke's bedroom window.

Caitlin held the swing steady. "How long have you known?"

"I've kind of known for a while, but I guess I'm

sure now. Just like I'm sure something has you spooked."

"Huh?"

"Don't bother telling me you're not. Tell me what happened, instead."

50

ATASCOSA, TEXAS

Caitlin had driven for a time after leaving the medical examiner's office, watching twilight darken into night. Before she could think twice about it, she'd activated her SUV's Bluetooth with a call to the Bexar County Sheriff's Department.

"This is Caitlin Strong of the Texas Rangers," she greeted the dispatcher who answered. "Please patch me through to Sheriff Pamerleau."

"Just give me a moment to track her down, Ranger," the dispatcher said, knowing better than to ask why or to argue the point.

A pause followed, in which the dead air sounded like the Gulf on a stormy day over her SUV's speakers. Caitlin had phoned the BCSD instead of San Antonio police simply because the sheriff's department was responsible for patrolling thirteen hundred square miles, almost all of it rural. The kind of land that was jam-packed with ranches like those belonging to Karl Dakota and Christoph Russell Ilg.

Susan Pamerleau, meanwhile, had been the first

woman sheriff to be elected in the county, in large part because she was a terrific administrator as well as a no-nonsense officer of law enforcement. And Pamerleau was apolitical. Caitlin was surprised as much by the skill of her campaigning as by the fact she'd decided to run in the first place.

There was a click, and then Sheriff Pamerleau's voice filled the cab.

"What can I do for you, Ranger?"

"Thanks for taking my call, Sheriff. I was just wondering if you'd had any reports that stick out as strange, the past day or so."

"As in . . ."

"Something that makes you think twice but leaves you short of dispatching the cavalry."

"You mean besides this spate of domestic abuse and sexual assault cases lately?"

"I do."

"Well, let's see. A ten-year-old boy stole his mother's car."

"Not that."

"Good thing, because he crashed the car. This morning we had a call about some bow hunters wandering off that Bexar County Bow Hunts place and going after bucks within range of an elementary school. Oh, and this afternoon a tourist filed a report about not actually seeing a ghost on the Silver Ghost tour last night. Then there's the farmer whose dogs went missing."

"Stop there," Caitlin told her.

* * *

Located in Atascosa, the four-hundred-acre Burlein farm had been in the family for generations. According to Sheriff Susan Pamerleau, Colt Burlein had called in a panic that morning, saying he'd heard horrible shrieking wails the night before and had woken up to the realization that his three German shepherds were missing. He'd called the sheriff's department, fearing foul play from one of the neighbors with whom he was constantly at odds, after he could find no trace of them anywhere on his property.

Caitlin squeezed through the fence rails onto Burlein's land in the moonless night, with no more than a flashlight to carve herself a path. The wind rustled through the trees and nearby corn crops, making her think of summer, for some reason.

Caitlin rotated her flashlight about the sprawl of the farm, her thoughts turning again to those kids who'd gone missing from Armand Bayou. If it had been a kidnapping, law enforcement or the kids' parents would've heard something by now. The fact that no one had heard a word suggested another factor here that she hadn't figured out yet. A hostile action, for sure, but one rooted in a motivation other than money.

Terrorism maybe? Some homegrown ISIS-like group, intending to make a show of executing the kids one at a time to frighten the country into submission? The possibility was chilling, although the actual logistics still suggested far-more-seasoned, even professional or paramilitary, involvement.

Caitlin stopped suddenly and moved the beam of her flashlight about. The wind had stopped; the trees and crops had gone motionless. But she heard a rustling sound, hollow and different than animals make, and the ground seemed to rumble beneath her feet.

Caitlin swept her flashlight one way, then back the other, then in a circle, trying to determine where the rustling was coming from. It seemed to be all around her and she froze, feeling for the SIG holstered on her hip.

The rustling dissolved into a pounding, a *thump-thump-thump* coming straight at her through the darkness, from the crops on her right flank. Caitlin twisted the flashlight beam about that way, revealing nothing.

Thump-thump-thump.

Still coming.

Caitlin turned. Ran. No longer feeling for the SIG. Her mind picturing whatever had descended on Karl Dakota's cattle out of nowhere and dropped them as they stood.

Her heart pounded her rib cage. Her lungs filled, emptied, and filled again. Then the gasps started, bred by panic and the unknown nature of whatever was chasing her down, the earth seeming to quake as if ready to open up and swallow her.

Something was coming. . . .

She'd been in more than her share of gunfights, situations where ambushes were more likely than not. But Caitlin had never known fear like this, not after a couple days of following leads that made no sense at all and confronted her with something between impossible and monstrous.

Ahead, the jittery beam cast by her swaying

flashlight caught the reflection of a still pond nestled in the center of the Burlein property. Could whatever was coming, whatever had eaten Dakoka's and Ilg's herds to the bone, swim?

Caitlin was almost to the water shimmering under the light of her flashlight beam, when a black wave swept over her and she went down.

51

SHAVANO PARK, TEXAS

"Stop laughing," she said to Dylan, when he broke up near the end of her story.

"It was the missing dogs, wasn't it? Those German shepherds."

"Damn things were blacker than the night."

"So Caitlin Strong has finally met her match: dogs!"

And he laughed so hard he almost fell off the swing, sent it rocking into a fresh sway.

"Everybody's gotta be scared of something, son."

"Okay, what am I scared of?"

"Waking up one morning ugly," Caitlin said, finally smiling herself. But it slipped from her face just as fast. "We were talking about Luke."

Dylan's gaze turned suddenly evasive. "About that," he said.

"Yeah?"

"When'd you figure things out?"

"I didn't, not totally. He told me last night."

"He *told* you?"

"Surprised?"

"He never told me a damn thing, even when I asked him. Just rolls his eyes and blows the hair from his face."

"You do that too, son."

"Roll my eyes?"

"Blow the hair from your face."

"No, I don't," Dylan said, doing just that.

"When you're nervous or on edge about something."

"I'm not nervous or on edge about this."

"No? How about how your dad is going to take the news?"

"Well . . ." Dylan's expression tightened, then grew questioning. "Luke really told you? On his own?"

"Guess I knew when I saw him and the other boy together in that office at the nature center. Something in their eyes."

"The way they looked at each other, you mean?"

"The way they didn't," Caitlin told him. "Like each was pretending the other wasn't even in the room."

"Is there anything you don't notice?"

"Well," Caitlin shrugged, "there were those dogs earlier in the night."

They smiled together this time, just before the screen door rattled open and, in the same moment, a pair of halogen headlights from Cort Wesley's truck hit the porch like a spotlight.

"What are you guys talking about?" Luke asked, emerging from inside just as his father parked his truck in the driveway.

52

Caitlin and Cort Wesley sat on the porch swing, the night silent save for the wind whistling through the trees and the slight creak of the swing's hinges from the rocking motion caused by their weight upsetting the delicate balance.

"How long have you known about Luke?" he said finally.

"We don't have to do this, Cort Wesley."

"We don't?"

"You should be talking to Luke, not me."

"I need some time to process this first."

"How do you think he feels?"

"I wouldn't know, because he didn't see fit to tell me."

"Maybe he thought you'd be pissed."

"And I am pissed, Ranger . . . that this is the way I had to find out."

Caitlin held to her calm, knowing Cort Wesley's emotions were all twisted into knots. "You want to blame me for that, go ahead."

"I want to blame you for not telling me as soon as he told you. Now answer my question."

"I don't remember it."

"How long have you known?"

Caitlin thought back to spotting Luke in the office at the Armand Bayou Nature Center, the incredible wave of relief she had felt starting to get washed away by the question of why exactly he and that other boy, Zach, had gone off into the woods alone the night before. She'd noticed something tense and uneasy in Luke's expression that was neither guilt nor fear so much as resignation. It happened the moment their eyes met and she saw in Luke's the same look a kid flashes when you find something you're not supposed to in a drawer or between the mattresses—not so much denial of the act as regret over not doing a better job at hiding the truth. But Caitlin knew she couldn't verbalize that for Cort Wesley and opted to tweak the tale a bit.

"Last night," she told him. "You were right. He wasn't asleep. He told me when I went upstairs. He also told me again about the lights he spotted in the woods. Got me thinking."

"Don't change the subject."

"I'm not. I was only telling you about our conversation. It stuck with me, but I didn't know why until just now."

"Why's that?"

"Because I think those boys got themselves turned all the way around, Cort Wesley. They thought the lights were coming from the west, but they were really coming from the east."

"The Gulf," Cort Wesley realized.

"That's right. Whoever snatched those kids did it by boat."

53

The revelation didn't seem to register with Cort Wesley or, at least, didn't seem to matter to him.

"Luke told you he was gay before me," he said, about something that did.

"Give him time, Cort Wesley."

"He's had fifteen years."

"I don't think you mean that the way it sounded."

"Nope," Cort Wesley sighed, "just the frustration talking."

"What's changed? He's still the same kid."

"It doesn't bother you, Ranger?" he asked, shaking his head. "Not at all?"

"Why should it?"

"My dad would've beaten me senseless if it were me."

"Then I guess it's a good thing you're not him."

"I just, I don't . . ."

Cort Wesley's voice tailed off and Caitlin didn't press him to continue, until he was ready.

"Did you ever suspect something was wrong? Tell me the truth."

"No, because there isn't anything wrong."

He shook his head, scolded her with his eyes. "You know what I mean."

"The answer to that is no, too. I never suspected

anything because he's a normal kid. Being gay doesn't change that."

"Well, it changes other things."

"Like what?"

Caitlin saw a vein start pulsing over Cort Wesley's left temple, as if he were trying hard to come up with an answer, without success, so she spared him the trouble. "I'm sorry."

"For what?"

"Being judgmental."

"I get your point," Cort Wesley told her.

"Do you?"

"You being judgmental with me like I am about Luke."

"Can't put anything over on you, Cort Wesley, can I?"

He almost smiled. "You know what's really bothering me here? The fact that you were afraid to tell me over how I'd react, the fact that you're worried about how I was going to deal with this. . . ."

"Well," Caitlin said, "you kind of proved my point."

"And the fact that I didn't see this for myself. How could I not have? I'm his goddamn father and I didn't even have a clue."

"Don't blame yourself."

"Can't help it, Ranger. If he'd come to me earlier, I can't believe this wouldn't have been easier on him. So I blame myself for not having the kind of relationship I thought I had with my youngest. That's why I'm sitting here steaming."

"Stop beating yourself up."

"Why is it easier with Dylan?"

Caitlin's mouth almost dropped. "'Dylan' and 'easier' in the same sentence? Do you really mean that?"

"In some ways I do."

"We comparing love lives of your sons here? Do I need to remind you about some of the romances Dylan's had that almost got him killed?"

"Why don't you just say what you mean?"

"You look at Dylan and see yourself, Cort Wesley."

"And what do I see when I look at Luke?"

"You shouldn't need to ask me."

"I just did anyway."

"You see his mother. When you look at him it gets you thinking about what your life might've been like if you'd made different choices."

"Like Luke did, you mean?"

"It's not a choice."

Cort Wesley lurched up out of the porch swing fast enough to crack one of the boards. "I can't think about this any more right now," he said, stopping short of the porch railing and squeezing his hands into fists. "What do I do about Zach? Do I talk to his parents, invite them over for dinner or something?"

"What makes you think you've got to do anything?"

"I don't know, Ranger; that's why I asked."

Caitlin looked away, then right back at him. "You hear from Jones?"

"While you were inside," Cort Wesley told her. "A building blew up on the campus of Kansas State University earlier tonight."

"What's that have to do with us, with all this?"

"Apparently, the building in question houses the nation's top biosecurity research institute."

"I've heard of it," Caitlin nodded. "Agriculture biosecurity, specifically."

"Which includes something else, Ranger: agroterrorism."

54

PENZA, RUSSIA

Yanko Zhirnosky felt the big SUV thump over the rut-strewn gravel road turned to mud by a recent storm.

"You still haven't told us where we're going," one of his political party's ministers said, impatience crackling in his voice.

"The future, that's where I'm taking you. Beyond that I don't want to spoil the surprise."

His armored SUV's run-flat tires took turns dropping into fresh divots dug out of the road, beyond which the thick tree line hid endless fields of scrub brush in Russia's Chernozem, or Black Earth, region. They had set out at dawn, neither Zhirnosky nor any of the four ministers of the Liberal Democratic Party of Russia informing even their closest aides of their plans or true destination. LDPR, of course, was a name left over from the party Zhirnosky had usurped and molded in his own ultranationalist image, to the point where Vladimir Putin himself began to fear his right flank, exposed by Zhirnosky's and the LDPR's growing popularity, as shown by the rising number of seats it now held in the Duma.

Zhirnosky's rise to such a standing was made even more incredible by the fact that he'd been one of the prime conspirators in an August 1991 attempted coup aimed at forestalling the collapse of his beloved Soviet Union. Working in concert with other, similarly minded Kremlin leaders, the conspiracy had been hatched with the help of Zhirnosky's mentor and then-head of the KBG, Valentin Krychkov. Ultimately, Zhirnosky had survived the fates suffered by his fellow conspirators by giving up Krychkov to Yeltsin's flacks. Zhirnosky took great pride in the fact that he'd never given in to the drunken fool, and he fretted only minimally over betraying his mentor, since Krychkov was a marked man anyway. Hell, Krychkov would've been proud of him for his actions, since they'd proved he learned his lessons well.

One of those lessons was to never give up on ultimately restoring the Soviet Union to its rightful place of prestige and power. And now, that goal was within his reach, with Zhirnosky himself installed as the nation's leader, once his plan was complete.

"But I can tell you this," Zhirnosky resumed. "Do any of you believe the future of our nation would not be best served by the fall of America as a superpower and the eradication of the American way of life as it is known today?"

His ministers remained silent and still.

"Does anyone object, then, to fully exploiting an opportunity that fortune has delivered onto us?"

"And what opportunity is that?" one of his ministers asked.

"The reawakening of something we gave up for dead," Zhirnosky told them all, "a long time ago, during the Cold War that may have ended but never entirely went away, as we have now seen. That is what this trip is about—to demonstrate to you precisely how we will seize upon that good fortune."

Zhirnosky was a short man, barely five and a half feet tall, who had long adopted a stiff-spined posture to make himself appear taller. His hair was slate gray and fit his scalp like a cap; none of the Liberal Democratic Party of Russia's ministers could recall ever seeing a single strand out of place. So, too, Zhirnosky held his expression in a perpetual scowl, born not only of the need to look stronger than anyone he was addressing but also of his mounting frustration over what he saw as the current government's lip service to the heritage and future hegemony of the Russian nation. In that respect, the party's name was a misnomer for the country's most ardent supporters of Russian ultranationalism. In increasing measures, Vladimir Putin was a peacenik when compared to the dogma of the LDPR.

"And what of our supporters in the Duma?" Zhirnosky continued, referring to the lower body of the Russian parliament that essentially ran the country. "What can we expect their response to be to our role in America's inevitable collapse and ultimate disintegration?"

"They are wary of opposing Putin," noted Igor

Lebedev, the party's chief deputy in the Duma, as the SUV thumped on through a wooded area that featured some of Russia's most fertile lands.

"Let me ask the question another way, then: if this had been a scheme hatched by Putin, what would they think then?"

"They would be leading celebrations in the street," insisted Oleg Malyshkin, a deputy comfortable working behind the scenes to ensure that the LDPR maintained its hard line at all costs and voted as a unified block. "But . . ."

"But what?" Zhirnosky prodded.

Malyshkin needed to force himself to respond. "We must consider how such open opposition to the ruling party will be greeted."

"You speak of the future."

"And the present, if our part in this is revealed prematurely. We all know that our president speaks like a nationalist while acting like a capitalist behind closed doors. He and his supporters will not be happy about the economic devastation wrought internationally by this."

"Only until they see the entire scope of the plan, something all of you are just about to see for yourselves," Zhirnosky explained. "We will use it to propel our party to a ruling position. The Soviet Union will be returned to all its previous glory as the true superpower in the world, the United States reduced to utter dependence on us for her very survival."

The ministers exchanged nervous glances, cushioning themselves against the jars and jolts that threatened to slam their skulls against the vehicle's roof. Around them right now there was only the tree line thickening into a forest in all directions as the convoy thumped up a slight hill.

"Goals achieved long after the plan's original implementation," said the lone female minister in the vehicle, Valentina Mironov, whose father had been a founder of the original LDPR but who had championed the move to radicalism upon his death. "I believe you were involved, at least peripherally."

"Peripherally, indeed. It was 1983," Zhirnosky scoffed, growing even stiffer. "I was a mere boy. I was responsible for the security details of the scientists involved."

"Protecting them," another minister wondered, "or watching them?"

"Both. Everything should have gone perfectly once the plan became operational."

"What happened?"

"We encountered circumstances that could not be anticipated. If you could grasp how close we came, how close we were to preserving our Union forever, how close to *winning*. Well, we are that close again— and to securing the power of our party for generations to come."

"Of course, our complicity in such a plot could be used against us before we are able to reap its rewards," Valentina Mironov agreed. "And we must also consider the detrimental, even catastrophic effects to our own economy of the likely collapse of international markets, once the operation's success becomes clear. We risk becoming pariahs, not heroes. We must have deniability here, plausible deniability, lest we risk our careers as well as our lives. And in that respect, comrade, I must question if your thinking is flawed."

Zhirnosky let himself smile. "That assumes you know what my thinking is. And what you're about to see should assuage any concerns and questions you may have."

Zhirnosky stopped there, as the SUV crested the hill and the driver slowed so the occupants could see what lay directly beneath them, stretching as far as the eye could see across a vast stretch of open, rolling fields.

"*Bo-zheh moy!*" Malyshkin managed. "My God. . . ."

"Can this be?" followed Lebedev in disbelief. "Am I seeing it right?"

"You are," Zhirnosky said, unable to restrain the grin that widened his jowls to bulbous proportions. "Behold the weapon we will wield to control our own destiny. Behold the means by which we will secure the destiny of the Soviet Union." He paused, smiled. "The *new* Soviet Union."

55

MIDLAND, TEXAS

"You have any idea the level of oil reserves in the Permian Basin, Ranger?" Calum Dane asked, picking up his pace slightly on the treadmill.

"I'm afraid I don't, sir," Caitlin told him, standing on a neighboring one that remained still. She could see a cup threaded over Dane's index finger, connected to an LED readout currently reading ninety-five.

"Thirty billion barrels," he said, answering his own question. "That's billion with a *b*."

"I know how to spell it, sir."

Dane's heart rate touched one hundred as he looked away from her.

"Anyway," Caitlin resumed, "I appreciate you seeing me."

She'd been waiting in the lobby of Midland's recently completed and lone skyscraper, the fifty-three-story Energy Tower, which was home to Dane Corp's international headquarters. Calum Dane's private gymnasium was located on the top floor of the old-fashioned slab-design of a building. The surrounding countryside's utter flatness allowed for a view stretching upwards of fifty miles, across pumpjack-littered oil fields currently producing more than a million barrels of oil per day.

"Didn't I also see you at the grand opening of the rechristened Midland International Air and Space Port?" Dane asked, turning to regard her again.

"No, sir," Caitlin told him, "I'm afraid I missed that."

"Guess I was mistaken, then. But you did hear we'll soon be offering suborbital space flights from just a few miles from here." Dane grinned. "A bit more exciting than riding on that helicopter that brought you here."

"The roof of your building here is plenty high enough for me, Mr. Dane."

"A building made possible by the fact that the

potential of our fields dwarfs other oil-rich geological formations, including North Dakota's Bakken and Texas's Eagle Ford Shale. It's not even close. You are standing smack-dab in the center of this country's biggest boomtown." Dane held his gaze on her, to the point where he stumbled a bit and had to grasp the treadmill's side rails for support. "I believe your grandfather spent some time in such boomtowns of his day, rode herd over them, I've heard told."

"I see you've done your research, sir. Things were different back in those days. It was the Depression, and men rode trains from everywhere to get where the work was, compared to today's oil workers, who make a salary that starts at eighty thousand a year."

"I see you've done your research, too."

"It pays to be prepared, Mr. Dane."

"I agree, Ranger, which explains why I was disappointed when you wouldn't be more specific about the reason for this meeting."

"It's not something easily explained over the phone," Caitlin told him.

"Like what?"

"I believe your life may be in danger, sir."

56

Calum Dane hit Pause on his treadmill and looked at Caitlin for what seemed like a much longer time than it really was, after she'd finished laying out for him the contents of the wall map in the murdered Alexi Gribanov's office.

"Farms and ranches, okay. What's that got to do with me, with oil, with Dane Corp?"

"You didn't let me finish, sir," Caitlin said, leaning up against the rail of her treadmill so her holstered SIG Sauer hung just beneath it.

That rail, in conjunction with the one on Dane's machine, created a barrier between them, a kind of invisible wall extending both up and down between their respective treadmills. The sun had just started streaming in through the north-facing glass wall, pricking Dane's eyes and forcing him into a squint that made him look even more uncomfortable.

"It's the potential perpetrators that have got me concerned, sir," Caitlin continued. "They seemed to have a specific selection of targets, and the evidence indicates you could be on that list."

"What evidence is that, Ranger?"

"I'm not at liberty to say, Mr. Dane," Caitlin told him, thinking of a property of his near Waco that had been identified on Alexi Gribanov's wall map. "I can say that four men were murdered yesterday and I believe their involvement in all this holds the reason. If you were on their target list, it stands to reason you might still be."

"Four of them, you said," Dane recalled, wedging a toothpick into the corner of his mouth, which he held between his teeth as he started up the treadmill again and jogged into the sun streaming into his eyes.

The same shaft of sunlight was just reaching Caitlin now. "And it's whoever murdered those men that's call for concern. You see, that wall map I mentioned also included some property in West Texas that belongs to you—your company anyway."

Dane grinned smugly, picking up his pace a bit. "Throw a stone from any window in these parts and you're bound to hit some land Dane Corp owns."

"I'm talking specifically about a former petrochemical plant, sir. Of course, you couldn't hit it with a stone, on account of the fact that it burned to the ground a few years back, after an explosion. Five workers were killed in the blast and seven firefighters in a secondary explosion that followed their arrival on the scene. Am I triggering any memories here?"

Dane's hands clenched into fists by his sides as they moved in rhythm with his pace; he was working his toothpick like a baby's pacifier. Caitlin noticed his heart rate was accelerating, up to one hundred twenty in bright red LED numbers. And his cheeks were now flushed with red, as if someone had smeared paint on them, when his previous exertion had achieved no such effect.

"You're no more the kind to mince words with me than your grandfather was when he tamed those oil towns in the thirties," he told her, his heart rate holding.

"The fire was labeled as suspicious," Caitlin told him. "But you already knew that, since the lawsuits are still pending against your company."

"That plant was actually owned by a subsidiary. We did a bad job of oversight, I'll admit that to you— but I'll deny ever saying it, if the statement comes back to haunt me one day. And, if it means anything, I reached out to the families of the men lost that night myself."

"The reports I've read indicated that plant manufactured pesticides."

"A business I'm glad to be out of," Dane said, dialing back his pace a bit by pressing a section of his treadmill's touch screen with a finger.

"Yes, I also read about the poisoning of those aquifers and resulting cancer clusters."

"*Alleged* poisoning, Ranger, *alleged* cancer clusters."

"My mistake, sir. But I'm sure you can understand my concern for your safety, given the connection between your petrochemical plant and these murdered Russians."

Dane seemed to perk up a bit. "I don't know any Russians, save for the business consortiums and investment groups I do business with."

"Any chance Alexi Gribanov was one of them?"

"Not to my knowledge, Ranger, and my knowledge of my own business dealings runs pretty deep. I'm not as good at delegating as I should be. I tend not to trust others to do a job I know I could do better. And

I don't like to do business with someone, especially important business, without being able to look them in the eye." He turned toward her atop the churning treadmill. "Does that sound familiar?"

"Is that what we're doing now, sir, business?"

"I figure you for the same kind of person, just like your grandfather Earl Strong was. A loner at heart. Someone who doesn't always play well with others."

"You could learn that much from reading the papers or watching the news."

"But it was the same for your father, too, and that was before the twenty-four-seven news cycle," Dane said, his cheeks still rosy but no longer flushed with red. "Jim Strong had a whole lot of folks at his funeral, I understand, but how many of them could he count as friends while he was alive?"

Caitlin reached over and plucked the emergency stop free of its magnetic hold. Dane's treadmill ground to an almost immediate halt. "You trying to scare me, sir?"

"I was merely sharing information, Ranger."

"Information about my dad and granddad, to make me think you're wearing the shoes here."

Dane reattached the metal disc against the magnet but stopped short of firing up the treadmill again. "I'm not sure I understand your meaning."

"You want me to believe you hold the upper hand so I'll hold my tongue in your presence. That's not going to happen, sir, not so long as you're implicated in four murders."

"Did you just use the word *implicated?*"

"You can substitute the word *connected,* if you

like. The point is I believe those men were killed because of the locations marked on a map of Texas, visible only under UV light. And your petrochemical plant that mysteriously blew up and burned to the ground, taking a dozen lives of working men and firefighters alike, for just doing their jobs, was one of those locations."

"I thought you came here because that made me a potential victim."

"I did, sir," Caitlin told him. "But maybe I had things wrong."

57

MIDLAND, TEXAS

"Those firefighters were volunteers," Caitlin continued. "How's that sit with you, Mr. Dane?"

Dane forced a smile. He'd worked up such a sweat that Caitlin figured if she reached out to touch him his skin would burn her hand, and she half expected the toothpick on which he was chomping to catch fire in his mouth. The sunlight streaming in through the north-facing window now caught both of them in a narrow shaft, like a spotlight shining from the sky.

"Their families were very well taken care of," he said finally.

"Out of guilt?"

"The plant was a subsidiary of Dane Corp, Ranger.

It was out of a moral responsibility—the kind nobody ever showed my family."

Caitlin remained silent, waiting for him to continue.

"When my father died on the last farm we share-cropped, in Glasscock County, nobody offered to do a damn thing except pay for his plywood coffin so he could be dumped in a pauper's grave with no head-stone. You know what I thought of when I made my first million dollars, Ranger? Picking cotton in those fields, the scars I've still got to show for it. You'd fig-ure I could put all that behind me, not bother looking back. But all I could think of was that farm, still up and operating with no regard for the workers out do-ing the picking. Time seemed to seize up whenever I thought about those days, to the point where nothing I was accomplishing seemed to matter, and wouldn't, until the farm itself was dead too."

"So what'd you do, sir? Kill it?"

Dane's gaze was still distant, reflective. "Close enough."

"And what were you thinking when you got word you were responsible for the deaths of a dozen men, Mr. Dane?"

Dane chomped down on his toothpick, the wood cracking audibly.

Caitlin had intended to leave it there, but more words raced up her throat before she could stop them. "Two years ago, right around the time of the fire . . . that would've been the same time that class action suit first sprang up, claiming one of your pesticides was making people sick."

The sun was continuing to move, one side of Dane's face lost to shadows.

"You came here to tell me my life was in danger," he said, his tone flat. He started to discard his toothpick, then changed his mind. "I appreciate the warning and can assure you I will take additional precautions." Dane stepped down from the treadmill and draped a towel that had been hanging from the front panel over his shoulders. "That should conclude our business, I believe."

"You don't find it strange, sir?"

Dane twisted the cap off a water bottle tucked into the machine's bottle holder and chugged half of it down. "Find what strange?"

"Like I told you, the sites marked on that wall map in Alexi Gribanov's office contained mostly farms and ranches. Kind of places known to use pesticides. What do you think I'd find if I checked which pesticide they'd been using?"

"I really have no idea."

"I'm sorry the connection escapes you, but I don't want to make this personal. A multibillion-dollar conglomerate like Dane Corp has tens of thousands of workers, and this connection to you that showed up in Gribanov's office could just as easily be someone else. I apologize if I led you to believe otherwise."

"This Gribanov, what's he do exactly?"

"Did, sir. Operated a strip club just off Harry Hines Boulevard. He's been in this country since 1983. Does that ring any bells for you?"

"Should it?"

Caitlin decided not to push that part of the issue. For now.

"Thank you for your time, sir," she said, as politely as she could manage. "I'm glad you'll be taking those extra precautions. But at least three of the men attached to your personal security team have done time on serious beefs. I thought you should be aware you have violent criminals in your employ."

"Who I hire is my business, Ranger."

Caitlin stepped down off her treadmill, the back of her shirt wet with enough sweat to make her think she'd just endured a workout of her own, eye to eye with Dane now. "I imagine any man who beats his own son would be comfortable in their company," she said, never taking her gaze off Dane.

Something flared in the man's eyes. Maybe it was the way the sun was hitting his face, but Caitlin could have sworn they turned as red as something out of a cartoon.

"Those baseless charges came out in my divorce proceedings," Dane said, the words seeming to hiss from his mouth. "The records were sealed."

"Not to me they weren't, sir. And 'baseless' isn't the way I'd describe those pictures of your son's injuries."

"Those were Photoshopped by my wife."

"What about that restraining order that forbids you to have any contact with your boy? Care to explain that?"

"Anything else, Ranger?"

"Just this, sir. I had an expert review the fire marshal's report on the explosion and fire at your plant.

He informed me that the items listed don't entirely jibe with the plant's shipping manifests, suggesting some of the actual contents got left off."

"You'll have to take that up with the fire marshal, Ranger."

"I intend to do just that, sir. But for now I was wondering if there was some way you could account for such an omission."

Dane drained the rest of his water, trying to make the motion appear relaxed and natural. "I wasn't privy to the plant's inner workings. Haven't I already explained that to you?"

"I thought you hated delegating. I thought you were the ultimate when it comes to hands on."

"I can't explain the discrepancy, Ranger. And I've already said far too much on the subject to suit my lawyers. I don't know what else to tell you."

Caitlin was backpedaling for the door now. "You didn't say anything about the significance of the year 1983."

"Are we back to that again?" Dane snapped, his demeanor starting to crack.

"It was the height of the Cold War. Gribanov came to Texas under a different name, to do great harm to both the state and the country, I believe. I also believe he was KGB and that his whole operation went dark before it ever got off the ground. But Gribanov changed his name, his identity, and never went home. He remained in place here, maybe waiting for another call. Maybe that call finally came and he didn't answer it. Maybe that's why he's dead. You listening to what I'm saying here, sir?"

"I don't think I like your tone, Ranger," Dane said rigidly.

"I apologize for that, but I wanted to give you an idea of what you may be up against. A bunch of guys who've done some time are no match for their kind."

"And you are?"

"Why don't you tell me, Mr. Dane? You seem to know an awful lot about my background."

Dane fought to show no reaction, but his lower lip dropped slightly, quivering. "Anything else, Ranger?"

"Another circle on that map I told you about included a site outside of Houston where a bunch of kids went missing two days ago. You wouldn't know anything about that, would you, sir?"

Dane took a step forward, close enough for Caitlin to smell the sweat soaking through his clothes and blanching his skin, its odor gone rank now. "So now I'm a kidnapper, as well as an arsonist and murderer?"

He held his ground, glaring at her as if surprised she hadn't backed off or flinched. Instead, Caitlin slid close enough to Dane to feel the heat of his breath as well as what felt like steam rising off him, with the dank stench. She thought she saw something waver in Dane's eyes, as if he was the one flirting with taking a step backwards in retreat.

"I was only wondering if you'd heard about it, sir."

"Of course I have. The whole state's talking about it. I think it's Muslims. Have you looked into that angle yet?"

"I'm sure the FBI will, sir," Caitlin said, angling for the glass-door entry/exit to Dane's private gym. She fit her Stetson back in place just short of it and looked back at Dane. "Any idea how missing kids might be connected to a pesticide factory fire and dead livestock?"

"I'll leave the answers to such questions to the professionals, Ranger."

Caitlin yanked the glass door open; the two plain-clothes security men standing there, facing the opposite wall, seemed to barely notice her. "You've got my number, Mr. Dane. If you think of anything, give me a call."

Two of Dane's security guards joined Caitlin in the elevator and escorted her to the rooftop helipad, where the pilot was waiting patiently for her return. He was already throwing switches and toggles, prepping for takeoff, when she closed the passenger-side door.

"Bit of a bumpy ride back to San Antonio, Ranger," he told her. "Gonna have to circle round a bit to avoid some sand storms that sprang up."

"No matter, because we're not going back to San Antonio yet. Got another stop to make first."

"Where's that?"

"Near Houston. Armand Bayou."

58

"Where we headed again, Bubba?" the ghost of Leroy Epps asked from the passenger seat, as soon as Cort Wesley pulled away from the house.

"To meet up with Jones."

"Leaving your youngest on his own again despite this peril he may be in."

"I trust Dylan to protect him, champ."

"Do you now? I never known you to trust nobody with something of such a magnitude."

"Dylan gets it."

"Gets what?"

"You know."

"Do I? Maybe you need to explain it to me. Maybe you need to explain a whole lot of things to me, starting with where we're headed."

"I told you, to meet up with Jones."

"That ain't a place; it's a person."

"I don't know where we're headed. Just that something big happened connected to what all this is about."

"And what exactly is all this about, Bubba?"

"Damned if I know."

Epps leaned back and eased his eyes closed, seeming to enjoy the feeling of the cool morning air blowing against his face through a window Cort Wesley couldn't remember sliding downward.

"You wanna tell me what else is eating at you, Bubba?"

"You weren't around to hear it for yourself last night?"

"Prefer hearing it from you."

"You gotta take a test to get your driver's license, gotta jump through hoops to cast a vote, and fill out a mess of paperwork to buy a gun from a legit dealer. But the only requirement for being a parent is knowing where to stick your pole."

"That's what's got your nads all twisted?"

"I'm still trying to process things, champ. If you weren't paying attention, that's not my fault."

"Why don't you refresh my memory, Bubba?"

"Agro-what?" Leroy Epps said, when Cort Wesley was finished with his tale.

"That's not what you asked me about originally."

"Well, I'm asking now."

"Jones hasn't explained everything to me yet."

Old Leroy rolled his eyes, the whites still creased by red streaks of veins bulged by his diabetes, which made it look as if the lower lids were drooping. *"The man's oily enough to dress a salad, Bubba."*

"No doubt about that, but he's also our best chance of making some sense out of all this."

Leroy's gaze wandered toward the empty cup holder. *"Say, you think we could stop and pick up a root beer on the way to wherever you're going?"*

"I don't think it works that way, champ."

"No, it don't, but twist the cap off and the smell will do me just fine. Ease the stress a bit."

"I didn't think ghosts had to worry about such things anymore."

"Most don't, Bubba. But most don't have you around them, neither."

Cort Wesley bought the biggest bottle of Hires Root Beer that would fit in his truck's cup holder, adding a pack of gum to ease his own dry mouth, when he got to the checkout line at the local CVS. The chain had stopped selling cigarettes, but for some reason, in Texas anyway, continued to sell snuff and chewing tobacco.

Just a pinch between your cheek and gum is sure to get you cancer. . . .

Old Leroy was nowhere to be found when he got back to his truck, so Cort Wesley tucked the root beer into a cup holder to await the ghost's return. His phone rang and he dragged it to his ear; he still hadn't figured out how to use the built-in Bluetooth device.

"Where are you, cowboy?" Jones demanded, not bothering with a greeting.

"Pulling off the airport exit now."

"Private terminal, don't forget."

"How's it feel to be back in the government's good graces, Jones?"

"Shitty, to tell you the truth, thanks to where we're going and why."

"Where would you like to start?"

"With a little field trip I made with the Navy SEALS to the caves of Afghanistan in 2002."

59

Caitlin approached the team of crime scene techs scouring the area of the Armand Bayou docks, which fronted the Gulf of Mexico. A trio of pontoon boats was currently moored in place, bobbing slightly atop the currents.

"Looks like your hunch was right, Ranger," said the head of the team, a man named Kilcoyne, who she'd met at a conference once with Doc Whatley. "So far we've got fresh paint scrapings and diesel fuel residue that's an entirely different grade than those pontoons use."

"What color were those paint scrapings?"

"Black."

"And the fuel would've been the kind recommended for high-performance engines?"

Kilcoyne took off his Houston Police cap and smoothed his hair back into place. "Looks like I could've just stayed home today."

"If you don't mind, sir, have your men sweep the woods leading up to the field those kids went missing from. There's a few trails that cut right through them," Caitlin said, turning to judge what the scene might've looked like to Luke and Zach when they got turned around in the nearby woods. "I think the kidnappers were shining flashlights ahead of them, the lights those boys spotted."

* * *

"I didn't know this case was Ranger jurisdiction," the young crime scene tech said to Caitlin a few minutes later, as she stood over him, shrouded by sunlight in the field the kids had vanished from.

"FBI's running point now, but we're still following up on a few leads," she told him, coming just close enough to the truth.

"Wait a minute," said the kid, who didn't look much older than Dylan, as he stood up slowly. "You're Caitlin Strong, aren't you?"

"Yes, sir, that would be me."

The kid extended his hand, forgetting it was sheathed in a plastic glove, and then pulling it back. Around him, the entire field had been staked off with yellow crime scene tape strung all the way around it. Uniformed officers were posted at regular intervals to secure the site; one of them had held the tape up so Caitlin could pass under it, as soon as he spotted her Ranger badge.

"Well, I'm not a 'sir.' Name's Robbie Fontaine."

"Nice to meet you, Robbie," Caitlin said, taking his hand anyway.

"Wow, they call you in special, on account of this is such a big case?"

"Nope, just doing my job. Following up a lead, like I told you."

Robbie's eyes strayed briefly to the SIG Sauer holstered on her hip. "So how can I help you?"

Caitlin had diverted the chopper here, unable to get parts of what Doc Whatley had said about his inspection of Karl Dakota's cattle remains out of her mind.

It's insect dung, better known as frass. What you're looking at is consistent with beetle frass, specifically bess beetles. I found it all over the skeletal remains of those cattle, which makes sense, since this kind of beetle uses its dung as a kind of defense mechanism.

"I was curious to hear if there were any new developments."

"Nothing specific." The young tech frowned, reluctant to continue. "Anyway, nobody seems to care."

"About what?"

"That the grass is dying, just like those fields over there," Robbie said, gesturing toward the interactive farmland Caitlin recalled from her last visit, which looked dried out and bleached.

Caitlin crouched and smoothed her hand around a patch of ground in the quadrant Fontaine was cataloguing and sampling in search of clues. "Looks green to me."

The kid crouched before her and plucked some blades from the area Caitlin had just smoothed. "See the browning here? Root system has been compromised."

"That common in these parts?"

"In a drought it would be. But we've had plenty of rain this season. And an external stimulus, like a pesticide or grass killer, would brown the grass from the outside as it kills the root." Fontaine rotated the blades he was holding to so Caitlin could better view them. "These are dying from the root up. How much you know about grasses, Ranger?"

"Well, Robbie, I know it grows. Beyond that, not very much."

The kid grinned, swiped a gloved hand across his brow. "Roots fall generally into two categories. The primary roots develop from the embryo during seed germination, while the adventitious roots emerge from nodes of the crown and lateral stems during the growth process. Now, the primary roots are pretty much history after the first season, but the adventitious ones stick around throughout the grass's entire life span."

"But not these," Caitlin noted, recalling something else Doc Whatley had said about Karl Dakota's plucked-to-the-bone cattle.

That farmer's herd wasn't wiped out by coyotes, wolves, mountain lions, or the boogeyman, Ranger. It was wiped out by something we can't identify, and what we can identify doesn't make any damn sense at all.

And here was something else that might not make any sense.

"No," Fontaine echoed, "not these. But the adventitious roots didn't die; they're gone. Another week or so," he continued, brushing off his gloved hands, "and this field'll be nothing but dirt. Just like that land over there," he added, gesturing toward the farmland that now looked like a desert.

"You got a shovel, Robbie?"

Fontaine produced a small trowel from his lab kit and handed it over.

"I have your permission to do this?" Caitlin asked him.

The young tech shrugged. "Hey, you're a Texas Ranger."

Caitlin worked the trowel slowly, careful not to disturb the ground any more than she needed to, until it sank into a gap between what appeared to be subterranean layers of the soil itself.

"What the hell . . ."

"Can you explain this, Robbie?" Caitlin asked him, jogging her phone to its video function.

"I majored in botany in college, Ranger, and I've never seen anything like it."

Caitlin hit Record, readying her trowel to widen the small trench.

"Hey, Doc, it's your favorite Texas Ranger," she said, after getting Doc Whatley on the line a few minutes later.

"I'm in the lab, Ranger. You got me at a bad time."

Caitlin followed the same path out of the field she'd taken in. "You need to have someone check something out at the field where that rancher's cattle got picked to the bone and get word to whoever we use in Zavala County to do the same with the fields where Christoph Russell Ilg's cattle were grazing."

"Sure, Ranger, and while I'm at it, how about I do your Christmas shopping for you? Anything else?"

"Yes," Caitlin told Whatley. "Get somewhere to look at a video I'm sending you."

"Why?"

"Because I think I may know why those kids got snatched from Armand Bayou."

60

His swagger back, with Homeland Security punching his time card again, Jones laid it out for Cort Wesley on the flight to Kansas State University.

"We had a firm lead on Bin Laden, probably only missed him by a few hours. He left in so much of a rush that he left a whole bunch of papers and documents behind, evidence of whatever they were still cooking up at the time."

"Which, I'm guessing, brings us to agroterrorism and the reason for *this* field trip, right?"

"As rain, cowboy. There were agriculture articles from American science journals, translated into Arabic. There were USDA documents. There was a comprehensive list of the most devastating livestock pathogens, like foot-and-mouth disease, hog cholera, and rinderpest. There was a separate rundown of crop diseases, like soybean rust and rice blight. And, most alarmingly, there were training documents detailing how to deploy these pathogens on farms."

"What about pesticides?" Cort Wesley asked, thinking about the suspicions Caitlin had shared with him the night before.

"You a mind reader now, cowboy?"

"Just answer the question, Jones."

"Yeah, there was plenty about pesticides. Leftover Cold War documents printed in Russian. By all indications, the Soviets had a plot to wipe out the bulk of our nation's food supply."

"Agroterrorism," Cort Wesley said, fitting the pieces together.

"Anton Kasputin was sent over here to fuck with America's farmland, when your father's original fence, Stanko, must've shown himself to be not up to the task. You wanna know why somebody wasted Gribanov, formerly Kasputin, and his gang, cowboy? Because one of them was talking. Turns out somebody in Moscow must've caught wind of whatever was going down in those locales he circled on that wall map you told me about, and ordered him to monitor the situation."

"While somebody inside was reporting back to you," Cort Wesley said, working it all out for himself. "Moscow figures out somebody's talking and sends a hitter to wipe Gribanov's entire organization out, just to be safe. Your informant anybody I know?"

"The big guy who swallowed his cigarette in the parking lot when you busted him up? That was my man."

61

SAN ANTONIO, TEXAS

Caitlin could see the shapes of men holding on to their hats, growing larger as the Ranger chopper settled into a hover over the Department of Public Safety heliport located near the intersection of Route 37 and the 410. Congressman Asa Fraley sharpened into view first, clear enough to make Caitlin want to remain on board.

Caitlin held firmly to her hat and crimped her knees beneath the still-slowing rotor as she climbed out, feeling the wash push wind and debris against her. She headed out across the small tarmac toward the field's single building, where Fraley was standing with his hands on his hips, flanked by a flunky on either side. One held an open notepad and the other a tablet, like it was glued to his hands.

"I'd hoped to have a subpoena ready for you by now," he greeted, expression trapped somewhere between a frown and snarl.

"You always serve them yourself, sir?" Caitlin asked him, as the rotor slowed to a stop and the debris it blew into the air stopped with it.

"I'm here putting out a brush fire you started, Ranger. Texas is littered with them. I swear, you're more dangerous than all the matches in the state combined."

"I'm guessing you received a call from Calum Dane, Congressman."

"I did indeed. You mind explaining your rationale for pissing him off no end? He just threatened to move a whole bunch of business out of the state, including the spaceport."

"Well, I imagine that would piss off plenty willing to pay a hundred grand in the hopes of meeting a Martian up there."

As she spoke, Caitlin noted assistant number one, the woman, jotting down notes feverishly, while assistant number two, the man, extended his tablet forward on an angle.

"Are you recording this, Congressman?" Caitlin wondered.

Fraley ignored her. "You mind explaining the purpose of your visit to Calum Dane to me?"

"I do, sir, on account of it's part of an ongoing investigation."

"Into Dane?" Fraley asked her, disbelief lacing his voice.

"He's a person of interest. That's all I can say on the matter."

"Dane said considerably more."

"I'm not surprised. Did he include the reason for my visit?"

"You mean, beyond harassment and intimidation?"

"I believed his life may be in danger."

"As part of this ongoing investigation?"

"That's right, sir."

Fraley mopped his brow with a balled-up handkerchief. He was wearing a darker suit today, which rode his plump lines like a shower curtain. His tie was the same orange-red color as the combed-over hair, which had been sprayed in all directions by the rotor wash.

"Mr. Dane reported that you came up just short of accusing him of complicity," Fraley told her, his final words partially lost to a sudden gust of wind that blew his comb-over backwards instead of forward.

"In what?"

"He wasn't specific."

"He couldn't be, because I never did, not directly anyway."

"What's that mean?"

"It's called police work, Congressman. I have reason to believe that Dane caused the fire at his own petrochemical plant to eliminate evidence."

"Evidence of what?"

"Being party to his pesticides making a whole lot of people across this state sick. Got any constituents who are recent cancer victims, Congressman, maybe part of a cluster of them?"

"So you accused one of the richest and most important men in Texas, in the whole goddamn United States, of giving people cancer. Have I got that right, Ranger?"

"Like I said, it's part of an ongoing investigation."

"You've got Calum Dane all wrong."

"Really? Maybe you should talk to the New York City police about that. Turns out a young man named Brandon McCabe, who lost a leg to cancer, was a part of a class action suit against Dane Corp for the same pesticides that were destroyed in that manufacturing plant fire in West Texas. McCabe shot his mouth off at the annual shareholders meeting at the Waldorf and hasn't been seen since."

Fraley pretended to be bored. "I imagine there's a point to that somewhere."

"There is, sir. I left out the part about security camera footage capturing McCabe entering his hotel. He disappeared that night. Just fell off the face of the earth."

"And does the NYPD share your concern?"

"There's a record of him checking out the next morning, so their interest is lukewarm, even though no clerk can verify the record. A detective I spoke with described his room as 'sanitized.'"

Fraley ran his tongue over his lips, then wet his fingers and tried to smooth his hair back into place. "Maybe they should talk to housekeeping."

"They did, Congressman. The maid insists she found the room in that condition, and McCabe hasn't been seen since. The ruckus he caused is up on YouTube."

Fraley's jaws moved as if he were chewing gum, uneasy with being informed of something he wasn't aware of. "Ruckus," he repeated. "Is that a law enforcement term?"

"Based on the current performance of Congress, I'd say it was a political one."

"Why don't you run for office, Ranger? With your popularity, you'd be a shoo-in. And if you grew unhappy with any of your colleagues, you could just shoot them."

"Maybe I should start now," Caitlin said, unable to help herself.

Fraley's eyes widened as his expression spread out into a grin. "You get all that?" he said to the aide taping their conversation on his iPad.

Before that aide could respond, a third one Caitlin hadn't noticed before rushed up to Asa Fraley, red faced and out of breath. He got close to the congressman's ear and said something too softly for Caitlin to hear. Whatever it was, though, must have pissed off Fraley mightily, because he shook his head, sneering.

"God*dammit!*" he hissed, swinging back toward Caitlin. "Someone sliced all four tires of my SUV. You wouldn't happen to know anything about that, would you, Ranger?"

"I didn't even know you were going to be here when I landed, Congressman. Maybe it was one of your constituents who's sick with cancer."

Fraley scowled and ran his tongue around the inside of his mouth as if trying to excise something bitter. "You're so far over the line there's no going back, Ranger. I'm going to have you served with a subpoena to testify before my committee in Washington about your methods and practices, so I can reveal the truth about Caitlin Strong to the country, even if that doesn't include shredding tires."

Caitlin fought back a smile, the truth dawning on her. "I thought you said they'd been slashed."

"They were. Before somebody tore the goddamn rubber off the rims."

PART SEVEN

One of my favorite quotes of all time is, "One riot, one Ranger," summing up that Texas Rangers don't come in big numbers, but when they show up, trouble is usually settled. I got to witness the Texas Rangers up close and personal this summer when I attended the annual Ranger Reunion, sponsored by the Texas Ranger Foundation. You talk about feeling secure. Being around both retired and active Rangers makes you feel no one in his or her right mind would offer a challenge. These guys are hard-bodied, steel-willed guys who are soft-spoken and courteous, but you know could blow up in someone's face if the predicament got dangerous.

—Bill Hartman, *The Madisonville Meteor,*
October 9, 2007

62

Calum Dane walked the now-barren grounds of his former petrochemical plant. He'd arrived early for his planned meeting with representatives of the insurance company that was still refusing to pay out his claim, due to the fact that the fire remained the subject of an ongoing investigation. Dane had made himself remain patient throughout the process, doing the right thing by paying all the medical bills of the injured out of Dane Corp's coffers, figuring he'd be compensated in due time.

But now due time had extended beyond two years, almost three.

Not far away, maybe twenty miles, the Branch Davidian compound, under the fanatical leadership of David Koresh, had burned to the ground too, in a fire sparked literally by the FBI. So Dane couldn't help but wonder if there was some curse or anomaly associated with the land. Kind of like a miniature version of the Bermuda Triangle.

If you asked him, Dane would've said the FBI had been too patient and waited too long to move on the

Branch Davidian compound. He hadn't made the same mistake here, when the toxic effects of Dane Corp's latest pesticide began to show up in people like the late Brandon McCabe, assigning to Pulsipher a job that should have come with relatively few complications. The fire should've been the end of it. The ammonium nitrate that had triggered the ensuing explosion wasn't even supposed to be on-site. Then, in the flash of an instant, five workers were dead, followed soon after by seven volunteer firefighters who were caught in a series of secondary explosions that pockmarked the sprawling plant. All because he needed to wipe out all trace of the pesticide's existence.

Walking the grounds of his former plant felt like traipsing through a graveyard, only with lots of places where an enemy could conceal himself. That made him glad he'd let Pulsipher bring along a full security team—four well-armed men, in addition to Pulsipher himself, posted about the grounds, all within Dane's sight, which meant, of course, that he was within theirs.

People like Brandon McCabe made him feel like an itinerant kid again. Worthless, smelling like shit, and no more than a face you pass by when driving on the road.

He could have sworn that a corrosive, chemical stench clung to the air around the former plant even now. It would've been easy to pass it off as rising out of the ground, or from the refuse of the fire, or from the wood, roofing, and clapboard of the remaining, now-abandoned buildings. But, truth be told, Dane actually believed the air itself was stained with scent no wind, rain, season, or time lapse could weaken. As if the explosion and fire had left something embedded there forever.

Dane shivered and wrapped his arms around himself, checking his men just to make sure they were still there. He walked through the ash clumps and piles, skirting the most dangerous husks of debris. The site's status as a crime scene prevented him from ordering a full-scale cleanup to give the land back to nature, but he didn't understand why the ash hadn't blown away or dissipated. Instead, there seemed to be more of it every time he came here, as if it were feeding off itself, a constant reminder of the site's squandered potential and profits that should have been expanded across a vast acreage instead of burned to the ground.

What had been produced here, after all, could've been far more valuable than oil or even gold. Food was the future—a commodity, soon to be a resource, to be valued like any other. It used to be that he who controlled the oil controlled the world. Just ask OPEC. But soon, he who controlled the food would control the world. And that should have been him, thanks to a concoction originally conceived, in principle, by his father and developed by Dane Corp's scientists. Fifty million dollars later and thanks to the latest in DNA and RNA technology, along with a whole bunch of other stuff Dane couldn't comprehend in the least.

He took a deep breath and spun his eyes around, suddenly realizing that his men were nowhere in sight. Even Pulsipher was gone from his post riding Dane's shadow, never more than fifty feet back. They were all gone, swept away in the brush of dust, dirt, and ash whipping along on the wind. He wanted to call for Pulsipher, wished he'd taken the walkie-talkie the head of his security detail had tried to give him. Dane hated the constant squawk and chatter, found it disrespectful to carry in a place he considered hallowed ground, no matter how soured by greed and death.

Then he spotted a huge shape walking toward him from the position Pulsipher should have been occupying. Walking with the sun at his back, forcing Dane to shield his eyes with a hand cupped to his brow to follow his approach. His height and width of his shoulders made him the biggest man Dane had ever seen up close, and that included a bevy of professional athletes from football and basketball. They were big, sure, but something about this man made them seem, well, small by comparison.

He realized the big man was holding a hand tucked behind his back. When he came close enough into view, Dane also noted his peaked cheekbones and protruding forehead and figured him for Slavic in origin, Russian maybe. He had crystal-blue eyes that seemed not to blink and ash-colored hair trimmed close to his anvil-shaped head.

"The insurance company isn't coming, Mr. Dane," he greeted, in an accent that was only vaguely Russian, his hand still tucked behind his back. "You'll be doing business with me, instead."

Dane reflexively swept his gaze about again.

"Don't bother," the big man told him.

With that, the man brought his hand around from behind him and tossed what he'd been holding onto the ground directly in front of Dane. It bounced once and then stopped, rocking slightly, with a pair of bulging eyes peering straight at him.

Pulsipher's eyes.

Attached to Pulsipher's severed head, which was shedding blood and gore in a pool around where it had come to a rest.

"You have something the people I work for want," the big man told him.

63

MANHATTAN, KANSAS

"You still haven't told me what we're doing here, Jones," Cort Wesley said, after a flash of Jones's ID got them through the crime scene barrier erected of tape, sawhorses, and concrete blocks around the rubble that had been Pat Roberts Hall the night before. "What this has to do with Anton Kasputin, aka Alexi Gribanov, and whatever it was my dad and Jim Strong were working back in eighty-three?"

Jones stopped just short of the rubble that had spilled out from the building's sprawling footprint. "Tell me what you make of what you see."

"Whoever did this has done it before," Cort Wesley told him.

"Brilliant. If I wasn't already on my feet, I'd give you a standing ovation," Jones sneered. "Now tell me something you think I might not know."

"You plan on answering my question?"

"That's what I'm doing. Now, what else does what you see tell you?"

Cort Wesley gave the rubble a longer look. "The bomber placed the explosives, shaped charges probably, in the basement. Six to eight of them would be my guess, planted at key structural points to achieve what you're looking at right now. How much of this building was taken up by that bioterrorism facility?"

"An entire floor, give or take. So security should've been tight. Metal detectors and bag searches, if I'm remembering correctly, which makes me wonder how he got those charges through."

Cort Wesley gave that some thought. "If it were me?"

"If it were you."

"I'd come disguised in the uniform of a campus or, better yet, local policeman. Maybe even highway patrol, something like that. Someone security guards wouldn't necessarily know but would respect, thanks to his badge."

"Makes sense."

"Any video feed to help us in that regard?"

Jones shrugged. "Just the cameras mounted outside, and we're checking them. Feeds from the interior cameras weren't backed up and were lost in the blast. And try this out for size: a female security guard was found dead in her vehicle outside a diner in town last night."

"Our guy, obviously."

"Sure as shit, unless she happened to swipe her ID to access what used to be this building maybe an hour after her death."

Cort Wesley figured that would be a stretch even for Leroy Epps and turned his gaze back on the rubble. The multitude of other authorities on scene, in addition to the rescue crews still desperately checking for survivors amid the rubble, gave him and Jones a wide berth, thanks to the Homeland Security IDs dangling from their necks.

"Whoever did this would know about the cameras," he told Jones. "He'd know about everything."

"Ever heard the word *agroterrorism* before, cowboy?"

"Not until you brought it up."

Jones joined him in surveying the rubble again. "Well, this place housed our best experts in the field. You are looking at the remains of the nation's biggest storehouse of brains and information on potential attacks on our food supply. They'd run the simulations, the scenarios. This was the NORAD of America's heartland, and losing the personnel and the knowledge based here is devastating to the cause."

"What about redundancy?"

"Cloud backup can't help you with interpretation or reactive strategizing. Assume what was happening in Texas had already registered on this facility's radar. We'll be able to dig up whatever findings they did share, but not their latest thinking on the subject or the kind of hypotheticals they were running. NORAD, just like I said. If you're going to launch an attack by air, you take out Cheyenne Mountain. If you're going to launch an attack on the land, you take out this."

"Suggests an expedited timetable . . ."

"Yes, it does."

"But still not what we're doing here."

"There was a survivor, cowboy, and he's waiting to talk to us."

64

SAN ANTONIO, TEXAS

Caitlin sat in her SUV for a time, letting the cabin cool before driving off. She ran the blower on high, still overheating inside from her exchange with Congressman Asa Fraley. She wasn't confused for one moment about how his tires had ended up scattered across the parking lot, and she couldn't resist staying until a flatbed arrived to truck his damaged vehicle away. A big, black SUV. Caitlin pictured him riding in the back, deluded by his own self-importance. When he finally left, it was in the back of a taxi, crammed inside with his aides. Their eyes met briefly when the cab pulled away and Caitlin couldn't resist casting him a wave.

Nice work, Colonel, she thought.

But the current lightness of her mood couldn't lessen the serious nature of being called to testify before a congressional committee chaired by someone who despised her. Fraley would have all the power in that scenario, committed to doing his utmost to destroy her. The Department of Public Safety and Austin in general publicly saluted her prowess and heroism, while privately bemoaning the spate of lawsuits against the state that she left in her wake. Gunfights caused damage, and parties were lined up three deep in state court with claims aimed at making Texas pay up for the losses incurred. There was even a hundred-million-dollar lawsuit currently stalled in the courts, brought by the stockholders of the former MacArthur-Rain company, who blamed Caitlin for its demise in the wake of the implosion of its corporate headquarters, which had also claimed the life of its CEO, Harmon Delladonne.

Sooner or later the cumulative effect of all that was bound to catch up to her. Asa Fraley knew that as well as Caitlin did, and confronting her with all the assembled facts and innuendo collectively might well be enough to move the State of Texas to finally take action.

Maybe she'd ignore the subpoena, let them come and arrest her instead.

She finally pulled out of the parking lot to head back to Ranger Company F headquarters, located a few miles from the Alamo, picking up the 410 just down the road from the heliport. She checked her phone yet again to see if an e-mail, text, or voice mail had come from Doc Whatley about what she'd asked him to check at the grazing fields of both Christoph Ilg and Karl Dakota.

She'd driven maybe two miles down the 410, from the Department of Public Safety heliport when she saw the construction worker standing in the middle of the road, brandishing a handheld stop sign. Looked like a dump truck had lost its load of gravel smack-dab in the middle of the roadbed, requiring a front loader or shovel to clear. A few cars ahead of her were threading their way through a narrow passage that took them to the very rim of the shoulder, beyond which lay a drainage culvert that had swallowed more vehicles than any auto salvage junkyard in the county.

Caitlin angled her SUV to follow them, the residue of her meeting with Calum Dane clinging to her like the stench of an oil fire from a blown-out rig. She'd been on the scene of several of those when sabotage was suspected, enough to know that no amount of hot water and soap could wash it off. It wasn't so much a smell as a residue that clung to the skin like stubborn beach sand.

Something about Calum Dane made Caitlin want to scrub herself clean. She'd gone up against more than her share of cold-blooded murderers, assassins, serial killers, and predators of all sorts. Dane was none of these but somehow worse than any of them. She felt in him a capacity to do virtually anything, under a complex and correct assumption that he could get away with it. That's what made him so dangerous and left her skin feeling coated by the grime of what he brought to the world. One thing all the monsters she'd confronted had in common was, deep down, they knew their days were numbered, that their time was borrowed and not owned. Calum Dane, on the other hand, was a portrait in vain self-assurance that apparently morally immunized him for taking a belt to his own son.

She'd been trying to think what bothered her so much about the brief glimpse she'd caught inside his office on the way to his personal gymnasium. The walls were utterly bare; no pictures, memorabilia, hangings—nothing at all. Caitlin took that as a symbol of him being a man who wasn't about to give anything away about himself, his true nature insulated by his great wealth, which left him capable of doing anything he felt his entitlement allowed. No compromise or quarter given. The kind of man who gives a million bucks to charities supporting the people whose lives he chews through and spits out.

It was finally her turn to slide onto the shoulder to move past the gravel pile and the traffic snarl it had caused. Caitlin was still thinking of Calum Dane when she eased her SUV forward, noticing in the side-view mirror the crew member holding the portable stop sign lowering it suddenly, attention focused on her instead of the cars stacked behind her.

That gave her the extra instant she needed to go for her pistol and drop down beneath the dashboard in the last moment before the gunfire started.

65

SAN ANTONIO, TEXAS

The shoulder harness held fast to her, and Caitlin barely managed to get it unclasped as shards of glass from the punctured windshield rained down upon her. The gunfire seemed to be coming from three sides at once, all but the rear, the echoes of it mixing with the pings and pocks of the glass breaking apart, the pieces clacking against each other as they flew. She heard the clang of metal dinging and the blare of horns sounded by the hands of stalled drivers desperate to escape.

She thought she might have been screaming herself, but she wasn't sure. She maintained the presence of mind not to fire off her drawn SIG blindly or to drop down out of the SUV, where the multiple fusillades would find her before she could do any worthwhile damage.

Rat-tat-tat . . . Rat-tat-tat . . .

Automatic fire now—or maybe it had been there from the start. She had a twelve-gauge stowed in the SUV's cargo bed. Reaching it meant climbing over the seat with bullets still burning the air in all directions, but Caitlin couldn't see winning this fight against five, maybe six shooters with only a pistol.

So she pushed herself up and over the center console, into the back seat, through the fury of fire that pushed air through her ears and left her actually feeling the heat buzz of the gunshots whizzing past her. The sound was deafening, banging off the SUV's interior in all directions at once now, the hot, sulfury smell burning her nostrils, a few of the bullets coming so close they seemed to singe her shirt. It was just as her father and grandfather had always said about how senses got "supersized" in a gunfight. That was her grandfather's term, even though she could never remember him eating at McDonald's.

She dropped a hand over the backseat, into the hatch. Caitlin managed to free the shotgun and draw it up and over the seat, rising just enough to steady it, with her gaze cast briefly out of the rear window pockmarked by shots pouring in through the windshield. Enough of the glass was still whole that she could spot a shape growing before her, seeming to fly over the twisted and tangled snarl of traffic like some dark-clad Peter Pan. Superimposed directly over the SUV's rear windshield wiper, which had somehow frozen straight up, at a ninety-degree angle, over the now-webbed glass.

Guillermo Paz held an assault rifle in either hand, balanced perfectly in his twin grasp as he leaped from one car roof or hood to another, the steel crinkling from his vast bulk. He was zigzagging as he opened fire, muzzle flashes flaring from both bores, though Caitlin couldn't hear his twin barrages above the constant din of bullets continuing to pound her SUV.

She burst upward when the sudden onslaught of his assault forced the enemy fire to abate just enough to tell her Paz's presence had been duly noted. Her first shot blew out the sunroof, deafening her as she crashed through the remnants of the glass.

Caitlin barely heard her next blast, or the two that followed. She'd vanished into the gunfighter's haze, which was brightened only by targets lit up like Christmas trees, cutting through the outskirts of her vision against an empty backdrop. She was conscious of the deafening crescendos of her shots, in contrast to Paz's staccato assault fire. Her skin felt clammy, her shirt moistened by sweat, not blood. Paz was firing from almost directly behind her now, the heat of his bullets whisking past her almost as close as the ones that had blazed through the vehicle.

The gunman who'd been wielding the stop sign was

wheeling her way, running for cover, when Caitlin blew half his head off with the twelve-gauge. Her SUV rattled under the fire of two remaining gunmen, who must've escaped Paz's fire, thanks to whatever cover they'd taken.

Screw this!

Caitlin dropped back down through the sunroof, snaring her shirt on a jagged shard of glass, behind the wheel again with a big chunk of fabric torn away behind her. The SUV's engine was still on, racing as if in panicked protest of the fate being suffered by the vehicle.

Ducking low again beneath the dashboard, Caitlin jammed the SUV into gear and floored the accelerator, tires first screeching and then finding purchase over the debris-strewn roadbed. Angling away from the shoulder, she felt a jarring impact against the vehicle behind which the last two gunmen were covered, forcing them into the open.

Then the cacophony of Paz's dual fire, one seeming to echo the other.

A few final shots from the area of spilled gravel before her.

Then, nothing at all.

66

Jack Jerry—PhD, according to his title—wasn't the only member of the bioterrorism unit housed in Pat Roberts Hall to survive, just the only one with the kind of security clearance indicative of someone involved in the most high-level projects, deemed to involve a threat to the homeland—in this case an agroterrorist threat, specifically.

Jones explained that was his specialty. "But according to security logs, he hasn't been to his lab in a week."

"Why?"

"Everybody who knows the answer to that is buried under maybe ten thousand tons of rubble," Jones said, as they stepped out of the sedan that had been waiting for him at the airport when they landed.

"You see him as a potential accomplice?" Cort Wesley wondered.

"I did initially," Jones said, leaving it there.

Jack Jerry lived alone in a University Heights cul-de-sac just off, or on the outskirts of, the Kansas State campus. The grass was so green and uniformly trimmed that it looked painted onto the ground. The house was easy to spot, due to the bevy of vehicles parked on the street before it and in the driveway—officials from local, state, and now federal agencies, here to keep Dr. Jack Jerry either safe or under guard. Cort Wesley couldn't ascertain which yet.

"People I spoke with hinted that Jerry may have mental problems, some sort of disorder," Jones explained, after they'd flashed their Homeland Security badges to those manning the first line of defense and proceeded up to the next pair, stationed before the front door. "There's some issue with his medication. Know what he does to relax? Plays a rodeo clown on the Chisholm Trail circuit here in Kansas."

"You're kidding."

"Let's find out," Jones said, flashing his ID to both uniformed officers standing on either side of Jack Jerry's front door. "You haven't asked what his specialty is."

"I figured you'd tell me when you were ready."

"He's an entomologist."

"I don't even know what that is."

"Insects, cowboy," Jones said, and knocked on the door. "The man's an expert in all things insects."

Dr. Jack Jerry answered wearing the greasepaint, colored face, wig, and clothes of his rodeo clown persona.

"Howdy, partners!" he greeted, smiling buoyantly behind eyes both glazed and glassy.

Cort Wesley couldn't tell if he was under- or overmedicated, but figured he must be suffering from bipolar disorder.

"Come on in! The show's about to start!"

67

MANHATTAN, KANSAS

The inside of Jack Jerry's house was freezing, the soft hum of the air conditioner creating background noise that reminded Cort Wesley of the sea heard from a distance. But it was the walls that claimed his attention. They were dominated everywhere by framed portraits and pictures of famous rodeo clowns, starting with Flint Rasmussen, who was a seven-time winner of the Man in the Can award.

"I prefer Johnny Tatum," Jerry told Cort Wesley, his eyes somewhere between him and Jones, as if unable to settle on which to focus on. "And this here's Quail Dobbs," he continued, pointing to a framed photograph blown up so much as to look grainy and out of focus. Then he moved to another. "But my all-time favorite is the great Slim Pickens here. Folks know him better as an actor, of course, but he made his bones, and broke plenty of them, as one of the best clown broncobusters ever. I heard he could entertain the crowd by hanging on upside down. Now folks look at him and all they think of is old Slim riding an A-bomb all the way to its Russian target in *Dr. Strangelove*, like it was bucking bronc."

Cort Wesley was having trouble focusing on the words coming through a pair of lips painted bright orange on a man smeared with greasepaint. It turned out Jerry wasn't wearing a wig, but his overly long, unkempt hair seemed to extend in all directions at once, more likely a result of poor grooming than a part of his costume. Whatever illness Jack Jerry, PhD, was afflicted with, he was definitely off his meds. Cort Wesley had heard stress could be a contributor there, too, and that was certainly the case here, making him wonder all the more what exactly Jerry had been working on at the lab that had been reduced to rubble the preceding night.

"I'd love to come watch you in action," Cort Wesley told him. "Bring my boys, too."

"Leave me your number. I'll call you when I book my next show."

"You been on the circuit lately, Dr. Jerry?"

"No, sir. Not lately. Been too busy. Lots going on, too much, lots of studies, projections, and scenarios I had to work up." Jerry narrowed his eyes, crinkling the greasepaint around them and cracking the portions that had dried too tight. "I'm allowed to talk to you, right? Being that you're from Homeland Security."

"Most definitely," Jones told him. "You should feel free to tell us anything. About these studies, projections, and scenarios you just mentioned."

"Which one most interests you?"

"Tell me about the most recent one," Jones said, trying so hard to sound comforting and reasonable that it seemed to actually hurt him.

"I can't." Jerry leaned forward, voice reduced to a whisper. "Top secret."

"We're Homeland Security, remember?"

"Oh, that's right."

STRONG LIGHT OF DAY 303

"So you can tell us."

"Better to show than tell."

"Show us what?" Jones said, stealing a sidelong glance toward Cort Wesley.

"Follow me," Jerry said, moving down the hall. "Right this way."

68

SAN ANTONIO, TEXAS

"Well, Hurricane," D. W. Tepper said, taking the seat next to her in the backseat of his truck, "it appears as if you've broken your own record. Over two hundred rounds fired, and still counting."

Caitlin didn't bother asking him if that included both sides. Tepper had left both doors of his truck open to keep air flowing through the cab and help her cool off, but so far she still felt like she was fighting off a fever.

"Here's a big surprise for you," he continued. "None of the gunmen were carrying IDs. You want to tell me who's got it in for you this time?"

"Calum Dane would be the most obvious choice, Captain, but this isn't his style."

"An ambush and gunfight on a major interstate, Ranger? Just whose style would that be?"

"My guess is their pictures and prints will come back Russian."

"How you figure that exactly?"

"Because it's the only thing that fits, where all this seems to be leading."

"Oh boy, those category ten winds are blowing this into an international incident now. Wasn't taking on China enough, or do you have to mix it up with every superpower on the planet?"

Caitlin had stripped off her shredded shirt to find streaks of color and threads missing, from bullet trails drawn that close over her frame. She'd slipped on a T-shirt over her sports bra, from a change bag Tepper always kept with him—maybe for a decade, judging by its dry mustiness. She gazed out of the open truck to find Guillermo Paz still standing on the other side of the roadbed, leaning against the wheel well of his massive truck, big enough to basically block the four-foot-high blackwall tire. Both his arms and feet were crossed casually, as if he were resting up for the next battle.

"Did you know he was riding your shadow?" Tepper asked her.

"Not until he shredded the tires on Asa Fraley's Suburban, back at the heliport."

"Yeah, I heard about that," Tepper said, massaging his scalp. "Report said something about down to the rims."

"Accurate, from what I saw."

Tepper slid back out of the truck, slammed the door behind him, and took a few steps back. Then he popped a Marlboro into his mouth and turned away from the wind to fire it up.

"You want one?" he offered, pressing the Lock button on his car remote to seal the door, in case she tried to throw it open.

"I'd rather let something worthwhile kill me, Captain," Caitlin said through the open window.

"I imagine that's what Congressman Fraley would like to do, but he'll probably settle for hauling your ass before that committee of his."

"The son of a bitch is in the NRA's pocket and he wants to embarrass me for excessive violence?"

"Something like that. But there's a long line ahead of him right now."

"How's that?"

Tepper gazed back toward where the bodies of seven gunmen had been staked off. Crime scene techs were busy scrutinizing every inch of road and vehicle, including the pile of gravel dropped in the road to set the ambush. Trace its origins and they'd be that much closer to the route taken by the gunmen to get here.

"Only seven bodies, by my count, Hurricane. I believe that leaves several hundred million more Russians for you to fix in your sights."

Caitlin got the door unlocked and stepped out. "How about you tell me more about the time my dad came up against them back in eighty-three?"

Tepper backed off, turning to the side to protect his cigarette from her. "What makes you think I know any more?"

"Because I'm figuring you must've been there, D.W."

69

"Who else knows about this?" D. W. Tepper asked Jim Strong.

"You're looking at him."

"So you've decided to fight the Cold War all by yourself."

"Somebody's gotta do it, D.W., and who better than the Texas Rangers?" Jim said, forcing a smile. "Hell, all these Indian marauders and Mexican bandits we've handled over the years—what's a few Russians?"

"That's not your call."

"Maybe it wasn't, but it is now. My man's the one inside, and I don't think he'd take kindly to working with anybody else."

"This being Boone Masters."

"The very same."

"You check his sheet before you decided to deputize him?"

"I didn't deputize him."

"Might as well have, Ranger. And what did you have to promise him to get him to cooperate?"

"To keep his son out of jail for being an accessory to his crimes."

"You got evidence that would stick?"

"Not even close. But Masters doesn't know that."

Tepper fired up a cigarette and offered up another

from his pack, which Jim declined. "Those'll be the death of you, D.W."

"You mean if you don't beat them to it. So what's the play?"

They went to lunch at La Fonda, San Antonio's oldest Mexican restaurant. Jim ordered the espinacas omelet with a side of hash browns while D. W. Tepper opted for migas La Fonda and a fruit cup that came out first.

They picked up their discussion with Jim explaining the rows of tanks labeled Propane that Boone Masters had spotted in Anton Kasputin's warehouse, all the stolen merchandise likely just a front for whatever the Russian was really up to.

"You mind telling me how you came by the information that the KGB was using Texas as a launching pad for some attack meant to level the country?" Tepper interjected, before he'd finished.

"I had a source," Jim Strong said evasively.

"Reliable?"

"FBI agent doing surveillance, pissed off that no one was acting on his reports that the Cold War was heating up right under our very noses."

"Maybe they ignored them because it's Texas. Been known to happen with the Feds." Tepper nodded, his mind sorting through all the complications. "Which begs the question, Why isn't the FBI sitting here with us? Tell me that. You can't, can you? And that tells me you don't have enough faith in the information to run it up higher on the flagpole, either."

"That what you think?"

"I just said it, didn't I?"

"And since when do you have an overwhelming desire to work with the Feds? As I recall, you've thought the same thing about them I have, since they squelched our investigation into those murdered college kids on Galveston Island a few years back."

"True enough, Ranger," Tepper conceded. "But I might be prone to make an exception in the interests of goddamn *national security.*"

"Problem being, my source really didn't have much to go on. I got more Shinola than shit to share, and my experience with the Federal Bureau of Bullshit is that they're more likely to fan a fire than put it out. They would've laughed me out of the office, or believed me just enough to spook Kasputin and his boys. So I figured, if there really was something here, only way to dig it out would be to handle the shovel myself."

Their meals came, the portions so large they were spilling off the plates.

"So what drove Kasputin and his boys to come in and wipe out that other gang?"

"I think Stanko was just biding his time, laying the groundwork. Once things turned operational, he became a liability, his contribution done and his worth a flat zero. They sent in the A team, and now that A team is behind whatever they intend to do with those tanks Boone Masters got himself a look-see at."

Tepper started to work his fork into his migas La Fonda, then stopped. "You read the reports detailing all the chemical and biological shit the Soviets are working on back home?"

"Nope."

"That's why you'll never make captain."

"Who needs all that administrative shit anyway? I prefer working a gun, not an office."

Tepper dug into his meal but didn't seem to enjoy it much. "Bump in pay might be helpful to a man raising a daughter. Old Earl still taking Caitlin to the shooting range?"

"More often than I'd prefer. She smells like gun oil, when most little girls are discovering perfume."

"The smell of which she'd probably hate."

"For sure, D.W."

Tepper leaned forward over his plate, seeming to forget about it. "Tell you what else is for sure, Ranger. We're gonna need more than just two of us to stage a full-scale raid."

"Who said anything about a raid?"

Tepper's only condition for coming on board was that he wanted no direct contact with Boone Masters, insisting he couldn't stand the sight of the man and didn't want to mix with him. So, the next day, Jim Strong met Masters alone at the Blue Bonnet Café for the pie happy hour the restaurant had been hosting almost since its founding in 1929.

"Why couldn't we just meet in a bar?" Masters said to him, seeming uncomfortable in such a mundane, homey setting.

"Someone like me meeting someone like you in a bar is bound to raise eyebrows. Could even get back to the Russians, which would do neither of us any good."

"That's for sure. You don't drink, do you?"

"Not a drop anymore. I'm done with those demons."

"My dad said never to trust a man who didn't drink."

"Is this before or after he beat you senseless?"

"Sounds like a man familiar with the scorecard," Masters told the Ranger.

"The mother of my little girl was murdered by Mexican druggers. I got myself in a bad way for a time after it happened, until I realized the booze made me not much good to myself or anybody else. I drank because it gave me the illusion I was in control, but I never really was. The booze was doing all the controlling." He saw Boone Masters look away and leave his gaze aimed away from him, as if afraid Jim might see something Masters was. "It would appear I've touched a nerve here."

"I've had some issues too."

"Past them, I trust."

"Or what, you'll arrest me?"

"Not so long as we're playing for the same team."

"That won't last, Ranger."

"I suppose not," Jim said, as a waitress set their pie plates down before them. "So let's make the best of it while we can."

"What's next?" Boone asked him. "What is it you need me to do, exactly?"

"What you do best, Mr. Masters: steal something."

* * *

Jim Strong and D. W. Tepper stood off the road a ways, what they judged to be a safe distance from Anton Kasputin's warehouse in Lolo.

"I can't see a goddamn thing," Tepper groused, lowering the binoculars. "How about a hill or rooftop, anything to better the angle?"

"There's a truck coming," Jim said, instead of responding. "It's Masters."

They watched Masters park the truck outside the darkened slab of an abandoned gas station, its pumps still advertising prices gone for more than a decade, in numbers placed manually on a once-lit marquee. Jim thought it said fifty-five cents, but couldn't be sure from here.

"Tell me again why we're not just raiding the place," Tepper said, handing the binoculars over.

"Because we can't be sure this is all the tanks that say 'Propane.'"

"What if they *are* propane, Jim?"

"Then I'm an asshole, and probably a former Texas Ranger, too, who got bit by excess diligence."

"Excess diligence," Tepper repeated. "I like that. You ever use it in court to justify a shooting?"

"I never had to justify a shooting."

Tepper turned his naked eye on the warehouse complex, following the shape of Boone Masters edging his way through the darkest reaches, all the way to the entrance. "First time for everything, like that little girl of yours becoming a Texas Ranger."

"That's her grandfather's intention, not mine."

"But how's it sit with you?"

"Well, that little girl is already as good a shot as I am, so I guess it sits just fine."

Boone Masters reached the same door through which his last boosted supply of major appliances had been loaded into the warehouse. The lock was a standard Master, which he worked his picking tools through with ease. It was fastened waist high in the door, latched to a security bar that extended across the door to prevent it from being raised. He worked in the dark, by feel, picturing the workings of the lock as he manipulated the tumblers into place.

While waiting for them to click into place, for some reason his thoughts turned to his fifteen-year-old son, Cort Wesley. Out here in the cold and dark, wondering if this was what he wanted for the boy twenty-five years from now. It wasn't a topic that crossed his mind much. But he'd been mostly sober for weeks, and working with the Texas Rangers to keep the kid out of jail had turned his thinking in that direction. Cort Wesley was a fine athlete and smart as a whip when he wanted to be. This whole experience had left Boone looking at his son a whole different way. He wasn't a man to preach change to himself or promise something to anyone he couldn't deliver.

It came down to a future he'd considered no more for his boy than he had for himself, never really thinking Cort Wesley could or would amount to any more than he had. No reflection on the kid as much as on himself.

Click.

The tumblers fell into place and Boone eased the lock off. Pocketing it, he eased the door up enough to scoot under and then slid it down quietly back into place again.

"Uh-oh," D. W. muttered beneath the binoculars he was holding against his eyes again. "We got one guard, no two, checking the entrance. Appears they noticed the picked lock."

No way, of course, Boone Masters could've locked the garage-style door behind him again, since the logistics required him to lower it back into place to disguise his presence.

"Your boy's a sitting duck," Tepper continued, extending the binoculars out toward Jim Strong.

Jim didn't take them. "My boy?"

"Would you prefer partner?"

"Just stay here and keep me covered," Jim said, slipping out toward the street.

"What exactly you planning on doing, Ranger?"

"You'll be the first to know, D.W."

At that moment, Masters was illuminating his path through the cluttered warehouse floor with a thin flashlight that fit in his pocket, the beam remarkably bright.

Merchandise, in the form of major appliances—fridges, washers, dryers, and ranges, mostly—was jammed in tight as sardines, no call or quarter given to potential damage. The whole scene, even in the dark, seemed to indicate that Anton Kasputin didn't give a shit about the stuff. That this whole gangster thing was just a front for his true purpose, rooted somehow in those tanks containing something other than propane.

But what?

Not his concern right now. He was here to keep his kid out of jail, so Cort Wesley could have a chance to do and be better than him. Strange how that never occurred to him while the boy was riding in a truck bed keeping stolen goods from toppling out the back. How old had he been the first time Boone had taken him on a job? Twelve maybe? Boone had been drunk that night and couldn't really say. He'd had his share of bad times, and the booze only made things worse. And he'd never told anybody, not a soul, that he'd really cut back 'cause of his kid.

The older Cort Wesley got, the more he started to look like his father, and that gave Boone even more cause to rethink his own choices. He didn't want the boy to look in the mirror in twenty years and see the same thing Boone did now. The reddish veins painting both cheeks, the bloodshot, tired eyes, the thick hair that seemed to hang limp all the time these days. Boone had never really thought or cared about embarrassing anyone, and now here he was, hating the fact that he might embarrass his son. Maybe he wouldn't be thinking twice about it if Jim Strong hadn't enlisted his particular services after their bar fight. He didn't really care about being a great father; he just wanted to make sure his son became a better man than he was.

Boone's beam finally reflected off the gray steel assortment of tanks stacked on shelves against the far wall. All he needed was one, and he let the flashlight guide him there to grab it.

Jim Strong could see one of the two guards raising the unlocked door as quietly as he could, then drew his gun as the other man led the way inside. He picked up his pace, first to a jog and then to an all-out dash. He reached the door to find it still propped up halfway, and he bent at the waist to slip beneath it inside.

Jim could see a single flashlight sweeping lightly through the air near a side wall half the length of a football field away. That light, added to the slight bit sneaking in from the parking lot, proved just enough to catch a glimpse of the guards and follow their motion across the floor littered with stolen merchandise. Local police would've had a field day with the contents, but this was about plenty more than that. There was a whole lot of hurt in whatever was really inside those tanks, and he was the only one right now standing between it and a whole lot of hurt, if he didn't do his job.

The two guards were hanging close, one leading the other forward. That was good because it provided an opportunity to take them out together, but bad because . . . he had to take the men out together.

Jim didn't give the situation much more thought than that. He had his Model 1911 .45-caliber pistol in hand, but he holstered it in favor of a jagged two-by-four that must've broken off a loading pallet or something. It was a yard long, the length of a baseball bat basically, which was just the way Jim intended to use it.

The Russian bringing up the rear never saw or sensed him. Jim cracked the stray two-by-four into his skull and felt the wood splinter on contact. That left him with less board than he'd started with but still enough to deal with the other man. The angle was all wrong for a roundhouse strike, so Jim jabbed the splintered end forward, driving it into the other Russian's guts hard. The man uttered a wheeze and doubled over, freeing Jim to shatter what was left of the two-by-four on the back of his skull. He crumpled over and hit the floor. Both men were down now, and neither had even gotten a decent look at him.

Boone Masters spotted Jim Strong before he noticed the bodies, rotating his flashlight from one side to the other.

"You been busy, Ranger," Boone noted, a single tank labeled Propane strung from his shoulder by a makeshift harness. "Any idea what's really in this thing?"

"Thanks to you, that's what we're gonna find out."

And that's when the warehouse's overhead lighting snapped on.

"Is this the way you do business, comrade?" Anton Kasputin asked Boone Masters.

70

Tepper stopped his tale when his phone beeped with an incoming text message.

"You're kidding, right?" Caitlin prodded. "You can't stop there."

Tepper held the phone farther away from his eyes and then tried squinting. "Looks like I got no choice. Doc Whatley wants to see you, and he's got Young Roger in his office, waiting right now. He put nine-one-one at the end of the e-mail."

"You mean text."

"Sure, whatever you say."

"You owe me the rest of the story, Captain."

"Speaking of which, you still haven't told me how exactly you know I was there."

"Because you'd be the only man my father would've trusted."

"Not counting your granddad."

"Earl was busy babysitting me at the time."

"And not doing a very good job at it, based on the fact that you ended up hiding in the back of your father's pickup when a gunfight broke out."

"Well . . ."

Tepper stuck a fresh Marlboro in his mouth but stopped short of lighting it. "Wait a sec. Earl *knew?* And he still let you go?"

"It was a vacation day, so it wasn't like I was missing any school."

"Tell that to Child Services, Ranger."

"I was born for this, D.W. My grandfather knew that. So did my dad."

"Was me, I would've put you over my knee."

"I was already pretty good with a gun, don't forget."

Caitlin realized she'd lost track of time while Tepper had been telling his story. Hearing it, thinking of her father again, had left her feeling more relaxed, the gunfight seeming very far away. Her shoulder and neck muscles had loosened and it no longer hurt her chest to breathe. She'd stopped perspiring and had the presence of mind to check her SIG and snap a fresh magazine home before sliding out from the backseat again.

"Toss me your keys, D.W.," she said, eyes falling on her shot-up SUV. "Doesn't look like I'll be using my vehicle for a while."

"They're in the ignition. And I'll be expecting you to return that shirt."

She climbed behind the wheel and fired up the engine. "Just like I'll be expecting you to finish that story," she said through the open passenger-side window.

"Where's all this headed, Ranger?"

"Nowhere good, Captain. But that doesn't mean we can't stop it."

PART EIGHT

Charlie Miller started out as a Ranger around 1920. He actually was a bodyguard at one time for Pancho Villa, and he was a tough, tough old guy. After he retired, he asked a Ranger I knew named Bob Favor to come see him, and Bob later told me this story. When Bob stopped by, Charlie Miller was laid up in bed with a broken leg he had set himself. He told Bob that his horse had kicked him in the jaw and busted a couple of his teeth. He said, "Go out to my pickup and get my pliers." Bob brought him the pliers, and Charlie Miller said, "Hand me that mirror there." Bob handed it to him. Then Charlie Miller stood there with those pliers, and he pulled out three teeth, one by one. He had no whiskey or tequila or nothing, and he didn't make a sound. He told Bob, "Pain's never really bothered me much."

—Former Texas Ranger Joaquin Jackson as told to Bruce A. Glasrud and Harold J. Weiss, Jr., eds., *Tracking the Texas Rangers: The Twentieth Century*

71

"Nice office," Beriya complimented, moving about the rows of windows on three sides, as if looking for the shades that had recessed up into the walls.

"You said I had something you wanted," Calum Dane said to him. "Care to tell me what it is?"

"It's not time yet."

"That tells me you're after something more."

Beriya stopped just short of the desk Dane sat at, trying to look comfortable. "Would you like to hear about the first person I killed?"

Dane didn't answer.

"I was fifteen at the time, in secondary school. A boy spied some other boys cheating on a test. The honor code required him to turn them in, so they paid me to kill him. You know the strange thing?"

Again, Dane remained silent.

"I don't remember how much it was. You'd think I would, but I don't. What do you think that says about me?"

"That you enjoy your work."

Beriya looked about him. "As you enjoy yours, comrade."

"I'm not your friend."

"Addressing you that way is a sign of respect. Would you like to know how I killed that boy? I did it with a plastic bag," Beriya continued, without waiting for a response. "I waited behind a tree on the path through the woods he took to get home. When he walked past me, I jumped out and jammed it over his head and pulled tight. He fought and fought, took his time dying, but I remember wanting it to last longer."

"How much would it take for you to come work for me?" Dane asked him, finding his voice firmly at last.

"The happiest moment of my life was feeling that boy die. I don't think I took any money from the boys who recruited me to do it. I think maybe that's why I can't remember how much I was paid."

"You'd remember the amount I could pay you," Dane said, leaning forward in his chair.

"You're wondering if I'm going to kill you after you give me what I came for."

"I'll admit the thought has crossed my mind today."

"But you're not scared."

Dane tried to hold the big man's stare, but couldn't for very long. "I haven't been scared in a real long time, since I planted my father's coffin in the ground. He used to get drunk and beat the shit out of me. Guess that's what he enjoyed."

"I watched my father die during the rebellion in Latvia. It was my first action as a soldier. Helped me to understand what war was really like, how not all enemies wear uniforms. You know why it's so easy for me to kill?"

"Because you picture the men who murdered your father?"

Beriya's eyes dulled, no longer appearing to look at anything. "Because he taught me so much of what I know, and I need to be worthy of his teachings. He didn't have to be in the square that day, battling the cowards behind the barricades. He felt it was his duty, that it wasn't right to order another man to do what he wouldn't do himself."

"You haven't quoted me a price yet," Dane said, instead of responding. "How much to put you on the Dane Corp payroll."

Beriya smiled. "I know you had the fire at that chemical plant set. I don't expect you meant to kill anyone, but I'm curious as to how being the cause of their deaths sits with you. After all, it makes you little different from me."

"Really?" Dane managed, finding his voice when the big man finally pushed the wrong button. "How many lives have you made better with your work lately?"

"That doesn't make *you* any less guilty, *pindo*," Beriya charged, using the Russian slur for Americans that had become popular during the peacekeeping mission in Kosovo. "But it does make you a coward. I wouldn't mention it to Comrade Zhirnosky if I were you."

"Yanko Zhirnosky, head of the Liberal Democratic Party of Russia?"

"I wasn't aware the two of you were acquainted."

"His people helped arrange some oil leases for me through Gazprom in Pavlodar."

"There's no oil in Pavlodar."

Dane managed to hold Beriya's stare this time. "So I learned."

"In any event, you're going to have the opportunity to thank him personally. Comrade Zhirnosky would like to meet with you."

"In Russia?"

"No, *pindo*, Texas. He's on his way here now."

72

MANHATTAN, KANSAS

They couldn't take off because of thunderstorms in the area and Cort Wesley was growing more antsy by the minute, especially when Caitlin's phone kept going straight to voice mail. He sat close to the front of the private jet. Jones was in the back, engaging in one call after another with various parties back in Washington, the man back in his element, seeming to grow taller and broader the more he talked.

Cort Wesley was stuck with his thoughts, starting with Dr. Jack Jerry leading them into what used to be his living room. Used to be, because all the furniture had been removed to turn the whole white birch floor into a map of the United States, drawn in the kind of Magic Marker, red and blue atop the white, that holds its pungent scent even after the ink has dried. Cort

Wesley remembered them from school, hadn't thought they actually made the markers anymore. The individual states weren't labeled, but the scale of the hand-drawn map was perfect, right down to the borders between them. Incredible really.

As was something else.

More marker, a ton of it, all in black, except for some stray flickers of white from the greasepaint Jack Jerry must've sweated through, which had flecked to the floor as he worked. Somehow he'd managed to create lighter and darker shades of black, the thickest swatches like tar blotching various spots in Texas in a pattern not unlike the one showcased on a different map, visible only under ultraviolet light.

In Alexi Gribanov's office.

"Beautiful, isn't it?" Dr. Jack Jerry had asked Cort Wesley and Jones hours earlier, standing somewhere around St. Louis on the map of the United States he'd drawn on his living room floor. "What a country!"

The room's bright lighting revealed the cracks in Jerry's greasepaint rodeo clown makeup, as if he'd been wearing it for too long. Cort Wesley focused on the black blotches, so far confined to Texas, where they were both big and dark.

"Maybe not so much anymore," Jerry added sadly, as an afterthought. "Maybe never again."

"Are you aware of what happened at the bioterrorism center on campus?" Jones asked him.

Jerry turned from Cort Wesley toward him. "Boom!" was all he said. "Bad, very bad—very, very bad. Now we can't stop them. We were working on coming up with a way to stop them."

"Stop what?"

"The invasion. That's what this is—an invasion." Jerry moved closer to Texas and began pointing downward at the darkest and largest blotches he'd drawn onto the floor. Cort Wesley noticed he was reluctant to step on them. "We were close to figuring out what created them, which is the key to figuring out how to stop them. Have to interrupt the breeding cycle, have to prevent them from reproducing. Before it's too late, before they kill it all."

Cort Wesley moved close enough to Jerry to make sure the man knew he was there. "All of what?"

"The land, the crops, the country, the world—take your pick."

73

San Antonio, Texas

"How exactly do you do it, Ranger?" Doc Whatley asked her, before he'd even said hello.

"Do what, Doc?"

"Come up with stuff that defies science, police work, and the Lord himself?"

"I'm guessing you're referring to whatever you found in those grazing fields used by Karl Dakota and Christoph Ilg."

"Same as what you found in Armand Bayou," Whatley said, shaking his head. "Near mirror images. Confirmed the direction my thinking was going in, all right; you just got there ahead of me, ahead of everyone. Same tunnels dug under the surface by whatever was killing the grass in Armand Bayou and the other places, too. Nearby crops, too, creating conditions passed off to a blight."

"I think I read about it."

"No one pays much attention to such things until they become all-out scourges, Ranger," interjected the man everyone in the Texas Rangers called Young Roger, "and that's exactly where we're headed with this now."

Caitlin didn't even know his last name. Young Roger was in his early thirties now, but didn't look much older than Dylan. Though a Ranger himself, the title was mostly honorary, provided in recognition of the technological expertise he brought to the table which had helped the Rangers solve a number of Internet-based crimes, ranging from identity theft to credit card fraud to the busting of a major pedophile and kiddie porn ring. He worked out of all six Ranger company offices on a rotating basis. Young Roger wore his hair too long and was never happier than when playing guitar for his band the Rats, whose independent record label had just released their first CD. Their alternative brand of music wasn't the kind she preferred, but Dylan told her it was pretty good. Caitlin figured he had a crush on a gal guitarist named Patty.

Doc Whatley, meanwhile, had opened a volume of an ancient scientific encyclopedia set shelved behind his desk, which he claimed contained information that had yet to reach the Internet.

"Remember where we left off last time, Ranger?" he asked Caitlin, turning to a page he'd bookmarked.

"With bugs, as I recall, specifically that frass you found present on the corpses of those cattle that had been picked clean to the bone on Karl Dakota's farm."

"Beetles, specifically," Young Roger elaborated for him. "Bess beetles, even more specifically."

"Got a picture here of one to show you," Whatley said, turning the book around so Caitlin could see.

The page he'd bookmarked featured a picture of a black tank of a bug so shiny it looked as if it was wearing a leather suit. The photo displayed was labeled "life size," which put the bess beetle at over two inches in length.

"Big bastard, for sure," Caitlin noted. "But what am I looking at here, exactly?"

"Your killer, Ranger."

Caitlin was still staring at the picture of the bess beetle in Doc Whatley's encyclopedia. "And this is what you figure wiped out those cattle where they stood?" she asked him.

"Multiplied by maybe a million, yes, I do."

"Did you say a million, Doc?"

"That was my estimate, based on how the herd had no time to cluster defensively or even panic. These bugs just came out of the ground and took them as they stood."

"Are you saying they were hiding there, disguising their approach, like predators?"

"Because that's what they are," Young Roger told her. "Predators—the perfect predator, especially given the genetic mutation they've undergone."

"We can't prove that at this stage, of course," Doc Whatley interjected.

"But it's the only thing that explains behavior that would otherwise be considered aberrant for this particular species," Young Roger reminded. "Somebody took nature's perfect organism and managed to turn them into monsters. Beetles are the most diverse group of any insect. There are over three hundred thousand species known to science, and probably many tens of thousands more that are still unknown. They're found on land and in freshwater all over the world, in just about every habitat. Some species live on plants, others tunnel or burrow, some swim."

"Did you say 'swim'? A bug?"

Young Roger seemed not to hear her. "They live in families, communicate audibly, and eat voraciously."

"Not cattle, though," Caitlin raised. "Right?"

"Not under normal circumstances," Doc Whatley told her.

"But these are not normal circumstances," said Young Roger. "Not even close."

"Because they're mutations."

"Their genetics have been altered. They're bigger, faster, even smarter."

"Smarter?"

"We didn't find one single carcass in the whole

grazing field where you found those cattle stripped down to the bone," Doc Whatley said grimly.

"You suggesting they hauled their dead away?"

"Ingested would be more likely," Young Roger answered before Whatley had the chance. "And we haven't even gotten to the best part yet."

"What's that?" Caitlin asked him.

"Reproduction."

74

MANHATTAN, KANSAS

"Colonies," Dr. Jack Jerry had continued from behind his greasepaint. "Based on the geographical proximities of the seven attacks we were studying, I estimated there were as few as three, as many as five, but that number is certain to multiply. Beetles have four different stages in their life cycle. Adult female beetles mate and lay eggs. The eggs hatch into a larval stage that is wingless. The larvae feed and grow and eventually change into a pupal stage. The pupa doesn't move or feed but eventually transforms into an adult beetle. Female beetles usually lay dozens to hundreds of eggs, reproduction timed to match the time of most available food. Some beetles collect a supply of food for their larvae and lay the egg in the ball of food. Some scavenger beetles even feed their babies."

"Like you said," managed Cort Wesley, trying to make sense of it all, "the perfect organism."

"Did I say that?" Jerry asked, looking genuinely confused. "When did I say that?"

"You said hundreds of eggs," interjected Jones, his voice growing impatient.

"I don't remember saying that, either."

"How many females in each colony?" Jones asked Jerry.

"What colonies?" the man asked, growing more confused by the moment.

"As many as five," Cort Wesley reminded, "as few as three."

"Based on crop ingestions and frass samples taken throughout the state, in the hot zones we identified denoting the largest infestations . . ." Jerry started, but then his eyes grew distant and confused. "Where was I?"

"Talking about crop ingestions and frass samples."

"Oh yes, based on those, I estimated the population of each colony to be between a hundred thousand at the low end and several million at the high, maybe tens of millions by now, allowing for further anticipated growth."

"Wait a minute," said Jones, moving from California to West Texas on the elegantly drawn floor map, "are you saying each of these dark blotches across the state of Texas represents as many as *ten million* of these things?"

"Not at all. Sorry to give you that impression. I meant *tens* of millions."

"Plural," Cort Wesley noted.

Jerry took a single step to the side on his floor map, placing him closer to Kansas City now. "These beetles only do three things: eat, screw, move, then eat, screw, and move again. At each stop more females lay their eggs, and the eggs grow into larvae, and the larvae grow into pupae, and the pupa becomes an adult beetle. So each stop on the map represents another potential colony." Jerry suddenly rotated his gaze between Cort Wesley and Jones, as if seeing them for the first time. "Who are you again?"

Jones flashed the badge dangling from his neck. "Homeland Security."

"Am I in trouble?"

"Not so long as you keep cooperating, Doctor."

"Cooperating about what?"

Cort Wesley wandered closer to Texas on the floor map, from Minnesota. He found himself standing over the general area of Armand Bayou, the site from which Luke's classmates had gone missing. Not too far to the southwest was one of the tar-black blotches denoting one of the colonies Jack Jerry had described.

"Dr. Jerry?"

"That's me!" the man beamed, swinging toward him.

"Have you ever worked the Texas rodeo circuit?"

"A few times. At least, I think I have."

"Because I think I've seen you in action. Maybe at the Houston Livestock Show and Rodeo or the Fort Worth Stock Show and Rodeo," Cort Wesley said, raising the two best-known ones.

"I believe I've worked both."

"There you go, sir. You're damn good, too."

"Why, thank you!" Jerry told him, beaming again.

"I do have a question."

"About rodeos?"

"About this map," Cort Wesley said, and stepped aside so Jerry could see him point downward. "This area around Armand Bayou, right here, just above this colony you've got just to the south of it. If there were a bunch of kids sleeping outside for the night right in the colony's path . . ."

"There wouldn't be anything left of them but bones, come morning." Jerry's expression brightened, becoming almost childlike. "So you've seen me perform."

"I have indeed," Cort Wesley lied.

"And I was good?"

"Best in the show."

Jerry's smile slipped off his face, even his clown makeup and painted red lips seeming to droop. "I think something bad happened." He twisted his gaze out the window at the phalanx of police cars. "I think there's been some trouble."

"It appears that way," Cort Wesley nodded.

"And I'll tell you something else," Jerry said, his voice so somber it started to crack. "There's going to be more."

75

SAN ANTONIO, TEXAS

"Here's my question," Caitlin said to both Doc Whatley and Young Roger. "Since when did beetles become carnivorous? I knew they ate plants, but flesh?"

"Actually," said Young Roger, clubbing his hair back into a ponytail and using a rubber band to hold it in place there, "they eat all sorts of things."

"Depending on the species, of course," Whatley interjected. "And, judging from the frass I had analyzed, this is the beetle the species we're dealing with most closely resembles."

Caitlin followed his finger back to the encyclopedia and the picture of what looked like a giant insect encased in a shiny shell of armor.

"*Odontotaenius disjunctus*," Whatley continued, "the familiar bessbug, native to the eastern US and Canada, but common pretty much everywhere. They're normally wood burrowers, but the frass I examined indicates they've been living underground instead, likely having adapted, since the colony's large numbers would've made securing enough stray logs impossible."

"In other words," Young Roger interrupted, "they've adapted to their environment. Very common for insect species, which explains how they managed to outlive the dinosaurs." He looked toward the medical examiner. "You want to tell her the real fun part, Doc, or should I?"

"Patience, son," Whatley told him. "Now, according to what I've been able to gather from the frass, this species crossbred with the coleoptera beetle more common in these parts."

"Is there any scientific precedent for them becoming carnivorous?"

"Over time, beetles can adapt to practically any kind of diet. Some break down animal and plant debris; some feed on particular kinds of carrion, such as flesh or hide; some feed on wastes, fungi, or plants. Some beetles are fruit eaters." Something changed in Whatley's expression, wariness replacing the childlike gleam. "And some are predatory, Ranger. I watched a video of a ground beetle attacking an earthworm that would freeze your insides."

Caitlin looked back at the picture. "And you're saying an army of these is what dropped those cattle in their tracks and chewed them up."

"Not exactly chewed," Whatley corrected. "Beetles don't have teeth; they have pincerlike mandibles that help them crush and eat food. But that's the idea, yes. And they're also a nearly perfect organism, one of the most survivable on the planet, even more adaptable than cockroaches—and far more formidable."

"What do you mean by that, exactly?"

"Well, bombardier beetles secrete a compound they can actually shoot, potentially injuring small mammals and killing invertebrate predators outright. And the *Anthiinae* family of beetles, meanwhile, can hit their targets with similar secretions from as much as ten feet away."

"How much of this did the two of you know a couple days back?"

"Not a whole lot," Whatley shrugged.

"I don't like sleeping much anyway," Young Roger added.

"At all, more like, in this case," Caitlin corrected. "One thing, though, Doc: cattle aren't small mammals."

"No, Ranger, they're not. But a million of these

things would be enough to cover a half-acre of land in a black blanket." His face paled a bit. "I can't even picture what a swarm of them feeding on a herd would look and sound like."

"What do you mean 'sound'?"

"The bess beetle is able to produce a recorded fourteen acoustic signals, more than many vertebrates. Adults produce the sounds by rubbing the upper surface of the abdomen against the hind wings."

"But they can't fly, right?"

"Not that we know of, no."

"That's a strange way of putting it, Doc."

Whatley's expression turned dour. Young Roger took a single step forward to place himself between the older man and Caitlin.

"Now comes the fun part," said Young Roger. "A picture out of the old encyclopedia is all well and good, except for the fact what we're facing here is as advanced beyond that thing as we are from cavemen."

"The boy can't prove what he's about to say, Ranger," Doc Whatley cautioned.

"But you agree with me on most of it."

"Some, son. Some."

Caitlin planted her hands on her hips, stopped just short of stamping her foot and firing her gun into the ceiling. "Will one of you get to the point?"

Whatley nodded. "We agree on the fact that exposure to something in the soil, air, or groundwater—maybe a combination of all three—led to a drastic mutation. We're guessing the mutation would've occurred over several life cycles. Since beetles ordinarily live around a year, whatever stimulus caused the mutation would date back three or four years, probably."

"This didn't happen overnight, in other words," an antsy Young Roger added.

"I'm talking here," Whatley groused at him.

"My turn now," Young Roger said, no longer able to contain himself. "These things aren't just mutations—at least I don't believe they are."

"Then what are they?" Caitlin asked him.

"Advanced on the evolutionary scale, Ranger. I think we're looking at what beetles would have evolved into after, well, maybe another ten thousand years or so."

"Just a theory," reminded Doc Whatley, "with no proof or data to back it up."

"The proof and data is in the cattle and crops they've been eating."

"They don't actually eat the crops," Whatley corrected. "They eat the refuse and, especially, the seeds."

"Same effect."

"Not really."

"So," Caitlin advanced, before the two men could start arguing again, "these crop infestations weren't really infestations or blights at all."

"No, ma'am," said Young Roger. "The crops didn't grow at all, or grew poorly, because the seeds had been damaged or destroyed."

"You can see where we're going with this," said Whatley. "Traditionally, beetles aren't migratory by nature. But these will go anywhere there's a food supply for them, in the form of crops or cattle—anything green or flesh and blood, really."

"The whole Midwest, in other words."

"Maybe just for starters. I've been doing some figuring, Ranger. Care to hazard a guess as to how many of these things there'll be in a year's time if this continues unchecked?"

"Not really."

"Neither can I, because the figures keep climbing. A trillion at last count, or three thousand for every American, according to the last census."

"Jesus Christ. . . ."

"Yeah," echoed Young Roger, "do the math."

"That's only part of the picture," said Whatley. "That analysis of the recovered frass I did also found plenty of crop waste, too, almost like, well . . ."

"Almost like what, Doc?" Caitlin pushed.

"Like these sons of bitches are eating everything in their path, Ranger."

76

MANHATTAN, KANSAS

"Cheer up, cowboy. How bad can it be?" Jones said, his voice a bit slurred by the third whiskey he was working his way through. Jack Daniel's poured neat, in an actual glass, since they were flying private.

Their jet had finally been cleared for takeoff, and Cort Wesley found himself unable to stop picturing the hordes of beetles, making up the growing number of colonies, overrunning the entire state of Texas before spreading out in all directions.

"This is the happiest I've ever seen you, Jones. If I wasn't the only one here, I'd suspect someone had slipped something into your drink."

"It's called purpose. I've got people taking my calls again. I'm back in the game. Fuck persona non grata."

Cort Wesley had his cell phone out. "I'm calling my boys."

"It's been, what, a whole two hours since you spoke with them last?"

"What part of my youngest maybe still being a target don't you understand?"

Cort Wesley turned away from Jones to hit "Dylan" on his Contacts list, remembering how his oldest son had lost his patience teaching him how to program all the numbers and e-mail. How long ago had that been? Maybe before the boy had gone off to college—an Ivy League school, no less. What were the odds?

"Everything's fine, Dad," the boy said by way of greeting, picking up after the first ring. "Just like the last time you called."

"Nothing suspicious?"

"Nope, other than those black helicopters circling overhead."

"This isn't funny."

"I'm not going back to school until it's over."

"Put your brother on."

"Can't you call him back on his own phone?"

"I'm paying for both of them. Now get him on yours."

It took maybe half a minute before Luke came on.

"I'm on my way home," Cort Wesley told him.

"You don't have to keep calling. I'm fine." But then a pause followed, heavy enough for Cort Wesley to feel the air over the line between them. "Any word on the kids from my school?"

"Not that I've heard. But you don't have to worry. Caitlin's gonna find them and bring them home."

Cort Wesley could hear Luke snickering on the other end of the line. "You talk to me like I'm ten. It's on TV twenty-four/seven. FBI's in charge now. Rangers aren't even involved anymore."

"This is Caitlin Strong we're talking about. Think that's gonna stop her?"

"The big guy was here," Luke told him.

"I know. His men still are."

"I can't see them."

"You're not supposed to. Neither will anybody stupid enough to come anywhere near the house."

"That's good." Luke paused, tension crossing over the line as Cort Wesley listened to him breathe. "Zach's parents picked him up."

"Okay," was all Cort Wesley could think to say, as opposed to something wrong.

"They didn't look too happy. I don't think they like me."

"Screw them."

"Yeah," Luke followed. "Screw them."

"I want to give them a call, tell them they've got a good kid."

"This all really sucks."

"You can't be blaming yourself."

"I wish I was bigger, I was stronger. What I'd like to do to whoever's behind this . . ."

"I know how you feel, son."

"Last year, when the big guy drowned those two men in my fish tank at school, it didn't bother me. I didn't feel anything, because I knew they were going to hurt me, and I was glad he did it. Is that okay?"

Cort Wesley almost said, wanted to say, a whole lot of things, but only a single word emerged ahead of his thoughts. "Yes."

"Can I ask you a question?" he asked Jones, once the call was done.

"Since when do you need to ask permission?"

"Last year, when you knew Luke was in trouble, you sent Paz to his school."

"Right," Jones smirked. "You're welcome."

"So you were watching him. You were watching Luke."

Jones ran his tongue around the inside of his mouth, said nothing.

"Anything you'd like to tell me?" Cort Wesley continued.

Jones looked a bit befuddled, even suspicious. "I told the Ranger he was in danger. I sent Paz to pick him up. What else are you looking for?"

"Never mind," Cort Wesley said, looking away.

77

"I'm no entomologist," Doc Whatley continued. "And, even if I was, I'd need living samples of these beetles to do a detailed study. But I can say, even absent of that, that this isn't remotely part of the natural order, leaving something *un*natural to blame for their behavior."

"As in . . ."

"Like I said before, genetic mutation would be the most obvious and likely, caused by exposure to something entered into their ecosystem that altered their DNA. Something that also accelerated their reproductive capacity and turned them into insatiable eating machines."

"Any idea what that could be?"

Whatley shrugged. "Right now, your guess is as good as mine. But if you're looking for a scientific precedent for what we're facing, check out army ants. When a colony exhausts its available food supply, it enters a nomadic phase where the ants set off to forage and consume any living thing in their path. I've read that a single colony can consume a hundred thousand animals per day."

"Hold on, did you say *a hundred thousand?*"

"I did indeed, Ranger."

"So how is it we've got something like that going on right under our noses and no one's seen these things?"

Whatley nodded, clearly having pondered that himself already. "Well, army ants march by night and rest during the day. I'd say the same could be true with these beetles, burrowing underground to nest during the daylight hours and emerging to feed on anything in their path at night."

"Sounds like they could be averse to sun or heat, maybe both. So they avoid the strong light of day."

"I guess. It could also be that these feeding phases are more sporadic than regular. And, under any scenario, the colony wouldn't have started at the level it's grown to now, remember. So any early incidents—compared to the more recent destruction of large swatches of crops, and now these livestock deaths—wouldn't have made anybody's radar."

Caitlin thought of the various areas throughout Texas where blights and animal kills were known to have taken place, including Armand Bayou, where Luke's classmates had disappeared. "One more thing, Doc. What would determine which direction these things followed?"

"Again, you're as much an entomologist here as I am. I think we'd be looking at environmental factors like soil condition—soft instead of rocky, for burrowing. And they would gravitate toward the largest sources of food supply. Remember, beetles rely primarily on their sense of smell, so it wouldn't be hard for them to move from one source to another based on which way the wind took them."

"Is there some food source that might attract them more than others?" she raised to both Doc Whatley and Young Roger.

"That's the rub, Ranger," Whatley said, jumping in first. "We don't know enough to even hazard a guess about that."

"In other words," picked up Roger, "everything we're postulating here is based on what we know about beetles, their habits and patterns. The problem is these aren't your daddy's bugs. They're mutations, genetically altered, thanks to some stimulus that disrupted their life cycle and created the superstrain we're facing now."

"Could you be a little more specific, Rog?"

"It's difficult, Ranger; all supposition at this point. But the common denominator is the farms and ranches known to suffer pest infestations, though obviously on a much smaller level."

"Pesticides," Caitlin advanced, nodding.

"Indeed," Whatley said, jumping in. "But most pesticides are essentially neurotoxins that kill everything they come into contact with. More modern methods, some of which are untested and experimental, rely on homing in on a genetic sequence that's unique to one species, thereby sparing others that are exposed."

"It's called RNA interference," Young Roger added, "and some say it's the key to eradicating all pests in the future, and perhaps hunger and famine along with them."

"What do the others say?" Caitlin asked him.

But it was Doc Whatley who answered. "That using it now, as a little paper called *The New York Times* reported, is the equivalent of using DDT as a pesticide in the 1950s—and look how that worked out." He looked toward Young Roger. "Why don't you tell her about the case that's most similar to what we may be facing with these beetles here?"

"Experiments were done with corn, incorporating a toxin into the crops that was supposed to kill root-worms. Worked like charm, for a while, until the rootworms developed a resistance to that toxin and everything else technology could throw at them. They'd become impervious to all efforts at eradicating them or even moderating their behavior. A superstrain, you might call it, that was eventually killed off by frost, if you can believe that."

"You think that describes what happened to our super-beetles."

"Not exactly, no," Young Roger told her. "Beetles aren't considered dangerous to crops, especially compared to other pests. I think the first generation of these beetles was exposed to one of these RNA compounds meant to alter the genetics of a different insect. I think it got inside them and, by the time it spread geometrically through the reproductive process, they weren't the same insects anymore. They're what you see now—an entirely different species, for all intents and purposes, and exceedingly dangerous."

"Cavemen and us," Whatley advanced, restating the metaphor. "That's the level of variance we're looking at and, unfortunately, we don't know any more about these beetles than we actually know about those cavemen."

"How much could the Soviets have known in 1983?" Caitlin asked them both, thinking of the case worked by her father, for which he'd enlisted the help of Boone Masters.

"Well, the technology wasn't there to pull this off on the level and scale we're discussing," Young Roger told her. "But they could have come up with something very close and very, very dangerous."

"Where you going with this, Ranger?" Whatley asked her.

"You don't want to know, Doc, believe me. But given what we do know, what exactly are we looking at if these things keep spreading?"

Doc Whatley swallowed hard, looking toward Young Roger, who was more than happy to respond. "The loss of a vast percentage of our crops and livestock throughout the Midwest and, before very long, California and Florida too."

"Okay," she said, "so these things are out there, and now we know it. So how do we go about stopping them?"

"How many bullets does your pistol hold?" Young Roger asked her.

"Fourteen in the mag, one in the chamber."

"Since that's a bit short of the trillion you'd need, Ranger, I'd consider calling nine-one-one."

Caitlin tried to smile but couldn't. "Normally, I'm the one who answers," she told him.

78

Caitlin sat in Captain Tepper's truck for a few minutes with the windows rolled down and the sun burning her face through the windshield. He never used air-conditioning, probably didn't even know his truck's was broken.

She'd parked in the sun outside the University of Texas Health Science Center, in which the medical examiner's office was located. Even with twilight closing in now, the cab was still warm, which helped to erase the layer of cool clamminess that seemed to have enveloped her skin during the course of her meeting with Doc Whatley and Young Roger. The minutes had literally melted into hours, but she'd still left with the anxiety of not knowing nearly enough. She couldn't recall a time when she'd been more frightened by what she was facing.

I think the first generation of these beetles was exposed to one of these RNA compounds meant to alter the genetics of a different insect. I think it got inside them and, by the time it spread geometrically through the reproductive process, they weren't the same insects anymore. They're what you see now—an entirely different species. . . .

Caitlin couldn't remember whether it was Doc Whatley or Young Roger who'd said that. Recalling it now triggered thoughts of something else, a missing piece just out of her grasp, which she couldn't quite get a handle on. Her mind flashed back to her earlier meeting with Calum Dane. He was the key to all this, somehow, starting a couple years before with the burning of his petrochemical plant—for which Dane, in Caitlin's mind, was no doubt responsible—to destroy all trace of the pesticides being produced there. And, just a few minutes before, Young Roger had suggested exposure to just such a pesticide had caused a genetic mutation that had unleashed a new breed of insects into the world, with the potential to destroy the entire heartland, with the devastating economic ramifications that presaged.

Like I told you, the sites marked on that wall map in Alexi Gribanov's office contained mostly farms and ranches. Kind of places known to use pesticides. What do you think I'd find if I checked which pesticide they'd been using?

Caitlin recalled posing that question to Calum Dane before she knew what she did now. A fresh chill grabbed hold of her, despite the steam-baked interior of Captain Tepper's truck, laced with the stench of stale cigarette smoke. She fished the cell phone from her pocket and pressed Tepper's contact.

"I can feel the winds picking up already," he greeted.

"I need you to call the land records office in Austin."

"Check the time, Hurricane. They're gone for the day."

"Then get somebody back. It's an emergency, maybe the key to this whole thing."

"Let me see, who can I piss off on your behalf? What is it you need?"

Caitlin told him.

"You're not kidding, are you?"

"Far from it."

"What is it with you? How is it you keep going from tilting at windmills to jousting with giants?"

"Not like you to wax poetic on me, D.W."

"I don't even know what that means, Ranger. Just stay by the phone and let me see what I can come up with."

79

SAN ANTONIO, TEXAS

Guillermo Paz stood outside the San Fernando Cathedral near Main Plaza in San Antonio, studying the plaque that proclaimed it to be the oldest cathedral sanctuary in the United States. Jim Bowie was married here before dying at the Alamo at the hands of Santa Ana, who used the building as an observation post. The cathedral claimed that Bowie, along with Colonel William Travis and Davy Crockett himself, had been ceremonially buried in the church's graveyard as their official resting places. But Paz knew of other locations that had made the same claim. Since the heroes' bodies had all been burned after the famous battle, he supposed anybody could claim anything they wanted to.

Paz mounted the stone steps to an odd feeling he couldn't quite identify. The double doors were open, allowing the scents of cleaning solvent and incense to pour out at once. A strange combination, for sure, and one that left Paz suddenly discomfited, his neck and shoulder muscles tensing the same way they did in the presence of an enemy.

The last time he'd been here, the floors had just been refinished with a fresh coat of lacquer, the wooden pews restored to their original condition as well. That was a source of great pride to Paz, given that the money he'd left behind on a previous visit had funded the renovation. He'd even done some of the work on the roof himself, enjoying the hot sun burning his naked back and shoulders, along with the view of the world provided from up on the hot slate. But something was off today, and he saw what it was as soon as he passed through the doors into the chapel itself.

The historic, pristine chamber in which he'd invested his money and passion, where he'd come to understand his new being and psyche, had been hit by vandals. The altar was awash in clutter, with broken pieces of the wooden statue of Jesus he'd refinished himself strewn about the shredded carpet. And, as he advanced up the aisle, past pews, knee rests, and book pockets that it looked like the vandals had taken an ax to in places, Paz was aware of a stench clinging to the air and resisting all attempts of both the solvent and incense to vanquish it.

Feces.

Someone must've have left piles of it smeared amid all the damage, maybe going so far as to pull down their pants and defecate right in the Lord's house.

Paz spotted his priest on his hands and knees at the

cathedral's front, swabbing the floor with a sponge drawn out of a bucket overflowing with suds. He was still wearing his dark slacks, shirt, and priest's collar, an ensemble to which he'd added fluorescent yellow rubber gloves.

The priest stiffened at Paz's approach, lurching back to his feet and almost spilling the pail of soapy water in the process. He looked old, his hair mussed and face reddened, the exertion plainly telling on him. His eyes had a haggard dullness to them that seemed sad as well.

"Oh, it's you," the priest said.

"Who did this, Padre?"

"If I knew that," the priest said, trying hard to smile, "I would've called you already."

"You don't have my number," Paz said, towering over him and blocking out a measure of the light coming from the flickering candles his priest had set upon the remains of the bema in a show of defiance. "So I'm going to give it to you."

This time the priest managed a slight smile. "Just a figure of speech. That isn't necessary, my son."

"I'm afraid it is, Padre. Have you ever read Aristotle?"

"Some."

"His writings were the first to turn me on to how I could find relevance to myself in the writings of others. To this day, his work still resonates the most of any of them with me, mostly because of what he had to say about friendship. Specifically, that 'without friends no one would choose to live, though he had all other goods.' When I started reading him, I didn't really have any friends, people important to me, like you or my Texas Ranger."

"Thank you, my son."

"No thanks necessary," Paz told him. "It's me who should be thanking you." He stopped and rotated his gaze about, embracing the revolting stench for what it said about whoever had done this. "Aristotle believed that friendship was all about two people engaging in common activities solely for the sake of developing the overall goodness of the other."

"That sounds like something God might say, doesn't it?" the priest asked, remarkably comfortable in Paz's presence outside the confessional that had once solely defined their relationship.

"That's the point, Padre, what all our talks have finally made me realize. 'To love another person is to see the face of God.'"

"Is that Aristotle too, my son?"

"No, it's from the musical *Les Miserables*. I forget exactly when I saw it. I had to leave early."

"What happened?"

"When the French troops stormed the barricades, I stormed the stage. Got carried away with the story." Paz stiffened again, his eyes churning through the scene around him. "Whoever did this needs to pay. I know you won't tell me to make that happen. You can even tell me not to, if it makes you feel better. But, see, I've got no choice, because I've got to make amends to you."

"For what?"

Paz turned his gaze downward, massive shoulders slumping in genuine embarrassment. "Because I keep seeking answers elsewhere—I just can't stop myself. First it was those college classes, then teaching English to immigrants. More recently I've been visiting a psychic."

The priest's expression tightened. "A psychic," he repeated, trying not to sound judgmental.

Paz shrugged. "I thought she could show me something I couldn't see on my own. A glimpse of the future, maybe. Or maybe I wanted to be connected with my mother so she could tell me I was a good man and that she was proud of me. That's what I've got to make amends for. But I always end up back here with you because, to paraphrase Aristotle, the great enemy of moral conduct is the failure to do what's right even in full awareness of what's wrong. People rely on me to do what's right now. Because there really are monsters that go bump in the night and people need me to bump back." He gazed about him again, nose wrinkling at the stench-laden air. "Like at whoever did this."

"This isn't your fight."

"If it's yours, Padre, it's mine."

"Aristotle again, my son? Or another musical, perhaps?"

"No, that one's all on me. I'm not asking you for permission or blessing here." He sniffed the cathedral's rank air again, his nostrils opening as wide as quarters. "It's a done deal."

"'God made the earth by his power,'" the priest recited. "'He founded the world by his wisdom and stretched out the heavens by his understanding. When he thunders, the waters in the heavens roar; he makes

clouds rise from the ends of the earth. He sends lightning with the rain and brings out the wind from his
storehouses.' Does that sound familiar, my son?"

"Jeremiah, chapter ten, verses twelve and thirteen."

The priest nodded, impressed. "Describing the Lord's
control over the forces of nature. Like you."

"Is that a good thing?"

"It's neither good nor bad; it just is. Like nature itself, my son." The priest seemed to shake himself from
a spell, finally peeling the yellow gloves from his
hands. "But you came here for something else. What
can I do for you?"

Paz grinned as his phone rang. "You already did it,
Padre." He checked the caller ID. "And I need to be
someplace else."

80

SAN ANTONIO, TEXAS

Cort Wesley saw Caitlin standing on the tarmac, halfway between the private terminal and the taxi ramp, as
Jones's private jet slid to a halt. Jones got up from the
other side of the plane, after unhitching his seatbelt,
and moved to electronically lower the recessed stairs
into place.

"I wouldn't be so set on deplaning," Cort Wesley
cautioned.

"Why's that, cowboy?"

" 'Cause it looks like we're headed somewhere else in a hurry."

"Why, Ranger," Jones greeted, his brain still buzzed by the whiskeys he'd drunk to celebrate his return to Homeland Security's good graces, "I'd like to say it's been too long, but . . ."

"Last time we were together, I saved your life, as I recall."

"That's right. After I got shot up because of you."

" 'Shot up,' " Caitlin repeated. "Sounds like something a Texan would say."

"Looks like you've rubbed off on me," Jones grinned. "I'm thinking of relocating on a permanent basis," he continued, butchering his impersonation of a Texas drawl. "Maybe you can recommend a real estate agent."

"Got just the man. Goes by the name of Baal Z. Bub."

"You know him from experience?"

"Nope, just reputation, but I think the two of you would get along just fine."

"You mind telling me where we're going on the government's dime, Ranger?"

"West Texas," Caitlin said, turning her gaze on Cort Wesley. "To find some missing kids."

"We should've secured a subpoena to get this information," Captain Tepper had said when he called

Caitlin back thirty minutes later, while she was still seated in his borrowed truck. "It won't be admissible in court now. No way, no how."

"I'm not looking to serve a warrant, D.W., don't worry."

"Worry about you? Why would I bother? . . . Can I ask you one question, Ranger? Just one question?"

"Yes, sir."

"Why does every single day have to end for you with a gunfight at the O.K. Corral?"

"Just tell me what showed up on those land transfers I asked you to check."

"Calum Dane's been a busy man when it comes to such things," Tepper told her. "There's pages and pages of them I got up on my computer screen right now, lost in the haze of the Marlboro I'm smoking. You hear that, Hurricane?"

"Must be from the pack stowed in that extra pair of boots you keep in the closet. I tossed out all the others. That's the pack I dipped in horse laxative."

She heard Tepper make a low guttural sound on the other end of the line before his voice returned. "I was able to roust a supervisor who was working late at the records office. Man didn't sound especially happy about it. Now, tell me what I'm looking for? There's tons of stuff, variances and the like, for that Midland skyscraper Dane built."

"Go back further."

"How far?"

"I don't know. Look for something under Glasscock County."

"There's fifty pages here."

"Do a search."

"Oh, yeah," Tepper said, and Caitlin could hear computer keys clacking, accompanied by the soft whir of the hard drive. "Got a hit here, all right. A farm in Glasscock County. Looks like Dane bought it two years ago, a whole lot later than the bulk of his other transactions. I didn't realize there were any farms left in Glasscock County, with oil having overrun the whole Permian Basin."

"There's a few, Captain, but Calum Dane didn't buy this one to grow anything but trouble."

"It's the only thing that makes any sense," Caitlin told Cort Wesley, after explaining what she'd learned from Captain Tepper, coupled with something Dane had said back in his office that she couldn't get out of her mind.

"You know what I thought of when I made my first million dollars, Ranger? Picking cotton in those fields, the scars I've still got to show for it. You'd figure I could put all that behind me, not bother looking back. But all I could think of was that farm, still up and operating with no regard for the workers out doing the picking. Time seemed to seize up whenever I thought about those days, to the point where nothing I was accomplishing seemed to matter, and wouldn't, until the farm itself was dead too."

"You figure that's the farm he bought two years ago in Glasscock County," Cort Wesley concluded. "And where he's now got the kids stashed."

"Will the two of you listen to yourselves?" Jones blurted out, words only slightly slurred, as if he were sobering up in a hurry. "You're talking about taking on one of the richest and most powerful men in America, effectively charging him with a crime that would put him away for life."

"That's just for starters, Jones," Caitlin told him. "I'm also looking at Dane for that fire at his Waco petrochemical plant from a few years back, along with the disappearance of Brandon McCabe in New York City five days ago."

"Who?"

"Young man who shot off his mouth at a Dane Corp shareholders meeting the same day he vanished."

"So you think Dane kidnapped him too?"

Caitlin's expression remained flat. "McCabe's hotel room had been sanitized by a crew of professional cleaners—the kind of crew you'd use, Jones. They got everything except some plastic shavings that a latter check I requested found stuck to the ceiling."

"Plastic shavings," Jones repeated, shaking his head. "Ranger, you never cease to amaze me."

"Then try this out: McCabe had an artificial leg. Those shavings were a match for the kind of plastic it was made out of."

"This just keeps getting better." Jones could only shake his head again, frowning. "Where's the nearest airport to this farm? I want to get going."

"We can't take off yet. Somebody else is coming."

"Not—" Cort Wesley started to protest, then veered his thoughts in midstream. "Why?"

"Because," Caitlin said, as a black pickup truck that looked more like a tank screeched to a halt in an area of the tarmac used by limousines carrying celebrities and politicians, "I think we're gonna be needing him."

And that's when her phone rang, the 202 area code of Washington, DC, flashing on her screen.

"How you doing, Congressman?" she greeted Asa Fraley, before he had a chance to announce himself.

81

SAN ANTONIO, TEXAS

"You will cease and desist on Calum Dane, Ranger," Congressman Fraley told her, his tone making it sound to Caitlin as if a snake had uttered the words.

"Sounds like something somebody else wrote for you, sir," she told him.

"Never mind who wrote it. I'm just a little ole country lawyer trying to do right for my people."

"And Dane doesn't live in your district any more than Christoph Ilg does."

"I'm talking about Texans in general, some of which clearly need to be protected from the likes of you."

"Why, I'm just a little ole Texas Ranger, Congressman. Who'd need protection from me?"

"Stow the bullshit, Ranger. I know you've been threatened with this before, but I've got the power of Congress backing me up. You don't back off this now, the president himself won't be able to save you from what's coming."

"This, or him?"

"Pardon me?"

"You started by telling me to back off Calum Dane. Now you're telling me to back off 'this.' What's 'this,' exactly, sir? Would it be my investigation into those missing kids?"

"That's not your jurisdiction."

"I'm a Texas Ranger. The whole state is my jurisdiction. And that's a fact, not a campaign slogan. Or maybe there's been concern expressed about my opening the books on that chemical plant fire. Now, Waco is part of your district, if I've got my geography right. That means a dozen of your constituents were killed in that fire, Congressman. Still want me to back off?"

"Why does everything have to be a show for you? You could've just walked up and arrested Christoph Ilg on those rustling charges, but you just had to play for the cameras."

"Not that you'd know anything about that, Congressman. And, speaking of which, how's your brother? I've got a call into his probation officer, just to make sure he's toeing the line."

Caitlin could hear Fraley's breathing intermittently over the line. "I'm writing up a subpoena as we speak. I'm gonna haul your ass before my government oversight committee with the cameras whirling. Let the whole country see what a loose cannon you are."

"Hey, Congressman?"

"Yes, Ranger."

"Boom!"

PART NINE

Since their inception the Texas Rangers have been shaped by the times in which they lived. In frontier Texas they were schooled by Jack Hays in irregular warfare against the Comanche. Under the leadership of John Jones, commandant of the Frontier Battalion, they gained a reputation as intrepid—and brutal—law enforcement officers. And in contemporary Texas, as amply demonstrated in the career of M. T. "Lone Wolf" Gonzaullas, who chased killers, tamed oil boomtowns, and became a specialist in forensic science, they have earned a reputation as shrewd detectives.

—"Texas Rangers," in *Violence in America: An Encyclopedia,* Ronald Gottesman and Richard Maxell Brown, eds.

82

"We have these all over our country, too," Yanko Zhirnosky, head of the Liberal Democratic Party of Russia, told Calum Dane.

"I know. We sold you the technology."

"Your company?"

"My country, Mr. Zhirnosky."

Zhirnosky smiled, his clothes as stiff as the burly frame they concealed. "Call me Yanko, Calum. After all, we're associates now."

"It's *Cay*-lum, *Yank*-o."

Zhirnosky grinned again. "There's an old Russian saying, *Cay*-lum: 'Little thieves are hanged, but great ones escape.'"

"I prefer the American one about people willing to buy oil from anyone, including Satan." Dane turned back to the drilling derrick that towered toward the growing night, the top of it almost lost to the dark. "Of course, that was before we became the world's largest producer of crude."

"A good thing, *Cay*-lum, because you're going to be needing every ounce of it very soon," Zhirnosky grinned, raising his voice over the loudening grind of the drill works. "To save what's left of your economy."

"Why don't you let me show you how this works?" Dane offered.

Zhirnosky turned his focus on the drilling operation, the steady *thunk, thunk, thunk* as a dozen workers labored in seemingly frenetic fashion about various stations. "I would like that very much, comrade," he said to Dane, an edge of suspicion creeping into his voice.

"Looks chaotic to you, I imagine."

"It does indeed."

"Well, my friend, for a long time, people figured this land was tapped out, the wells gone bone dry. Then we came up with new technology that allowed us to drill down deep enough to uncover new reserves that dwarfed what the Permian Basin had produced before. You're standing in what plenty say is the biggest oil field in the world," Dane explained, capturing all of Zhirnosky's attention. "Virtual armies of oil workers have flooded the area, since these new techniques in deep drilling fostered a fresh oil boom. Cheap roadside motels in Midland now fetch three hundred dollars per night, thanks to the blocks of rooms rented out on a permanent basis to drilling and oil companies boasting unlimited budgets to sap as much crude from the ground as they can. Rooms are at such a premium, in fact, that crews often have to double up in them—as one pair of men is leaving for the fields, another pair is returning from them. And that's even with oil prices going as low as they did."

"Others shut down or reduced their operations, I believe."

"They did, indeed, with an eye on the short term instead of the long. Those prices will come back up; they always do. And when that happens I'll be poised to control the market."

Zhirnosky smiled thinly. "I like the way you think."

"I've purchased tens of thousands of additional acres *since* prices sank. It's all about the future, and I can afford to wait."

"For just the kind of economic crisis that would force oil prices to spike, perhaps?"

"The thought had crossed my mind," Dane told him. "Real recently, in fact," he added, leaving it there.

"I must say, comrade," Zhirnosky responded, seeming to hold the breath in his cheeks, until they puckered with a sound like air escaping from a balloon, "I'm very impressed."

Dane let his eyes stray back to the derrick. "I believe I'm on the right track, given whatever that crack about us needing every drop of our oil was referring to."

The Russian's cheeks inflated again, joining Dane in looking back toward the derrick. "How deep are you drilling here?"

"Oh, we're probably down fifteen thousand feet by now. According to the seismic studies, we should hit soon. At that point, the well is capped and a pumping rig is brought in to replace the derrick."

"How many of these do you own and operate?"

"I couldn't tell you. And even if I could, it varies by the day, as some drilling stations pull up stakes because the oil wasn't there and others set up shop over fresh finds." Dane joined the Russian's gaze toward the derrick. "So tell me what brings you over here, what makes you so impressed with what I'm about?"

"Oil is only one precious commodity, comrade, and your country is about to lose another: food."

"Pretty big commodity," Dane managed.

"What do you think brought me here?" Zhirnosky continued.

"I was waiting for you to tell me."

"A plot thirty-five years in the making, dating all the way back to the height of the Cold War. We couldn't win an arms race with you, so we tried a different track. A team was sent here with a compound capable of destroying crops and eroding the soil across your heartland."

"Obviously you fucked it up."

Zhirnosky bristled at Dane's use of profanity, the disrespect it showed. Dane was glad the big man named Beriya was hovering out of earshot, along with the other guards who'd accompanied Zhirnosky.

"Circumstances worked against us, yes," he conceded. "But the head of the team managed to survive and has been lying in wait all these years. Then, what does he learn? He learns someone else is suddenly doing our work for us. Someone else is killing America's crops."

"Me."

"Inadvertent, I'm sure, but impressive nonetheless. When our agent informed us of what was transpiring here, we did . . . how you say? . . . our due diligence and learned about the fertilizer your company withdrew from the market. The rest you know."

"You mean the part about how your ape over there killed my bodyguards?"

"Ape?"

"*Zool,*" Dane repeated in Russian.

"You speak Russian," Zhirnosky grinned.

"I've got substantial business interests over here. And it sounds to me like that's what you're suggesting, a business proposition."

"Am I?"

"I don't think you understand how useful we can be to each other."

Zhirnosky remained silent, waiting for Dane to continue.

Dane did, finally. "The worse this gets, the deeper the economic crisis across the globe, the more money my stockpiled oil will be worth."

"Just the thinking I'd expect from a man with the proper ambitions and resources."

"I've got plenty of both, Yanko," Dane said, pronouncing Zhirnosky's first name correctly this time. "And I'll tell you what else I've got: stores and stores of that fertilizer, hidden away, just in case I have use for it again down the road."

"Well, comrade," said a beaming Zhirnosky, "it appears you now do. You will become richer than your wildest dreams and I will get my country back."

Dane extended his hand. "Guess we've got ourselves a deal."

Zhirnosky took it. "A marriage of mutual convenience."

Dane smiled at him. "In that case, there's something else I'd like to show you."

83

GLASSCOCK COUNTY, TEXAS

"What the hell is this place?" Jones groused, as they slid forward under the canopy of a moonless night.

Before them was the overgrown refuse of what had once been a farm—cotton, specifically—recognizable from the buildings that had collapsed in on themselves. They'd landed at a military airfield twenty miles from the site, kept open just to service their flight, evidence of Jones's return to the good graces of Homeland Security.

"The last farm Calum Dane's family sharecropped," Caitlin said, just loud enough for Jones and Cort Wesley to hear. Guillermo Paz lingered a bit further back to secure their rear. "We're just a few miles from the grave where Dane smelled oil when he buried his father, the site of the first well he ever dug."

She went on to detail briefly how Austin had confirmed her suspicions, Captain Tepper learning that Dane had indeed bought this land five years ago, in cash, through a shell company he created just for that purpose, to avoid any connection whatsoever to Dane Corp. And the ruse held everywhere except the land record office, where the paper trail was clear enough for anybody who knew where to look.

The land was overgrown and likely riddled with varmints, though the only thing visible right now was a herd of wild horses that had appropriated the farm as its private pasture. Caitlin continued to lead the way up toward what had once been a fence line, judging by the remnants of stray posts rotting in the ground. She stopped when she saw a thin flicker of light through the trees and overgrowth, in the area of a barn that remained whole amid the collapsed buildings toppled by wind, storms, and disuse.

"You can see that shack line back over to the east," she said, even softer. "Dane and his family must've lived in one of those."

"That still doesn't tell us what we're doing here, Ranger," Jones said again.

Caitlin looked at him and then at Cort Wesley, but she waited for Paz to draw even before she responded. "I think it was Dane who snatched those kids from the Village School, Jones. And I think this is where he's holding them."

More flickers of light flashed from the area of the barn. Someone lighting a cigarette, maybe, or sweeping a narrow-beam flashlight about.

Guards watching the perimeter. Just as she expected.

"Remember those lights Luke said he saw?" Caitlin

whispered to Cort Wesley, after they'd ducked down to stay out of sight of the guards. "I think Dane's men came by boat and used flashlights like the ones we see now to find the camp. I think Dane knew the bugs were coming and got the kids out before they got there."

"And brought them here," Cort Wesley whispered back. "I get that much. What I don't get is what he figured on doing with them at that point. Hell, seems like he'd have been better off just letting the bugs do their thing."

"Yeah," Caitlin acknowledged, "I'm still working that part out."

Jones looked over at them, shaking his head. "How the hell do you do it, Ranger?" he asked.

"Just lucky, I guess. I also think Calum Dane burned his own petrochemical plant in Waco to eliminate any trace of the pesticide that turned these beetles into monsters."

"Wait a minute," Cort Wesley said suddenly, "where's Paz?"

Caitlin fixed her gaze ahead toward the wild horses and patches of scrub between them and the barn. "Getting things started."

84

Moving about without detection, especially in the dark, was a skill Guillermo Paz had mastered as a boy, when he needed to steal food for his brothers and sisters and escape the gangs who wished to enlist him in their ranks. To this day, he wondered if the *bruja* vision and witchlike foresight he'd inherited from his mother also enabled him to move like a ghost, a *sombra,* immune to detection.

Paz barely registered the kills, just as he never even considered merely incapacitating the guards as an alternative. Killing them was much easier and less complicated; the number of lives he took was as meaningless as the lives of those men themselves, in his mind. They were nothing to him, soulless creatures who sealed their own fate by being party to doing harm to children. Paz never bought into the pass-down effect of acting under orders, believing above all else now that man was the master of his own fate, as opposed to the other way around.

His vast size and bulk, moving through space lacking sufficient cover, should have rendered a stealthy approach an exercise in futility. Yet Paz stalked his prey with ease. Even when the guards seemed to be looking straight at him, they indicated no acknowledgment whatsoever of his presence or existence. With each snap of a neck or twist of a blade through bone and cartilage, he again pondered the level of magic he'd inherited from his mother.

The psychic Madam Caterina had offered to bring his mother forward so he could speak to her as an adult for the first time. Paz had declined, because the truth was that the prospect of such a conversation frightened him, especially if his mother expressed displeasure with the man he'd become. He regretted that decision now and, since he'd turned away from such things in favor of his priest again, had likely squandered the opportunity for good.

Look at me now, Mamá. . . .

Paz began to wonder in earnest if perhaps the tales his mother had told him had more credence than he had let himself believe. Beyond the visions he was convinced were true, maybe there was something to be said for some having been blessed with phantom-like abilities, to be both man and *sombra* at the same time.

Paz approached the next guard from the rear, massive hands swallowing his head in the last moment before a crack that sounded like a thunderclap resonated through the air.

"The guards are gone," Cort Wesley said, sweeping the mini binoculars about the now-weed-infested cotton fields that Calum Dane had worked as a boy. "I can't see a single one."

Caitlin tried not to smile. "Paz . . ."

"I can't see him, either."

"You will when we need him. Time to move."

Cort Wesley had moved the binoculars to the left, looking toward the wild horses. "Something's wrong about this."

"Where'd you like to start on that note, cowboy?" Jones asked him.

Cort Wesley lowered the binoculars. "There are no wild horses in these parts."

The three of them moved straight across the sprawling field, keeping to the thickest patches of scrub for cover, on the unlikely chance that Paz had somehow missed one or more of the guards. Caitlin figured there'd be three or four more inside the barn. No way to take them by surprise the way Paz had dropped the perimeter guards in a matter of a few short minutes. And as far as she knew, the barn had only a single entrance. How to storm it, how to gain entry and secure the hostages without bullets starting to fly their way through the kids . . .

"I've got an idea," said Cort Wesley, as if reading her mind.

85

GLASSCOCK COUNTY, TEXAS

The guards Paz had killed were dressed uniformly in black commando gear courtesy of 5.11 Tactical, the best such outfitter short of the military. Cort Wesley and Jones stripped off the black pullover tops and flak jackets of guards Paz had dropped in his tracks, and pressed on toward the barn together, still hunched low. Caitlin clung to the best cover she could find, maybe thirty feet behind them.

When they drew within sight of the barn—and a watcher likely stationed in the hayloft—Cort Wesley wrapped an arm around Jones's shoulder, pretending to drag him desperately forward as Jones limped and sputtered along. Both kept their eyes down, clearly much the worse for wear as they approached the closed barn door, feigning having been the victims of some kind of attack.

They didn't have to knock or cry out. The big barn door opened with a creak when they drew close, flickers of lantern and generator light emerging, along with a pair of similarly dressed men wielding M16s.

The light didn't strike Jones and Cort Wesley until it was too late, until each had his pistol palmed and steadied. They could have tried to face the guards down. But with no idea how many other gunmen they were facing, and the hostages to think about, they couldn't risk giving any quarter at all.

So they fired, and kept firing, as Caitlin surged past them into the barn and the elongated circle in which the captive kids and their chaperones had been arranged. She sighted in on two additional guards, SIG churning and spitting before she'd zeroed them firmly, locking them down and aiming in the same thought merging into action. The gunmen were standing and then they weren't. The echo of her gunshots was lost in the screams and wails of the terrified students of the Village School, who hadn't yet processed that they were being rescued.

Even then it wasn't over. The thump of footsteps pounded in the hayloft overhead, and Caitlin trained her aim on the ladder, waiting for the shape of a man to emerge.

But Cort Wesley and Jones weren't nearly as patient. They opened up with pistols, dual streams fired upward to pulverize the dried wood into sawdust, which sprayed from the holes their bullets punched in the hayloft floor. There was a thud, and then the footsteps stopped.

Caitlin spun, eyes running over the hostages who, but for a strange quirk of fate, would've included Luke Torres. She again found herself wondering what had moved Dane to take such a risk. Linking him to an attack on these kids, or any of the others, by the marauding hordes of beetles would've been damnnear impossible. Yet he'd still risked everything to get the students from the Village School out of Armand Bayou before the swarm descended upon them.

Sobs and whimpers replaced the screams as the hostages clutched and held each other, a few emerging from behind positions of cover they'd managed to find. Caitlin wanted to tell them it was all right, they were fine and going home, except that she knew it wasn't true. The experience itself, and then the violence that had finally ended it, would leave an indelible mark for the rest of their lives. More nights than they could count would see them lurching up from the bedcovers, drenched in sweat from a nightmare they couldn't remember and never would, because nothing could best the reality of what they'd just witnessed.

"I'm a Texas Ranger!" she called anyway. "And all of you are going home!"

Something changed in that instant, the heaviness in the barn's air receding in favor of what felt like a soft breeze. She smelled the stink of fear and stale sweat for the first time, glad for the scents her revived senses conjured, since it spared her the coppery odor of blood from the men she, Cort Wesley, and Jones had just killed. Her eyes recorded cans of gasoline that had been fueling the generators, along with a pair of tractors, attached to industrial-size sprayers, which the previous owners of the cotton farm had used to fertilize their crops, backed up against a rear corner of the barn.

Caitlin felt her breathing even out, her lungs and heart steadying, as it always was in the aftermath of a gunfight. She'd been in far tougher ones than this, though the stakes involved—thirty-four high-school kids—were unparalleled.

"Let's get a move on," she said through the silence that had settled around her. She was preparing to lead the kids from the barn when she saw Guillermo Paz standing a few feet in front of the open barn doors, board stiff, his gaze focused straight ahead into the black ribbon of night beyond. "Hold on a sec," she corrected, hand held in the air to keep the former hostages in their tracks.

Caitlin slid past Cort Wesley and Jones, who had stayed on their guards, with guns ready. She could feel the heat radiating off Paz as she drew closer, was almost able to actually see the hackles rising on his neck.

"What's wrong, Colonel?"

"Trouble, Ranger," he said, without turning toward her, gaze fixed on the fields beyond. "Just like my psychic warned. I can see it now, even though there's no strong light."

And that's when one of the horses grazing before them started whinnying, an instant before it went down, disappearing into the scrub as if its legs had been yanked out from beneath it.

Followed by a second horse.

Then a third.

86

GLASSCOCK COUNTY, TEXAS

There are no wild horses in this area, Cort Wesley had said. These must have come from a nearby farm, spooked by the advance of the deadly colony of beetles. They'd ended up here, taking comfort in some brush to eat, with the false security of the night around them.

Paz backpedaled with her and slammed the barn doors behind him so none of the kids would be able to see what was coming. Cort Wesley couldn't see it either, but one look at Caitlin was all he needed.

"You've gotta be kidding."

"Coming straight toward us, Cort Wesley."

Jones holstered his pistol, getting the gist of what was happening. Paz just stood before the now-barred barn door, seeming as big and broad as it was.

"What'd you see, Ranger?"

Cort Wesley had reached her side without Caitlin realizing his presence; she could only look at him and speak in a voice that sounded like someone else's.

"A black wave, Cort Wesley, darker than the night."

"How big?"

"Everywhere."

Someone else's voice again.

"Let's move now," Jones put forth. "Take our chances out the rear."

"We'll never make it. They'll chase us down."

Jones's gaze fixed on the ladder leading to the hayloft. "Up there, then. Take our chances up there."

"I don't like those chances."

"What," he shot back at her, "these bugs can climb?"

"We're food, Jones. They'll do whatever they have to."

"Hold on a sec," Cort Wesley said, his gaze fixed in another direction.

"This is crazy!" Jones said, trailing Cort Wesley to the tractors tucked into the barn's rear corner.

"Just shut up and follow the plan," Caitlin told him, toting a pair of the gas cans that had been used to fuel the generators.

"Plan? You call this a plan?"

"Colonel," she started, Paz picking up from there.

"He says another word, and I'll cut his tongue out," Paz said, looking toward Jones.

"Close enough," said Caitlin. She turned her gaze on the twin dark SUVs parked alongside the tractors. "Make yourself useful, Jones, and check the navigation devices in those. Let's see if we can figure out exactly where they came from."

"We don't have much time," she said to Cort Wesley as they each poured gasoline into the tank that fed the tractor attachment's fertilizer sprayers.

Outside, the sound of the horses' wailing had stopped. Another sound, though, filled the air beyond the barn, something like a million fingernails clacking together. A fecal smell seemed to trail it, permeating the barn with an odor so sharp it had some of the kids, bundled together in the center of the barn by their chaperones, retching or vomiting.

"Whatever it is, we'll make it enough," Cort Wesley replied. He watched Guillermo Paz finish tightening the works of one tractor engine and move on to the next. "Hope you know what you're doing there, Colonel."

"So do I, outlaw," he said, head buried in the second tractor's engine.

"It's an address in Midland," Caitlin heard Jones call out, as he slammed the SUV's door. "South Country Road."

"That's just off Interstate twenty," she noted, fixing the placement in her brain. "Not much in the area besides warehouses and fulfillment centers."

"Well, that's where the gunmen we shot drove here from. By the way, Homeland was able to find facial recognition matches on a couple of those guys you shot up on the four-ten outside San Antonio. Ex-Russian special ops."

"Mobbed up?"

"Available for hire, but no organized crime associations in their files."

"And you're just telling me this now?"

"I only got the news on the plane while you and the cowboy were reminiscing."

Caitlin looked past him, at the SUVs he was standing between. "How many can those carry?"

"As many as eight, maybe ten passengers, Ranger."

"I wasn't talking about just passengers inside."

87

GLASSCOCK COUNTY, TEXAS

The stench, Caitlin figured, must have something to do with the frass Doc Whatley and Young Roger had explained the beetles smeared over themselves. It grew overpowering while she supervised the effort of squeezing as many kids into the SUVs as humanly possible. Jones climbed in behind the wheel of the lead SUV, and a chaperone took the wheel of the trailing one. The remaining chaperones and the oldest and most athletic kids would ride the roof of the trailing

SUV, saving the roof of the lead one for Guillermo Paz alone.

Since his role was the centerpiece of the plan they'd desperately hatched.

All told, there were thirty-nine hostages, literally squeezed into place by the time they were ready to roll. The sounds of the approaching horde of insects had grown into an all-out rattling din, like teeth chattering together times a billion, evidence the first wave of the beetles was almost to the barn. By that point, Caitlin and Cort Wesley sat in the driver's seats of the old tractors currently parked side by side, their engines rumbling and black smoke belching from their tailpipes at the front of the convoy. After initially sputtering, those engines had caught, then rattled for a time, before settling into uneasy idles.

The loudening clacks of the beetles, combined with the twin racing engines, would've made being heard difficult, had there been anything to say. As it was, Caitlin and Cort Wesley tensed as Paz yanked off the plywood stretched across the barn door and pushed the door open to the night and the endless black wave, darker than the night sky beyond.

Cort Wesley threw his tractor into gear, first, and felt it lurch forward before its tires found reasonable purchase on the barn floor. It rolled on, Caitlin working hers into gear immediately behind it, while Paz took his place atop the roof of the lead SUV, still in the process of fastening a plastic shoulder tank into place and testing the heft of a six-foot spraying wand.

Caitlin turned her gaze from him and started rolling

too, staying back about ten feet from Cort Wesley. Ready with the hand controls to work the attached sprayer, having already familiarized herself with them, gasoline poured in the rusted steel drum, instead of fertilizer.

She surged from the fetid, rank conditions of the barn into the cool of a night braced with a powerful, spoiled stench that hung over it like a cloud. The entire landscape before and around her for as far as she could see was nothing but black. But it was a peculiar black, shifting in apparently uniform fashion, as if the ground itself was moving en masse. Caitlin found herself wondering how many beetles this colony actually numbered and how many layers of them had piled atop each other, sniffing out their next meal.

She didn't have time to wonder long, though, because she saw Cort Wesley activate his sprayer and did the same with hers. Instantly, the acrid scent of gasoline claimed her nostrils, battling the frass stench shed by the beetles for control of the air. Her stream fired to the right, covering a fifty-foot swatch of land, while Cort Wesley sprayed to the left. The result was to inundate the dried scrub, weeds, and overgrown brush where cotton fields had once flourished with gas, forging a makeshift path through which to escape.

Caitlin stole one last look at Paz standing atop the roof of the lead SUV as Jones revved the engine almost directly beneath him, inside the cab. The colonel also had filled a portable pesticide tank with kerosene siphoned from a fifty-five gallon drum used to refill the lanterns supplying the barn's light, and she watched him touch a flaming lighter to the tip of the spraying wand attached to the tank by a flexible hose connection. Fire sparked at the wand's tip, creating what was essentially a jerry-rigged flamethrower. She had no idea how Paz could possibly manage the task while standing unsupported atop the SUV's roof, but she had stopped questioning his capabilities, along with his intentions, long ago, about the same time she began wondering if he was even human.

Her senses contorted, each engaged in a battle for supremacy of her attention. There were smells, sounds, and sights all fighting for control, but Caitlin let instinct guide her to better focus on the task at hand. She was just starting to record the click-clacking clatter of her tractor's tires crushing the hordes of beetles she was driving over, the chattering of the remaining bugs seeming to intensify, as if they were enraged by her actions.

She'd drawn fifty feet from the barn when fresh revving of the SUVs' engines told her they'd emerged to follow the path carved by the gasoline. She heard a loud *poof* as Guillermo Paz squeezed the activator on his wand, shooting a line of fire left, right, and back again, igniting the vibrating black mass on either side of the makeshift road they were forging through the swarm.

A much louder *poof* sounded, followed by another. And then the night was aglow with an almost day glow brightness.

Paz felt as if he was experiencing a rare moment of crystal clarity as the flames burst into the air like a vast curtain spreading out, drawing all around him. He realized the point of the message the psychic Madam Caterina had relayed to him, all the messages gleaned from the tarot cards as well as in his other sessions. And if she'd been right, if there really was a great beyond out there, if Paz's mother really did listen when he spoke, then all he held dear toward the purpose that drove him was vindicated. *He* was vindicated, along with that purpose that defined his very reason for being.

The Chariot is one of the most complex cards to define, Paz remembered Madam Caterina saying. *It implies war, a struggle, and an eventual, hard-won victory over enemies, obstacles, nature, the uncertainties inside you. But there is a great deal more to it. The charioteer wears emblems of the sun, yet the sign behind this card is Cancer, the moon. The moon suggests it will shine somehow at night. That's symbolic of an enemy that can't be seen.*

As in invisible? he had asked.

More like out of sight. Hiding from view. Does that mean anything to you?

It will, Paz had said, assuredly.

And now it did, all of it, every bit. The invisible enemy had been revealed and, in this wondrous moment of clarity, he came to understand the true meaning of the psychic's most vital message to him.

There's a light, a strong light, a blinding light. Everywhere at once, swallowing everything.

Fire was that very light, slaying and swallowing the evil around him. Or maybe he needed to tweak that thinking a bit. Maybe *he* was the light, hope against the great evil, the ridding of which he'd claimed as his purpose. It wasn't just about his Texas Ranger, it was about the threats to her that needed to be vanquished before those threats could turn the strong light of day dark.

In an endless black wave of insects that seemed to have no beginning and no end. A circle as opposed to a square, Paz standing at the center point to provide balance.

Madam Caterina had been right. Darkness *was* everywhere. But Paz's light shined through it, melting it away, returning the darkness to the depths of hell from which it came.

Caitlin's breath caught in her throat as she got her closest, clearest look yet at just one of the insect colonies marauding through the state of Texas, ingesting whatever crops and livestock showed up in its path. She recalled the picture of one from Doc Whatley's ancient encyclopedia, magnifying the creature in her mind while reducing the horde to that single image of a shiny black creature, encased in rough armor that left only its legs and mandibles protruding. A still shot multiplied a million times to form the single, unbroken wave that stretched before her in a dark ribbon that looked like mud churning over the countryside. The horde seemed to move as one, and Caitlin half expected its shapeless composite to form into some kind of massive creature the size of an aircraft carrier, intent on swallowing anything that got in its way.

She shook the illusion aside and focused on the

actual nature of the enemy engaged against her in a battle to the death. Their advance was terrifying in its simplicity and perfection of movement, each individual pest seeming to act as part of a greater whole, moving in eerie synchronization, ready to devour anything in its path. She imagined what the scene might look like if it were fertile crops before them instead of land already dead from disuse and age and unprotected against the relentless elements. There was no trace of the horse herd ahead, not even their skeletal remains visible from this angle and distance.

Accident or design, plot or fortune, the origins of this colony and the others, along with the part Calum Dane had played in this, mattered not at all now. The night brightened further under the growing shroud of orange light shed by the flames blossoming on both sides of her, as Paz continued to rotate his flame-thrower from left to right and back again. Caitlin heard a constant clatter of crackling and rippling sounds, like popcorn roasting in a microwave, as the fire consumed the bugs, devoured them just as they would've sought to devour whatever lay before them. The odor of the beetle frass merged with the smoke, wafting through the air and seeming to intensify it to a stench so powerful that each breath sent ripples of nausea through her stomach. The scene before her was like some cosmic battle, something you read about in the Bible and were never sure had really happened.

But this was really happening.

And they were winning.

Until Caitlin saw the tractor Cort Wesley was driving seem to drop into a pit on its right side. It corkscrewed one way, then the other, and Caitlin realized the old thing had thrown a wheel, grinding on an axle as it fishtailed across the field and came to a halt, blocking the route out.

88

GLASSCOCK COUNTY, TEXAS

Caitlin hadn't thought much about her tractor's brakes until that very moment. They didn't seem to engage at first, so she pumped the pedal in rapid motions in the hope they'd catch. They finally did, and she felt the tractor's tires sinking into the soft ground when it ground to a halt. Only it wasn't ground it had sunk into, it was a fluid black wave that looked like liquefied tar pooling beneath her. The bright orange glow of the flames belching huge black plumes of smoke and stench into the air left her with the feeling she was trapped in the midst of some biblical apocalypse. The endless black wave of beetles looked shiny in their glow, in contrast to a starless, empty sky that made her think, almost whimsically, that heaven had shut down for the night.

If she dropped down now she had no idea how deep she'd sink. Up to a foot, maybe, judging by what she could glimpse of the tractor's tires. She was trying not to picture how easily a wave of these bugs could bring a person down, based on what they had done to those horses.

And Karl Dakota's cattle.

Caitlin rose in her seat, careful to keep her boots firmly planted in the tractor's rubber footrests.

"Cort Wesley!" she yelled to him, listening to the SUVs braking to a halt behind her.

He was balanced precariously on the tow assembly, between the tractor and the tank of gasoline it was hauling, trying to adjust the nozzle of the sprayer to continue holding the bugs at bay on his designated side.

"Just keep firing, Ranger!" he yelled back, without looking her way.

Caitlin realized she'd disengaged her sprayer when she braked her tractor to a halt. "These aren't bullets!"

"They are tonight!"

Caitlin looked down and saw the swarm had now climbed past the halfway point of the tires. She reengaged her sprayer a moment after Cort Wesley did his, Guillermo Paz hitting both mists of fluid from left to right and back again, making it seem the air itself had caught fire. The flames dropped with the dewlike mist, turning fresh waves of the swarm ablaze and filling the air with a rancid stench worse than a week-old corpse left smoldering in the heat. The clacking of the bugs continued to push forward into the flames, without pause. It had grown loud enough to bubble her ears and drown out whatever sounds or pleas might have been coming from the SUVs behind them.

This wasn't going to work. They weren't getting out of here.

Pictures flared through her mind of the swarm

swallowing the SUVs in their spread, shutting off all light and air. Only a matter of time before Luke's classmates suffocated or tried desperately to escape, opening a door to let the deadly horde in. There was no safe quarter here, no alternative to escape.

Caitlin had never run from a fight in her life; neither had her dad or granddad. The three of them were used to going all in, against any and all odds. But that was against men—humans, anyway—and not some genetic nightmare spawned in a science lab. She stood no more chance of winning here and now than she did of besting a Texas funnel cloud as it churned over the countryside, sucking up everything in its path. She was hardly arrogant and brash enough to believe she could escape its fury, any more than she could escape the marauding menace intent on turning her and those kids into their next meal.

And that was the thing: those kids. Fail and they were dead, whatever she'd accomplished in her life and career paling by comparison with a defeat that would come to define her legacy. The last of the Strong line, five generations of Texas Rangers for a lineage, done in by a swarm of bugs capable of leaving nothing but bone behind.

No.

That's what she thought.

No.

A blast of heat shook Caitlin, the back of her neck singed by a gush of what felt like hot breath against the back of her shirt, which was already stuck to her skin by sweat.

"Get the vehicles ready to move, Ranger," Guillermo

Paz called to her, drawing even with her tractor as fire spit in all directions from his jerry-rigged flame-thrower, holding the swarm at bay.

It was the only chance, Paz reasoned, at least for the kids, and that was enough to satisfy him. Because it wasn't the flames that formed the strong light Madam Caterina had seen in her vision.

It was Paz himself.

The fire of his own passion, illuminating his soul with purpose and direction. He had faced his own mortality more times than he could possibly count, but had never accepted it before. Doing so was like holding his breath until he passed out. Normally, instinct seized the moment, eliminating the need for thought, rational or otherwise.

Not tonight. Tonight was about facing an enemy with no emotion or purpose beyond the perpetuation of its own existence. No ulterior motives, no careful planning, no government to seize or protect. Survival and nothing more. Life at its most primal.

Paz almost envied the swarm's simplicity of purpose, its mindless pursuit of what lay directly ahead, without need of peripheral vision or any quarter given to what lay behind. A perfect existence, in many ways, dominated by the most base desires and breeding and nothing more.

He felt his combat boots crunching over the charred, still-smoking piles of darkness his flames had already fried in their sweep. He thought the vast black wave might be receding in his path, learned behavior teaching it in some primitive collective sense that death awaited its continued push forward.

Paz stopped just in front of the outlaw's tractor, continuing to rotate his flames as a cry from his Ranger burned his own ears.

"Cort Wesley!"

"I'm a little busy here, Ranger!" Cort Wesley yelled back to her.

"I can see that! Are you crazy?"

Still balanced precariously, Cort Wesley worked to free the fittings attaching the tank, to dislodge it from its bonds.

"No choice I can see."

He started to rock the tank to spill it over. Caitlin realized she'd misjudged his original intention and crawled back along the length of the tractor to do the very same thing.

89

GLASSCOCK COUNTY, TEXAS

"You know what to do, Colonel!" she yelled to Paz over the swarm's incessant clacking, which had deafened her to everything else.

Caitlin had forgotten about the older kids clinging to the roof of the trailing SUV, couldn't imagine the panic and terror compounding the plight of so many squeezed into such tight spaces for the journey that had now stalled. Their screams and cries pierced her ears, rising over the clacking of the horde, now that the tractor engines had quieted. She heard sobs and pleas, too, and only wished she could answer them. Because how long would it be before the swarm climbed past even the windows and reached the roof, if they tried to hold out here?

But Paz was in motion by then, backpedaling while firing off his flames more deliberately and judiciously, to clear his own path and save whatever fuel he could for the final rush. Caitlin watched him signaling the plan's intentions to Jones behind the wheel of the lead vehicle. Then, though, instead of climbing back to his perch on the roof, he jogged forward through the slog of darkness that moved and grew as more of the swarm rolled over the corpses Paz had fried.

"Colonel!" Caitlin cried out to him, as he passed.

"It's the only way, Ranger!"

His words reached her softly and calmly, maybe transferred by thought instead of voice—who could say anymore? Paz moved ahead of Cort Wesley's stalled tractor to take point, just as Cort Wesley managed to tip his tank over and spill the remains of his tank over the advancing storm. The land's natural grade left the fuel running downhill, spreading outward on one angle, while hers, once tipped, would spread in the other.

But the old metal tank proved too heavy for her to do much more than budge. She heard a *thump*, felt the frame of her tractor rock, and saw Cort Wesley's shape bent at the knees, rising to join her at the assembly's rear.

"On three, Ranger!"

And on three, together, they managed to tip her tank over, barely hearing the slosh of gasoline hitting the ground to begin its spread along the land's natural grade forward. Then the two of them slid along the rusted steel frame, reached the tip of her tractor, and jumped together back onto Cort Wesley's, before which Paz continued his fiery stand.

The colonel looked back at them long enough to acknowledge their presence, then swung again to the front, without seeing Caitlin whip her hands around in the air to signal the SUVs on. The wave of bugs had almost entombed the entirety of their tires, stretching over the wheel wells in patches, and Caitlin wondered if they'd even be able to find traction. But there was a lot to be said for having four thousand pounds under you and, after an initial bout of fits and starts, both SUVs started rolling, sweeping around the stalled tractors.

Jones and the other driver both accelerated through the flames, Caitlin jumping onto the running board of one and Cort Wesley the other, both holding to the luggage rack while pinning their feet higher against the frame to stay above the beetles. That left Paz to continue clearing a path for them, black waves parting for the route of his flames like the Red Sea did for Moses. No way their SUVs would have any more chance than the horses, if it weren't for him. And Caitlin had to shake off the illusion that thinner waves of the black swarm scurried from his own path blazed through them, as if frightened and intimidated by Paz's mere presence.

Caitlin felt heat that reminded her of dipping her hand into scalding water, as the flames clawed at her hair and grazed the fabric of her clothes. She sucked in her breath to make herself as small as possible, trying not to think about the possibility of the fire stealing her in its grasp. Pressed up tight against the SUV, she watched the world through the flame-shrouded reflection in the vehicle's windows.

Guillermo Paz shrank in that reflection, his huge shape dwindling from sight when she turned to look directly toward him, while still clinging to the roof rack for dear life. She stole a moment to glimpse Cort Wesley doing the same, the incessant clacking chatter of the beetles starting to lower in volume the closer they drew to the road.

Caitlin looked back toward Guillermo Paz again to find nothing but a shifting darkness and shroud of flames within the reach of her vision, no sign of him anywhere among them. The SUVs thumped and bucked past a trio of mailboxes, the sound and smell of the swarm decreasing until only the night itself lay before them.

90

GLASSCOCK COUNTY, TEXAS

"The address in question is a warehouse, and it belongs to Dane Corp, all right," Captain Tepper told Caitlin, Cort Wesley, and Jones over the speaker of her cell phone.

They were riding in one of the SUVs after a brief stop at a service station five miles up the road from the farm, where authorities were already en route to meet them. The first order of business was to get the kids reunited with their families. Everything else, all the explanations and such, could be sorted out later.

For her part, Caitlin needed to get to that address in Midland, where, hopefully, she'd find Calum Dane himself.

"Wish I could tell you more," Tepper continued. "What's the play here, Ranger?"

"Let you know when we make it, D.W."

"For once, just for once, can you let me send in the cavalry before you storm the place?"

"No, sir, because it could risk squandering the advantage we have on Calum Dane right now. He's the key to all this, Captain—everything, including those goddamn bugs. We're thirty minutes away. You tell me you can get the cavalry ready to charge by then and we'll talk."

"Well, you're going to do whatever you want, no matter what I say, so I'm just going to tell you to have at it and don't shoot any more men than you have to."

"You can tell Cort Wesley and me something else, sir. The rest of the story about what happened to our fathers."

91

LOLO, TEXAS; 1983

"Is this the way you do business, comrade?"

Boone Masters swung with Jim Strong to find Anton Kasputin standing twenty feet away, a trio of thugs flanking him on either side with guns drawn.

"Call the play, Ranger," Boone said, just loud enough for Jim to hear.

"You're all under arrest," Jim Strong said, hand over his still-holstered .45.

Kasputin grinned and broadly waved his finger in Jim's direction. "I've seen cowboy movies about men like you. They shoot and never miss. That gun fires eight bullets. There are seven of us. I like our odds."

"All the same," Jim said, not even flinching, "you're still under arrest, sir."

"What's the charge, exactly?"

"I'll throw a whole bunch in a hat and pick one out. Let's start with receiving stolen goods and move all the way up to possession of a deadly weapon."

"And what weapon would that be?"

"Whatever's in all those tanks, Sergei."

"That's not my name."

"But you look like a Sergei to me," Jim told him, fingers still dancing over the butt of his holstered .45. "And, you're right, maybe I won't be able to get all your men with my eight bullets, but I'll get you for sure."

Kasputin's gaze moved from side to side, then forward again, assessing his prospects. "You could just walk out of here, and we go about our separate ways."

"That the way it's done back home in Russki land? Not so here in Texas. When I walk out of here, it'll be with you in cuffs."

The smile slipped from Kasputin's expression. "Take your best shot, Ranger."

"Exactly my intention."

But it was D. W. Tepper who opened fire first, his presence catching the Russians utterly by surprise. He pushed all eight shots from his .45, diving to the floor behind a column of packing crates to snap home a fresh magazine. He was pretty sure he'd dropped two of the Russians with those shells, though it was hard to tell.

Because Jim Strong used his initial shots to take out the overhead lighting, plunging the warehouse into darkness.

"Kill them! Shoot them!" Kasputin cried out to his still standing thugs. "Don't let them get away!"

By then, Boone Masters had unslung the tank labeled Propane from his shoulder and sent it rolling down the aisle, straight at the Russians. He had his .357 Magnum out in the next instant, firing toward the sound of the thing's roll and the slight gleam its shiny steel made in the darkness. If the contents had really been propane, a *boom* and accompanying flame burst would've followed. Instead, there was a hiss of something contained under pressure escaping, something that felt like a liquid and a gas at the same time, bringing a harsh chemical odor with it.

The light sneaking in through the hold door Kasputin had left open was enough for Boone to spot him and his men scurrying away, still with superior numbers and firepower, even with the addition of a second Ranger's gun.

"Ranger!" Boone yelled out to Jim Strong.

"We need to waste those tanks!" Strong's voice chimed back through the darkness.

"I got a better idea."

Boone's shape flitted through the darkness, illuminated in splotchy fashion by muzzle flashes trained his way. The darkness of the warehouse swallowed him, as the two Rangers kept Kasputin and his thugs at bay in a crossfire that would last only as long as their bullets.

"Masters!" Jim cried out.

When no response followed, he slid sideways, ducking down one aisle, between stacked major appliances, and then up another. It was like being trapped in a maze, his ears burned by the constant din of the Russians returning their fire on D. W. Tepper. Jim was down to his last magazine, eight bullets, with the pounding steps of Russian gunmen tracing him through the dark. He couldn't see them, meaning they couldn't see him, meaning . . .

Thought and action merged, Jim leaping up onto

the irregularly stacked crates and firing down on a trio of thugs who'd been converging upon him. They dropped like ducks in a shooting gallery, not about to rise again, when Jim's .45 locked open and empty. In the same moment a torrent of machine-gun fire flared his way. The shells penetrated the crates and clanged against the metal of the appliances inside. The sound puffed out his ears, Jim recognizing the distinctive din as coming from a Thompson, of all things, drum-fed .45-caliber shells turning fridges and ranges, washers and dryers, to paste.

The fire of a second Thompson blared his way from another angle, the tinny, echoing blare reaching him in stereo now. All he wanted to do was drop and cover his ears. Instead, he kept darting and weaving atop the crates, twin streams of fire blistering the air around him. He thought he might have been screaming, was conscious, too, of the barrage aimed well in front of him, around where D. W. Tepper must've made his stand. He thought there must be gunmen who escaped his original count, wielders of the Thompsons, held back by Kasputin to slice him down once he'd risked exposure.

Man was smarter than he thought. KGB for sure, and Jim cursed himself for underestimating his opponent, not putting enough stock in the brutal, merciless manner in which his men had gunned down Stanko and his gang in a park fronting the MacArthur-Rain building in Houston as he and Boone Masters had looked on from the rooftop level of the parking garage.

Along with his daughter, Caitlin, who'd hidden under a tarp in the bed of his truck.

Thinking of her recharged Jim's batteries but left him assessing the dire nature of his plight, the reality that he was never going to see her again. There were just too many Russians, and they were too well armed, to expect he and D. W. Tepper would be able to take them alone.

Only they weren't alone.

Jim Strong heard an engine grinding an instant before Boone Masters burst through a stack of appliances, piloting a massive, large-capacity pneumatic forklift running on four truck-size tires. Its scaffold was piled high with tanks balanced precariously upon its lift forks, looking ready to tumble off at any moment. Jim wasn't sure of Boone's intentions, until he spotted the lit cigarette in the man's mouth. Only one hand was on the wheel, while the other clung fast to what looked like the wand of an acetylene torch. Jim watched him jam it forward, toward the tanks that he now realized were shiny and wet with something Boone Masters must've sprayed or doused them with.

Jim had just recalled that the inventory of one of Masters's more recent heists included a bevy of remanufactured kerosene stoves, when the forklift smashed through the crates on which he was perched, sending him flying. His last thought before he hit one toppled box and rolled down onto another was of the rich scent of something like lighter fluid hanging in the air. He'd lost sight of Boone Masters by then, but pictured him touching his cigarette to some makeshift fuse soaked in kerosene, then watching it flare and burn down toward the similarly soaked tanks.

The flame burst that blinded him on the floor was more like a flash, the tanks rupturing in a series of rumbles instead of a single explosion. The entire front section of the warehouse was awash in white-hot flame that spread like a curtain over the floor, blocking the path to the hold door through which they'd entered. There were exits behind them as well, but Jim Strong didn't even look toward them, charging into the heat and flames, dancing past the fire pooling on the floor and setting the stolen merchandise ablaze.

He found D. W. Tepper first, aiming his empty .45 at nothing, his eyes glazed beneath eyebrows that had been burned from his face. Jim got a shoulder under Tepper and dragged him along until he spotted Boone Masters lying half on and half off a stack of appliances tumbled by the blast, his clothes and hair soaked by whatever had sprayed out of those tanks marked Propane. It had a bitter, corrosive, chemical stench to it, something like a mix of turpentine and motor oil that rode Jim, too, all the way to a rear exit that he burst through with both Tepper and Masters in tow.

"Neither of you is gonna die on me tonight, hear? Neither one!"

He dropped them down in the cool of the night to catch his breath, then resumed dragging them far as he could from the warehouse before the blast he was anticipating came. Fortunately, the back portion was spared the initial inferno that spread in rippling fashion from the front, the roof seeming to peel away and the walls blown both out and up. Jim dropped over both Tepper and Masters to shield them, woozy from breathing in whatever had soaked Boone to the gills from those tanks, now gone forever.

Jim watched Masters's eyes flicker, fixed on him when they finally opened. "Well, this oughta keep my boy Cort Wesley out of jail, anyway."

"Who's Cort Wesley?" Jim asked him, the two of them somehow managing to share a smile.

92

SAN ANTONIO, TEXAS

"I take no pleasure in telling you all this, Mr. Masters," Tepper said, his voice sounding tinny over the cell phone's speaker. "You deserved to hear the truth a long time ago, but your dad made Jim Strong promise him you'd never hear it from him or any Ranger."

"He must not have wanted me to think of him that way."

"As a hero, you mean?"

"Because he did it for me. He wouldn't want me to bear the burden of his death. Would've preferred me hating him for the way he went out. Wasting away to nothing, all weak and all."

"Guess it makes perfect sense when you say it that way," Tepper told him.

"Maybe he didn't just do it for you, Cort Wesley," Caitlin said suddenly.

"How's that, Ranger?"

"Your dad boosted appliances. He carried a gun, showed it a few times, but never shot anybody in the commission of one of his crimes. I don't think the poison in those tanks made him sick. I think he was already sick, and this was his way of trying to go out on his own terms."

"Without telling me, even from his hospital bed?"

Caitlin shrugged. "Part of those terms. We think we know our parents, Cort Wesley, but we don't, not any better than our kids know us."

"Or we know them," Cort Wesley said pointedly, Luke back on his mind.

"I suppose," Caitlin agreed, whatever she'd meant to say, instead, frozen in her throat. "Anton Kasputin didn't die in the explosion, obviously, Captain."

"No, Ranger," Tepper confirmed somberly, "he didn't."

She looked toward Jones in the backseat. "This jibe with your thinking on Alexi Gribanov?"

"Perfectly. As Kasputin, he manages to survive that battle and ends up staying here. Setting up shop while awaiting a call from Russia he never figured would come."

"Wait a minute," interjected Cort Wesley. "How's he connected to those documents on agroterrorism you found in Afghanistan?"

"The plan targeting farmland in 1983, the formula and schematics al-Qaeda got their hands on, was virtually identical to what's happening now," Jones said to both of them. "The pesticide stockpiled in that warehouse your fathers blew up wasn't intended to create a superstrain of bugs, it was only supposed to kill the soil, make it impossible for it to absorb water."

"Oh, that's all?" from Captain Tepper, over Caitlin's phone speaker.

"So what Dane came up with at his petrochemical plant had nothing at all to do with it," Caitlin said.

"Only so far as Gribanov must've reported to somebody back in Russia what was happening, not realizing that one of his own men was already talking up a storm. So in comes your invisible man to secure the intent of the original plan."

"Which was?"

"Wiping out three-quarters of our nation's food supply. Turn us from exporters into importers as our economy goes in the tank."

Cort Wesley started to run his hands through his hair and got only halfway. "And this invisible man comes here accompanied by that hit team on the interstate, and almost surely more."

"Which is sure to complicate things once we get to Midland," Caitlin added.

"Just the way you like them, Ranger," Tepper noted over the speaker. "Gives you a whole new nationality to wipe out. We'll just call it payback for them having the bad sense to try to smoke you in that ambush. Had no idea they were about to get caught in the path of Hurricane Caitlin. Just make sure you've got enough bullets to blow their way."

"Always, Captain," Caitlin told him.

93

"I must tell you," Yanko Zhirnosky said to Calum Dane, after the demonstration was complete, "I'm glad to be doing business with you."

"We still got some bugs to work out," Dane told him, glad he'd instructed the Bass brothers, Frank and Fred, to keep things at level one, to lessen the odds of another screwup in their demonstration of the immersive video game technology they'd developed for Dane Corp. "But the potential is unlimited—internationally."

"Everything is international these days, and about to become even more so. What do you call this again?"

"Immersive video gaming. Means that the game is played from within."

"You have vision, comrade, as do I. I know what I want out of this. Less clear is what you do."

"My oil fields aren't going anywhere," Dane told him. "But they're not going to make me history's first trillionaire by themselves."

"And you think this will?"

Dane grinned so broadly he could feel his cheeks pinch. "Here's the thing, Yanko. I'm dog shit to the ruling class, like I can't wash the smell of oil off myself. In their minds, I got lucky with a shovel. You see where I'm going with this?"

"No, I don't."

"These men own the country, like your oligarchs back home, only multiplied by ten. America isn't a democracy and hasn't been, really, since the railroads and robber barons. Only I grew up more like a worker on those rails than the foremen holding the chains. Because here's the thing: I spent the early part of my life working on behalf of those who still think I'm dog shit today, and too much of the rest of it kissing their asses to get where I am, while I lost one boy to war and another to the temper I inherited from my own father. Know what, though? I'm there now, and nothing would give me greater pleasure than the lot of them kissing mine instead."

Zhirnosky grinned back, jabbing a finger at the air. "You're going to short their stocks. You're going to short shares in their companies so when the rest of that pesticide is released you'll effectively own them. The world's first trillionaire. . . . Has a nice sound to it, very nice."

"When this is over, you'll be running your country . . . and I'll be running mine."

And that's when all the lights in the warehouse went out.

94

MIDLAND, TEXAS

Caitlin, Cort Wesley, and Jones had driven slowly past the warehouse linked to the address from which the guards at the Glasscock County farm had driven, then retraced their route back before stowing their SUV out of sight off South Country Road.

"How many vehicles you make in the parking lot, Ranger?" Cort Wesley asked her.

"Seven."

"I counted eight."

"The eighth was an old truck with flat tires. And I think Calum Dane himself's inside that warehouse."

"How the hell you figure that?" Jones asked her.

"You notice how those vehicles were parked?"

"No."

"Four of them abreast, away from others, where the sun would've been shining during the day. That tells me they showed up in a convoy after nightfall. You want to try telling me who else would be showing up in a convoy at night?"

Jones rolled his eyes, his big, anvil-shaped head seeming to puff up further. "We've got three pistols between us, and maybe a few extra clips."

"Magazines, Jones. They're called magazines. Man with your field experience should know that."

"You're a piece of work, Ranger."

"Let's talk about that field experience of yours," Caitlin said, watching Jones shaking his head now. "As I recall, you know your way around an electrical transformer."

Caitlin and Cort Wesley slid up to the fence line enclosing the flat-roofed slab warehouse of a building that Captain Tepper explained had belonged to a now-bankrupt distributor of industrial plumbing parts. Ten thousand square feet, and they had no idea how the interior was laid out, or any modifications to the original design that Dane might've made.

"I make two guards outside the front door," Cort Wesley told her. "Nobody else."

"They look Russian to you?"

"How can I tell?"

"I was kidding, Cort Wesley."

He didn't even smile. "We mount the fence on an angle they can't spot us from. Take them out first, as soon as Jones turns out the lights."

"Lots of men sure to be inside," Caitlin reminded. "As many as four truckloads."

"You sound like Jones."

"He was talking guns, I'm talking targets."

"A lot to ask of what bullets we've got, Ranger."

"So what else is new?"

"That wasn't us," Fred Bass said.

"Emergency generators should be kicking on any second," Frank added.

Beriya stepped out of the shadows, flanked by Zhirnosky's eight private guards. "It's an attack."

"That's a load of crap," Calum Dane scoffed. "Nobody even knows we're here."

"It's the Texas Ranger," Beriya persisted, seeming to sniff at the air.

"How can you know that?"

"Because we failed to kill her when we had the chance. This is hers."

"Then finish the job," Zhirnosky ordered. "Do it right this time."

Beriya shook his head, his hair looking like ash-colored straw matted to his scalp in the thin spray cast by the wall lanterns that had automatically flashed on. "First I will see both of you safely on your way."

"Sounds like a plan," Dane echoed.

"Except you're not coming, comrade," Zhirnosky told him.

"I thought we had an arrangement."

"If Beriya is right, then you led this Ranger here somehow. What is it you're not telling me? Because if she's after you, that means she's after me, too."

Dane snapped his toothpick in two with his teeth. "We're talking about a single bitch here, one bitch," he said, thinking of killing the kid with the prosthetic leg who'd messed up his shareholders meeting, just as the shooting started outside.

Eliminating the two guards stationed before the doors had fallen on Cort Wesley. Using the night, finding the pockets of the deepest darkness. Just like he'd done on infiltration missions back in his days with special ops, which seemed like a hundred years ago, the memories feeling like somebody else's.

The two guards never knew what hit them.

The third man, who they hadn't seen perched on the roof, was something else again.

Caitlin heard his heavy steps clanging across the flat tin roof, glimpsed the assault rifle in his grasp as she fired off four shots and hit him with three, tearing his feet out from under him. Not bad under normal circumstances, but tonight those bullets were gold she couldn't afford to spend.

But Cort Wesley retrieved the downed guards' AR-15s and tossed one to her.

"Where's Paz when we need him, Ranger?"

"I was just thinking the same thing, Cort Wesley."

And they burst through the warehouse's front door with guns blazing.

Calum Dane felt as if he were drunk, the world swaying around him, all out of kilter. As the gunshots burned the air before him, he felt he was about to slide off the world into some bottomless abyss. He actually wondered if he was asleep, since the entire experience was marred by a kind of soft focus, viewed through a fog that had settled before his consciousness.

He mind flashed back again to killing the kid in New York, the hyperfocus and exaggeration of every one of his senses that he'd felt—from the smell of blood and urine when the kid pissed himself to the shiny brightness of that blood as it splashed everything and everywhere in the room. This was the opposite of that. The world had turned heavy and slow on its precarious perch, and Dane had the sense he was sliding downhill on ice, unable to stop.

He knew it was Caitlin Strong, just as he somehow grasped something else: she *knew,* knew about *everything,* from his beating the kid to death in New York, to the petrochemical plant that couldn't remain standing, to the real reason he'd snatched those kids up from a field trip to save their lives.

How had she found him here?

What if she'd found the kids? What if the guards he'd left at the farm had given the location up?

Things were going from bad to worse. Survive Caitlin Strong and he'd still have Zhirnosky to contend with. Both men were committed to using each other—a fine prospect, until things turned sour and the world tilted on its axis, trying to spill him off. Zhirnosky's mere presence in the United States, not to mention his reason for coming here, would make him vulnerable to his many enemies, who'd give no quarter—Putin in particular. If this all got out, Zhirnosky was finished.

Which meant the Russian would use the small army he'd brought along to finish Dane as well.

He spotted the Bass brothers cowering in the corner, behind the control panel for the immersive game system prototype, and steered himself their way.

Cort Wesley heard the echoing whir of the emergency generators kicking in, through the gunfire, the cavernous warehouse suddenly aglow in faded light, as if someone had activated a dimmer switch. It reminded him of the first light of dawn, the world coming to life, as the AR-15 danced in his grasp, a pair of magazines taped together jungle style by the make-believe Rambo he'd shot dead outside. That gave him sixty shots in total, and he'd likely need them all, judging by the fierce fire from at least eight enemy gunmen, maybe more.

And that's when time froze, as it always did in moments like this, nothing but the staccato bursts of sound and glimpses of movement registering with him at all.

Here we go again. . . .

Time changed. Places changed.

But not battle, one exactly like the last and the next. Context, location, and purpose always distinct, while sense and mind-set remained the same.

And Cort Wesley took to this one just as he'd taken to all the others. Nothing was forgotten; each piece of every other battle he'd ever fought had left an indelible mark. There was the sense of the assault rifle vibrating slightly as it clacked off rounds, warm against his hands, steady in his grasp. The sight of the muzzle flash, strange metallic smell of air baked by the heat of the expended shells, and his own kinetic energy. The world reduced to its most basic and simple. There was the gun, his targets, and nothing else. Welcome and comfortable in its familiarity, with all thinking suspended and instinct left to command him.

* * *

Bodies fell. How many, Caitlin couldn't say or tell. It felt like a crazed arcade game, right down to the moment her AR-15 clicked empty and she saw "RELOAD" flashing across the screen in her mind. Only she had nothing to reload with. She was back to where she started, with maybe a half-magazine jammed home and a single spare to replace it.

She'd taken cover behind a thick concrete pillar a moment before her assault rifle stopped firing, and now she felt chips of it flying off into the air in small clouds that dissipated as quickly as they'd come. The sensation grated at her teeth, left her gnashing them, as if the whole experience was happening from the inside of her out, instead of the exact opposite.

She spotted a burly, squat man riding the protective shadow of a massive shape that made her think of Guillermo Paz, when she had spotted him that last time, waging war against an insect horde that might've been plenty more than a million strong for all she knew. In Caitlin's mind, Paz was going to come bursting through the ceiling at any moment to stop the flight of the giant and whoever was riding his shadow. She thought she'd glimpsed Calum Dane briefly, couldn't be sure, but knew he was here someplace.

In contrast to the battle against the swarm of beetles back on the farm, this one smelled of nothing but the heat flash of the gunfire and something like superheated wires. Then the world went dark again, pierced almost immediately by slabs of light that somehow sprouted form and substance as the impossible grew before her eyes:

An army of chiseled, well-armed men charging to

her rescue amid a landscape dominated by giant insects that seemed to walk on hind legs. Like something she'd seen Luke lay waste to with controller held in hand before the big screen television in the living room.

Like something out of a video game. And that's when Caitlin realized she was inside one, moving from one hellish scene straight into another.

95

MIDLAND, TEXAS

"This is whacked, man, seriously whacked!" one of the Bass brothers whined to Calum Dane.

"Shut your hole, man!"

"Fuck you, Fred!"

"Fuck you, Frank!"

The brothers argued, but they continued to keep the game running and the projector beams firing as the artificially intelligent video beings of their own creation waged fake war in the midst of a real one. Would have made a great commercial for an upcoming release of a game system worth tens of billions of dollars, if it hadn't been so absurd.

Viewing that bizarre counterpoint of the real versus the fanciful made Dane realize just how incredible this system really was. Impossible to tell, really, which figures were real and which weren't. Except for the giant bugs, of course, which made Dane think of the disaster he'd unleashed across the state of Texas, destroying his reverie and renewing the survival instincts that might guide him safely out of this mess.

Still, the perfection of the game system's functionality, the thought of how much money it had taken to compose every computer-created dot that formed the matrix of the figures inside the game, claimed his mind. Until, anyway, he heard a pop and red lights began flashing all over the massive game console prototype.

"Oh, shit." From Frank.

"Oh, fuck." From Fred.

It took Cort Wesley an elongated instant, the length of a long breath, to realize he was inside some kind of video game, projected everywhere around him. He'd never done a single drug in his life besides booze, but he knew plenty of people who had, and he wondered if this was what being on an acid trip felt like. The world turned fantastical from taking a hit of LSD.

Only he imagined that people on acid didn't have to contend with real-life bullets and bad guys.

Stepping over the bodies that his or Caitlin's fire had downed was the easiest way, in Cort Wesley's mind, of telling the real from the unreal, even as he began using the projected images and game landscape for cover.

Didn't have anything like this in Iraq or the other places I served. . . .

War was war, but this, this—

Cort Wesley's thinking froze abruptly when actual fire hissed through the air past him, instantly recognizable from the fake forays of fire—thanks to instinct bred of actual combat as opposed to make-believe. Something primal distinguished the real threats for him.

Still, more than once before he emptied the second magazine of his assault rifle, he'd had to remind himself not to fire at the giant insects rampaging his way. Dying in some life-size video game, after all, beat dying for real.

Amazing, though, truly amazing, how the all-too-real-looking depictions of special ops soldiers skirted his position as if aware of and acknowledging his presence. Twice Cort Wesley was sure the figures had actually met his gaze, and one had actually winked at him.

Did the games his son Luke played do that? Did Luke play video games with his . . .

Oh boy!

. . . friend Zach?

That wasn't so hard, was it, Bubba? Fuck it all and let the chips fall where they may!

You're damn right, champ! thought Cort Wesley.

Beriya led Zhirnosky through the projected city landscape. They were immersed in it as soldiers as big as him fought a war against giant bugs that seemed to walk upright like men. He had to remind himself they were neither friend nor foe, because they weren't real, no matter how much to the contrary their life-size projections seemed to indicate.

In his mind, none of this was any different from the barricades in Riga where he'd watched his father die. Everything was coming full circle, one impossible image converging into another. For that moment, memories, visions, and video game landscapes all seemed the same.

His father had failed in Riga. He would not fail here. He'd spirit Zhirnosky away, back home to Russia, where he'd be a much bigger hero than his father when the man's political party rose to power.

Beriya had an exit door in his sights when the landscape projected over the naked warehouse changed suddenly to a primordial jungle, the soldiers and aliens from the original game still battling each other. Then, massive shadows fell over both him and Zhirnosky.

Caitlin was thinking of the ambush that had almost punched her ticket, as she stalked the big man, still half expecting Guillermo Paz to drop into the scene when something else did instead.

Dinosaurs, or at least dinosaur-size creatures, which stormed the landscape with roars that bubbled her ears. Sound from whatever crazed video game this was had been blaring all along from unseen speakers. And the cityscape suddenly morphed into the other game's jungle landscape, before the two of them seemed to merge, one transposed upon the other in rotating fashion, as the figures from the dueling games converged. This was the first time she'd noticed the ferocity and realism of it all. If someone had dropped her in here and told her to open her eyes, Caitlin would've thought it was all real, every bit of it.

She lost track of the giant who'd been shepherding the stout Russian figure she took for the leader through the make-believe carnage. Amazing to have been party to such scenes in real life, only to experience one bred of fantasy and reality at the same time, the struggle to discern one from the other playing out in real time, moment by moment.

Caitlin realized her path was blocked, figuratively anyway, by figures converging on each other from both games at once, the landscape flickering, fighting to hold to the primeval landscape while the city backdrop flashed onto the scene like a strobe. The game figures, though, seemed not to care. The soldiers, who looked so real she could practically smell their sweat and feel the heat pouring from their bodies, started shooting at the monster-size creatures, some as tall as the warehouse ceiling—depictions that reminded her of the monsters in pretty much every horror movie she'd glimpsed Luke or Dylan watching.

Real bullets whizzed by her and Caitlin continued on, pistol in hand now, in place of her empty AR-15, wishing she could have grabbed a plasma rifle from one of the pretend shooters, when a hand grasped her from behind and pulled.

Cort Wesley rushed through the city as it became the jungle and then seemed to switch back again. A few times, absurdly, he had to remind himself not to shoot at images his bullets would've passed straight through, no matter how real they looked. For a few moments, he was running in stride with the special ops soldiers forced to battle monsters they hadn't been programmed for, in a terrain to which their artificial intelligence allowed them to adapt.

Had he been bonked on the head? Was this actually happening?

Combat inevitably created its own skewed version of reality, but all this stretched way beyond that. He wondered if Leroy Epps himself might show up when the game reached the next level, gun in hand, firing away at targets both computer generated and flesh and blood.

How about that, Bubba? I'm pretty good, ain't I?

He caught a glimpse of two figures of the flesh-and-blood variety darting about amid the clash of games and landscapes and opened up on them. His bullets pushed straight through the scene before him, clanging off the steel warehouse's walls as a door opened briefly to the night and then closed again.

Zhirnosky backpedaled through the night, wondering if Calum Dane's creatures might burst through the warehouse walls to continue their battle in the real world. Beriya had managed to get him out, but then returned to eliminate the threat posed by the female Texas Ranger he'd been warned about. She'd seen him, could identify him—certainly enough to cause more of an inconvenience in the United States, as well as back home, if she survived.

In that moment, the shock of it all spared Zhirnosky awareness of the abject failure into which this had degenerated. Here he was, so close to seeing the dream of a restored Soviet Union rising on the back of a demoralized and dismantled America, only to now find himself wishing that the walls of the warehouse would crumble before an onslaught of pixilated monsters released into the real world. A fantasy, as much as his whole vain attempt to topple America from the pedestal the country occupied, raising the restored Soviet Union up in the process.

Zhirnosky saw that now, in his mind, along with the indelible, grit-smeared face of a woman wearing a badge he'd glimpsed shining against the video projections he only wished were real.

Caitlin twirled, had her pistol righting on the figure that had grasped her. She recognized Calum Dane just before she fired.

"He was about to shoot you!"

"Who?"

"The big guy. His name's Beriya. I saved your life."

"Who was he trying to lead out?"

"Yanko Zhirnosky. This is all on him. You got here just in time."

"I think you're full of shit," Caitlin said, sweeping her gaze about the dueling landscapes and rampaging creatures in search of Cort Wesley.

She'd started to move, when Dane grasped her by

the shirt once more. "You've got to get me out of here, Ranger!"

"Grab me again and I'll shoot you, Mr. Dane."

Figures drawn from history had joined the mix now as well, Cort Wesley realized. Fugitives from a more urbane game, who had no idea what awaited them here. He watched presidents, a man he thought might be Churchill, and another he recognized as Napoleon scooped up by the monsters' gaping jaws. The thud and thump of them moving was powerful enough to make the floor feel as if it were shaking.

Well, Bubba, if you can't beat 'em . . .

This time, Cort Wesley did swing around, toward where he thought Leroy Epps's voice was coming from, but there was nothing there besides the lesson the ghost had imparted. While bullets passed through the game figures, light didn't, which meant they could continue serving as camouflage for him, cover.

Cort Wesley had known combat in both jungle and urban environments, but no one knew combat in an ever-shifting depiction of both at once. He treated the scene and everything in it as if it were as real as his weapons, going so far as to tear his shirt down the middle and expose as much of his torso as those of the special ops team.

He began mixing with the troops that had survived both the alien invaders and the dinosaurlike monsters. He flinched and closed his eyes when one that looked like a giant squid balanced on its tentacles thrust its twin whips out for him and then reared up to swallow him.

Cort Wesley surged right through it, pistol coming up when the game thing was behind him, and saw the big man poking a pistol out from a nest of thick greenery superimposed over a smoking city grate.

Their guns came up together, both ready to fire, when a snarling, bloblike creature separated in two, the halves converging on the big man from either side. Not real, but it didn't matter, because he hesitated, just for an instant.

Cort Wesley didn't hesitate, but the blob monster had stolen view of his target from him, so all he could do was shoot into the computer-generated, gelatinlike mass. He put his last five bullets into whatever it was concealing, moving in for a better look at the result, when the giant burst out of the projection and slammed him against a wall that wasn't really there.

The Russian giant, all too real and almost as big as Paz, and Cort Wesley continued to twist about, struggling for purchase on each other, as the background whirled from city to jungle and back again. The man-size alien bugs were now fighting the dinosaur-size monsters, while the gunmen who were no more than products of a video feed from both games seemed to have joined forces against them.

Cort Wesley felt the giant slam him up against a projection pillar that turned out to be real this time. Impact rattled his spine and stole his breath. He felt a blow pound his midsection and just managed to twist aside from a vicious punch to his face.

The giant had a knife out by then, and Cort Wesley

actually had to remind himself it was real and not some game-generated prop. The giant lashed it one way and then back the other in expert fashion, his teeth stretched into a grin that shined in the naked light of the multiple projectors. Cort Wesley felt icy-cold streaks that quickly turned red hot where he'd been gashed.

Finally, tearing his belt from his pant loops, he whipped the heavy buckle across the giant's face, catching him totally by surprise, feeling something in the man's cheek or jaw crunch on impact. Then he used the same buckle like a short whip to deflect the next series of knife lashes that followed, more than holding his own, when he had the misfortune of ignoring the downed prop form of one of the projected gunmen.

Because it was a real body, not a prop at all, and Cort Wesley tumbled over it, hitting the floor hard. The giant was tearing a pistol from beneath his jacket and was sweeping it steady when—and Cort Wesley had to blink to make sure this was really happening— the game's unified teams of gunmen seemed to record the giant as a hostile threat and opened up on him with weapons both traditional and futuristic. He was swallowed in a constant spray of light, splashing and flashing around the entire building. Cort Wesley could see the giant's steely eyes waver, suddenly trapped in confusion and uncertainty.

Cort Wesley seized the moment to go for the gun pinned beneath the dead man's body. But the strap caught, and the giant was righting his pistol again, when the biggest shape of any of the projected warriors rushed the giant, certain to go right through him.

But it didn't.

Instead, the giant was there and then he wasn't, lost to a massive shape even bigger than him, swathed everywhere in what looked like steaming tar and smelling of something Cort Wesley's memory told him was that beetle shit.

He couldn't tell what was real and what wasn't real anymore. He half expected Dylan and Luke to join the fun—and Leroy Epps, too, since this whole crazy environment would probably suit him just fine. He tried to remind himself to focus, and managed to lock his gaze on the sight of the giant's hands and feet twitching, halfway up the pillar directly over Cort Wesley, where the dark figure coated in tar, real or unreal, had impaled him.

He realized the air smelled like an overheating car engine. He heard a *poof,* after which the creatures and landscapes vanished. The blank warehouse scene returned, with only a whole bunch of bodies littering the floor. Then Caitlin was by his side, still wary and ready with her pistol.

"Paz," Cort Wesley managed. "I think I saw him."

"Just settle down, Cort Wesley. You're bleeding."

He reached up found the warm blood spilling from the gash on his forehead, more of it leaking out through his midsection, where the giant's knife had grazed it. Caitlin helped him to his feet and supported him as her eyes swept about the confines of the warehouse, empty save for the eight or so bodies spilled on the floor, testament to the carnage the real bullets had left behind.

"Well, Cort Wesley," she said, gun still held at the ready, "I know one thing the boys aren't getting for Christmas."

PART TEN

I think the reason the Rangers have survived since 1823 is our ability to adapt. The Rangers went from single-shot pistol to the Colt, from the horse to the automobile, and now we've grabbed onto the computer age, DNA, and new crime scene technologies. You know, you can move forward or you can stay still and die.

—Former Texas Ranger Tracy Murphree as told to Bruce A. Glasrud and Harold J. Weiss, Jr., eds., *Tracking the Texas Rangers: The Twentieth Century*

96

"It was Paz, Ranger," Cort Wesley insisted, "it had to be. He'd smeared that beetle shit all over him to confuse the sons of bitches. I'm telling you, he was in that warehouse."

Caitlin stood next to him over the grave of Boone Masters, a few days later, after picking him up at the hospital, where he'd been treated for blood loss and a concussion. "If he was, you were the only one who saw him, and I haven't heard a word from the colonel, not a peep."

"How many human skeletons did they find at that farm in Glasscock County?"

"Nobody's talking much."

"Paz is alive, Ranger," Cort Wesley said adamantly, "and he saved my life."

Caitlin gave him a closer look, especially the bandage covering the stitched wound on his forehead and the bulges where similar wraps covered the slash wounds under his shirt. He was moving the slowest she'd ever seen him, each step seeming to bring a grimace.

"You suffered a concussion, Cort Wesley," she told him. "Why don't we pass what you think you saw off to that?"

"Then how . . ."

He let his words trail off when they both spotted Captain Tepper approaching slowly over the grass, smoking a Marlboro, which he discarded and stamped out with a boot as he neared them.

"I tried to switch to those e-cigarettes," he said, "but I couldn't find the goddamn switch." Tepper regarded the small headstone quickly, then looked back at the two of them. "I figured you'd be here. Brings back faded memories of my own dad's funeral. Son of a bitch was so ornery even the undertaker couldn't coax a smile out of him."

Cort Wesley didn't remember his father's funeral very well, the memories shrouded in a fog of guilt over not feeling the kind of regret he felt now. Boone Masters hadn't been the churchgoing type, but it turned out he'd given more than his share to the diocese—enough so a spot was reserved for him here in the Holy Cross Cemetery, located a mile outside Loop 1604, on Nacogdoches Road. It was a beautiful site, the graves taking up only a small portion of the spacious, beautifully landscaped grounds, which looked even more pristine because most of the sites featured ground-level headstones. Somehow, standing here today, the setting seemed to fit Boone Masters for the first time.

"You didn't come out here to enjoy a picnic lunch, Captain."

"Nope," Tepper told them both. "I'm here 'cause I wanted to hear how your little talk went with Calum Dane, firsthand."

97

MIDLAND, TEXAS; EARLIER THAT DAY

"It's good to see you alive, Ranger," Dane had greeted, when Caitlin caught up with him at an oil well just about to strike, halfway between Midland and Odessa in the Permian Basin. "Good to see both of us alive."

"That's why I wanted to thank you in person for your help the other day, sir."

"Any sign of Zhirnosky?"

"None, I'm afraid. He's probably back in Russia by now, which makes him their problem."

"He killed some of my men. He tried to take control of my company. Maybe we should go over there, hunt him down together. He told me something I think might help."

"What's that?"

"You think wiping out most of this country's farmland was all he had in mind? Far from it, Ranger."

"Can you be a bit more specific, sir?"

Dane spit a half-chewed toothpick to the ground and wedged another between his lips. "Why don't you tell me about those two men in the car parked next to your truck first."

"They're New York City police detectives," Caitlin told him. "They've got a few questions for you. I'd recommend you have a lawyer present."

"You brought them here."

"They asked for my help. Professional courtesy."

"Am I missing something, Ranger?"

"Not here, back in New York," Caitlin said, reaching out to pluck the fresh toothpick from his mouth. "One of these, sir."

Dane shook his head. "This about the young man who disappeared after disrupting my shareholders' conference?"

"It is. Your people did a great job of sanitizing the crime scene. Problem was, they forgot to check the elevator. That's where the NYPD found one of these," Caitlin told him, flashing the toothpick she was still holding. "Those detectives are here with a warrant for your DNA. If it matches the toothpick that was found in the elevator, I'd say you're gonna be in a heap of trouble, Mr. Dane."

Dane smirked, pretending not to be particularly bothered by that notion. But then the smirk slipped from his expression, which flattened to the point where his face suddenly looked frozen in a still shot.

"Anything you can do on my behalf with them, Ranger?" he asked her. "As a fellow Texan?"

"Help a man who beats his own son?"

Dane scowled, shaking his head. "We back to that again? You should've seen what my daddy did to me."

"For different reasons, I suspect."

"What's that supposed to mean?" Dane said, stiffening.

"Those pictures I saw of the damage you did to your boy didn't include his face. But a few others I dug up did. I believe his name is Zach, isn't it?"

98

SAN ANTONIO, TEXAS

"Zach, as in . . ." Cort Wesley let his words tail off, still processing what Caitlin had just said.

"That's right."

"The kid who got lost in the woods with Luke!" Tepper realized, stopping just short of slapping himself in the head.

"Dane beat him because he was gay. The boy as much as told me so, without mentioning names."

"Oh," Tepper said, fidgeting a bit.

"Explains why Dane risked everything to save those kids in Armand Bayou. He knew his son was on that field trip," Caitlin said, leaving it there. "Anyway, Dane's fighting the warrant."

"Well, Ranger, at least you didn't shoot him."

"That was my second choice, Captain. We can't get him for the chemical plant fire and we probably can't get him for the billions of dollars in damage his bugs did to the state. But New York can get him for killing that kid with his prosthetic leg. Kind of fitting, I guess."

"Why's that?"

"Because Dane Corp manufactures the plastic it was made out of."

The three of them looked each other, struck by the twisted, macabre irony of that.

"And what exactly did Dane give you on Zhirnosky?" Tepper asked her.

"You owe me something first."

"What's that?"

"The rest of the story, Captain. What you and my dad did to those Russians who got Boone Masters killed."

99

SAN ANTONIO, TEXAS; 1983

Jim Strong stood over the bed of Boone Masters in San Antonio's University Hospital.

"It's blowing up a storm outside, Ranger," Masters noted, gaze drifting to the window.

"Thanks to Hurricane Alicia, ready to make landfall around Houston."

"Bitch of the bunch, it seems." Masters turned from the window. "Thanks for getting me home," he said, more of a message in his eyes than in his words.

"Least I could do."

"Well, there's something on top of that you can do, too. Nobody ever needs to hear about how all this went down, least of all my boy."

"He won't hear it from me, Mr. Masters."

"Call me Boone . . . Jim."

"Guess after stopping the Soviets in their tracks, we should be on a first-name basis."

"For a time, anyway." Masters's expression sombered. "I'm not gonna ask you to look out after my boy."

"I would, if you did."

"I know that, but it'll do more harm than good in my mind. I like the fact of him not thinking too fondly of me, so my being gone won't cause more than a blip in his life. I've lived my life without regret, Jim, and I'd like Cort Wesley to do the same."

Jim Strong shrugged. "Just because you lived it that way doesn't make it right, Boone."

"Best I can do, all the same."

Masters's gaze turned steely against the infamous criminal once more. "We didn't get all of them, Ranger."

"What happened to 'Jim'?"

"Business is business and you need to finish this."

D. W. Tepper stopped in the doorway, looking toward Jim Strong like Masters wasn't even in the room. "We've got a lead."

They literally raced the storm to Houston, heading north along an otherwise abandoned highway, while the lanes heading south were a parking lot of cars that had followed a late evacuation order. The rains and wind were already bad, and got steadily worse the closer they drew to the city, until the torrents came in sheets that seemed to pucker the windshield glass and freeze the wipers midsweep, time after time. The visibility had turned so bad it was like driving through the smoke of a brush fire.

Closer to Houston, D. W. Tepper's truck was hammered by flying objects big and heavy enough to obliterate the fenders and hood and to smash the windshield to the point where the windswept rain hammered them in the cab, soaking both men clean through to the upholstery. Jim looked over then and spotted Tepper lighting a cigarette.

"You're kidding me, right?"

"Always told you smoking would never kill me."

"But you thought it'd be a bullet instead."

"Nobody's right all the time."

In response to their all points bulletin, a report had come in from Hobby Airport in Houston about four Russian-speaking men buying plane tickets in cash. One of them matched the description of Anton Kasputin and, since the airport had been officially declared closed, he wasn't going anywhere. Jim Strong had instructed Houston officials to stand down until his arrival, told them that this was Ranger jurisdiction.

"You want Kasputin for yourself," Tepper concluded, voice a bit gnarled by the cigarette clenched between his lips as his hands hung on to the steering wheel for dear life.

"Least I can do for Boone Masters."

"Old school never goes away, does it?"

Jim Strong looked across the soaked seat toward him, swiping a wet sleeve against his even wetter face. "We're driving through a hurricane to get into a gunfight. You tell me, D.W."

*   *   *

The normally bustling airport was eerie in its desolation, closed to air traffic but not shut down, due to the mass of travelers stranded there. The gates remained open and functional, but no planes were coming in, and almost all those that had been grounded had been flown out to airports further inland, to avoid being damaged.

Hobby's naked exterior belied the congestion of the stranded inside. Hurricane Alicia was bearing down on the city with a force that could leave tens of billions of dollars of damage in its wake; the Lone Star State offered no protection against natural disasters.

D. W. Tepper parked his truck in a red zone and stepped out with Jim Strong into the teeth of the hurricane's mounting winds, rain hammering them in waves that soaked through their rain slickers. On top of everything else, the storm had already produced a series of tornadoes, and more were expected. Toppled trash cans rolled down the airport access road, the lighter ones lifted airborne by the increasing gales, one missing Jim's head by no more than an inch. Their former contents whipped about in a steady swirl, all manner of paper cups, plates, and food wrappers filling the air like snow. It was all the Rangers could do just to get inside the terminal through the still-functioning automatic sliding doors, even as a tornado warning alarm blared somewhere close by.

Jim Strong and D. W. Tepper shed their slickers, once inside, dropping them where they stood and spotting the airport security chief, who was waiting as instructed. He didn't notice the Rangers right away because he'd been deluged by passengers on the verge of panic, looking for any reassurance they could find—probably that the whole terminal building wasn't on the verge of blowing away itself. The sour smell of fear and anxiety hung in the air like dried sweat. The stranded passengers were pale, wide eyed, and not even seeming to blink, to the point where they looked like zombies.

The airport security chief, a tall, gaunt man with a thin mustache, finally spotted them and broke away from the crowd to approach.

"They're on the Pan Am concourse, waiting for a flight to New York," he reported. "I've got two of my men watching from a distance, just like you said."

"I said one man," corrected Jim Strong, just before the shooting started.

Somewhere in the back of his mind, Jim Strong registered the tornado warning alarm blaring inside the airport now, as well as Hurricane Alicia battering Hobby with such force that the view beyond the wall-length windows was obliterated. Worse than night, because of the howling beyond and the occasional crash of something slamming up against the glass, as if hurled by some giant creature beyond. Thunder crackled. Lightning flared.

As he rushed down the Pan Am concourse toward the intermittent sounds of gunfire, Jim was also conscious of the world darkening beyond those windows. His ears had started popping and he felt a low rumble in the pit of his stomach. The drastic and sudden change in pressure told him a tornado must be bearing down on the airport now, certain to swallow up whatever aircraft remained on the tarmac, along with jetways, food trucks, and just about anything else that wasn't bolted down.

He and Tepper rushed through a stampede of already-panicked would-be passengers now running for their lives.

"Son of a bitch, son of a bitch!" Tepper kept saying.

"I warned them, D.W. I warned them!" Jim followed, drawing closer to the clatter of gunfire.

He spotted Kasputin first. He and five of his thugs, as opposed to the three they were expecting, were holed up in a terminal bar, making full use of both the counter and toppled tables for cover. Two of the gunmen were squeezed between one of those tables and the window glass itself, which looked like it was melting from the waves of rain running down it. Jim Strong knew there was no sense in wasting bullets trying for an impossible shot, especially with innocent bystanders clinging to cover they might abandon at any moment, so he decided to flush the Russians out instead.

He put three bullets into the glass over and behind them.

The big .45 shells exploded with a deafening roar and sent the bulk of bystanders scurrying away, their footsteps echoing in hollow fashion against the concourse tile in the sudden silence that followed. The bullets blew right through glass that spiderwebbed and blew inward behind the force of the storm, exposing the terminal to Hurricane Alicia's effects. Glasses, menus, mugs, plates, and all manner of silverware were hurled into the air, adding to the maelstrom and forcing the Rangers to duck or dodge to avoid being struck. But the storm's onslaught and entry had the dual effect of forcing the first two Russian gunmen from their perch. Jim Strong and Tepper opened up together, the big bullets blowing the Russians' bodies backwards until the wind pushed them back forward, ultimately holding them upright for a split second before catching them in a swirl that threw their corpses forward. Their blood whipped about with the loosed ice and contents of drinks abandoned on tabletops when the gunfight began.

An onslaught of fire erupted from behind the bar, forcing the Rangers behind the cover of toppled trash cans that had collected against a men's room entrance across the way. Jim recovered his senses just in time to spot Kasputin himself leading his three remaining men out a door marked Emergency Exit Only, which led out onto the tarmac. An alarm immediately began to squeal in insane counterpoint as the Rangers fought the buffeting winds toward the same door, emerging just as an almost preternatural calm fell over the field, accompanied by a hint of sunshine.

"Holy shit," Tepper muttered, "is that a . . ."

"Yup," Jim Strong picked up, "a funnel cloud."

* * *

The tornado bred by Hurricane Alicia seemed to grow and widen as it swooped down over the airport tarmac, sucking up everything in its path while coughing out tires, food wagons, stray luggage, and signs ripped right out of the ground. The door had slammed behind the Rangers, denying them any thought of reentering the terminal, while bullets smacked off the concrete facing behind them. The howl of the approaching tornado drowned out the sounds both of the gunshots and of their impacts, making Jim Strong feel he was acting out a scene in some nightmarish silent movie, even as the funnel cloud sliced across the patchwork of runways like a black vortex, swallowing everything before it.

The world seemed to vanish in the tornado's wake, two of the Russian gunmen trying to flee its path too late. Jim Strong and D. W. Tepper watched the funnel draw the Russians in and spin them around, and then they were gone, as if merged into it and no longer visible. A final gunman had stayed with Kasputin, the two of them pinned against a toppled luggage cart, holding on to the restraining straps for dear life.

The Rangers approached, fighting the winds at the periphery of the funnel cloud, which kept twisting them one way and then back the other, firing shots silenced by the impossible crescendo of sound pitched enough to sting their ears. Jim realized he was having trouble finding breath amid the torrents of rain that seemed to provide no quarter for air.

Can you drown on land?

Crazy thought, he knew, but that's what it felt like.

"Ranger!"

He heard a portion of Tepper's desperate call and realized he was behind him, taking a firm hold of Jim's clothes and trying to pull him back. But Jim was hearing none of it, with Kasputin right there in his sights, the grasp of his final gunman the only thing keeping Kasputin from being vacuumed up. Then the funnel cloud grabbed that gunman in its grasp and seemed to pick him up by the boot strings, whipping him about upside down before the darkness swallowed him altogether.

Jim found himself propped up against a terminal bulkhead door, Tepper tying himself to the latch with a belt. The slide of Jim's .45 locked empty. Kasputin struggled to right his pistol on him while desperately clutching a strap with the other. Jim thought he recorded a final series of muzzle flashes before the pistol was lost to the vortex of wind sweeping it away. By then, Jim had gotten his own belt fastened tight through the latch, his body pressed up tight to the bulkhead door. He felt it rattle and buffet against him. He looked back toward Kasputin but could see nothing now, the world erased by the funnel cloud that was upon the terminal.

Jim Strong thought he might've been screaming, but he couldn't hear himself, couldn't hear anything. The tornado had stripped him of breath and pushed him into the air, the belt wrenching but holding. He saw D. W. Tepper's belt snap, and he latched a hand to Tepper's waistband and drew him in, with an arm tucked around his chest, battling the funnel cloud for him. He tried to find Kasputin through the black swirl, but it gave up nothing and seemed to be everywhere at once.

Jim pushed Tepper between him and the bulkhead door, pressing himself against it for dear life. The latch still wasn't giving, so he stripped Tepper's holstered .45 free and fired the final two rounds against it. Sparks flew, the wind swallowing everything, including his thoughts. But the latch gave and he jerked the bulkhead door open, feeling the sweep of the funnel cloud, just starting to tear both him and Tepper away, when Jim pushed both of them inside the terminal.

The door itself was torn free and whisked away as if weightless, leaving nothing beyond them but a swirling blackness that was everywhere at once. Jim forced his gaze through it, looking for Kasputin, but the Russian and everything around him looked to have been sucked up by the storm by the time the vortex finally cleared.

"We get him?" a still-dazed D. W. Tepper shouted from the floor, over the winds that continued to rage.

"Nope," Jim Strong said, still gazing into the carnage the tornado had left behind on the tarmac. "Guess we didn't have to."

100

SAN ANTONIO

"Explains why Anton Kasputin needed to disappear, become another man entirely, after somehow surviving all that," Caitlin said when Tepper had finished. A graveyard was an oddly appropriate place to hear the rest of the tale.

"In a hurricane yet," Tepper followed, shaking his head. "Am I the only one who finds that about as fitting as it gets?"

"Might've been my father's most famous gunfight, the day he shot it out with a tornado," Caitlin said, recalling parts of the tale now. "But I never could pin him down on exactly who he was shooting it out with. Guess I know why, now."

"It was hushed up all the way from the White House," Tepper told her. "Whole story was concocted that held up well enough, and when men get swept up by a tornado, there's not normally much evidence to process. What was left of their remains was found maybe ten miles away by a farmer, when he went to check on his herd, if you can believe that."

Caitlin looked toward Cort Wesley. "After all this, I can believe anything."

"It's your turn now, Ranger," Tepper said to her. "What exactly did Calum Dane tell you about Zhirnosky and how we can finish this once and for all?"

"Well, Captain, it involves a trip to Russia on Homeland Security's dime. Jones is making the arrangements."

"Russia got any idea what's headed their way?"

"There's one Russian in particular who does. . . ."

Before Caitlin could elaborate further, she spotted a dark-clad man heading toward them, skirting the grass in favor of the concrete walkway that sliced through the graveyard. All three whipped their guns out when he dipped a hand under his jacket, ready to shoot before the man took his next breath.

"Hold on! Hold on!" he cried out, terrified, jerking a pair of trembling hands into the air. "I'm just here to serve a subpoena! I'm not even armed!"

Tepper moved forward, still holding his .45 at the ready. He stripped a trifolded set of pages wrapped in a blue cover from the man's inside jacket pocket and regarded them quickly.

"Looks like it's for you, Ranger," he said to Caitlin.

IOI

WASHINGTON, DC; TWO WEEKS LATER

"Raise your right hand, please," Asa Fraley, chairman of the Committee on Oversight and Government Reform, said, his own hand in the air as he addressed Caitlin. "Do you swear the testimony you provide at this hearing shall be the truth, the whole truth, and nothing but the truth, so help you God."

Caitlin made sure to tip her mouth toward the microphone "I do."

"Please be seated, Ms. Strong."

"It's Ranger, sir."

"Excuse me?"

"Just like you like to be addressed as 'Congressman' . . . *Mister* Fraley."

"Acknowledged, *Ranger* Strong," Fraley relented, clearly enjoying himself as cameras whirred, flashed, and clicked. "You have been called to testify for us today on the excesses of law enforcement and the tendency to expand the mandate of duties you are duly sworn to perform. In other words, how far is too far to go in the purported pursuit of justice, and how are we to hold our law enforcement officials responsible for exceeding their authority in that regard and taking innocent lives in the process of this excess."

"Was that a question, sir," Caitlin started, when Fraley lapsed into silence, "or just a mouthful?"

"Let me pose it as a question for you, Ranger: How many men have you shot?"

"I don't keep count of such things, Congressman."

"Then maybe you should. Would you like to hear the number, Ranger Strong, before we enter it into the record?"

"That isn't necessary, and the number you're referring to likely isn't accurate."

"Could you explain that last statement, please, for the record?"

"I've shot plenty more than shows up in the reports before you. For the record."

Fraley banged his gavel dramatically when a murmur spread through the crowd. "And how many more would that be?"

"Like I said, sir, I don't keep count. It just comes with the territory."

Fraley covered his microphone to confer briefly with the ranking member from the minority party. "Ranger Strong, we can't help but notice that no legal representative has accompanied you here today."

Caitlin looked at the empty chairs on either side of

er. "I'll stand behind everything I've done in service o the Rangers and the State of Texas," she said into the microphone. "In my experience you only need a lawyer f you've done something wrong."

Laughter and a brief ripple of applause filtered hrough the chamber, Fraley just short of rapping his ;avel.

"And it's you who may need a lawyer, Congressman," she added.

"And why's that, Ranger?"

"Because it so happens a criminal complaint has been filed against you back in Texas." Caitlin withdrew a folded set of pages from the inside pocket of he lightweight denim jacket she'd worn for the occasion. "I have it right here. The charge is conspiracy."

"This hearing isn't about me, Ranger," Fraley said, struggling hard to manage a smirk.

"Why don't you let me speak my piece? Unless you've got something to hide, Congressman."

"Proceed, Ranger Strong."

"I believe you're acquainted with Christoph Russell Ilg, the rancher who believed he could graze his stolen cattle for free."

"I am."

"Him being a rustler didn't sit well with me. A moocher and lowlife for sure, but a rustler who'd bother rebranding the stolen cattle? No, that didn't seem his style at all."

Fraley sat stoically on the raised dais before her. Caitlin was certain he was clutching his gavel, even though she couldn't see it from this angle.

"So I paid him a visit before I came down here," she

continued. "He was none too happy to see me, until I threatened to revoke his bail. He sang your praises Congressman, had a lot of nice things to say. Like you telling him he didn't need to pay his grazing fees, that you'd take care of things on his behalf."

"I never said anything of the sort!" Fraley roared, over the hum of words being exchanged in the hearing chamber.

"And where do you think he said he got the cattle to replace the ones that had died, threatening to stop the plan you hatched in a real hurry?"

Fraley rose slowly, his tinted hair looking orange under the bright lighting as he pointed the heavy end of his gavel straight at Caitlin. "Texas Ranger or not, this committee will entertain no more of these baseless allegations meant to distract us from doing our duty."

"Does your duty include cattle rustling, sir? Because you may be interested to know that the local sheriff's department just arrested the alleged perpetrator. I hear they got security camera footage to help make their case."

"Caitlin Strong, you are out of order!" Fraley repeated, louder, banging his gavel over the murmurs spreading through the gallery and the press suddenly turning their focus on him. "These charges are not worthy of being entered into the record. Please strike all comments made by the witness in that regard from the record."

Caitlin waited for the chamber to quiet again before resuming. "Then can you tell me how it is, Congressman, the rustler in custody happens to be your brother?"

"How could I not know about this?" President Vladimir Putin said into his headset, as the helicopter cruised over the vast expanse of crops filling out the Black Earth region of southern Russia, looking like an endless ribbon of beige stretched atop the countryside.

"We'd run out of fuel before we got to see the whole of these fields, sir," Caitlin told him. Jones had arranged for her to join a law enforcement delegation to Moscow, along with this private audience with the Russian president. "I'm told it's somewhere around twenty million acres, capable of yielding ten thousand metric tons of wheat per year, putting Russia on par with the United States and China in terms of production. With America's heartland turned into a wasteland, Zhirnosky would've used these crops as a springboard to succeed you as president. He even found himself a distributor, in the person of Calum Dane."

Putin sneered at that. "So now I've received two gifts from you," he said, in a fashion hardly in keeping with his fearsomely cold reputation. "But I must say, the horse was much more pleasant to receive."

"It's a Driftwood quarter, Mr. President, bred at Green Creek Ranch. Not much for speed, but great for riding, and tough as nails. I've heard a pair of them can plow as much as four acres in a single day. I saw one crush a possum flat as a pancake once."

Putin grinned. "Sounds exactly like the fate soon to befall Comrade Zhirnosky, Ranger."

EPILOGUE

The legendary Texas Rangers occupy a unique place in American history both as lawmen and as larger-than-life heroes, occasionally even antiheroes. Historically the force has reflected the values and shortcomings of the Texas society of the time. As a statewide enforcement agency the Rangers have been wielded as a political instrument by elected offices in times of social and economic discord. At times actions by Rangers enforced inequitable and even violent causes, often dictated by Texas law. Today the Rangers still reflect the direction and values of the state but modern Texas itself has adapted, sometimes imperfectly, to a more diverse culture and peaceful, often technological, solutions to the challenges of the twenty-first century. So too has the modern Ranger force . . . adapted and today operates as a team of professional and respected lawmen—but lawmen with a colorful history.

—Bruce A. Glasrud and Harold J. Weiss, Jr.,
Tracking the Texas Rangers: The Twentieth Century

SAN ANTONIO, TEXAS

"You have that talk with Luke?" Caitlin asked Cort Wesley, on the drive from the airport where he'd picked her up after she flew back from Moscow by way of New York.

"Not yet. Keep putting it off. Hey, don't look at me that way."

"What way is that?"

"Like you think I'm avoiding the issue, Ranger, sticking my head in the sand."

"That is what I think," she told him.

"Well, I've started the conversation maybe a dozen times, but it keeps going off the rails. I'll finish it next time, I promise."

"Sure, Cort Wesley, whatever you say."

"You don't believe me?" he said, and whipped out his cell phone. "I'll up and call Luke right now, I swear I will. Have that talk right now for you to hear on speaker."

"I thought you said he was back in school."

Cort Wesley stuffed the phone back in his pocket. "Later on, then."

"Sure."

"Stop saying that. Anyway, Zach's mother and stepdad finally showed up."

"You say anything to them?"

"As little as possible for now."

"Even about Calum Dane?"

"I figured I'd leave that to you, Ranger."

"When the time is right."

"Speaking of the right time, I've got a little present here for you," Cort Wesley said, lifting what looked like a matchbox from the console.

Caitlin took the box from his grasp and slid it open, finding inside a dead beetle that looked exactly like the ones they'd battled after rescuing the hostages on Calum Dane's former cotton farm in Glasscock County. Seeing it in this condition made for a pleasant contrast with the vision of the picture from Doc Whatley's encyclopedia, come to life in those fields.

"Turns out there was a survivor from the blast Zhirnosky engineered in Kansas, a doctor who moonlights as a rodeo clown," Cort Wesley explained to her. "He came up with the means to kill all those bugs by putting a little present in some food bait. They'll be a nuisance for a while, but they're all gonna end up exactly like the one in that box."

Caitlin slid the box closed again and placed it back in the console. "You look tired," Caitlin said, as they turned onto East Main Plaza, going through the city, thanks to both an accident and construction on the 410.

"I haven't been getting much sleep."

"You're a damn good father, Cort Wesley."

"It's not about Luke so much as his friend Zach. I

keep thinking of his son-of-a-bitch father beating him on account of he's gay."

"It's not about that," Caitlin corrected. "It's about the kind of man Calum Dane is. Love doesn't mean a damn thing to him—I don't think it ever did. For him, power is everything, and asserting it over anyone in his world is like breathing to him. Google 'bully' on the Internet and his will be the first face that comes up."

"How do we find these people, Ranger?" Cort Wesley asked her, shaking his head.

"We don't. They find us, through their actions. There's too many Zachs out there, and too many Calum Danes too."

Cort Wesley took a deep breath and glanced across the seat. "What about Paz?"

"Haven't heard a word from him. I don't think any man could've survived what I saw behind us on that farm," Caitlin said, elaborating no further.

"That's assuming Paz is a man."

"He wasn't in the warehouse, Cort Wesley. That was your imagination, turning one of the game figures into him."

"The smell of beetle shit included?"

Caitlin just shrugged.

"So the Russian giant who ended up impaled on a spike?"

"You," Caitlin told him. "You did it. You were slumped under him when I found you. You don't remember it that way, but that's the way it happened."

Cort Wesley saw no point in arguing the matter further. "I was thinking of paying a visit to that psychic

Paz was seeing, check if maybe she's still tuned in to the same frequency."

"Paz doesn't have a frequency, he's got his own goddamn bandwidth."

"Present tense, Ranger?" Cort Wesley said and checked the rearview mirror.

They hit a traffic snarl a few blocks before San Fernando Cathedral, the church Guillermo Paz was known to frequent. At first, Caitlin and Cort Wesley passed it off to too many cars funneling off the highway, but drawing closer they saw an intersection before the church awash in flashing lights, traffic being detoured onto adjoining streets. They noticed the shapes hanging from matching telephone poles on either side of the street, just short of the church, passing them off initially as the product of a prank.

Initially.

Cort Wesley leaned forward, squinting behind the wheel. "Is *that* . . . are *those* . . ."

"Yes, I believe they are," Caitlin acknowledged.

They were close enough now to clearly identify the shapes as bodies swaying lightly in the breeze; what looked like baling wire was looped under their arms and knotted over spokes protruding from the poles. The corpses' sagging pants hung low enough on their hips to expose their boxer shorts, and bandanas dressed in the colors of whatever gang they'd run with were stuffed in their mouths.

Cort Wesley looked across the seat. "Didn't you tell me that church—*Paz's* church—was vandalized recently?"

"I did."

"Then I guess it's safe to assume the offenders have been punished," Cort Wesley told her.

"We shouldn't be smiling about this, Cort Wesley."

"But we still are."

"All things being relative."

"That's my point, Ranger. That's my point."

AUTHOR'S NOTE

The headline in the January 27, 2014, edition of *The New York Times* read, "Genetic Weapon Against Insects Raises Hope and Fear in Farming," and with it, this book was born, almost a year to the day before I finished it. I saw the headline and, even before reading the article, the two greatest words for a writer popped into my mind: What if?

That's where all thrillers are born. In this case, what if something went wrong with that kind of genetic weapon—I mean *really* wrong?

As a kid, maybe the best short story I read was one called "Leiningen Versus the Ants," by Carl Stephenson, about a Brazilian plantation owner who learns that a horde of army ants, *marabunta,* is headed his way. It was made into a damn good film for its time, called *The Naked Jungle,* starring the great Charlton Heston. In both versions, Leiningen decides to stay and fight the scourge, resulting in a brilliant last hour featuring amazing effects, before anyone even knew what computer animation was. I guess I'd always wanted to do my version of that tale, and that *New York Times* article gave me the chance.

The idea for a gunfight staged within a video game came after I read a similar Web article on "immersive gaming." I was shocked at how close Samsung actually is to showcasing a first-generation version. I kid you not. And the concept also reminded me of the classic short story "The Veldt," by the great Ray Bradbury. Given his recent passing, I saw the scene as a way to pay homage to one of America's greatest writers, at any time or in any genre.

I'm working up the concept for Caitlin's next adventure now. Guess it's time, with the anniversary of finding the last one just about upon me. So let's make a date to get together at the same time next year, and be well until then.

Providence, Rhode Island; January 26, 2015

Read on for a preview of

STRONG
COLD DEAD

Jon Land

•

Available in October 2016 from
Tom Doherty Associates

A FORGE HARDCOVER

I

EAST SAN ANTONIO, TEXAS

"Nobody goes beyond this point, ma'am," the tall, burly San Antonio policeman, outfitted in full riot gear, told Caitlin Strong.

"That include Texas Rangers . . ." She hesitated long enough to read the nameplate over his badge. "Officer Salazar?"

"That's *Sergeant* Salazar, Ranger. And the answer is yes, it includes everyone. *Especially* Texas Rangers."

"Well, Sergeant, maybe we wouldn't need to be here if a couple of your patrolmen hadn't gunned down a ten-year-old boy."

Salazar looked at Caitlin, scowling as he backed away from her Explorer. A few blocks beyond the checkpoint, a grayish mist seemed to hover in the air, residue of the tear gas she expected would be unleashed again soon. That is, unless the youthful crowd currently packed into the small commercial district at the near end of Hackberry Avenue dispersed, which they were showing no signs of doing. The third night of trouble had brought the National Guard to the scene, in full battle attire that included M4 rifles and flak jackets. Caitlin could see that more floodlights had been set up to keep the street bathed in daylight brightness. They cast a strange hue that reminded her of movie kliegs, as if this were a scene concocted from fiction rather than one that had arisen out of random tragedy.

Sergeant Salazar came right up to her open window, close enough for Caitlin to smell spearmint on his breath as he worked a wad of gum from one side of his mouth to the other.

"Those patrolmen found themselves in the crossfire of a gunfight between a neighborhood watch leader and gangbangers he thought were robbing a convenience store where most pay with their EBT cards. The clerk who chased them down the street just wanted to return the change they'd left on the counter for their ice cream, but the watch leader, Alfonzo Martinez, saw the scene otherwise and ordered the bangers to stop and put their hands in the air."

Neighborhood watch leader Martinez, a lifelong resident of J Street, who'd managed to steer clear of violence all his life, started firing his heirloom Springfield 1911 model .45 as soon as the gangbangers yanked pistols from the waistbands of their droopy trousers. The only thing his shots hit was a passing San Antonio Police car. The uniformed officers inside mistook the fire as coming from the gangbangers, and the officers opened up on them so indiscriminately that the lone victim of their fire was a ten-year-old boy who'd emerged from the same convenience store.

It was almost dawn before everything got sorted out and the investigative team, comprising San Antonio police and highway patrol detectives, thought they'd managed to get control of the situation. Then, relatively peaceful protests by day gave way to an eruption of violence at night, spearheaded by rival gangs who abandoned their turf wars to join forces against an enemy both of them loathed. Violence and looting reigned, only to get worse by the second night, when eight officers ended up hospitalized—one injured by what was later identified as a bullet rather than a rock. And now, the third night found the National Guard on the scene in force, along with armored police vehicles from as far away as Houston, barricading the streets to basically shut the neighborhoods of east San Antonio's northern periphery off from the rest of the city.

"You're still here, Ranger," Sergeant Salazar noted.

"Just considering my options."

"Only option you have is to turn your vehicle around and leave the area, ma'am. You're not needed or welcome here."

"On whose orders, exactly?" Caitlin wondered aloud.

"Mine," a female voice boomed, a moment before Caitlin heard a loud pop, like a shotgun blast, crackle through the air.

2

A few blocks beyond the checkpoint, one of the spotlights fizzled and died, more likely the victim of a well-thrown rock than a bullet. Caitlin was out of her Explorer by then, hand instinctively straying to her holstered SIG Sauer P-226 in anticipation of more shots to follow.

"Get back in your vehicle, Ranger," said Consuelo Alonzo, deputy chief of the San Antonio Police Department, as she strode forward, red-faced from the exertion of rushing to the scene from the police line upon learning of Caitlin's arrival.

"You got a problem with getting some more backup?" Caitlin asked her.

"I do when it comes from you."

"Why don't you catch your breath and hear me out?"

"Because there's nothing you have to say that can possibly interest me right now. In case you haven't noticed, we're sitting on a powder keg, one spark away from blowing San Antonio to hell. We don't need you providing that spark, Ranger. No way."

Instead of settling down, Alonzo's agitation continued to increase. Her face had grown redder, her words emerging through breaths that were becoming more and more rapid. She had risen quickly through the ranks of the department, the youngest woman ever to make captain, three years prior to her recent promotion to deputy chief. And she had been rumored to be in line for the job of public safety commissioner, which came with a plush Austin office and would make her, among other things, chief overseer of the Texas Rangers. Alonzo had no doubt relished that particular perk of a job certain to be hers—until the death of a Chinese diplomat, exacerbated by Caitlin's solving of the murder while Alonzo was dealing with more politically oriented ramifications, led to her being passed over.

Alonzo had overcome an appearance that was often referred to as "masculine," even by her supporters, and much worse than that by her detractors, who seemed to put no stock in the fact that she was happily raising three young children with her husband, who was a professional boxing referee. This was Texas, after all, where a woman needed to work twice as hard, and be twice as good, in a profession ruggedly and stubbornly perceived to be for men only. Caitlin and Alonzo had had their differences over the years but had mostly maintained a mutual respect defined by their professionalism and the sense that their own squabbles only further emboldened those who sought their demise.

At least until Alonzo assigned Caitlin all the blame for Alonzo losing out on a job that was likely never going to be hers now. Since then, Alonzo had used her position as deputy chief to wage subtle war on the Rangers' San Antonio-based Company F whenever possible, seizing upon any bureaucratic conflict or jurisdictional dispute she could in a hapless attempt to make Caitlin's life miserable.

Alonzo ran a hand through her spiky hair. She was heavyset and had once set the women's record for the bench press in her weight class. She'd also done some boxing and was reputed to be the best target shooter with a pistol in the entire department. But Caitlin had beaten her three times running when they'd gone up against each other in state-sponsored contests, winning the overall title in two of those, instead of just the women's division. Caitlin had stopped entering after her most recent victory, figuring the last thing she needed was to draw more attention to herself than her exploits already had.

"You're not moving, Ranger," Alonzo told her.

Caitlin gestured toward a figure pressed tightly against the waist-high concrete barrier erected to close off the street to unauthorized vehicles. "See that woman there? That's the mother of the boy who was killed by the fire of those SAPD officers. She's the one who called me, asked me to see what I could do about the violence being done in her boy's name. She doesn't want the city to burn on his account. She wants this resolved peacefully."

"And you think I don't?"

"No, ma'am. It's a question about how you're going about things."

"And how's that?" Alonso asked, not sounding as if she was really interested in Caitlin's answer. "We got a full-scale riot brewing back there. What exactly do you think you can do about it that we can't?"

"I've got an idea or two."

"Care to share them?"

"Ever hear of Diego Ramon Alcantara?"

"Can't say that I have."

"He goes by the nickname Diablo. Leader of a gang running drugs for a Mexican cartel that sees the riots as their opportunity to solidify their hold on the business throughout the state. And Diablo Alcantara has united the city's normally warring gangs toward that purpose, on the cartel's behalf. I take him off the board, all this goes away."

Alonzo shook her head, her expression a mix of resentment and disbelief. "You alone?"

"That's right. Just give me a chance. What have you got to lose, Deputy Chief?"

"How about this city?"

Caitlin turned her gaze in the direction of the rioting. "Seems to me it's already lost. Thing at this point is to get it back."

Alonzo's lower lip crawled over her upper one, her cheeks puckering, until she blew out some breath that hit Caitlin like a blast from a just-opened oven. "We've got five hundred personnel on scene who haven't been able to manage that."

"Would it really hurt to listen to what I've got to say?"

"It hurts me, standing here right now instead of commanding the front line. The governor just approved an assault. We move inside the next hour, if the crowd doesn't disperse as ordered."

"Just give me a chance."

Alonzo shook her head again. "You know the saying 'stone cold dead,' Ranger?"

"I do."

"Maybe you haven't heard that among Texas law enforcement types it's called '*strong* cold dead' now."

Caitlin smiled slightly. "Is that a fact?"

Alonzo was left shaking her head. "Tell me, when you look in the mirror, how big's the army that looks back?"

"Well, you know how the saying goes, Deputy Chief," Caitlin said, backpedaling toward her SUV. "'One riot, one Ranger.'"

3

EAST SAN ANTONIO, TEXAS

Caitlin skulked about the outskirts of the neighborhoods just outside the riot zone. Through windows not boarded up or covered in grates, she spied more than one family following the simmering violence just a few blocks away on their televisions while they huddled against a wall.

According to the information she'd obtained from a trio of informants, Diablo Alcantara was running the show from his sister's home, near J Street, two blocks from the brewing riot's front lines. The cartels had trained Alcantara well, had taught him the tricks of their own trade, to inspire everyday people to turn to violence to the point that it came to define them. By the time a person found himself on this road, he was too far down it to turn back. So here, in east San

Antonio, closing the schools for the day had turned hundreds of teenagers into virtual anarchists, looting and destroying for its own sake. Right now, Caitlin could still smell the smoke from a Laundromat that had burned to the ground after local firefighters and their trucks had been chased back by crowds hurling bottles and rocks. Three firefighters had been hospitalized, and one of the engines had been abandoned at the head of the street, where it too had been set ablaze.

The chemicals and detergents stored in a back room of the Laundromat had turned the air noxious for a time, the strange combination of lavender soap powder mixing with the corrosive bleaches to form the perfect metaphor for the city of San Antonio. Watching those white curtains of mist wafting through the flames to chase the rioters away—more effective than any efforts the authorities had mounted—had given Caitlin the idea to which Deputy Chief Alonzo had refused to listen.

Holding her position against a house, in view of the main drag, Caitlin checked her watch, then the sky, and finally her cell phone, to make sure she had a strong signal. Because word was the gangs were communicating via text message, there had talk of shutting down the grid, but nobody could figure out a way to do it quickly—something Caitlin was glad for now.

Above the fire smoke and tear gas residue staining the air in patches, the night sky was clear, and she made out a collection of news choppers, their navigation lights flashing like the stars millions of miles beyond them. Creeping closer to J Street and the home of Diablo Alcantara's sister, Caitlin froze. She was just beyond the spray of a streetlight, which showcased a block packed with gang members proudly and openly displaying their colors.

Amid the gangbangers unified in this unholy alliance was a stocky figure, more bulk than muscle, holding court near the rear. Diablo Alcantara had gotten into a knife fight while in high school and had ended up losing an eye to a slice that split the left side of his face right down the middle. Even in pictures, it was hard for Caitlin to look at the jagged scar, and the translucent orb visible through the narrow slit Alcantara had for an eye socket, without feeling a flutter in her stomach.

Caitlin knew that the stocky figure was Alcantara the moment he turned enough toward the streetlight for its spray to reflect off the marble-like thing wedged into his skull in place of an eye. She counted fifty bangers in the vicinity, armed with assault rifles and submachine guns no intelligence report had made mention of, meaning such firepower must have only just reached the scene, courtesy of the cartels.

The bangers, under Diablo Alcantara's leadership, looked ready to launch the assault that would push the rioting from this neighborhood into the city proper. They were intent on turning San Antonio into Juarez. Caitlin's plan hadn't accounted for going up against heavy weaponry, but the reality made the plan's implementation all the more necessary. Giving the matter no further consideration, she lifted the cell phone closer and pressed out three words in a text message: *Come on in.*

Caitlin figured she had three, maybe four minutes to wait. She spent the first of them following the gang members' antics in preparation for what was to come. Some of them wore military-grade flak jackets, in odd counterpoint to the pungent scent of marijuana smoke gradually claiming the air. She watched beer bottles drained and smashed, a few stray shots fired into the air to the cheering of the most chemically altered in the bunch.

Caitlin checked her watch one last time before she stepped out from the darkness and into the street, light glinting off her badge, holstered pistol in plain view as she continued toward the center of the block.

"I'm a Texas Ranger," she called out to the gang members, whose gazes fixed on her in disbelief. "All of you, stay right where you are."

4

EAST SAN ANTONIO, TEXAS

Caitlin stopped thirty feet from Diablo Alcantara and swept her gaze across the other fifty or so gang members, who were armed to fight a small war.

"Diego Alcantara?" she called, breaking the silence that had settled over the block.

"Who wants to know?" Alcantara asked, emboldened by having a veritable army to back him up.

"Texas Rangers, sir. You're under arrest."

The silence returned, until it was broken anew by

laughter. Just a ripple at first but quickly spreading, some of the gang members literally doubling over, slapping their knees, their assault weapons all but forgotten.

Alcantara joined in, clapping. Closer up, Caitlin saw he had a bullet-shaped head to go with the horribly scarred face, which seemed to come to a point at the top, where his black hair was bunched together with dried gel. Caitlin thought she could actually smell the oily pomade from this far away, the aroma not unlike the Brylcreem her grandfather Earl Strong had used every day until his last.

Alcantara's eyes, both the good one and the bad, were set too far back in his head, as if some cosmic force had realigned the sockets while he was still in the womb. Caitlin watched the good one narrow.

"Hey, you're that famous bitch Ranger," Alcantara said in recognition. "The one put a whole bunch of men in the ground."

Caitlin's mental clock continued to click down. The gang members started to encircle her, still giggling and chortling, seeing no threat whatsoever in her presence. The dueling aromas of weed smoke and stale sweat intensified as they drew closer.

Alcantara approached through the crowd, his misshapen features tightening and one eye narrowed, like a dog trying to figure out what it was seeing.

"You're a bitch with balls, I'll give you that, and now you're gonna have to—" He stopped midthought, puzzlement sprouting on his features. "Hey, anybody else hear that?"

The gang members exchanged glances, shaking their

heads uniformly, providing no relief for Alcantara, who swept his eyes about the night sky.

"What the fuck, man. What the fuck . . ."

The faint buzzing Caitlin too had detected on the air had now grown to a whine, and finally a screech. Only then did the gang members swing around from both Caitlin and Alcantara to look farther east, toward the sky. Still unable to see anything, because the crop duster was flying without any lights. It was, for all practical purposes, invisible, until it opened its dual tanks to send the first wave of a thick, white, paste-like cloud dropping toward the ground.

By the time Alcantara had swung back toward Caitlin, she'd pulled a plaid kerchief soaked in her dad's old cologne up over her nose and mouth. And two, maybe three seconds later, the dense white cloud unleashed by the crop duster settled over the area like a blanket, spreading straight down the street toward riot central, at the head of the neighborhood's commercial center.

Of course, it wasn't called crop dusting anymore, Caitlin knew. The new term was "aerial application," and the plane that had just soared overhead, not more than fifty feet off the ground, cost more than a million dollars and was outfitted with an advanced turbine engine and sophisticated GPS system to allow for just this kind of flight. The pilot was a former Texas Ranger who'd taken up the practice to supplement his pension. He also had come up with an especially noxious formula that mixed corn starch and soap powder with a scent most closely resembling skunk oil. He'd used a version of it to repel a riot of his own, back in the day, and was more than happy to come out of retirement to return favors done for him by both Earl and Jim Strong, Caitlin's grandfather and father.

"Hell," he'd told her, "they saved my life more times than I care to remember. Just tell me where and when, Ranger."

He didn't own a cell phone, so Caitlin had provided him with one, to ensure he could receive her signal via text message.

Caitlin made her way through the vapor, which was thicker than any fog, brush fire, or West Texas dust storm she'd ever seen, dodging bodies, to Diablo Alcantara's last position. The gang members were desperately fleeing the street all around her, grunting and gasping, some doubled over with nausea from the stench. Those sounds drowned out the last of the crop duster soaring overhead, the fading drone of its turbine engine matching the cadence of its arrival on the scene.

She reached Alcantara just as he managed to unsling the assault rifle shouldered behind him. Caitlin clocked him on the side of the skull with the butt of her SIG Sauer and watched his grasp go limp as his knees buckled. She caught his dazed form halfway to the roadbed and dragged him from the street with one arm, the whole time keeping her SIG ready in her free hand.

The soupy, stink-riddled mist had dissipated enough for a few of the gang members to clear their watering eyes and follow the trail Caitlin blazed toward the thick congestion of houses and yards. She shot two, and then a third, in rapid succession, all shots aimed ow, for the legs, since incapacitating the bangers was as good as killing them, under the circumstances. More followed those three, and then still more, until Caitlin felt she'd entered some crazed video game, she was clacking off so many shots.

Everything was going just fine until a police helicopter sweeping overhead blazed its spotlight down over the scene. The beam pierced what was left of the thick, soupy vapor and exposed her for all to see. A dozen bangers, maybe, left to give chase. More bullets needed than she had left in the magazine, Caitlin thought, as they struggled against their own retching to sweep their weapons around.

The police chopper was hovering directly over them, its spot as big as an oversize truck tire, carving a cone-shaped ribbon of light into the night. Caitlin aimed her SIG up toward it, instead, and clacked off three shots. A *poof* sounded, as the big bulb exploded and a shower of glass rained down onto the remaining gang members, slowing them up enough for Caitlin to continue dragging Diablo Alcantara into the dark cover of a yard adjoining a pair of multifamily houses.

Her back slammed into the frame of an aboveground swimming pool sturdy enough to steal her breath, just as Alcantara regained enough of his senses to try to wrench himself free of her grasp and then to launch an elbow backwards. It struck Caitlin in her left cheek, rattling her jaw and smacking her teeth against each other.

Alcantara managed to tear free, but instead of running, he launched himself at her, so enraged that his one functioning eye looked ready to bulge out of his head. Caitlin tried to bring her gun back around only to have him knock it from her grasp. She tried to snatch it out of the air, then heard a plop as it smacked the pool water, which looked like a pocket of refined oil shining in the night.

Alcantara came at her again, and Caitlin realized he'd never gone anywhere at all—he was latched to her by a watchband that had become ensnared in her denim shirt. The shirt was soaked with perspiration and dappled with vapor spots that dragged the rancid stench with them. Alcantara fired a jab-like blow, which she managed to deflect. But his next strike landed in the side of her neck.

Caitlin shrugged off the stinging pain just in time to duck under the next blow and shoulder him hard into the aboveground pool. Her intention was to spill Alcantara over into the water, but the impact buckled the framing and, instead, unleashed a torrent of water from a tear she'd cut in the liner. Its force separated and pushed both of them backwards, Caitlin feinting one way and then launching a palm strike from the blind spot created by the marble-sized fake eye wedged into his eye socket, straight into his nose.

Bellowing in pain and blowing out a torrent of blood from his nose to match the water still cascading around him, Alcantara barreled in toward her, his one working eye as big as an eight ball. Caitlin let him get close—close enough that he practically rammed that big eye straight into the thumb she plunged forward and twisted.

Caitlin had never heard a scream as deep and as shrill as Alcantara's. She grabbed hold of both his

houlders when he sank to his knees, and began dragging him toward the side street parallel to J Street,
where the bangers had gathered. The fight had stripped
her cologne-soaked bandanna free. The stench and bite
of the old Ranger's skunk-stench concoction pushed
ears from her eyes.

Caitlin could barely see when she reached the side
street. Sirens were screaming everywhere, and bright
lights poured through the haze that had settled before
her vision.

"Stop right there!" an SAPD uniformed officer
screamed at her, pistol trembling in his hand instead
of steadying on her. "Stop, or I'll shoot you dead!"